The Art of
Misdirection

Isles of Illusion

Book One: The Promise of Deception
Book Two: The Art of Misdirection

The Art of Misdirection

Isles of Illusion

By
Jessica Sly

MOUNTAIN**BROOK**FIRE

The Art of Misdirection
Published by Mountain Brook Ink under the Mountain Brook Fire line
White Salmon, WA U.S.A.

The website addresses shown in this book are not intended in any way to be or imply an endorsement on the part of Mountain Brook Ink, nor do we vouch for their content.

This story is a work of fiction. All characters and events are the product of the author's imagination. Any resemblance to any person, living or dead, is coincidental.

ISBN 978-195957-27-6

The Team: Miralee Ferrell, Alyssa Roat, Tim Pietz, Kristen Johnson, Cindy Jackson
Cover Design: Indie Cover Design, Lynnette Bonner

Mountain Brook Fire is an inspirational publisher offering worlds you can believe in.
Printed in the United States of America

Dedication

To Mom and Dad

Chapter One

London, 1914

I STOOD ALONE BEFORE A SET of closed double doors. Delicate, sheer curtains blocked the full-length windows to the outside, but soft music drifting in from a string quartet calmed my thundering heart and teased what lay beyond. Anticipation filled me despite the quivering of my hands. I drew my cascading bouquet of white lilacs to my bosom and squeezed the thick stems as its syrupy sweet scent tickled my nose.

Less than a year ago, I'd stood before a similar set of doors, dreading what crossing the threshold would bring to my life. Manipulation. Fear. Submission. A marriage for which my heart had yearned but that a master schemer had forced upon me. The reason? To compel his son and I to produce heirs to carry on the family name. It had only been through the grace of God and a bold stand on our part that we had escaped that fate.

This time was different. This time, I had chosen this path willingly. Excitement abounded so strongly that I could barely control its threat to burst out of me. I rolled my shoulders back and sucked in a deep breath, but the high beaded neckline and rigid corseted bodice of my ivory gown kept my body in a state of tension.

A gentle whisper reached my ears, drawing my gaze back over my shoulder. Percy Ford guided his grandson, a young child of about five or six, to the end of my gown's bejeweled train. Percy helped the boy lift the lacy edge and grasp it tightly in his little hands. "That's right," Percy said with a nod, his voice deeper and huskier than that of his younger brother—my dashing groom. "Hold it just like that."

The juxtaposition of the boy's pudgy cheeks and sleek suit stirred amusement in me, which escaped in a quiet snort.

Noticing my attention, Percy pressed a kiss to the boy's head before straightening and circling around to stand before me. "It's nearly time. Are you ready?"

Palms perspiring, I released the bouquet with one hand and flexed my fingers. "Ready for this to be over."

The mustache wrapping around his jaw widened with his smile as he picked up the edges of my veil, pulled it over my head, and allowed it to drape in front of my face. "Be sure to enjoy this moment. It only happens once in a lifetime—or so one hopes." He took his place at my side and offered his arm.

I slid my hand into the crook of his elbow, but as I did so, the gratefulness I felt for his presence became tainted. Deep longing tensed my muscles. My father should have been the one standing here, not Percy. I'd always dreamed of the day when my father would walk his only child down the aisle, but he'd been violently stolen from me. Though almost two years had passed, the hole his death had left in my life only seemed to grow larger with the passing of time.

Anger churned amidst the loneliness, anger for the moments and memories that had been snatched from me. Father had a right to be here, and I had a right to walk down the aisle beside someone who loved me.

Yet, there *was* someone who loved me and who eagerly awaited the chance to escort and welcome me into his family. I leaned against Percy, head bowed. "Thank you for being here for me."

He covered my hand with his and squeezed. "It is my honor."

The music beyond the doors paused a moment, then eased into a soothing hymn. The knobs turned before the doors swung outward, allowing bright afternoon sun to spill around us. I blinked until my eyes adjusted and I could view the comforting sight of the garden stretching between my home and the Fords'. Today, our garden had been adorned with extra flowers and two aisles of chairs. Standing people filled the rows. They all faced me, watching intently.

I stiffened and shut my eyes, convinced my heart would crash straight through my chest with its erratic pounding. Lightheadedness weakened my knees.

"Breathe," Percy whispered, bracing to hold me upright.

Obeying, I cycled through several deep inhales and exhales. The dizziness lifted.

"Good." Percy's arm tightened and guided me forward. "Take it one step at a time."

Somehow, my numb feet carried me down three stone steps and onto the white runner that lined the middle aisle. I surveyed the crowd, its occupants eager and smiling, some even crying. Serving as my matron of honor, Emily awaited my approach with a broad smile while my mother occupied the first seat of the front row and held tightly to Emily's one-year-old son, Basil Allan. Across the aisle, Superintendent Richard Whelan and other members of the Metropolitan Police stood at attention. Tenderness glistened in the gristly superintendent's eyes.

Near the edge of the space, separate from the group on the groom's side, Mr. Ford stood rigid. I locked my gaze on him, paying no heed to the wife at his side. Harsh shadows cast by the sun overhead made his face appear more wrinkled, more weary, but his expression held his usual indifference. He and I exchanged a cold stare before I severed our connection, determined not to let him detract from the festivities. Why should he, of all people, be cross about this union? It's what he wanted, wasn't it? The only difference was we were no longer beholden to his demands. He should be grateful we had even permitted him to attend.

Finally, I allowed my gaze to track the rest of the length of the aisle to the fanciful but minimalistic arrangement at the back of the garden. Ivy trailed the entire span of a rounded arch positioned above Reverend Phillips holding a leather Bible loosely in his hands. At his feet rested two cushioned hassocks primed for when we would kneel in prayer.

And before him stood my husband-to-be, my best friend, my love—Baze.

When our eyes met, Baze's chest swelled with a large breath and held. The sun's rays lit his brown irises and made them glow nearly amber in hue. A full smile brightened his face—but it faltered with a flush of his cheeks as tears brimmed in his eyes and his chin quivered.

Standing to Baze's left, his brother and best man, Frederick, whispered something inaudible and clapped a hearty hand on his shoulder. Baze rubbed at his eyes, but the emotion remained present and palpable on his face.

I pursed my lips to hold back my own tears. *Oh, Baze, you have such a tender heart.*

Excitement chased away all trepidation. I leaned forward and took an extra step, but Percy's arm tightened around my hand and braked my advance. "Slowly," he said under his breath.

Emitting a small growl in the back of my throat, I forced myself to take gradual strides and rolled my eyes in Baze's direction. He shook his head, and his shoulders stiffened as though he suppressed a laugh.

When Percy and I finally completed the procession, Emily came forward to accept my bouquet and beamed in encouragement before she retreated to her station. Then I turned my focus upon Baze, peering through the veil's translucent material, and the world around us faded as though we were the only two who existed. Myriad emotions of every extreme contorted my stomach and constricted my chest. In mere moments, I would be a married woman, joined to the man I couldn't fathom being able to love any more than I did. Unable to help myself, I swept my thumb against Baze's cheek to brush away the last of his tears.

The quartet's music faded, and the reverend softly cleared his throat. Clasping my hands before me, I faced the minister. Baze, however, held me in his stare for a long, poignant moment, then eventually matched my posture and turned as well. Love and peaceful strength exuded from him. Though we couldn't yet hold hands, I leaned as close to Baze as public decency would allow until our elbows grazed together, sending anticipation skittering through me.

The reverend instructed the audience to sit, waited for the shuffling of guests to subside, and then spoke in a mellow baritone. "Dearly beloved, we are gathered together here in the sight of God, and in the face of this congregation, to join together this man and this woman in holy matrimony . . ."

The reverend's words faded into a low murmur punctuated by birdsong and a rustling breeze. I peeked toward Baze and took in every detail—his slicked brown hair, black frock suit, white waistcoat and gloves, vibrant corsage, bow tie, and single dimple. His own gaze made its way across my face and beyond.

"You look handsome," I said in the tiniest whisper.

"Shh." His dimple deepened as his eyes flicked to the reverend, then back to me.

I clamped my mouth shut and faced forward. Closing my eyes, I tried to block out my surroundings and put my heart into a state of praise and thankfulness. *I never thought this day would come. Thank you, Lord. Thank you for letting us come to this moment and for bringing us together.*

A year ago, when we had confronted the charming magician and sinister killer, Cornelius Marx—or Ciaran O'Conner, as we had learned to be his real name—I truly didn't think we would survive. We almost hadn't. We'd lost our dear friend Bennett, Baze had been injured, and my mind remained plagued by darkness in the form of night terrors—but we persevered. We had proven that no matter how deep the darkness, how strong the opposition, the soul-cleansing power of the Almighty could prevail over any evil.

I cast a glance at Baze, and a single tear escaped and rolled down my cheek.

When he noticed my attention, concern furrowed his brow. "Are you okay?" His words barely reached my ears.

I grinned and gestured to the revered with my eyes. "Shh."

Baze sighed and opened his mouth to respond, but the reverend's tone grew commanding. "Basil Alistair Ford."

At the utterance of Baze's full name, we clamped our mouths shut and looked to him with bated breath. However, rather than offer a reprimand, Reverend Phillips glanced between us, amusement coloring his rosy cheeks. With an encouraging lift of his eyebrows, he nodded to Baze. "Wilt thou have this woman to thy wedded wife, to live together after God's ordinance in the holy estate of matrimony?" Baze stiffened and concentrated on me. "Wilt thou love her, comfort her, honor, and keep her, in sickness and in health; and, forsaking all other, keep thee only unto her, so long as ye both shall live?"

Baze swallowed, then answered with a strong, clear voice. "I will."

Tilting his head toward me, the reverend repeated the query, replacing mentions of "wife" with "husband." When he stopped to allow for my reply, I could hardly hear due to the great rushing of blood in my ears. Somehow, I managed to say, "I will."

The reverend straightened. "Who giveth this woman to be married to this man?"

Fulfilling his pledge to carry out what would have been my father's duties, Percy took up my right hand in his and passed it to Reverend Phillips, who, in turn, placed it into Baze's right hand. The feel of his strong, sure fingers spread warmth up my arm and throughout my body, hushing my roaring heart and embracing me with peace.

Our eyes never left one another's as Baze began to recite his vows after the reverend.

"I, Basil Alistair, take thee, Adelynn Elizabeth, to my wedded wife, to have and to hold, from this day forward, for better for worse, for richer for poorer, in sickness and in health, to love and to cherish, till death us do part, according to God's holy ordinance, and thereto I plight thee my troth."

Then came time for my vows. I clutched Baze's hand in mine and spoke confidently. "I, Adelynn Elizabeth, take thee, Basil Alistair, to my wedded husband . . ." Emotion began pressing on my throat as I continued, tears welling until my vision blurred, but I managed to endure until the very end and concluded on a resolute, "And thereto I give thee my troth."

We exchanged smiles and relaxed our shoulders, the bulk of the ceremony now complete.

Baze rotated to accept a simple gold band from Frederick. Then, he lifted my left hand and slid the ring onto my fourth finger, speaking the accompanying text after Reverend Phillips's prompting.

I bit my lip and stole my gaze away from Baze to admire the adornment, eager for the moment when I would pair it with my engagement ring, the one Baze had had made using a pearl from my father's necklace.

Reverend Phillips tipped his head. "Let us pray."

When I looked back to Baze's face, a shadowed figure over his shoulder, beyond where Frederick stood, snagged my attention. Overcome by curiosity, I glanced in the figure's direction—

Cornelius.

The Irishman reclined against the side of the Fords' home, arms folded, head tilted forward. Though his top hat and disheveled raven hair cast sharp shadows across his face, his glacial eyes gleamed from beneath the hat's brim. A devious grin distorted his features, revealing his sharp incisor.

Breath fled from my lungs. I mashed my eyes shut, prickling gooseflesh racing across my body. *No! You're dead. You can't be here. Not today.*

I waited a beat, then two, before peeling my eyes open. He had vanished. The space he had occupied only a moment ago sat empty. Was he truly gone? Or was this another of his deceptive magic tricks? Chilled unease swirled in my stomach. I'd watched him die, had thought I'd accepted the reality that he had departed this earth without repentance. So then why did he still torment me? No matter what I tried, how hard I prayed, could I never escape him?

Baze's fingers stroked my chin through the veil and tilted my face toward him. His eyes searched mine, brows drawn in worry.

Tipping away from his reassuring touch, I faced forward and knelt upon the cushioned bench before us. Warring emotions consumed my being and produced a shiver. *I can't tell him. Not now. Today of all days. If he knew that Cornelius still lurked in the recesses of my mind* . . .

Baze's focus lingered on me a moment longer before he dropped beside me.

"Those whom God hath joined together let no man put asunder." Reverend Phillips lifted our right hands and joined them once more. As he made his way through the benediction, I looked at Baze, and he at me, and we allowed our gazes to become lost in one another's. His fingers squeezed mine resolutely as the reverend proclaimed, "And by joining of hands, I pronounce that they be man and wife together, in the name of the Father, and of the Son, and of the Holy Ghost. Amen."

Chapter Two

APPREHENSION FOLLOWED ME AS BAZE AND I stole away to separate rooms to change and allow the crowd to filter out of the garden. My hands trembled as I helped Margaret, my steadfast maid, shed the wedding gown and don a traveling suit. She must have noticed my unease, for she grasped my hands and kissed my fingers, then beamed with wide, bright eyes.

I tried to return her excitement with a genuine smile but only managed a twitch of my lips. "Thank you, Margaret." She needn't know the true reason for my disquiet, that Cornelius yet lurked in my mind.

Mother and Emily found us as I was shrugging into my coat. Margaret curtsied and took her leave as Mother glided to my side, her lavender satin gown swishing at her feet. Tears sparkled in her deep green eyes as she fastened the last of my coat buttons before drawing me into a strong embrace. I rested my head on her shoulder and took a deep breath, then allowed my emotions to filter out with a long exhale.

When Mother pulled back, she cupped my cheek and smiled. "I'm so proud of you, darling. Your father would be as well."

I nodded, and the lump in my throat pinched my words. "I know."

She kissed my cheek. "Enjoy your holiday. Make sure Baze drives safely. It will be dark before you arrive."

I chuckled. "Of course."

A tiny grunt drew my attention to little Basil Allan. Emily had set him on the floor and held him upright with one hand. He clung to her and swayed on his feet while gaping up at me, four teeth protruding from his gummy mouth. His wispy blond curls and bright hazel eyes featured the likeness of his father. The toddler lifted a foot and leaned toward me.

"Oh, come here, my love." I crouched and reached out.

Basil Allan pumped his legs, and Emily helped him toddle into my hold. I swept him up into my arms, supported his weight on my hip, and pressed a series of kisses to his chubby cheeks. He squealed, tucked his chin, and buried his head into my shoulder as though to escape my affection.

"I don't know how he'll possibly survive without Auntie Adelynn all this time." Emily shook her head and scratched his back. "A month is a long time."

"I shall think of him every day." I tipped my head against his. "Not to worry, little one. We'll be back before you know it."

Emily drew me into a side hug. "Be sure to call if you need anything. Truly." Her mischievous blue eyes twinkled. "And check your trousseau as soon as you arrive. I've left you a gift."

I raised an eyebrow. "How curious."

"It's nothing of consequence." She winked and reached for her son. I surrendered him, and then we exchanged another hug. Emily kissed my cheek. "God bless you, my dear friend."

Baze tugged the wrinkles out of his coat and donned his hat, heart racing. They had only just been together, but this brief separation from Adelynn as they prepared for their journey deepened his longing for her. The quicker they gathered their things, the quicker they could be on their way.

Adelynn Ford. My wife. I'm a married man. Heat radiated from under his collar and scorched across every limb. He liked the sound of that . . . and could hardly wait to experience all that it entailed.

Giving a final glance about the room, he swiveled toward the door, and his gaze fell upon the hooked cane propped against the wall. It brought him to a halt. The delight in his heart darkened. His pounding pulse traveled to his right leg and throbbed, reminding him of the pain that he had managed to forget during the day's celebration. The forgetfulness rarely lasted, and today was no different.

Baze extended a hand toward the cane but couldn't bring himself to grasp it. Adelynn had seen him use it before—many times—but things had changed. He was a husband. A provider. Using that cane would only show her his weakness, but could he endure the pain that came if he rejected it? His opium prescription only did so much to stave off discomfort, and it didn't last long.

Caught between decisions, Baze gritted his teeth and snatched up the cane, but rather than lean on its support, he hung it over his arm.

The grinding of a clearing throat yanked his attention to the door. Alistair Ford slipped into the room, his erect posture, slicked silver hair, and stark black suit exuding an air of indifference. He targeted Baze with a steely stare and stopped several paces away. The air staled between them.

Baze firmed his jaw and tried not to let this disturbance taint the happiness of the moment. "I haven't much time, Father. We're supposed to leave in a few minutes."

"Yes, well . . ." Alistair rocked on his feet and clasped his hands before him. "I suppose congratulations are in order."

Baze snorted. "You suppose."

"Yes. You should be proud of what you've accomplished. A wife will grant you the power to truly make something of yourself, to give you heirs to carry on your name, to—"

"Stop." Baze slashed a hand through the air. "You know that's not why I got married."

"But it is still the natural progression of such things. It is only a matter of time before—"

"I'm not focused on that right now. I've only just said my vows." Baze sighed. "I don't want to talk about this anymore, so drop the matter. Please."

Alistair looked at his feet, jaw muscles pulsing, but remained silent.

Baze narrowed his eyes. Was that indecision he saw cross his father's features? No. The man never wavered. It had to be something else.

"I know you don't understand why I did what I did." Alistair's voice rumbled low. "But perhaps once you've enjoyed the advantages of marriage, once you've begotten your own son, you'll come to see my perspective."

Anger surged through Baze's veins and snapped his hands into fists. It took every ounce of resistance to keep from popping the man in the nose, as Baze had done when he'd first learned of his father's blackmail. How could Alistair still cling to the notion that he had done nothing wrong?

Because Baze's three brothers had somehow sired only daughters, their father had tried to force Baze and Adelynn to marry for the pure reason of producing a son to carry on the Ford name. How could the man continue to justify the torment he'd put them through?

Still, even after all that, Baze had clung to a sliver of hope that his father would see the error of his ways. Clearly, it had been foolish to hope.

Alistair moved forward and extended his arms.

Alarmed, Baze stumbled back, tweaking his leg in the process but managing to avoid the man's touch. Alistair had never shown affection through physical means. Why now? Baze bit back a curse. "What do you think you're doing?"

Something akin to confusion washed over Alistair's face. His gray eyes grew dim. "You're my son, Basil."

"That we're flesh and blood means nothing." Baze jabbed a finger toward his father. "You have no right to waltz in here and pretend as though nothing happened. If you want to have any hope of remaining a part of my life, then swallow your pride. Admit you were wrong. Apologize to me *and* Adelynn. And be sincere."

Alistair blinked, and for a moment, Baze allowed his hope to rear its irrational head again, that perhaps the man would still repent—until the all-too-familiar coldness crept into Alistair's eyes and stiffened his features.

Baze exhaled and rubbed the bridge of his nose, the crooked bone yet another reminder of why Alistair would never be the father Baze wished him to be. He straightened and brushed past the man toward the door.

"If I did?" Alistair called.

Baze stopped short but didn't turn.

"Apologize." Alistair's voice sagged. "You would forgive my actions?"

The question gave Baze pause. Vulnerability was an emotion his father didn't possess. He had learned that the hard way. So, more than likely, this was merely another form of manipulation masquerading as humility.

Baze twisted slightly and looked at his father askance. "The problem with that is I don't believe you capable of sincere remorse. You've trampled my trust to the point where I don't think it's possible to rebuild." He faced away, a boulder of guilt weighing his gut. "Farewell."

Rather than wait for Baze by the car primed for our departure, I stole away one final time to the place that had provided so much comfort as a child, through my adolescence, and now even as an adult—the hedge, its twisted interior still arched with barely enough room for me to crawl inside.

I hugged my knees to my chest and rested my chin upon them. Adelynn Ford. How could one go through a whole lifetime assuming a particular identity and then, in a brief flash, change that identity? Would Adelynn Ford be the same as Adelynn Spencer? She couldn't be . . . and that's what stirred fear in me now. I had to change, had to embrace this new identity—whatever that meant. It would take some adjusting, but in that, I was certain of one thing. My new identity had been proclaimed before God and the masses. I belonged to Baze now, and he belonged equally to me.

Emotions crashed through me in waves—thankfulness, doubt, fear, happiness. The moment I left this hedge and accompanied Baze to our destination, my life would be different. Of course, we had been together for the last year, but now we were *together*. I couldn't be the independent soul I was accustomed to being, for I no longer *needed* to be independent. I would have to learn to lean on someone else for strength.

The edge of the hedge rustled, and Baze's head popped through the opening. "I thought I might find you here."

I laughed softly. "Am I that predictable?"

"Typically, no." As he clambered in and settled at my side, he flashed a cheeky grin. "This is quite a welcome surprise, actually."

"Well, enjoy it. I won't be this easy on you all the time." My smile lasted but a moment before I let it fade. I snatched up his hand, hugged it to my chest, and rested against his shoulder. We sat in silence, listening to the gentle whisper of the breeze and the delighted trills of the birds flitting about in a nearby tree. After a while, I craned my neck upward and examined his face, tracing his profile with my eyes—his sloped forehead, the slight defect in the bridge of his nose, his strong square jaw. Despite his stoic expression, thoughts brimmed behind his eyes.

I wiggled his hand. "What are you thinking about?"

As though snapping from a trance, Baze smiled and began massaging my palm with firm, adept fingers, knowing exactly where to trigger pressure points that released my tension. "I'm merely thinking about how I'm the luckiest man in the world."

I rolled my eyes but couldn't help being set alight by his silly statement. "You flatter me." I squeezed his hand. "But you're deflecting. What else?"

His smile wilted. "Nothing."

Indignation flared. "Oh, I don't think so. We're not about to start this marriage with secrets." I dug my fingernails into his palm. "Out with it."

"Ouch!" He yanked his hand from my attack. "Good gracious, Adelynn, it's nothing."

I wrangled his hand back into my lap and held it securely in place. "If it's nothing, then it doesn't matter whether you share it. Tell me."

His Adam's apple bobbed. "It's simply that this is new territory for me. My father didn't teach me much in the way of how to be a husband—a *good* husband. I don't want to muck it up."

I released my anger as my heart warmed. "I don't know how to do this either, so I'm sure we'll both muck it up at some point. Either way, everything's about to change."

He nodded and picked at the spindly weeds growing at his feet. "Oh, things will change. Lots of things. But they're going to change for the better. Of that, I am certain."

I half-grinned. "I am envious of your certainty."

He breathed a laugh and pulled his hand free. "Now you're the one thinking too deeply about this, Al."

"But what if—"

Baze twisted, took hold of my face, and captured my lips in a deep kiss—our first as man and wife. Thoughts of doubt fled, chased away by his touch. I weakened into his arms. Fiery desire had begun flickering to life when he pulled back. "I love you," he murmured. "That's all that matters."

Craving more, I tilted my face up and stole my own kiss, sliding a hand behind his neck so that I could keep him in place and fulfill my heart's yearning.

Eventually, I pushed against his chest to force us apart. My cheeks flushed and my skin tingled despite the cool breeze filtering through the foliage. "I love you too," I whispered and traced a finger over his forehead, between his eyebrows, and down the crooked bone in his nose. Baze shivered and leaned in once more, but I stopped him with a finger to his lips and smirked. "We shall have to retreat and find solace within our new bedchamber if you seek more."

Baze closed his eyes and breathed in and out, slowly, deliberately. The vein pulsing in the side of his neck began to slow. Finally opening his eyes, he raised his eyebrows and held out a hand, palm up. "Ready?"

Taking a steadying breath, I nodded and dropped my hand into his. "Ready."

Chapter Three

THE EVENING SUN DOUSED LONDON IN warm rays as Baze drove us through its boroughs, heading west toward the countryside and our destination of the quaint Cotswold town of Bath. A wave of exhaustion poured over me. Lulled by the purr of the engine and gentle vibration of the motorcar, I sank deeper into the seat and clung tighter to Baze's hand in mine. Through half-shut eyes, I watched the darkening scenery speed by—the hedgerows, the castle ruins, the farmland.

Answering the enticing beckon of sleep, I let my eyes slide shut and surrendered my mind to the pull. Evening's golden light shone through my eyelids, but soon, darkness blotted it out. Dreams evaded me as I fell further into the clutches of unconsciousness. A cool sensation bloomed near the base of my neck and slithered over my shoulders, across my arms, down my spine. Somehow, that chill—that power—I had encountered so many times before in Cornelius's presence had found me once again and bound my body in place. The mind-numbing tendrils poked at the far reaches of my thoughts, and then the outline of his tall figure emerged from the shadows.

You can't escape, sweet cailín.

Something tugged my hand.

With a jerk, I bolted upright. Heart pounding, I gaped out the windshield. We sped across the dim road stretching before us, brightened by the artificial beams of the car's headlights. The vehicle quivered beneath me as its wheels emitted a crackling hum.

"Sorry to startle you." Baze's voice eased through the silence, amusement coloring the tone. "I've never seen you doze so soundly. You were utterly comatose."

"Yes, well"—I shivered and rubbed my hands together to warm them—"you didn't have to wake before the sunrise in order to endure hair styling and makeup."

"You've got me there." Baze centered his hands on the top of the steering wheel. "We're nearly there. I didn't want you to miss the entrance into the city."

I surveyed the road before us. In the distance, a regal skyline loomed, its stone buildings reflecting the coolness of the sun's dying light. Within several minutes, we'd crossed the threshold into the city.

Well-dressed men and women strolled along the pavement that ran the length of the road. A majestic abbey on our left drew my attention to its lofty windows and pointed spires. A busker stood near its fountain, playing a tune on his violin. To our right lay a green expanse of trees and a groomed lawn populated by lounging couples. Beyond that, a thick stone rail separated the park from the tranquil River Avon. Farther up the road ahead of us rose a grand building constructed of the same sandy stone that I assumed was the famous Bath stone for which the city was known.

"That's our hotel." Baze pointed. "Take a look at the roof. Its design is meant to represent a cottage, a house, and a castle to signify the mixing of the different classes."

I snorted. "Look at you, so full of arbitrary knowledge."

He grinned. "I do try."

I swallowed, still perturbed by the odd sensation lingering from my slumber—or whatever that had been. Fortunately, my visions had died with Cornelius, freeing me from the curse of seeing his victims as he killed them. This was the closest I had come to feeling that way since his death. What could have triggered it? I supposed we *were* approaching the one-year anniversary of Cornelius's demise, so perhaps my subconscious was merely trying to make sense of it.

Baze eased the car up to the end of the hotel entrance's wrought iron canopy. A suited valet awaited us as we stopped. He opened my door and extended a white-gloved hand. "Welcome to the Empire Hotel, ma'am."

The Empire Hotel. The name triggered a new twinge of fear in me, its cadence too similar to the Empress Theatre—the opera house that had served as a deranged magician's lair and the setting where Baze and I had almost met our ends.

I took a deep breath. This wasn't the Empress. This was a different place entirely, and I wouldn't let the past ruin the prospect of a fulfilling future.

"Don't keep the man waiting, Al," Baze whispered.

I glanced at the valet. "Thank you, sir." As I accepted his help and climbed out, Baze came to my side. He tipped the valet before offering me his arm. We passed beneath the canopy, through the entrance manned by two doormen, and into an impressive lobby. Oriental rugs stretched toward an imposing staircase boasting an intricate design mixing several types of wood. Tapestries adorned the marbled walls. A passageway to our left opened to a dining room, while a lounge occupied the space to our right.

A slender man in a decorated suit approached us. He bowed, and when he smiled, his thin mustache stretched. "Welcome. How may I be of assistance?"

"We have a reservation under Ford," Baze said.

"Ah, yes, we've been expecting you." The man ran a hand over his short, kempt hair. Speckles of silver highlighted the otherwise dark strands, with a few thicker streaks rimming his ears. His kind, gray eyes shifted between us. "I am Cecil Everett, and I will be at your service for the duration of your stay. Should you need anything, no matter how inconsequential, don't hesitate to send for me." He swept an arm toward the staircase. "Now, if you would follow me to your suite."

As we ascended, I tried not to lean on Baze so as not to aggravate his leg, though he seemed oblivious to my actions. Mr. Everett led us down the left hallway a short distance and popped through one of the rich wooden doors. We entered an elaborate sitting room decorated with a sofa, a pair of chairs, and various side tables and cabinets. An ornate but cozy fireplace occupied the wall in front of us, with tall arched windows spanning the rest of the wall and opening to a view of a lush garden. I peered through an adjoining door into a master bedroom. Several trunks, which contained our effects, surrounded the lavish bed.

"I hope you find your accommodations agreeable." Mr. Everett clapped his hands together. "May I offer you a tour of the grounds?"

Sudden weariness weighed my limbs. "Actually, I would like to get settled. Thank you."

Baze raised his eyebrows at me. "Well, one of us should get a lay of the land. Do you mind?"

My first instinct was to shoot down the bold notion. How could he be so eager to abandon me after we'd just been married? Yet, my fatigue quelled my argumentative nature, and I chose not to press the matter. "Of course. You can give me the details when you return."

He grinned and lowered his voice. "Wait up for me?"

Cheeks flaring, I very nearly smacked his arm, but I smiled sweetly instead. "Hurry back."

If Mr. Everett picked up on our suggestive exchange, he did a fabulous job hiding it. "Right this way, Mr. Ford. I think we'll start in the drawing room."

Baze followed the man out, shutting the door and leaving me alone in the unfamiliar space. I took a moment to close my eyes and collect myself. *Thank you, Lord. For Baze. For our marriage. For this new life. Give me the courage to be the wife he needs me to be.*

I opened my eyes and planted my hands on my hips. "Right," I said to the empty room.

Inside the bedchamber, I checked one of the two wardrobes and discovered a row of my gowns hanging within—and I surmised that the second contained Baze's shirts, coats, and trousers. After rearranging the dresses into a satisfying order, I turned my attention to the trunks on the floor, more specifically to my trousseau. Though I already knew what it contained, having selected a special array of jewelry and family heirlooms to bring on holiday, I decided to rummage through it, if only for something to keep me occupied. Besides, hadn't Emily hinted that she had left something for me?

Sure enough, when I opened the lid, my gaze fell upon an unfamiliar object—a folded ruby-red garment topped with an envelope addressed to me. The note inside bore a short inscription: *May your marriage be everything you have ever dreamed and more. This isn't much, but I couldn't resist the opportunity to play a small part in the beginning of your union. Be blessed, my dear friend. Love, Emily.*

Burning with curiosity, I set aside the note and lifted the garment. It unfurled to reveal an ornate lace nightgown . . . a sheer nightgown. I clutched it to my chest, giggling as my stomach twisted and my skin heated. "Emily, you scamp."

I most certainly couldn't.

Then again . . .

Mind made up, I laid the negligee aside, tugged the pins out of my hair, and scrambled to wriggle out of my dusty traveling suit. For a moment, as I struggled with the buttons, I wished we hadn't chosen to forgo a maid, but eventually, I managed. It was one thing to fasten a corset oneself, a technique I'd had to learn out of necessity, but loosening it proved a joy. Once I stashed my evening wear, I slipped into the nightgown. Cool air moved freely through the lace and made me shiver. As I examined myself in the full-length mirror—and, more importantly, imagined Baze seeing me in this state—an inner flame chased away the chill.

I folded my arms across my bosom as though to reclaim some decency. *What am I doing? I haven't the faintest idea what I'm doing, that's what. This is absolutely ridiculous.*

Laughter bubbled in my chest as I crossed to the bed and sank onto the plush mattress. Whether prompted by the comfort of the bedding or the fact that I finally had a moment to be still after such an overwhelming day, exhaustion washed over me and weighed my eyelids. *No, I can't fall asleep now . . . But perhaps I could rest . . .*

Almost involuntarily, I lifted my legs onto the bed and laid my head upon the down pillow. I heaved a deep sigh as the mattress conformed to my curves. My eyes drifted shut. Light from the dim lamp created colorful shapes on the backs of my eyelids. The figures twisted and darkened as my body grew heavier. Thoughts fled and made way for sleep.

Soft lyrics filled my mind. Father was singing "The Parting Glass." His beautiful tenor vibrato poured love and longing over me. But as he continued, his voice distorted and morphed into a new one—commanding, sweet, and familiar. Cornelius. Fear swirled within the music. He stopped singing. The words echoed and faded to silence. Then he whispered in a gentle Irish accent, "Be alert, sweet *cailín*. Your trials are far from over."

A pinprick of light appeared in the distance and grew larger until a scene within an elegant dining hall faded into view. I passed by a table bearing ornate place settings. A middle-aged man and woman sat at the table, deep in conversation. Hair swirled into a tight updo adorned with beads, the woman sipped from a dainty teacup. As she listened to her husband, her complexion grew increasingly pink, sanguine even. Then she grasped at her throat. Her mouth gaped and gurgled. As her husband and onlookers responded to her behavior, she toppled out of her chair and writhed on the floor.

The scene flickered, dripped to black, then lit again, back to the same scene. This time, Cornelius stood beside the woman in the center of the chaos. He stared only at me, his glacial eyes fixed and frightening.

Discovering that I could move my feet, I sprinted in the direction of the lobby. A force thumped me from behind. It sent me sprawling. Firm hands flipped me onto my back. I thrashed, rolling and kicking, but Cornelius lunged atop me, crushing my stomach. Air punched from my gut.

Tears jumped to my eyes as I looked wildly at the other patrons, pleading for their help. But no one even glanced my way.

The lights dimmed until Cornelius's face became a mere shadow. I kept struggling, fighting with all my strength. "Leave me alone! Please."

"Adelynn!" he shouted, catching my arms and crisscrossing them over my chest.

"Stop, please!"

"Al, wake up! It's me," he shouted again, but this time, the voice distorted and morphed.

Pulse roaring, I froze and stared hard at his face through the darkness. Fog clouded his bright blue eyes. A dark color bled into them bit by bit until they settled into a warm brown, and the features transformed to match.

"Baze," I squeaked out as the whole scene dissolved back to reality. Night had fallen. We were alone in our room, and Baze held me pinned to the bed.

"You were kicking and screaming." His hands tensed around my wrists.

Sweat cooled on my skin. I panted and let my heart rate come down before attempting an answer. "It was a nightmare."

"It seemed more than a nightmare." His voice grew quiet. "Has this been happening to you ever since we stopped Cornelius?"

I swallowed. "Yes."

"Every night?"

"Nearly."

Baze's shoulders collapsed. Ever so gently, he released my wrists and slid off of me, settling cross-legged at my side. "What can I do?"

I shook my head, wiggled into a sitting position, and leaned against the headboard. "There isn't anything you can do, I'm afraid. It's a battle I have to fight on my own." As his face fell, my stomach soured. I'd had nightmares consistently since our last confrontation with Cornelius, but nothing so vivid as this one . . . and certainly not one framed like my visions had been.

Baze picked at the bedding. "You should try to get some sleep if you can. Exhaustion won't help the matter if you're already on edge."

I frowned and froze as I took in his wardrobe—a loose-fitting nightshirt and striped trousers . . . and I still in the sheer nightgown Emily had so kindly gifted. Face flushing, I clutched my arms to my chest and realized that our wedding night had come and gone. "I fell asleep," I breathed. "I can't believe I fell asleep. I've messed it all up."

"No, you haven't. You were completely knackered." Baze gave a small smile. "And to be quite honest, my body was begging for rest by the time I returned from the tour. You've done us both a favor." He yawned. "Now, if you don't mind, I'd like to get back to sleep." He rolled onto all fours, clambered to the other side of the bed, and burrowed under the covers. When he noticed that I hadn't moved, he raised an eyebrow. "Planning to sleep upright, are you?"

A scorching heat crawled from my toes to the crown of my head. In a quiet voice, I said, "I've never shared a bed with a man before."

He chuckled. "On the contrary, you've been sharing a bed with a man for the past several hours." When I balked, he frowned. "I hope you haven't been expecting me to sleep on the floor all this time. If you have, there's been a gross misunderstanding of what marriage entails."

"Right . . . yes, you're right," I stammered. Regaining control of my limbs and cramming aside my unease, I scooted under the covers, hyper aware of his presence next to me. Before I could talk myself out of it, I edged toward him and nestled into the crook of his arm. He tensed slightly as I rested my head on his shoulder. Soon, our breathing harmonized, and our bodies relaxed into one another.

I closed my eyes and listened to his steady heartbeats vibrating against my ear. It felt safe, it felt right, as though I'd always belonged here. Heaving one last contented sigh, I let sleep claim me again and, sheltered in Baze's arms, experienced a night of rest without the nightmares that had plagued me for so long.

Morning light peeked through a slit in the drapes, allowing me enough illumination to observe Baze sleeping beside me. True peace relaxed his expression as a warbled snore emitted from his nose.

I smiled, wanting to rouse him, but refrained, if only to let him enjoy unadulterated rest for a little while longer. With the softest movements I could muster, I crept from the bed and snuck to the vanity. Conscious of his presence, even though he still slept, I threw off the nightgown, tugged on my combinations in haste, and fastened the ribbons over my shoulders. Then I slipped on my stockings and readied my corset. Once I wrapped it about my torso, I set to fastening the busk at the front.

"You're up early." Baze's voice rasped with sleep.

I whirled, flushing. He sat upright in bed and observed me with a crooked grin, hair in disarray.

"How long have you been watching me? I thought you were asleep."

"I'm a light sleeper." He slipped to his feet and stretched. "Have been since becoming an officer, I'm afraid."

I turned back to the vanity and finished buckling the corset, but I kept an eye on Baze in the mirror. He crossed to his wardrobe, then reached behind his neck and tugged his nightshirt up over his head. Muscles rippled across his broad back as he crumpled the shirt and tossed it onto the floor of the cupboard.

My cheeks flared. I averted my eyes, ashamed of the response it had aroused in me. Then I chuckled at myself. *This is ridiculous. He's my husband. I can admire him as much as I please.*

Emboldened, I looked back to the mirror . . . and found him staring right back.

He wagged his eyebrows. "You can't keep your eyes off of me, can you?"

I bristled, annoyed that he was right. I lifted my chin and reached behind me to grasp the laces of my corset before targeting him with a challenging stare. "Mind giving me some assistance?"

He pointed at his chest. "You want *me* to do that?"

"I could do it myself, but it's much easier for a second person, and since we chose not to bring any staff for our holiday, you're the only one I have at my disposal. Come." I wiggled the laces. "It will do you good to learn anyway."

As he approached, I glanced at his bare chiseled chest before deliberately focusing on his eyes. His fingers brushed mine as he took the laces from my hands and sent gooseflesh up my arm. "So how do I do this?"

Sliding a foot out front and bracing my legs, I said, "Tug on those long laces. Once it's as tight as you can go, pull up on the top and bottom laces. Then pull the long ones again to tighten. Keep repeating. I'll tell you when to stop."

Baze pursed his lips and set to work. The first violent jerk caught me by surprise and forced a gasp from my lips. "Sorry," he mumbled.

"Not that hard." I shook my head and focused on breathing and shifting my ribs into place as the garment grew tighter and tighter.

"This is barbaric," Baze muttered. "You do this every day?"

I fought off a grin at the defensiveness in his voice. "I have been doing this every day since I was an adolescent. It's what society expects of women."

Baze paused a moment, frowning at the laces. Then he resumed his task, but this time, when he tugged, the corset loosened.

I pressed a hand to my stomach to hold it in place. "What are you doing? That's not—"

"You're not going to do this today."

"That's absurd." I nearly laughed out loud. "I'll be the subject of city gossip if I venture into public without it."

"You needn't worry about that. Trust me." Baze grasped my hips and spun me to face him, then placed his large hands over my ribs and used his thumbs to pop open the busk.

I grasped his wrists, another protest forming at the tip of my tongue, but he'd already finished and tossed the corset aside. Tilting away, I gaped. "You're completely incorrigible, Basil Ford. If you think—"

Baze's mouth on mine sent the last of my objections spiraling into nothingness until all that remained in my conscious thoughts was the smooth melding of our lips together. He kissed me hastily at first, then slowed, his gentle hands exploring places of me that a God-ordained union now encouraged him to go. Knees weakening, I shivered and savored each tender touch.

As his kisses traveled down my jaw, to my neck, one of his hands drifted to my shoulder and tugged loose the ribbons holding up my combinations. Instinctually, I clapped a hand to my chest to prevent their fall, then nearly giggled at the silly notion of clinging to modesty in the presence of my husband.

Baze leaned back and traced a finger along my chin, his cheeks flushed. "I love you, Adelynn. So much."

Rising on the tips of my toes, I clasped his face with both hands and whispered, "Enough talking."

Chapter Four

STEAM ROSE FROM MY TEA AND twirled before my eyes, but I stared through the smoky tendrils, my strategic location at a side table in the dining room allowing me a direct view into the lobby. The Fords—handsome Baze and spirited Adelynn—had emerged from their room moments ago, right as the sun had begun its descent toward the horizon. They'd wasted the entire day away selfishly indulging in the pleasures of marriage.

I lifted the teacup to my lips, observing them over the cup's delicate edge, and inhaled the nutty scent before drawing in a dainty sip. As the couple approached Mr. Everett, they absolutely reeked of affection. Their suggestive glances and stolen touches likened them to lovesick teenagers, but the host either didn't notice or chose not to acknowledge the distasteful display.

Though the contented conversation and the ambient piano music of the dining room made it impossible to hear the couple from so far away, I focused on their lips and managed to make out part of their exchange.

"I trust your stay has been enjoyable thus far." Mr. Everett bowed his head.

Adelynn's face twisted in a smirk. "You could say that." Her husband pinched her side, and she responded by flinching and leaning against him, cheeks reddening.

Bitterness tightened my stomach and soured the taste of the tea. They should know better than to flaunt their status, to partake in public displays that would turn up the noses of any respectable gentleperson and loosen the tongues of gossips.

Mr. Everett gestured toward the dining room, then led them within and to a table across the room from where I watched. I tilted my head, studying them. Baze had an attractive face and muscular but lean build—but those sympathetic brown eyes and pronounced limp robbed him of the ability to exude full strength.

And then there was Adelynn. She held herself confidently, her violet velvet gown modest but tight enough to accentuate her slim waist and shapely hips. Though her face lit with happiness, there brimmed an unspoken affliction behind her pale blue eyes—an affliction of the mind. Yes, she had bested Ciaran O'Conner, or Cornelius Marx as he had presented himself to her, but little had she known how powerful his dark gift would prove to be.

Chills enshrouded me as a young waiter skirted to the front of my table, blocking the giddy couple from view, and placed a delectable plate of braised salmon and Brussels sprouts before me. "Enjoy, madam."

I lashed out and caught the waiter's sleeve before he could pull away. He stiffened as I held him in place and stared into his eyes. His colorless irises drowned behind a thick haze, and wisps of darkness oozed from his arm onto my hand. Grimacing, I released him and sat back. The waiter nodded, then retreated without a word.

But the darkness remained.

I wasn't sure why the revelation that he was being controlled disturbed me—after all, it was why I had ventured into this space—but there seemed to be no method for growing accustomed to watching an individual's mind bend to the will of another. I shot a look at Adelynn. Did she sense it too? Had she witnessed what was about to happen in her visions?

Well, if she didn't yet realize what was to come, she was about to.

My stomach rumbled in response to the hearty aroma of steaming soup and seared meat permeating the dining room air. "I am utterly famished," I grumbled and folded my arms over the table in exasperation, then eyed Baze. "How are you not wasting away?"

He grinned and patted his stomach. "Because Mr. Everett was kind enough to offer me several hors d'oeuvres last night."

I targeted him with an indignant glare, my empty stomach releasing a supportive growl. "And you didn't think to bring anything back for your new wife?"

Skin paling, his smile faded. "My apologies. I didn't think . . . I mean, it merely slipped my mind."

"Well, you shall have to make sure it *doesn't* slip your mind again." I kept him locked in my stare until I grew satisfied by his squirms. Then, groaning, I tapped a foot on the floor and cast my gaze around the room, observing several of the other guests—a table of six middle-aged gentlemen who appeared nearly ready to take a cigar, a young starry-eyed couple likely here on their own post-wedding holiday, and a lone woman in a wide-brimmed hat sipping tea near the opposite corner.

I paused on the woman, struck by the stark contrast of her flaming red hair against her deep green evening gown. Was she here alone? The long gloves she wore covered her ring finger and prevented me from deducing her marital status. As she leisurely drank her tea, her gaze roamed across each supping guest. Then, abruptly, it snapped to mine.

An involuntary inhale sucked through my lips. Apprehension prickled at the small of my back as we stared at one another, her dark eyes direct and unblinking. That feeling. I'd felt it before . . .

The connection cut short when a waiter arrived with the first course of butternut soup. Consumed by the hunger pains in my stomach, I tossed aside thoughts of the woman and snatched up the spoon. The creamy broth nearly scalded my tongue, so I paused just long enough to let it cool, then slurped it up. Within a few minutes, I had gulped down all of the soup and tried to scrape every last drop from the bottom of the bowl.

Watching me, Baze's single dimple appeared as he grinned. It took him a few moments more to finish his own serving, after which he pushed the bowl aside, rested his forearms on the table edge, and scrutinized me.

Dabbing my mouth with a serviette, I raised an eyebrow. "What?"

"Nothing." He shrugged. "Can I not admire my new bride?"

"No." I raised my chin. "It's impolite to stare unless you have something to say."

A sweet smile spread his lips as he cocked his head, but he continued to hold me in his gaze.

I cleared my throat. "Very well. While I have your attention, we may as well talk about some things. Like children, for one. Society expects couples of our standing to start producing as early as possible. We don't need to begin straightaway, but it's something to keep in mind. On that note, you'll need to return to your job before others begin whispering that you can't provide. Of course, *I* know that's not the case, but we can't start out this marriage in the negative eye of the public."

Baze shifted his jaw. "Since when have you cared about bowing to the standards of society?"

"Since last year." My throat grew tight. "After the story about Cornelius and our involvement spread through London, our families and friends have been harassed and swarmed by the public. I know we could endure it, but I don't want our loved ones to continue suffering. So, if blending in is the best way to help them escape the scrutiny, then I'll do it."

Baze flattened his lips and tilted back a bit, growing pensive as he usually did when his head swam with conflicting thoughts.

While Baze pondered, the waiter whisked away our empty bowls and returned with steaming plates of braised quail.

Baze lifted his fork and prodded the cooked bird. Then he set it down, reached across the table, and scooped up my hand. "The time for dealing with that will come, but right now, I want to focus on you—and on this holiday. *That* is all I care about at this moment."

The resolve in his voice and the directness of his words stunned me into silence.

His voice lowered. "I had also hoped to be further along in treatment for my leg before our wedding, and especially before returning to the force, but I think this may be my opportunity to find an effective remedy for the pain. The myths surrounding Bath indicate that the hot springs here have healing properties."

I let out a deep breath. "I hope you're not pursuing this on my account. Neither of us is perfect and never will be. If your leg must remain in its current state, it doesn't reduce my love toward you."

"It's not only for your sake." He frowned. "How do you think I feel hobbling around like a cripple? Do you not want me to be well?"

"I do." A touch of nausea curdled my stomach. "But your doctor said it's not likely that there's anything more—"

"Not every doctor knows everything." His free hand slammed down on the table. "I refuse to believe that I've exhausted every option."

I let my shoulders slump, my heart aching due to the hopeful shine in his eyes. "Baze, you shouldn't—"

A strained cry sliced through the air.

Conversations ceased. Heads turned. As though controlled by an outside force, I lurched to my feet. Another cry sounded and dragged my attention to a table near the middle of the room.

A middle-aged woman quivered in her chair, clutching at her throat with both hands. Her mouth opened and closed like a fish sucking in oxygen. Her eyes bulged. She jumped up, but her quavering legs failed to support her weight. She toppled to the floor and writhed. The man beside her fell to his knees, collected her in his arms, and looked about with wild eyes. "Someone get help." The woman seized. "Get help now. Please!"

Numbness ripped through my body as the scene progressed in slow motion. *No, this is impossible. This shouldn't be happening.* That was the woman . . . the same woman from my dream. Yet here she was, fully real and dying in exactly the way I had seen.

But Cornelius was dead. *How* could this be happening if Cornelius was dead?

Blood drained from my face. My ears began ringing, and my vision grew fuzzy. All feeling left my limbs. Sensations of the outside world faded away for a brief discombobulated moment until I rudely jerked back into consciousness—and found myself in Baze's arms.

The hallway listed as he carried me through the door of our room. Sweat gathered on his forehead, and his jaw clenched as he limped prominently beneath my weight.

Mind spinning, I whispered, "What happened?"

"You fainted." He held his breath as he bent and laid me atop the sofa. He propped my feet on a pillow, then pulled up a nearby chair and sat beside me.

I covered my face with both hands and breathed heavily, willing the dizziness to cease. Sorrow paralyzed my muscles, which lasted but a moment before escalating anger chased it away. My visions—and the trail of murders—were supposed to have all died with Cornelius. So how could this have happened? And why?

Baze lay a firm, comforting hand on my stomach. "I'm sorry you had to witness that."

Uncovering my face, I shook my head. "It's not that." I grasped his wrist, if only to stop my hand from shaking. "I knew she was going to die."

Baze frowned. "I don't understand."

"My nightmare last night. It seems it wasn't only a nightmare." My throat grew tight. "I saw her die."

Slowly, Baze pulled his hand from my grip and sank back into the chair. Color faded from his cheeks until it appeared he was the one about to black out.

I elbowed into an upright position and swung my legs over the side of the couch. "I don't know how, but my visions are back."

"But . . . but Cornelius . . ."

"I know. I don't understand either." Convinced that I could stand on steady feet, I rose and turned to the door.

Baze stood and caught my arm. "Where are you going?"

"I saw a woman die, Baze," I snapped. "I have to know more. I have to know why."

He shook his head, skin still pale. "I can't let you go out there. It's absolute chaos."

"Then you go." I poked his chest. "Maybe you can learn something from the police when they arrive. Find out what happened and why she died."

"I could try, but I don't have any jurisdiction here."

"But you're an officer. That has to count for something." As Baze's focus grew distant, I grabbed his collar and wrenched his attention back to me. Anger swirled so strongly within me that I expected it to burst straight through my chest. Somehow, I managed to speak steadily. "If you don't go, then I will. Please. I need to know what happened."

Chapter Five

BAZE STRAIGHTENED HIS COLLAR AS HE shuffled back through the hall toward the dining room, the last place he wanted to go. They were supposed to be on holiday, supposed to have seen the last of these horrific crimes after they defeated Cornelius, but if Adelynn was telling the truth—and he had no reason to doubt her this time—then he couldn't ignore this. Yes, Adelynn had begged him to investigate, but his curiosity burned every bit as strong.

Rounding the corner, Baze heard the ruckus before it came into view. Uniformed officers had taken control of the room. Several used the lobby to interview hotel guests, and another team gathered in the dining room. Baze focused on the deceased woman as he drew closer, noting that her face had turned a ghastly shade of red. Before he could form another thought, words flowed unbidden through his mind, an annoying but blessed habit that Bennett had bestowed upon him.

Almighty God, commit her spirit into your hands. Bring agents of evil to justice and heal the pain of this dark world.

"Excuse me." A tall officer stepped in Baze's path. "Unless you have a statement to give, I must ask you to vacate the premises. This is the scene of an investigation."

Baze glanced up and took quick stock of the man's appearance—short blond hair, a muscular but lean build, and a strong bearded jaw—before responding. "Could you point me to the commanding officer on duty?"

The man regarded Baze a moment before tipping his head. "Detective Chief Inspector Sydney Whitaker at your service. How might I assist you?"

Trying not to allow his surprise to manifest on his face—he hadn't expected to encounter a higher-ranked officer—Baze reached into his coat pocket and flashed his badge. "Detective Inspector Baze Ford with the Met."

Whitaker sized Baze up. "I appreciate your concern, Inspector Ford, but we have everything under control. You may return to your usual activities."

When Whitaker started to turn, Baze stepped in his way. "I apologize, sir, but I thought I might be of assistance. I've some experience investigating murders."

Whitaker raised an eyebrow. "What makes you conclude it is a murder from a mere glance?"

Baze jutted his chin at the woman. "Discolored complexion. Seizing muscles. She collapsed only after drinking from her teacup. I watched it happen, sir. It's likely poison."

Recording the information on a notepad, Whitaker nodded. "I appreciate the information and your eagerness to help, but I assure you, we have everything under control. So please, take your leave." The chief inspector's eyes flashed with warning. "I won't ask you again."

Baze bit the inside of his cheek as Whitaker rejoined his men. As much as Baze wanted to argue, he didn't have the jurisdiction nor the rank, and he couldn't risk defying the order of another superior officer. He'd already suffered enough reprimands for doing so in the past.

Sulking from the dining room, Baze tried to determine what he would tell Adelynn, how he would explain that he'd walked away without any new information. As he headed across the lobby, he caught a glimpse of a younger couple striding away from an officer, likely having just given a statement. Baze glanced Whitaker's way. The man's attention seemed directed at the dead woman for now.

Making a split-second decision, Baze hastened to the couple and cut off their retreat. "Excuse me." He flashed his badge quickly so they couldn't look too closely. "Detective Inspector Ford. Might I ask you a few questions about what you witnessed?"

The young man stopped in front of his wife, their eyes swimming with confusion and shock. "Sorry, sir, but we've already told—"

"Yes, I realize that, but we like to be thorough." Baze fished out his notepad. "Now, if you would, please describe what you saw."

The couple hesitated before the woman said, "We didn't see too much. The lady had been drinking from the same cup all evening. Then a new waiter, one we'd never seen before, came by and refilled her drink. Right after that, she . . . she . . ." The woman covered her mouth with her hand, and her husband placed an arm about her shoulders.

Baze nodded. "This new waiter. Can you describe him?"

"Yes," the man said. "He had a slight build, dark shorn hair, pale skin."

"When the woman began to choke"—Baze flipped to a new page of his pad—"did you notice anything else?"

"No, we were so taken aback by what was happening—"

A sharp whistle pierced Baze's eardrum. Detective Chief Inspector Whitaker appeared at his side, demeanor incensed, and flicked a hand at the couple. When they'd scurried away, he stood chest to chest with Baze, hands on hips, glaring down his straight nose. "I am going to assume that your intentions are pure, Inspector Ford, but you must understand that you are grossly overstepping your authority and deceptively impeding an active police investigation. I realize that you city police might look down upon our methods as primitive or simple, but we have been successfully policing Bath for decades and do fine on our own." Whitaker firmed his jaw. "Now, leave, Inspector Ford, else I shall ring Scotland Yard and report your insubordination to your commanding officer."

Picturing Superintendent Whelan's wrath, Baze stashed his notepad and held up his hands. "I apologize, Chief Inspector. I won't interfere again."

"See that you don't."

Fighting against the shame brought upon by the admonishment, Baze withdrew from the superior officer and hurried up the grand staircase. His calf spasmed, but he gritted his teeth and suppressed the limp until he rounded the corner out of sight of everyone. Then he stumbled against the wall and used it as support to take pressure off his leg. He craved the opium Frederick had prescribed, its effects long worn off. He'd chosen Bath as the location of their holiday for the sole purpose of finding healing in the Roman hot springs, but now this new development threatened to rob him of that chance. Would he never find relief?

God, I've tried to be faithful. Why are you allowing me to keep suffering?

Within their suite, Baze found Adelynn pacing in the sitting room. She had her arms folded against her chest, her thin form wrapped in a snug, silk robe. Her loose, flaxen hair breezed around her neck with each of her spins.

When she noticed him, she stopped in her tracks. "Well? What did you learn?"

He grimaced. "Not much, I'm afraid. The chief inspector ran me off before I could ask too many questions."

Adelynn blew fringe out of her eyes and flattened her lips. "Perhaps I should speak to him."

Were it not for the severity of the moment, Baze would have laughed. "You will do no such thing."

Her eyes flashed. "And why not?"

Sighing, Baze crossed to her. "The man didn't seem keen on entertaining interference by civilians. You'd risk inciting his wrath and keeping us from learning anything at all. We have to approach this carefully." Pain radiated up his kneecap. He gripped the back of the sofa to relieve the weight on his leg. "Though perhaps we have nothing to worry about. Perhaps this vision was a lone occurrence, a fluke caused by remnants of Cornelius's power. Who's to say this means anything?"

She scrunched up her face. "The visions had meaning then, and I believe this one has meaning now."

Baze touched her shoulder, pulled her into an embrace, and tucked her head beneath his chin. "Don't let this be a burden upon you. We already put this behind us." She relaxed against him but didn't speak. He exhaled. "I'm exhausted."

"Me too," she whispered.

"We should get some rest. We can revisit this in the morning."

Adelynn remained quiet, then nodded. Moisture soaked through his shirt as she buried her face against his chest. "I love you."

He squeezed tighter. "I love you too."

Father's favorite song, "The Parting Glass," hummed in the back of my mind as Cornelius's form materialized before me. A dying candle cast weak light across his amused features. Grinning, he sat facing me on a backward chair, arms rested on the top rail. We were back in that room where he had sequestered me at the Empress Theatre before our final confrontation on the stage.

"What be you plannin' to do, sweet *cailin*?" His voice echoed and distorted, then faded.

"About what?" I whispered, my own voice hollow and distant.

His gaze bored into me. "Those visions of yours. Surely you didn't think you were done."

I bared my teeth. "Get out of my head, Cornelius."

A smirk twisted his lips. "Say it as though you truly mean it in your heart, *cailin*. After all, is God not on your side? Or have you already forgotten?"

He laughed a resounding, maniacal laugh.

I tore from the grips of sleep with a jerk, eyes wide, chest heaving. The bedcovers coiled around my body as though trying to bind me as Cornelius had done. I reached for Baze, but my hand fell upon an empty pillow. Alert, I sat up and searched the room. Shadowed lumps loomed in the darkened space, but none of the silhouettes belonged to Baze. *Where has he gone?*

Panic began edging into me until I heard a faint rustle coming from the adjoining room. Trembling, I slipped from the bed, donned a silk robe and slippers, and followed the sound.

Though the sitting room sat veiled in darkness, my well-adjusted vision allowed me to make out the shapes of the furniture. Near the far wall, with his back to me, Baze stood before the cabinet. As I crept toward him, he lifted something to his mouth and threw his head back, then swallowed.

"Baze?" I whispered.

His body jolted. He spun. A glass tumbled to the floor but remained intact, its fall softened by the rug. Baze stooped to retrieve it. "I didn't hear you approach."

"What are you doing up at this hour?" The sharp sent of alcohol laced with something sweet filled my nostrils. I frowned, the smell arousing recognition. "Is that laudanum?"

He took a long, deep breath in through his nose. "The pain was keeping me awake."

"I didn't know you were still taking it. I thought Frederick said you should seek out something weaker. He was concerned—"

"I got a second opinion." Baze smacked the glass down on the cabinet. He closed his eyes and stood still for a moment, as though letting the effects of the medicine wash through him. "The smaller dose wasn't working for me."

My stomach tightened. "But—"

"The dosage is irrelevant. That it takes away my pain is all that matters." He slid a hand down my arm and grasped my hand. "It allows me to be fully present for you. Isn't that enough?"

My emotions of alarm and relief warred against one another. To see him released from his pain, even temporarily, lightened my heart in ways that encouraged me not to press any further on the matter. Still, he had been on medication since the accident—first morphine and then a potent tincture of opium. The surgeon had expressed confidence in the drug's ability to subdue pain, but Frederick reserved judgment, having explored recent literature citing its addictive effects . . . and how difficult it was to break that addiction.

I ran my thumb over his fingers. "Promise me you'll speak to Frederick once more when we return home."

Baze's expression brightened into amusement. "You worry too much, Al. This is a *good* thing, and I'm sure Frederick would say the same. Besides"—his eyes grew tender—"without it, I couldn't do something like this." He grasped my waist and hoisted me into his arms.

Squealing at the upward momentum, I clung to his shoulders and locked my legs around his hips to keep from falling. "Stop. Put me down. You'll hurt yourself."

He laughed, eyes sparkling with euphoric delight. "It's *okay*." He spun us around. "See?"

"No, you shouldn't be doing this. That medicine only masks your—"

His mouth cut off the rest of my words. A nagging feeling of concern prodded my belly as I tasted the sweet yet bitter concoction lingering on his tongue, but I forced it away, trying to quell my doubts and allow his joy to settle in me.

Chapter Six

PINPRICKS OF COLD RAIN STUNG EMILY'S face as she hefted her basket on one arm and braced her son in the other. The Clock Tower tolled the six o'clock hour. Blinking against the precipitation, she crossed the pavement and ducked into the shadow of New Scotland Yard. Her stomach turned as she wrestled to get the door open. Every time she saw the familiar, red-bricked façade of police headquarters, it sent her mind spinning with memories—both heartening and melancholy.

A rush of warm air mixed with the odor of cigarette smoke and mildew greeted her upon entering. Without thinking twice, she boldly weaved her way through the well-known halls, having walked this track countless times before . . . with Bennett.

Superintendent Richard Whelan's office came into view, situated at the front of several rows of desks where officers worked. Whelan leaned against the doorjamb, speaking to another man, when he looked up at her approach. His graying mustache and thick mutton chops spread as he smiled wide. "Emily!" he boomed, drawing the attention of his men. "Twice in one week? You spoil us."

With a shrug, Emily said, "I have to keep busy somehow."

Whelan slapped a hand to his hefty paunch and guffawed. "It appears you've made it your personal mission to expand our waistbands." He winked. "Seeing as how I'm well taken care of in that regard, I'll have to leave the rest for the men. Sorry I can't natter on, but I'm in the middle of important business. You understand."

"Of course."

Whelan and his companion disappeared into his office.

Hiking Basil Allan farther up her hip—eliciting a small protest from him—Emily sought out the nearest desk. She set her sights on the space belonging to the newly promoted Sergeant Rollie Bounds, his bright red hair serving as a beacon among the sea of other officers, and thumped the basket down upon it.

Rollie jumped. Then, realizing who stood before him, sprang to his feet and saluted. "Emily . . . er, Mrs. Bennett. It's good to see you. I mean . . ."

"I brought your favorite." Emily chuckled and pushed back the linen keeping the baked raspberry scones warm and fresh. "All for you, Rollie."

Without further hesitation, he reached for a scone and sank his teeth into the golden-brown pastry. His eyes rolled shut, and his freckled cheeks flushed.

The enticing aroma attracted a throng of other officers from around the room. They crowded around the desk, eyes wide and lips smacking.

Emily stepped back and let them have their fill, nodding at their praise and "thank you, ma'ams." She leaned her head against her son's, enjoying the softness of his hair against her cheek, and watched the officers enjoy a brief moment of delight. "Thanks for all you do," she whispered.

"Mrs. Bennett?"

A deep rumbling voice pulled her attention to a tall officer approaching her. Sergeant Rees Andrews—the man who had led the charge and accompanied Adelynn into the Empress Theatre when they were trying to flush Cornelius out and the same man who had taken it upon himself after Bennett's death to see to it that Emily was well looked after.

Sergeant Andrews nodded toward Basil Allan and raised his eyebrows. "Might I take him off your hands for a minute? Give your arms a rest?"

Emily's stomach clenched as she tried to determine how to accommodate his request without planting more seeds of hope within him. Yet, her arms begged for a reprieve, and anytime she could find a moment to rest without her son, despite her unwavering love for him, she leapt at the chance.

"I appreciate it. Thank you."

Sergeant Andrews bent the significant distance between them and scooped up Basil Allan in his large, muscular arms. Emily marveled at how easily he hefted the child—as though he weighed nothing—and tried to picture what Bennett would have looked like carrying their son.

Basil Allan pushed against Sergeant Andrews's broad chest and frowned up at his face. The sergeant flashed an overexaggerated expression. "What do you think, little man? Not quite the same as your mum, huh?"

Basil Allan continued to stare, his displeasure resolute in the crinkle of his forehead and the pucker of his lips.

Sergeant Andrews laughed. "He has a more intimidating appearance than most of the police officers I've come across."

"He certainly knows what he wants." Emily scratched her son's back with light fingers.

The sergeant drew closer, his spiced masculine scent engulfing her. Longing ignited within her, followed by a cold loneliness. "If you don't mind my asking, how are you?"

After taking a moment to gain control of her voice, Emily craned her neck so she could peer up at him. By the sincerity in his brown eyes, he seemed truly concerned—that she didn't doubt—but here wasn't the place to make her feelings known . . . and not to him.

She forced a smile. "I am well. I've managed to regain some of my lost clients, so I've been able to work."

Sergeant Andrews watched her a moment before leaning even closer, and Emily fisted her hands to keep herself from retreating from him. "But how are you really? It's been nearly one year since—"

"Yes, I know." The words burst out sharper than she'd intended, but she was pleased by the effect it had, as Sergeant Andrews stepped back, expression apologetic. Emily sighed to tamp down her rising anger. "I am well, Sergeant. Really. And I appreciate your asking." She held out her arms for her son. "It's time we were on our way."

After handing over the child, Sergeant Andrews rubbed the back of his neck. "I apologize, Mrs. Bennett. I overstepped."

"No harm done." She squeezed Basil Allan to her chest, finding comfort in his dense warmth and sweet baby scent. "I will return later to fetch the basket."

As she headed for the exit, she passed Whelan's office and caught a clip of conversation through the slight opening in the door.

"The blighter's one of those IRB spies, isn't he?"

"It appears so."

"Well, keep looking into it. Find out if they're connected—"

Emily managed to keep walking, but her agitation swelled with each passing step. The IRB—the Irish Republican Brotherhood—the name under which the monster who shot her husband had been working. They were the reason for all of this. The reason she faced each day with anxiety and emptiness. The reason her son would never know his father.

What were they doing back in London? Were they continuing Cornelius's work? Well, now that he was dead, they should take their fight back to Ireland where it belonged and stop involving innocent civilians or diligent policemen.

As she imagined the violent nationalists leaving the city, her mind drifted to another Irishman who had chosen to journey back to his homeland.

Finn.

The deluge of anger raging inside her eased as she pictured the Irish magician, with kind eyes and gentle accented voice. Where was he now? She prayed that he had safely completed his passage home to Liscannor. She tried to envision him working in the quaint seaside village, living a modest and peaceful life—yet, for some reason, she couldn't quite bring herself to imagine that he had settled down with an Irish lass.

Allowing the images of Finn to fade, Emily hailed a cab and traveled home. Though she lived within walking distance of New

Scotland Yard, she had taken to traveling by cab of late, the streets having seemed more ominous and unsafe since the loss of Bennett's stalwart, protective presence.

The cab dropped her at the front stairs of her house, its walls sandwiched on both sides by other narrow residences. She stared for a moment at the green door—noting the stray green flecks on the handle that Bennett had accidentally splattered when he'd repainted it—before willing herself to trudge up the steps.

Basil Allan's unconscious form weighed down her shoulder. She hugged him tighter as she pushed through the front door. When it swung shut, silence and darkness enveloped her. Dusty sunbeams tried to penetrate the curtains but only managed to cast a thin sliver across the wall. Sharp ticking from the wall clock interrupted the otherwise unadulterated silence.

Standing before the empty room, Emily dragged her gaze across the lone armchair by the window where Bennett used to sip coffee in the wee hours of the morning before work so he wouldn't wake her, across the sofa where she and Bennett had spoken tender words about their unborn child before he had walked out the door for the last time.

Loneliness swallowed her, and she allowed the last of the façade that she carried when out in public to dissipate fully. Her body trembled in response.

Why do I keep coming back here? There's nothing here for me anymore. I should just sell the lot, retreat into the country, and be done with it.

Yet, as painful as it was to reside alone in a place she had once shared with her love, the thought of losing the place where they had built the beginning of their lives together proved unbearable.

Drawing a shuddering breath, Emily padded on numb feet to the bedroom—not the one in which she and Bennett had delighted in so many sweet nights, but the guest bedroom. Basil Allan's crib sat next to the plain bed. She leaned over the rail and placed him gently within. He twitched but remained deep in slumber.

Emily brushed aside his silky hair and traced one of his eyebrows. She tried not to let her mind wander to what Sergeant Andrews had reminded her of—not that she ever needed reminding of the day Bennett had been ripped from her life. She didn't fault him for the sting his words had caused, but she wished he had never uttered them all the same.

Emily's nose burned as her eyes filled, and Basil Allan became no more than a blur of colors. She cleared her throat and managed to maintain control, then crept from the room. Shivering, she headed for the kitchen to put the kettle on, but the dim light and her tear-filled eyes obscured the path forward. She tried to gauge the location of the furniture as she passed from the sitting room into the kitchen, but her toes caught the claw-foot leg of a table. She spilled forward. Her palms and knees skidded on the hard floor. The table collapsed, launching its contents everywhere, and a piece of it snapped off with a sharp *crack*.

Emily stilled, listened. Miraculously, Basil Allan stayed quiet.

Then tears came swift and thick, her emotions finally crashing through the dam that had been holding them back. She embraced herself and rocked. After enduring so much, after pushing down so many emotions, how could *this* have been the trigger needed to make her break?

"I'm not strong enough." She whimpered. "I'm not strong enough to do this, Lord. Why would you let me go through this? Why would you take him?" She trembled, and her limbs and feet throbbed. "*You* let this happen. So you must help me get through this. You owe me that much."

She had never uttered such hostile, demanding words to the Creator, but for the moment, she didn't care. It was the only thing that gave her some sense of control. After all, weren't the ancient Psalms filled with pain and petition, of David lamenting countless times to the same Creator? If the king of Israel was allowed moments of weakness, why not she?

When she finally quieted and her knees began to complain for having knelt upon the hard floor, Emily dried her cheeks with a sleeve, breathed in a renewing breath, and stood. She righted the table and began collecting its spilled contents. Most of it was the post she'd been ignoring for several days. As she stacked it in her hands, she glanced at the names just for the sake of it—a letter from her mother, another petition from the local ladies' guild trying to secure her membership, her monthly compensation so generously provided by Baze, and a letter from Frances Ford.

Emily paused at Mrs. Ford's note. Though she had been acquainted with Baze's mother for only a short time, the woman knew Bennett almost as well as Emily did, having watched him grow up at her son's side. Mrs. Ford had reached out after Bennett's death and consistently called upon Emily each week since.

Though her heart warmed at the older woman's letter, Emily hadn't the strength to read it—not today—so she continued on. Near the bottom of the stack, she came across an envelope constructed of crude tan paper. The postage appeared unfamiliar, so she glanced curiously at the name, its handwriting blocky and unsure.

Finn O'Brien.

Emily gasped and dropped the stack. The letter landed faceup, the name big and bold as though screaming for her attention. Finn . . . The last time she'd seen him, she had requested that he write to her so she would know he made it back to Ireland safely. That had been nearly three months ago. She hadn't expected anything in the first month, figuring it would take him a while to settle, but as the weeks continued to pass, she gave up expectations that he would ever reach out. She assumed he had become so integrated in his new life that he no longer cared for those he'd met in England.

But now . . . what could have prompted his correspondence? What could he possibly have to say—and to her, no less?

Gingerly, she lifted the letter as though any sudden movement might make it crumble in her fingers. She turned it over and opened the seal. The envelope contained two full pages of Finn's writing, beginning at the top with a delicate, "Dear Emily."

Emily found herself barely breathing. It was real. He had indeed written to her. Clutching the letter to her chest, she struggled to her feet, left the strewn post on the floor, and hurried to the armchair for a more appropriate and formal setting.

Preparing her heart, and battling through her fear, she finally took the letter in both hands and began reading to herself.

Dear Emily,

It has been several months since you instructed me to write to you of my arrival in Ireland. I apologize for the delay and hope that you will be receptive to my correspondence. Enough time has passed that I wonder if you have forgotten me. In fact, imagining that you had moved on with your life nearly prevented me from drafting this letter, but I wanted you to know that I have not forgotten you. Not for a moment.

I made landfall in Ireland not long after I departed from you. I will admit, stepping onto my homeland conjured more emotion than I was prepared for. I went immediately to Liscannor, to home. My parents' house still stood, albeit in degrading condition. I have spent this whole time repairing and improving it, and it is finally in a livable state. The house is situated just north of town, overlooked by the ruins of Liscannor Castle. I wish I could take you for a stroll by the bay, where rock formations rise above the water and the lush green hills roll across the countryside. And the smells are exactly what I remember smelling so long ago—the salty spray from the ocean, earthy pastures harboring flocks of sheep, and slats of fish sold by merchants nearby.

Emily closed her eyes to imagine the scene he described. Then she continued reading.

I have found modest work. A local carpenter took me on as an apprentice, as I had never learned a trade apart from magic but still wanted to work with my hands. I host magic shows for the local children every so often to keep my skills sharp. I do not know why I cannot let it go. Perhaps one day I will return to it full time, but not yet.

Now, you have no obligation to write back to me. To believe that you have read this is enough to put my heart at ease, but I truly wish to know that you are well, you and your son. The demons of the past continue to haunt me, and I can only imagine that they torment you even more. I have been through intense pain, as have you, so if you allow, I would like to help, both in word and in prayer.

I will leave this letter here, Emily. I think of you often, heartened by the fact that you have your son to carry on Inspector Bennett's legacy. Be well, and may God's blessing be upon you.

Sincerely,

Finn O'Brien

Emily reread the letter once more, savoring the care he put into each word. Then she pressed the wrinkled paper to her chest and closed her eyes. When he hadn't written to her right away, she had surmised that he'd forgotten about her, or perhaps even consciously tried to banish her from his thoughts—for thinking of her also meant remembering the horrors they had endured. However, this was proof she had never left his mind . . . and he had never left hers.

Fighting off a smile, Emily rose and hobbled into the kitchen. She fetched a blank sheet of paper and a pen before sitting at the table. She paused and stared at the broken edge of the wood, her heart pounding. Then she poised the writing instrument and scrawled, "Dear Finn."

Chapter Seven

ARM IN ARM, BAZE AND ADELYNN stepped into the majestic shadow cast by the morning sun shining on the ancient Roman Baths. Nearby, at the corner of Bath Abbey across the square, a busker performed a classical tune on his violin, the music a jovial accompaniment to the conversation rising from the vast crowd of ladies and gentlemen who promenaded through the streets and awaited entrance to the baths.

When Baze and Adelynn entered the baths, two suited men greeted them. The older of the duo tipped his head. "Ma'am, you will find the ladies' quarters that way." He pointed to the right. "I shall take you there. Sir, if you would follow my assistant."

As the staff members turned to lead the way to their respective baths, Baze held Adelynn back and stole a kiss. "If only we could bathe together," he murmured just loud enough for her to hear.

She swatted his chest. "No one forced you to come. We could make an escape back to our hotel room if you feel so strongly."

"Don't tempt me." He tasted her lips once more and winked, but as he spun to follow the man, he sobered, chest tightening. No, as much as Baze longed to spend his every waking moment with Adelynn, he needed to do this. The legends said the hot spring waters had been providing healing to the sick and wounded for centuries. For what seemed like the thousandth time since he woke, Baze prayed that there was some truth to the tale and that he would find permanent relief.

The staff member led Baze to a dressing area and left him with instructions. After yanking on a bathing suit, Baze followed a short passageway that opened into the bathing area.

As the bath came into view—a massive rectangular structure filled with dark blue-green water—Baze found himself marveling at the ancient architecture of the structure. Thick ornate columns lined the bath's edge, supporting a covered area that wrapped around the outer perimeter. The middle of the ceiling gaped open, exposing the water below to the bright sky above. How could something so old have survived for so long while being unprotected from the ferocious elements?

Baze shook his head and focused on the water. Enough stalling.

Submerging himself in the hot liquid, Baze winced as he put pressure on his crippled leg. He grabbed the rough edge of the bath wall and leaned all his weight onto his good leg, trying to ignore the pompous stares of the well-to-do men who lounged about in the pool and wishing once again that he and Adelynn could share their own private bath.

He closed his eyes and forced his mind away from the tingling in his leg. The feel of the water lapping around his chest recreated a memory from his childhood—one of the rare instances when he and his three brothers had all been together. They'd gone to the beach in the summertime. As the humidity closed in and the sun shone down, they had splashed gleefully in the shallow water for hours, carefree and closer than they'd ever been . . . until a nearby family had begun screaming. Baze had stared in horror as an adult dragged an unconscious boy from the water and breathed into the child's mouth. Frederick was quick to whisk Baze away.

"What's he doing, Fred?" Baze had whimpered, straining to watch the scene over his shoulder.

Frederick dropped to his knee and gripped Baze's face to force his attention from the commotion. "That man is trying to save the boy's life."

Baze gaped in fright. "Is he going to die?"

"I do not know." Frederick's features fell. "Artificial respiration is the only technique that has had any success in saving a drowning person, but it is not always effective."

Baze's leg spasmed, yanking him back to the present. Flexing his foot, he clenched his jaw in frustration. Thankfully, he still clutched the side of the pool and hadn't gone under himself while distracted. If anything, the pain had grown worse the longer he soaked. Why had they come all this way to seek healing from these waters if they weren't even going to heal him?

The sound of a gravelly throat clearing snapped Baze out of his reverie. He glanced to the side to find an elderly man, perhaps late sixties or early seventies, standing beside him. The first thing he noticed was the shock of white hair, surprisingly full for a man of his age.

Baze tried leaning away but ran up against the pool wall. "May I help you?"

"I couldn't help but observe your limp as you entered." The man's thick eyebrows rose. "You wouldn't happen to be seeking the bath's healing powers, would you?"

Before Baze could form a response, a group of older men nearby guffawed. "Let the young man alone, Sebastian. You've enough test subjects," one of them shouted with a laugh.

The white-haired man waved a hand at the gentlemen and scoffed, then smiled at Baze, gray eyes sparkling and thin skin wrinkling across his brow and temples. "Do not pay them any mind. I am a physiotherapist, retired of course, but I have taken quite the interest in these mythical Roman springs. I have lived my entire life in Bath, so I have seen countless people travel from across the world to have a taste of these waters." Sebastian gestured to Baze's leg. "Now tell me. What sort of ailment afflicts you?"

Baze's head reeled. Why was this physiotherapist asking strangers about their personal sufferings? Did he have no boundaries? Yet, something in Baze wanted to trust the man. Maybe it was his jolly, grandfatherly build. Or maybe it was his gentle tone, which reminded Baze of the tone Thomas Spencer, Adelynn's late father, had once used—succinct, articulate, and kind.

"I was injured last year, and there were complications after surgery," Baze found himself saying.

The man stroked his white bushy mustache. "Ah, and what kind of injury?"

"A compound fracture. Suffered on the job." Baze bit the inside of his cheek. Why was he sharing this information with a stranger?

"My heavens." Sebastian widened his eyes. "What do you do that would put you in such a harrowing situation?"

Baze hesitated, then said, "I'm an officer. Detective Inspector Basil Ford."

"Charmed." Sebastian swirled his hand with a small bow. "I am Sebastian Cutler." He tilted his head as he straightened. "Ford, you say? I recognize the name. Were you not involved in the investigation of that string of murders in London last year? A right shame, that." His eyes grew cloudy. "I can't imagine what that feels like. Taking a man's life. I swore an oath to protect life, so aside from the unavoidable medical mishap, these hands have never stolen a life."

The sound of a firing gun punctured Baze's skull as the image of Cornelius's body flying backward flared to life. Baze grew nauseous. "It's not something I recommend."

Sebastian smiled. "Well, you did what was necessary, so don't think any more on the matter." He made a grabbing motion. "Now, if you please, I'll see that leg now."

Baze frowned. "I beg your pardon."

"Your leg. I should like to examine it. I have more than forty years of experience in my field, and I must have something to keep me busy in retirement. Perhaps I can help increase your rate of healing."

Baze glanced at the cluster of men, but Sebastian tsked. "Don't pay them any heed. They're of no consequence. They've seen me do this countless times."

"That's what he wants you to believe," one shouted amidst more laughter.

Sebastian kept Baze pressed under a soft stare. "If you knew something had the potential to take away your pain, would you not at least give it a try?"

Baze snorted. "That's why I came here, as you said—for the healing waters."

"A little reinforcement couldn't hurt." The physiotherapist winked.

Caressing the bridge of his nose, Baze pondered. What *could* it hurt? Letting the therapist look at it wouldn't stop him from seeking the bath's powers. Then again, what if the therapist told him something he didn't want to hear?

"Come on. Let him have a look," one of the other men shouted. "He'll never leave you in peace if you don't."

"Humor him," another hollered.

Baze sighed. "Very well."

Leaning against the bath wall, Baze draped both arms over the edge to hang on and floated his right foot up into Sebastian's waiting hands. The therapist made quick work of it, massaging the irregular tissue of his calf, prodding every inch of flesh, as Baze tried to tamp down the unease brought on by having a man handle him like so, and in public no less.

Sebastian grasped Baze's foot with one hand while supporting his calf with the other. "Now, tell me if this hurts." He flexed Baze's foot toward him.

The muscle tightened and popped. Baze sucked in a breath and clutched at the bath edge.

Sebastian grunted. "That's a yes, then."

"Yes," Baze said through his teeth. He yanked his foot away and submerged his leg. "What have you learned?"

"Well, you sustained a nasty injury, that is obvious, and the surgery complications certainly did you no favors. Tell me, how have you managed to operate in the day to day, especially in your occupation?"

Baze averted his eyes. "I've found ways to manage the pain."

The therapist folded his arms. "How much opium are you taking?"

Baze's mouth grew dry as he tried to remember the dosage the doctor had first prescribed him. "A thousand drops twice a day."

A knowing smile peeked out from under Sebastian's mustache. "And how much are you taking presently?"

Baze swallowed, stubbornness rising. "Enough to quell the pain."

"I see." Sebastian tapped his chin. "Now, I do believe I could be of service to you. Some orthopedic exercises could help and allow you to live with minimal pain and medications. Come." He gestured to the bath steps. "Take a drink with me in the Pump Room, and we can discuss the matter further."

Pebbles in the uneven floor tickled and poked my bare feet as I padded through a short passage lined with Corinthian columns. The thick air grew humid and plastered the thin shift I now wore to my skin. Clutching my tray of salts and soaps that a maid had bequeathed to me, I passed from the shadowed hall to a bright bath area and squinted. Steam hovered above the circular pool, and the warm air filled my lungs and nose with the scent of earth and minerals. Several groups of women relaxed and conversed in hushed tones, some still wearing their opulent hats despite having changed into bathing attire.

Taking a readying breath, I crossed to the stairs disappearing below the water's surface and stepped in. As the water rose to my calves, my skin prickled with heat. I nearly leapt the rest of the way in and let out a delighted gasp as the warm water enveloped me up to my neck. I closed my eyes, reveling in the moment of absolute bliss. Whether or not the healing rumors were true, I now understood how many had come to believe such claims.

Time became lost to me as I relaxed, spreading the fragrant salts over my skin and allowing the water to lull me into an intense state of calm.

I tilted my neck over the edge of the bath, eyes shut, and wondered if Baze was experiencing the same delight as I . . . and if the waters were helping his leg.

Oh, Baze. That I could take his pain away. The ache always seemed to haunt him at every turn, tightening his expression and coloring his tone despite his best efforts to hide it. Forget that he lived in perpetual pain—it also kept us emotionally distant, as he had never expressed his true feelings toward his injury, only apathy.

Yet, he had also never been more vulnerable to me than in these recent days. Through the shared events of the past, through our blessed union, we had drawn closer together than we had ever been, in every sense—in thoughts, in emotions, in body . . .

The temperature spiked, and my cheeks flushed. I sank lower into the water until it lapped just beneath my eyes, then blew bubbles through my nose in amusement. How was it possible that my heart could hold so much love without bursting?

Haze swirled before my eyes as the atmosphere continued to warm, soon reaching an uncomfortable level. I stood fully upright to let my skin cool in the air—the water dropping below my bosom—but it had warmed too much, even for that. *What is happening? Is this normal?*

Fanning my face, I glanced at the other women to see if the temperature affected them too, but they carried on with their conversations, oblivious. My head spun with the intense heat. I rose to my tiptoes to achieve any kind of relief from the sweltering liquid and made for shallow waters. *I need to get some air. I need—*

Darkness struck. My consciousness lurched from my body and into the point of view of another.

I loitered near the perimeter of a grand room stretching beneath a vaulted ceiling. Well-dressed gentlefolks occupied the many decorated tables, snacking on scones and enjoying afternoon tea. Near the entrance of the room stood an ancient stone fountain spewing streams of water out of three fish-shaped holes in each of its sides. A waiter stood beside it, speaking to a red-headed woman dressed in an ivory lace gown and wide hat. The man tipped a crystal glass beneath the fountain's flow, then handed it to her.

Holding the glass with both hands, the woman raised it to her red lips and drank. She wrinkled her nose and handed it back to the man with a laugh. "Terrible as always. I don't know why I ever think differently."

She turned from the fountain, then halted. Her skin flushed as she gripped her stomach and doubled over. Her intense green eyes locked with mine before she collapsed.

The scene melted away.

I spasmed and gasped. Water filled my lungs. Thin fingers yanked on my shoulders and scooped up my arms. I burst through the surface of the bath. Racking coughs consumed me as my body tried to expel the inhaled liquid.

Three women supported me as I continued to hack until my airway cleared. My head pounded and my lungs ached. I tried to push the women away, aware that all others had turned to stare, but they held on with surprising strength.

"Easy, dear one. You appear to have fainted. You must rest."

"No." I shook my head, coughing again. "No, I have to . . . I have to go."

This time, with a firm downward swing of my arms, I managed to escape the group and began wading for the stairs, the water's fierce resistance only fueling my muscles. The Pump Room. Based on key features—namely the strangely shaped fountain—that scene had occurred in the Pump Room adjacent to these baths. I don't know why I was determined to dash to the scene when every time before had ended in tragedy. Maybe, just maybe, this time could be different . . .

I splashed out of the pool, rushed to my garments, and haphazardly threw everything on, not even bothering to properly lace my corset or fasten all the buttons on my dress.

Then I ran, following the signs that pointed me to the Pump Room. Water flung from my limbs with every pounding step. Homed in on a distant door, I swiped wet strands of hair from my face, braced for impact against the door, and burst into the Pump Room. Several people gaped at me. I ignored them and scanned the area.

There. Against the far wall—the red-headed woman. Baze and an elderly gentleman stood nearby, but I only had eyes for the woman as she raised the glass to her lips.

"No!" I shouted as loudly as I could muster and lunged at her. She spun toward me. I batted the glass out of her hands. A cacophony of gasps and shouts rose from the crowd.

I held my breath, exchanging horrified stares with the woman. I waited one moment, then two. Still, she remained standing.

Air stole from my lungs. Each of my previous visions filtered through my mind's eye. Each victim's face appeared as vivid as the day I had witnessed their deaths. They had all perished, every last one, my visions having seemed the catalyst that signaled their inevitable fate. And yet, here she stood, the most recent victim. Alive.

Chapter Eight

TIME DRAGGED TO A HALT. ERRATIC heartbeats roared in my ears. All eyes in the Pump Room pierced me. Hushed, accusatory murmurs rippled through the crowd as I tried to figure out what to do next. The woman whom I had seen die a moment ago stood before me—hale and hearty, as though she hadn't sipped from a poisoned glass and keeled over. But *how*? How had I arrived in time?

Eyeing the spilled glass on the floor, then tracing her gaze up the length of my body, the woman raised her eyebrows a tick. "All right, there?"

I blinked and squinted through the hair hanging in clumps around my face. Did she not realize what just happened? Here I stood, soaked to the bone and shivering uncontrollably, having burst through the door and attacking her without warning.

A gentle hand pressed against my back, then Baze whispered, "Al, what are you doing?"

His touch snapped me out of the initial shock and loosened my lips. "I have reason to believe that water has been poisoned," I blurted, eliciting gasps and more urgent mumbles from the crowd.

The woman narrowed her eyes before throwing a quizzical glance to the server beside the fountain. "Trying to off me, are you?"

The young man's face paled, but before he could respond, the woman erupted in sharp laughter, bending over at the waist and placing both hands on her stomach. Everyone fell silent as she carried on, the mood tense despite her mirth.

I whirled, caught a fistful of Baze's coat, and whispered, "I saw her die, Baze. She was supposed to die. That water is poisoned."

"Carry on, ladies and gents," the woman called, drawing my attention back her way. She straightened and brushed her hands down the front of her gown, carrying herself erect and lifting her chin. "'Twas a simple misunderstanding, I'm sure. My guardian angel here was confused." She waved a graceful hand toward me. "The horrid events at the Empire the other day have her a touch on edge. Nothing a good hot tea can't fix."

The woman glided up to me and wound a comforting arm about my shoulders. "Let's get you cleaned up," she said with a low, soothing tone. "You look a right mess."

As the woman pulled me along with her, I turned back to Baze, briefly pausing our progression, and flashed him a look of urgency in hopes that he would investigate the matter. He nodded and mouthed, "I understand."

Satisfied, yet chased by the niggling feeling of danger, I allowed the woman to whisk me through the hallway and into the ladies' washroom where I had first readied for the baths. Clicking her tongue, she situated me in an empty section of the room a good distance away from the nearest patron. "Wait a moment," she said with a wag of her finger and breezed from the room.

My head reeled. It was vexing enough that the woman had managed to escape death, defying everything I thought I knew about my visions, but now, she tended to me as though *I* had been the one targeted by poisoned water. *God, what are you doing? Why did you allow me to save her? Is she important somehow?*

About five minutes passed before she returned, a pale green gown tucked in her arms. She sized me up, mumbled, "That should do," and laid the gown atop a nearby bench.

When she reached for me, I held up a halting hand, finally bottling my chaotic emotions and grasping hold of good sense. "Why are you doing this?"

The woman raised an eyebrow. "We ladies have to look out for one another. You're troubled, that much I can see, so I refuse to let you look anything but your best while in such a state."

"But I've just made a fool of you in front of those people. For all you know, I could be a complete madwoman."

"We're all a little mad sometimes, angel." Her amused dark eyes caught a ray of light that illuminated her irises' deep emerald color. They twinkled like a pair of rare jewels. She extended an open hand. "Katherine Quinn. Drifter. Journalist. Occasional madwoman." She winked as she shook my hand. "I heard that handsome man of yours call you Al, but I assume that's merely a cute pet name he fabricated for you."

I suppressed the urge to roll my eyes. "Yes, I'm Adelynn. That was my husband. He's called me that since we were children."

"How sentimental of him." Katherine spun me and began unfastening my gown. "Honeymooners?"

My face flushed. "That's quite the bold supposition."

"Oh, angel, there's not much to suppose. It was written all over his face and in those pretty brown eyes of his." She laughed. "It's clear he's enamored with you. You chose well for yourself."

My heart warmed. "Thank you. I think I'll keep him around for a while."

As she helped replace my soiled combinations and corset cover with dry ones, then wrapped my torso in the corset, I sobered. "You mentioned the events at the Empire Hotel when a woman fell dead in the midst of the evening meal. That happened only recently. How did you hear about it?"

"I make it my business to know the goings on in the place I'm currently occupying." She clad me in the new gown, a lace ensemble adorned with elaborate beading. "Care to fill me in on what that was all about in the Pump Room? What brought you to believe the water was poisoned?"

I very nearly divulged the true reason for my suspicions, but I managed to bite my lip. I'd grown accustomed to having Baze and Emily know everything about my gift, but they were the exception. I couldn't go yammering to just anyone, especially considering I barely knew this woman—and didn't yet know the reason she had escaped unscathed. Best to tread carefully until I knew more.

"Well, it was like you said. The woman from last night has me on edge. I witnessed her death, you know. Saw her foam at the mouth and drop dead."

"How awful!" She combed her fingers through my damp hair, twirled it about, and secured it at the back of my head. "I hope you are able to find healing from such a horrible thing."

Katherine directed me back around to face her. Then she unpinned her hat, placed it atop my head, and fastened it in place. Now free from the shadows cast by the hat's wide brim, her bright red hair shone with a fiery glow, complementing her freckled, milky skin. Fine lines etched her forehead and the corners of her mouth, suggesting her age was older than I'd first estimated, perhaps late thirties.

"There." She swiped at my shoulder. "Good as new and absolutely radiant."

"Thank you." I felt the brim of the white hat and peered down at my new adornments. "I don't know how I shall repay your kindness." Our eyes locked, and familiarity struck me with realization.

Recognition also piqued behind Katherine's own eyes. Jaw tightening, she gave a curt tip of her head and spun on her heel. "Look out for yourself, angel."

"Wait!" I threw out a hand, clutched her sleeve, and forced her to turn back. I stared, absorbing every detail of her face. Lowering my voice, I said, "You were there." A statement—not a question—for her features were now unmistakable. She was the woman who had been sipping tea in the corner of the dining room, the one who had first alighted my senses and hinted that something out of the ordinary was about to transpire. I squeezed the fabric in my hand. "You witnessed the woman's death at the Empire too. Now you're here. That can't be coincidence. Why—"

"Sally Lunn's," she said, her voice a pitch lower than mine. Her shoulder came up in a lopsided shrug, but her expression remained impassive. "Tomorrow. Four o'clock. Don't be late." She yanked from my grasp, flourished her hand with a curtsy, and dashed behind a pillar, out of sight.

Back inside the Pump Room, I spotted Baze pacing near the tainted fountain. Several of the patrons had vacated their tables, but others remained in place, leaving the room more than two-thirds full. Two officers loitered nearby, speaking to a pair of guests.

Aware that wary eyes followed me, I hurried to Baze's side and grasped his arm in relief. "The police are here?" I said through my teeth.

"Someone must have called them after your outburst. I had to give a statement." Baze directed us closer to the edge of the room. He paused, noticing my new hat and gown. "Where did you . . ." He shook his head and changed course. "Al, what *was* that?"

I took a deep breath before words tumbled from my mouth. "I experienced another vision while I was in the bath. Very nearly drowned me, wretched thing. In it, I saw that woman die after drinking water from the fountain. Something came over me after that. I can't explain it, but despite everything I've experienced before, a small voice whispered that perhaps this time could be different. So I ran. I ran faster than I've ever run before." I squeezed his arm. "Baze, she survived. No one has ever survived before, not after appearing in my visions. I don't know what to do with that."

Baze flattened his lips, eyes hazing over in thought.

"That's not all," I continued, quieting my voice. "I recognized her. She was there the other night in the dining room when the other woman died."

Baze's eyes focused a touch. "What if she was *supposed* to survive?" he said gradually, as though processing aloud. "What if she's not a victim . . . but the very person orchestrating all of this? Why else would she have been in both places you experienced a vision?"

Not the victim—but the perpetrator? Resolve quivered in my

muscles. "I may be able to find out. When I confronted her about her whereabouts, she stated a place and a time before fleeing. I'm to meet her there. It could be my chance to obtain answers."

His chest swelled. "Good. I'll come with you."

I grimaced. "No, I should go alone." When he opened his mouth, I knuckled the bottom of his chin to close it. "I'll likely get more out of her if we're by ourselves. You know, woman to woman. You may think you're unassuming, but your masculine presence could put her off."

Baze frowned. "Al, I can't let you—"

"I've done this before, Baze." I pressed my palm to his chest. "And it turned out all right."

He leaned forward against my hand. "That's only because Bennett was there to—"

"Excuse me!" A voice called out. We turned toward a new officer approaching. As he slowed before us, he checked a notepad in his hands before looking between us. "Mr. and Mrs. Ford?"

Transitioning from an appearance of annoyance to one of inquisitiveness, Baze stepped in front of me and shifted his weight onto his healthy leg. "How may we help you, officer?"

"Detective Chief Inspector Whitaker wishes to speak with you regarding today's incident."

"Told him already, did you?"

The man sniffed. "He likes to stay apprised of everything that might disturb the citizens of Bath." Stashing his notepad, he gestured with his head for us to follow. "Come."

I made to march after the officer, but Baze pinched one of the back buttons of my dress to slow my gait and fell in step with me. He whispered out the side of his mouth. "Leave the talking to me."

Bristling, I linked an arm through his. "What exactly are you insinuating?"

"Only that you have . . . a unique gift for conversation." His dimple appeared. "I'm simply asking you to reserve that skill for another time."

I rolled my eyes. "I shall do my best, and that is all I can promise."

My gaze came to rest upon the fountain as we passed, mesmerized by the smooth liquid spouting from its three small openings. So inconspicuous—yet fatal. In the churning water below one of the streams, a speckle of blue flashed. I squinted, trying to make it out before the distance between us became too great. Five tiny petals gave away its identity. A flower?

Slow gooseflesh swept over my body. Not just any flower. The spring gentian—Cornelius's flower.

The muscles in my legs stiffened, but Baze's supportive arm carried me forward, and the fountain passed from view. I moved rigidly, tongue paralyzed, as the officer led us to a motorcar parked near the abbey.

He drove us the short distance to Orange Grove to a stately building constructed of the sandy Bath stone, and I realized we were within shouting range of the Empire Hotel. A pair of green doors opened onto the main walkway. Inside a room midway through the hall, a thin officer in plain clothes and sporting trimmed blond hair sat behind a hefty desk. Tidy paper stacks consumed one side of its surface, while the opposite side held a lone informal portrait of a smiling trio—the officer, a woman, and a little girl.

The man stood as we approached and extended a hand toward Baze. "Good to see you again, Inspector Ford."

Baze accepted the greeting. "You as well."

The man nodded at me. "Pleased to make your acquaintance, ma'am. I am Detective Chief Inspector Sydney Whitaker."

"Thank you." I nodded, chafing at being called "ma'am" but reserving my rebuttal for another time. "I'm Adelynn Ford."

"Please, have a seat."

As we settled in, Chief Inspector Whitaker rocked back in his chair and crossed one leg over the other. The office space reminded me of Superintendent Whelan's, but unlike Whelan, the chief inspector didn't exude the same intimidating aura—rather, he displayed a more level-headed, composed authority.

Chief Inspector Whitaker stroked his full groomed beard. "Basil Ford." He paused as though mulling over his words. "I thought the name sounded familiar, so I gave an acquaintance at Scotland Yard a ring, and sure enough." His pale blue eyes softened. "You've had quite the year, Inspector. Both of you have. All of us throughout England were fixed on London last year as that serial killer wreaked havoc." His lips tightened. "My condolences for the loss of your partner."

Baze tensed. "Thank you."

"London is in your debt for taking that psychopath down." Chief Inspector Whitaker laced his fingers over his stomach. "One should hope never to encounter such an individual in his lifetime. However, it seems you've been dragged into this once again, not by anyone's choice—but fate's." He studied Baze. "I would like you to come on as a consultant in this case."

Baze hesitated. "I don't understand, sir. You told me—"

"I know what I told you." The chief inspector straightened and opened one of the desk drawers. "But that was before I realized who you were . . . and before we found this." He extracted something from the drawer and placed it on the edge of the desk facing us—a small slip of paper marked with a single sentence: *Give yourself up or these Killings will continue.*

After reading the note another time, Baze frowned. "Do you think this is connected to the crimes of last year?"

"I don't know what I think quite yet." Chief Inspector Whitaker leaned farther back in his chair, eyes on the note. "I had Scotland Yard send me the case files from your serial killer. Mr. Marx seemed keen to leave notes, but I also read his postmortem report. He's good and dead. All I know is that a year ago, you and your wife ended a serial killer, and now the night after you showed up in Bath, a woman turned up dead. So, are they connected? That I can't say yet. But I don't believe in coincidences."

Memories swept me away from the room and into the hospital, when I had sat with Baze after his surgery and discovered that Cornelius had etched the numeral one on himself, indicating that he was the last to die in a descending count of his victims. We had never learned if he had done that to himself . . . or if there was someone else involved, perhaps even pulling the strings behind the whole thing. If it *had* been someone else, could they have made their way to Bath?

The chief inspector crossed his arms again. "Inspector Ford, I'm prepared to open our files and allow you access to investigate with us."

I straightened. "What about me?"

His jaw firmed, though not unkindly. "You're a civilian, Mrs. Ford. I can't involve you. I apologize."

My mouth dropped open. "But I—"

Baze clamped his hand down on mine, flashed a chastising look that said, "Don't argue," and nodded at the chief inspector. "We understand, sir. Thank you."

I fluttered my eyes, displeased, but obeyed.

Chief Inspector Whitaker looked from me to Baze, then nodded. "Do you have time for a thorough debrief, Inspector Ford?"

"If you would allow me to escort my wife back to the hotel, I will return immediately."

"Very well." The chief inspector tapped a finger on the note, muscles pulsing in his temples. He heaved a sigh. "I don't know what we're about to get into, but if you don't already pray to a higher power, I suggest you start."

Chapter Nine

WHEN BAZE AND I EXITED THE police station, he offered his arm to me, silent. I accepted and followed his lead. Rather than head back to the Empire Hotel, however, he coaxed me across the street and down a large stone staircase leading into a lush park beside the River Avon. The sinking sun cast golden rays through the trees and onto the river's swift, sparkling waters.

I flattened my lips and matched Baze's uneven pace as he directed us toward a paved path running parallel to the river's winding procession. Though his eyes drifted across the scenery, his expression remained pensive.

As we drew nearer to the river's edge, Baze pointed to a shallow waterfall no higher than a man's waist cutting diagonally across the river in front of Pulteney Bridge. Two men stood at the waterfall's edge, fishing poles in hand. "That weir was built to prevent flooding in the city, you know," Baze said, voice weary.

I cocked my head, watching the fishermen a bit more before looking at Baze's distant gaze. "Interesting as that might be, I don't quite believe that's the reason for our stroll."

Baze cast his eyes to the path before us but didn't offer explanation. It took every ounce of self-control not to probe for more information.

We passed another strolling couple and then a gentleman with a dog. Children played near a gazebo situated in the center of a large green lawn, their delighted squeals joining the pleasant rush of the weir's falling water to create a blissful atmosphere. Somewhere far in the distance, the wind enhanced the lone notes of a busker's violin.

"Bold of the chief inspector not to include me," I ventured. "After all, were it not for my visions, we wouldn't be involved in this mess. You shall have to divulge every detail you learn."

Baze grunted. "I'll tell you what I can."

I pursed my lips so as not to argue, then huffed. "Well, we should talk about my rendezvous tomorrow. I need to be alert so I can learn everything about our Miss Katherine Quinn."

"Who?"

I wiggled his arm. "The woman from the baths. Remember? I'm to meet with her tomorrow for tea. Any advice on how to make someone talk?"

Baze's eyes brightened slightly as we rounded the path's corner and headed toward the middle of the park, back to where we had come.

"If she was indeed there the night that woman died, you need to figure out how she might be connected. Does anything link them as victims of attempted murder? Then learn about her family, about any spouses, any children." He watched the youngsters playing near the gazebo while he spoke. "And if she ever gives a short answer or doesn't speak, stay silent for a moment . . . if you can." A slow grin replaced the worry on his brow with lines of amusement.

I bumped his shoulder with mine. "I know how to stay silent!"

Rolling in his bottom lip as though to hide the smile, he cleared his throat. "Providing that's true, you should be able to use it to prompt her to say more than she first intends. It's an excellent tactic to coax out information people otherwise would not have shared."

"Providing that's true," I muttered. "Anything else?"

"You need to remain calm and act as though you're engaging in regular conversation. If she realizes you're interrogating her, she may refuse to give up too much. And . . ." His free hand came up to stroke the bridge of his nose. "I want you to stay in public areas. If she's a target, it could be dangerous for you to be around her." He lowered his hand and placed it atop mine.

I leaned my head against his shoulder. "I don't think she's dangerous."

His grip tightened around my fingers. "*She* isn't who I'm worried about."

We approached the wide stairway that led up to the hotel, our enjoyable jaunt in the fresh air nearly at an end. An arched alcove lined in pillars stretched to the right of the stairs, supporting the street above. It wrapped around and followed the river toward Pulteney Bridge.

I sighed, allowing the weight of our conversations to settle within me. "And here I thought we would be able to enjoy our honeymoon in peace."

Baze came to an abrupt halt.

I grunted as his arm jerked me to a stop. "Baze, what are you—"

He lowered his supportive arm, clasped my hand in his, and tugged me away from the stairs and under the shelter of the columned alcove. My stomach lurched as he swung me into one of the small recesses behind a column. Just when I formed another protest, his mouth crashed down on mine. Chills raced from my scalp to my toes, followed by a sweeping heat as he kissed me thoroughly, deeply.

Finally, he drew back, allowing me to gulp in a series of ragged breaths. He gripped my face with both of his hands and stared into my eyes. Muscles in his jaw clenched. "I thought we were done with all this, Al. I thought we would finally have time to heal from what we endured and be able to simply focus on learning how to live as husband and wife." His voice cracked. "I don't want this."

"I know." Throat tightening, I slid a hand over his wrist. "I know."

He drew a long breath in through his nose. "But if we must, then I want to commit to this fully. Last time, you and Bennett investigated without my knowledge."

I winced as I recalled our partnership and how I had lied to Baze. "I'm sorry . . ."

"That's in the past. I've forgiven you." His thumb stroked my cheekbone. "But we're in this together now, you and I. No secrets. We'll share anything we learn, and we'll bring down this monster who has dared target the innocent, just as we did with Cornelius."

"I'm with you." I smiled and squeezed his wrist. "I commit fully. No secrets. No going it alone. We'll solve this together."

Baze sighed, visible relief bowing his shoulders, then bent his head toward mine. Before our lips could meet again, an incredulous gasp startled us apart.

Motionless on the path that looped beside the alcove where we stood, a middle-aged woman clad in extravagant clothes and accessories gawked at us. Her wrinkled, angular face reddened. "You should be ashamed of yourselves. Such immodest conduct is not suitable for public display." She waved a bony finger. "Shame on you!"

I ground my teeth, a rebuttal welling up, but Baze took a backward step away from me. He gave a small bow. "I apologize, ma'am."

She scrunched her nose. "See that it doesn't happen again, young man, else you risk leading pure, innocent minds astray should they witness your irreverent spectacle."

A blush tinted his cheeks. "We didn't realize anyone could see. Truly. We won't—"

Stubbornness flared. I seized Baze's collar, yanked him toward me, and kissed him squarely on the mouth. As we stumbled, he threw out a hand against the column behind me to avoid crushing me into it. Adding dramatic flair for our judgmental audience, I mussed his hair and ran my hands all across his face, his neck, and his chest. With a final loud smack, I pulled back and held his flushed, mortified face in my hands, then cast a defiant look at the woman.

With ashen skin, gaping mouth, and eyes round as saucers, the woman's very soul appeared to have fled her frail body.

"I suggest you move along and mind your own business, ma'am," I said, out of breath. "We have only just begun."

Sputtering, the woman tried to respond, then must have thought better of it, and scurried away.

I looked back to Baze.

Face as red as rouge, he stood stock still, arm yet braced on the pillar. His bulging eyes sparked with incredulity.

Giggling, I straightened his collar and smoothed his ruffled hair. "That should certainly teach her to keep her snooty little nose out of places it doesn't belong."

"I swear, Al"—he cleared his throat, his voice having risen several pitches higher than his usual timbre—"you're going to be the death of me someday."

"Oh, come now." I grasped his jaw and shook it a bit. "A part of you enjoyed that, and you'll never convince me otherwise."

He popped his index finger over my mouth and raised his eyebrows. "Promise me you'll never do that again."

I smirked against his finger. "If I may remind you, *you* started this montage of public display."

"And I can put an end to it." He clasped my shoulders and steered me out from under the alcove.

Laughing, I spun from his hold, came back around, and looped my arm through his. As we fell in step, shoulder to shoulder, I glanced up at him. Though his cheeks remained flushed, a smile teased the corners of his mouth.

My heart swelled, overcome with adoration for this man, but that emotion darkened as the pact we'd agreed upon stormed to the front of my mind. Oh, that our holiday could stay filled with sweet moments like this. Unfortunately, we were about to charge into a new battle, and there was no telling what we might encounter. *Thank you for the moments we've shared thus far, Lord. But I need to ask that you protect us now . . . and help us keep our bond intact.*

Baze followed Detective Chief Inspector Whitaker through the police station, trying to keep pace with the man's long strides without revealing that his leg screamed for him to stop. He and Adelynn had made the most of what little time they had after he escorted her back to their room, and every aching fiber of his being had protested at his abrupt exit. But they'd agreed—if they were to commit fully to the case at hand, he needed to bend to the whims of the Bath Police.

"The woman's name was Mary Sands." Whitaker spoke over his shoulder as he walked. "She'd recently passed sixty summers. She was a wealthy socialite from Oxford on holiday with her husband. Only had one more night to stay, God help her."

"Any idea why she died?"

"Caine should be able to shed some light on that subject." Whitaker pushed through a door, which opened into a narrow, brightly lit room. Sterile, chemical-laden scents irritated Baze's nostrils as he trailed Whitaker inside.

Tables scattered with an array of medical instruments filled the area. At the far end of the space, a short man faced the wall, peering into a microscope, his neck bent and shoulders hunched. He paused a moment, grabbed a pencil, and jotted several notes on a pad that sat among a cluster of crumpled papers and strewn photographs. Then he returned his eye to the instrument.

Whitaker halted them a few paces away from the man and cleared his throat. "Caine?"

The man glanced over his shoulder before turning back to his work. "One moment." His soft, even-toned voice was nearly imperceptible. He checked in the microscope again, then recorded another note, and finally rotated to give them his attention. Even when he straightened, his upper back retained a slight curve, as though he carried a great weight upon his shoulders.

Whitaker waved a hand from Baze to the man. "Inspector Ford, this is our toxicologist, Charles Caine. He's been analyzing what killed Mrs. Sands. Caine, Detective Inspector Basil Ford has been providing assistance in this case."

Baze extended his hand, but the toxicologist only stared at it and massaged his own hands together. Unsure how to recover from the uncomfortable moment, Baze shoved his hands into his pockets.

Eyes unblinking, Caine held Baze in an unnerving stare. "Are you sure it is wise to involve the city police in our affairs, Chief Inspector?"

"I thought the same, but I believe that he has the background and the skill set to help us solve this murder." Whitaker gestured to the toxicologist's workspace. "Would you mind informing the inspector about what we know so far?"

"As you wish, sir." Caine turned on his heel and bowed over his microscope.

Baze frowned and glanced at Whitaker. The chief inspector tilted his head toward Caine and knuckled Baze's shoulder in encouragement before taking his leave.

Clenching his teeth against the bittersweet memory conjured by the motion—the same one Bennett had so often made—Baze approached Caine. "You've already determined it was a murder, then?"

"Considering we found traces of cyanide in the woman's drink and in her blood, yes, we have determined it was a murder."

Baze hesitated, detecting annoyance in the quiet, matter-of-fact tone. Though his knowledge of poisons barely scratched the surface of what a dedicated toxicologist had at his disposal, Baze retained enough information to know that cyanide was not to be trifled with. Several queries formed at the tip of his tongue, but doused in the hostile presence of the toxicologist, the most senseless question tumbled out. "Do you think that's what killed her?"

Caine looked at him askance. "What *else* would have killed her, Inspector?" Letting out a loud sigh, Caine twisted his fingers in his palm. "I have determined the compound to be sodium cyanide—or cyanide salt, as you might call it. Do you know anything about cyanide, Inspector?"

Not wanting to make a fool of himself again, Baze chose a safe response. "I know that it kills quickly."

"When administered in high doses, yes. It appears that Mrs. Sands ingested a potent blend of the compound and suffered acute poisoning within minutes." Caine let the words hang between them. "Cyanide is a terrible poison, Inspector. It forces your cells to retain their oxygen, starving the bloodstream and thus your body of needed energy. You begin to convulse, to breathe rapidly. Your face turns beet red. Then you collapse into a coma. Or death. In essence, you suffocate."

Filling his lungs and holding the air for a prolonged beat, Baze shuddered. In an attempt to diffuse the tension building in the atmosphere, Baze lightened his tone and said, "Is that all?"

Judging by the toxicologist's furrowed brow and pinched mouth, Baze's effort to lift the mood fell flat. "I don't know how you city policemen conduct yourselves, but here in Bath, we take the deaths of our citizens seriously."

"Of course. Apologies." Baze's cheeks burned. He thought of Bennett, of his knack for being able to read a situation and knowing when to inject humor. Clearly, Baze lacked such a skill.

"I have been with the Bath Police longer than you've been alive, Inspector." Caine faced his microscope and adjusted a dial on the side. "I'm good at what I do, and we catch criminals because of it. I didn't get to where I am by making light of a serious situation. You are here to flush out a killer. I suggest you hop to it."

What had gotten the toxicologist in such a temper? Was he carrying the weight of the murder especially deeply, or was this his usual demeanor? Either way, it was clear he had no interest in making pleasant chitchat.

Hands tightening into fists, Baze occupied himself by scrutinizing the contents on the table beside Caine. Several vials of liquid were grouped around the microscope. Among a cluster of stacked notebooks, he noticed a small photograph lying partially covered by other papers. A little boy, perhaps five or six years old, peered out with bright eyes and a crooked smile that revealed a missing front tooth. Though he carried the pudginess of youth, the boy's oval jaw resembled Caine's.

Baze touched a finger to the photograph's corner and slid it out from under the paper. "Is this your son?"

Caine kept his eyes downward, face stoic. "He was."

A final nail strike in the coffin of their acquaintanceship.

Baze winced. "I'm sorry."

Caine removed a clear slide and placed it beside the microscope, then sent Baze a pointed look. "Is there anything else I can assist you with, Inspector?"

The man's fiery gaze sent shivers through Baze. "No. Thank you. This was helpful."

"You should expect nothing less from me."

Chapter Ten

HAND PROTECTED UNDER QUILTED OVEN GLOVES, Emily plucked a tray of biscuits from the stove and plopped them on a burner. Steam spiraled off of the golden-brown pastries and carried the comforting scent into every nook of the kitchen. She glanced over her shoulder to check her father's progress. He sat upon the floor, tools strewn about in a semicircle, working to repair her broken table. "How are you?" she asked.

"Nearly there, Emmie." He grunted with a twist of a wrench. "It'll be good as new in a flash."

"Well, let me know if you need a respite." She tossed her oven gloves onto the counter. "The biscuits have finished baking."

He laughed and slapped his stomach. "You're too good to me."

Emily returned his smile. Then the delighted sounds of a toddler's squeals drew her toward the living room. She leaned against the archway and peered inside.

Mother had Basil Allan draped faceup across her lap. She hovered her hands above his round, exposed belly. He bit his fingers and grinned in anticipation of the tickling attack. Then she struck, scratching his tummy with her fingers, and he squirmed and screeched in delight.

Emily's heart grew larger, nearly bursting with each of his high-pitched laughs.

Mother looked up and noticed her. "Why don't you lie down for a while, Emily? Get off your feet. Basil Allan and I are getting on swimmingly."

Emily nodded, aware of the aches in her bones threatening to collapse her right then and there. "Thank you for coming, Mother."

"No need to thank me. I will accept any chance to see my grandson."

Emily sighed with a weary smile. "I think I will lie down." She pushed off the archway and headed toward the second bedroom, but as she passed through the entrance, a knock sounded on the front door. She groaned inwardly and changed course.

"I can get it," Mother called.

"No, it's fine." As she passed by her son, she made a silly face at him, then sobered once out of his view. She prepared her heart for more company before swinging the door open.

Sergeant Rees Andrews stood at attention in his full police blues. Even though he had stopped on the step below the top landing, his eyeline was level with hers. Her empty basket hung from his fingers, dwarfed by his large hands. "I hope you don't mind my intrusion. I know how busy you must be with your son, so I thought I'd bring this round and save you the trouble." He offered up the basket.

Gathering her wits about her, Emily accepted it and flashed a half-hearted smile. "'Twould have been no trouble, I assure you. I am sorry you had to come all this way."

He waved a hand. "You're but a quick jaunt from New Scotland Yard. I was happy to do it."

Silence bloomed between them. Body tensing with the uncomfortable shift in atmosphere, Emily motioned with the basket. "Well, thank you again."

Sergeant Andrews made no move to leave. Rather, he wrung his hands and placed a foot upon the landing. "If I might, I should like to make a proposition."

Emily's heart thudded. She stepped across the threshold and pulled the door half-closed behind her, hoping to keep whatever he was about to ask from her mother's prying ears. "I don't know if now is a good time, Sergeant Andrews."

"I won't take long." He clasped his hands behind his back and scuffed the concrete landing with the sole of his shoe. "I realize how hard the past year has been for you. Inspector Bennett, God rest his soul, was a force to be reckoned with, and we are all the worse for the wear without him, but your courage and resilience are inspiring. You have faced adversity and loss with the greatest of poise. Yet, I know that raising a son alone, without a male presence especially, must be incredibly difficult."

Emily passed her dry tongue over her front teeth, heart pounding in her throat, knowing where he was headed but unable to construct a tactful way to stop him.

"I wish to ensure you are taken care of. That you should want for nothing. That your son would have the father figure he needs to mold him into a respectable young man." Sergeant Andrews lifted fully onto the landing, dowsing her in his shadow and his masculine scent, and searched her face intently. "I was hoping . . . rather, it would be my honor . . . if you might consider a courtship with me."

Melancholy memories snatched the breath from Emily's lungs and transported her back into the moment when Bennett had asked her to go steady, beneath the romantic willow tree that had become such an integral place for their dalliances. Her heart had sung in anticipation— quite the opposite reaction from what she experienced now.

A ball of emotion rose in her throat as she grappled for words. "I-I am flattered by your interest, Sergeant Andrews. I am. But—"

"Wait." He reached out a hand, nearly touching her shoulder, but refrained. His square jaw firmed. "Before you give an answer, I ask that you ponder it. Pray about it."

Oh, she had. Countless times.

But his expectant, nearly fraught expression tugged on her heartstrings. All instincts within her urged her to say no, but she couldn't bring herself to let him down, not after it had likely taken all of his courage to simply ask her such a thing.

She swallowed. "I shall think about it."

His shoulders relaxed. "Thank you."

Eager to avoid further awkward conversation, she gestured back to the door. "I appreciate your dropping this off, but I must tend to my son. You understand."

"Of course, of course." He backed down the stairs, his gaze lingering upon her face. "Be well . . . Emily."

Though she hadn't given him permission to use her Christian name, she didn't bother correcting him. Not waiting for him to disappear, she retreated inside. In a daze, she wandered toward the couch and set the basket on the floor. Her pulse still raced. The sergeant's attraction toward her certainly didn't come as a surprise. A few months after Bennett's funeral, he had begun consistently showing interest, but she *was* surprised he'd decided to just go for it, especially when she'd been confident that she'd made her disinterest clear.

"A courtship?"

Emily looked to her mother, whose attention was fully on Basil Allan beaming in her lap.

"Don't you think it's a tad soon for such things?"

Emily's stomach tightened. "I didn't answer in the affirmative, Mother. You needn't worry."

Her mother's jaw shifted, her mouth a straight line. Emily recognized the woman's common look of disapproval, but something more lingered below the surface of her mother's silence.

Emily huffed. "What is it?"

Mother tilted her head. "I had merely hoped that you would search for a new mate outside of the police profession."

Emily tensed. "What exactly is wrong with it?"

"Nothing, per se. It is a noble occupation." Mother tickled Basil Allan, but her expression remained rigid as he giggled. "However, I did warn you when you married Bennett that his life would be fraught with constant danger. It pains me, Emily, that my words proved true."

Emily's hands quivered with anger as she balled them into fists. Yet, she managed to keep her voice calm. "I can't believe you would gloat over my husband's death."

Mother frowned and finally looked at her. "Darling, I'm not gloating, but all of this heartbreak could have been avoided if you had heeded my words from the start."

A hot tear fell down Emily's cheek. She moved in front of her mother and glared down at her. "I would rather have spent only a short time married to Bennett than to live my entire life bound to a man whom God did not intend for me."

"Of course, darling, I understand that, but now that he has passed, you have an opportunity not to make the same mistakes in your next relationship."

"A *mistake*?" Her calm tone evaporated, and her chin trembled. "You think my marriage a mistake? You think Basil Allan a mistake?"

"That's preposterous. Of course not."

As though sensing the rising tension, Basil Allan began to whimper and squirm.

Mother held him still. "I was merely saying—"

"All finished!" Father lumbered into the room, a look of satisfaction on his face. "Your table's better than when you first purchased it. How do my lovely ladies fare?"

Emily and her mother sat locked in a glare. Still trembling, Emily bent and snatched her son from her mother's arms and clutched him tight against herself. "I think you should leave."

Father sighed. "Esther, what did you say to her?"

"Nothing!" Mother gaped. "Can't I show concern for my daughter's well-being?"

Emily pointed to the door. "Go."

Her skin reddening, Mother rose to her feet and silently stalked toward the door. Father began to follow but lingered when he reached Emily. "I'll talk to her, Emmie." His soft tone drew out the little girl in her who used to curl up in his warm, protective lap—and who longed to return to such security.

"Thank you," she whispered back, managing to tamp down her pain. "And thank you for repairing my table. Truly."

He patted her shoulder, tickled Basil Allan's chin, and exited after his wife.

Chapter Eleven

RAUCOUS APPLAUSE THUNDERED IN MY EARS as I stashed my deck of cards in my reticule and collected all of the coins strewn across the rickety table before me. I tallied the total in my head and smiled. The men had been generous tonight.

A warm cloud reeking of sweat and spilled alcohol grew stronger within the circle of men who had gathered around me in hopes of witnessing sleight of hand. My own skin felt slick and sticky, made worse by the multitude of layers holding my torso erect. The evening had nearly expired, so it was about time I fled and sought a warm bath and reveled in my spoils.

"One more, sweetheart," a man shouted, followed by more clapping and jeers from the others.

I brought my glass tumbler to my lips and enjoyed a slow sip of beer, letting the suspense hang in the air. Then I chuckled. "Oh, very well." I aimed a finger at a nearby man who held a steaming bowl of stew in his hand. "I'll have that spoon, if you please."

Without hesitation, the man removed the spoon from the stew, clacked it on the side of the bowl, and handed it to me.

Dramatically, I placed the spoon in my mouth to suck off any remnants of the salty stew, drawing several low whistles from the men. Then I downed the rest of my beer. As the alcohol shivered through my veins, I flipped the tumbler over in my hands and examined the bottom of it. "It appears this is a special patent filter tumbler." With the opening of the tumbler facing my body, I held it near the base while lifting the spoon in my other hand. "In case you were unaware, that means that there's a hole in the bottom. Allow me to demonstrate."

The group drew closer as I lifted the objects. I tapped the spoon against the solid bottom of the tumbler and then in one quick movement, I thrust the spoon between my palm and the tumbler until the end protruded through my fingers, which would appear to the spectators as if I had passed the utensil through the opaque glass.

Whoops and claps rose from the crowd as they cast more coins upon the table.

After making a show to pull the spoon back out of the tumbler, I tossed it among the coins and collected the currency. As I plunked them in my reticule, I gave an exaggerated sigh. "I'm afraid that's it, boys. I must retire for the evening."

They groaned and tried to convince me otherwise, but I stood and turned, fastening the reticule to my hip. Head down, I made a move toward the door. When feet stepped in my path, I drew up in time to avoid a collision. "Excuse me, sir, but I told you—"

"Just one more, miss." A soft Irish accent accompanied by the familiar scent of citrus and spice cut through the unpleasant stench and racket of the pub and engaged every sense in my body.

Within seconds, his stark blue eyes held me captive—utterly vulnerable to his charm. He raised one of his dark, arched eyebrows and jutted his chin. "Your parlor tricks are cute, but you have more in you. Impress me."

My nostrils flared, and though the room seemed to grow warmer, I shivered with an isolated chill. Before I could respond, a few of my audience members stepped forward. "The lady said she's done," one snarled.

I let out a laugh and pulled out my trusty deck of cards. "It's quite all right, boys. It's clear our new friend here is skeptical of my abilities. I'd be happy to smack that smug look right off his face." The men laughed and taunted in agreement as I fanned the cards out before me and forced myself to look back into that intense gaze. "If you would, sir, take a card."

He plucked one from the deck and glanced at it, mouth tipping up on one side.

"Good. Now return it."

He did so.

I pulled the deck back toward me and, with a quick movement of my fingers, palmed his card. Flashing it in my periphery confirmed he had chosen the card I'd intended. "Now, you may have noticed that I don't have the standard sleeves or waistcoat that a man does when performing, so this may be more difficult for me to execute. I implore you to be patient." Confidence filled me despite my misleading words.

While I shuffled, I allowed his card to fall discreetly into my reticule, then flattened the deck and handed it back to him. "Could you find your card, please?"

Pursing his lips, he flipped through once, then a second time. Now his whole mouth curved in a smile. "It isn't here."

"A curious thing." Maintaining eye contact, I reached two fingers down the front of my dress, between the corset and corset cover, and felt the card I had planted earlier for such a trick as this. His eyes narrowed a touch, his smile widening, but he kept his gaze fixed upon my face even as the men around us unashamedly ogled my bosom.

I extracted the card and flourished it toward him. "Is this your card, sir?"

He shook his head and clapped slowly three times. "Excellent work."

I swallowed against the lump in my throat as the rest of the crowd joined his applause. Returning the card to my reticule, I swept my gaze across the crowd. "It's been a real treat, everyone. Tomorrow night, then?"

Ducking my head, I sidestepped and hurried through the crowd and out the door. The dim streetlamp cutting through the night's darkness greeted me. The fresh, clean air chased the last of the pub's odor—and his tantalizing scent—from my lungs and renewed my energy. Aware of the ever-growing threats of the night, I stepped into the streetlamp's protective halo.

Footsteps clipped on the pavement behind me and stopped a few paces back.

Invisible tendrils of cold lapped at my feet. I steeled myself. "How did you find me, Sully?"

"You may think you're clever, Kate"—his voice, though a whisper, sliced through the night's silent atmosphere—*"but I've been trackin' you since you left Edinburgh, driftin' from city to city, never stayin' in one place for too long."*

"I think I've been quite clever." With a half-smirk, I twirled to look Sully in the eye. He lurked partially in the shadows, which deepened the sharp, masculine angles of his face—features I could still conjure perfectly in my memory despite the years that had separated our last meeting. "You'll never catch me. Try as you might. Of that, I'm quite certain."

His hands hung jadedly at his sides, fingers loose and relaxed. Yet, his voice held an edge. "You have to be stopped. You might have been able to escape thus far, but this is where fate will catch up to you."

I shrugged one shoulder. "Fate holds no sway over my life."

"But it is comin' for you, nonetheless." He tilted his head forward slightly, and his strong brow cast a shadow over his threatening eyes. "I will kill you."

"Not if I kill you first." Smiling sweetly, I fluttered my eyelashes. "I know your tricks just as well as you know mine, lest you forget. So I will ask you once and only once. Stop following me. Give up your vendetta. The work I am doing is for your good as well as for the good of Ireland." I allowed my pleasant expression to stiffen. "It's time you let me go."

Resentment—and perhaps disappointment—overtook his features. Then, ever so slowly, a grin twisted his mouth. He touched his fingers to his forehead and bowed. "May your days be many and your troubles be few, mo ghrá. *Sleep well." The grin still plastered on his face, he straightened, stepped backward, and dissolved into the shadows.*

Chapter Twelve

BAZE ROSE EARLY—BEFORE THE SUN had broken the horizon, before Adelynn had roused from slumber. He dressed quietly, casting wary glances at her to ensure he didn't make too much noise. Once finished, he crossed to her side of the bed, bent, and pressed a gentle kiss to her forehead. A tiny moan emitted from the back of her throat. She stirred but didn't wake.

Caressing hair from her face, he smiled and took a moment to absorb her beautiful features—her full lashes, her smooth skin, her round lips. Then he whispered, "I love you," before sneaking from the bedroom. He limped heavily to minimize the pain in his calf as much as possible as he crossed to the cabinet. Why did it seem the aches worsened in the morning? Perhaps the medication faded during the night. No matter—it was a problem he was about to remedy.

Baze opened the cabinet door and retrieved one of his last vials of laudanum. He tilted it to his lips and drank, estimating the correct amount by the number of his swallows—but perhaps ingested a little more than his doctor had recommended. A light, airy sensation expanded in his chest as the tingling effects of the drug swept over his body and wrapped around his leg. The pain dulled to an inconsequential throb. His head spun, though not enough to put him off balance.

He bent, intending to return the laudanum to the cabinet, but paused. What if he needed it later in the day? The opium had been less effective of late, so he'd had to take it more frequently and in higher doses to achieve the desired outcome—but he was also running out. What then? It had been several months since he'd felt the full pain his leg was capable of inflicting, and he wasn't keen on repeating that horrid experience anytime soon.

No, he'd simply find more. Better to be prepared.

He slipped the tincture into his coat's inner pocket and quit the room, hurried past Cecil Everett—did the man never sleep?—but didn't slow to trade pleasantries. Baze stepped outside and headed toward the Roman Baths.

At such an early hour, with the night's chill still clinging to the air and a few stubborn stars yet winking above the horizon, the street lay bare. Only a few stragglers milled about near the park. Baze hobbled slowly, inhaling the floral springtime scent and absorbing the peaceful morning ambience. Making his way across the street, he set his sights on the baths and sent up a quick, forthright prayer. *You led me here, God. You say in your Word that you would give to those who ask. Well, I'm asking. Heal my leg. Let this be the method by which you allow it to happen.*

Feeling renewed hope, Baze approached the entrance to the baths. He found it odd coming to this place with no one about, but Sebastian Cutler had assured him it was acceptable. Sure enough, when he found the door, it opened without hindrance. Exactly as he'd said, Sebastian awaited him in the foyer.

The therapist's eyes lit as Baze approached. "Welcome, Basil. So glad you could make it."

Baze sighed. "You may as well call me Baze. It's what everyone calls me."

"That's kind of you." Sebastian patted his arm. "But I don't bother with nicknames. I prefer to use your real, God-given name."

Baze suppressed a grimace. God-given it was not. The choosing of his name had all been Alistair Ford's doing. Still, Baze respected the therapist's preference for formality.

"Now, let us begin. I shall meet you inside once you've changed." The therapist shuffled away.

Baze ventured to the men's area and donned his bathing suit. Now that the opium had had time to take effect, the pain in his leg was but a mere memory, allowing him to walk nearly unhindered. His head rushed with excitement, and his muscles slackened in extreme relaxation. He hoped that wouldn't alter the therapist's treatment.

Inside the bath area, Baze's skin grew clammy with the humidity. Delicate steam swirled above the water. Bubbles rose to the surface in several areas of the pool.

Sebastian had already entered the water and beckoned Baze to join, then gestured to a spot between himself and the wall. "If you would, please stand here."

Skin prickling with the heat, Baze waded to where the therapist pointed and awaited further instruction. "You're certain it's all right for us to be here?"

"Of course. I have a longstanding relationship with the owners of the baths. They allow me to use them for treatment so long as I do it when they don't have any patrons." Sebastian situated himself before Baze, swiping the top of the water with both hands as though treading water, even though it only rose to the middle of his torso. "Now, I want you to balance on your injured leg and bend your knee, then come up. I shall demonstrate." He lifted one leg, extending both arms out to the side, and rested his foot above the knee of his anchored leg. Then he squatted and came right back up. "Don't go too low. You may use the wall for balance if you have need of it."

Baze narrowed his eyes. "I can barely walk with this leg and you want me to put all of my weight on it?"

"The buoyancy will keep you afloat so that it doesn't strain your leg. That's why water is one of the best mediums for physiotherapy. It allows for low-impact motions without further hurting yourself. Now, let's give it a go, shall we?"

Moving slowly, Baze held out an arm. He refused to grab the bath edge but kept his hand close—just in case. Then he lifted his good leg, tightening the muscles of the other one to keep balance. Dull pain rushed through his calf and wrapped over his knee, the usual sharpness likely blunted by the opium.

"Good." Sebastian nodded. "Now bend your knee ever so slightly. Stop if you feel discomfort."

Baze snorted. "And if I already feel discomfort?"

"Minor discomfort is normal, but if you feel sharp pain, do not strain yourself."

Biting his lip, Baze bent his knee slightly—and a burst of pain shot through him. He grunted and fell back against the bath wall. His fingernails scraped the stone, and his chest heaved as anger began to build.

"That's quite all right." Sebastian clasped his hands together. "We've only just begun. This simply tells us that we need to start you off with the basics." The therapist paused, wrinkles crumpling in a frown. "However, I do wish to set your expectations before we continue."

A barrier came up inside Baze, defensive, bracing for undesirable news. "What kind of expectations?"

"Expectations for what this treatment can accomplish for you."

Baze flexed his foot to try to take the edge off the pain—and to distract him from the words he was about to hear.

"This is not a cure, Basil. I want you to hear that clearly."

The therapist's tone, akin to a father scolding his child, made Baze bristle, but he stared at the ripples in the water and kept his mouth shut.

"This treatment may lessen your pain. It may even, hopefully, restore some of your mobility." Sebastian tilted his head. "But the damage you suffered is irreversible. We have come a long way in the realm of medicine, but clearly, we yet have a great distance to go. If you can keep your expectations realistic, it will help you accept whatever outcome we are able to achieve."

"I appreciate your honesty, Sebastian. Thank you."

Yet, Baze steeled himself, deflecting the words before they could settle within him. *I don't need his treatment to heal me. It only needs to help. God, you're the one I'm trusting for this. Work through Sebastian to bring me full healing. I know You are able.*

Sebastian smiled, compassion lingering in his expression. "Now, if you are ready, we can begin."

For the next hour, Sebastian led Baze through a series of low-impact exercises and stretches, aided by the buoyancy and warmth of the water. By the end, perspiration coated Baze's face and chest. Though his leg throbbed, it exhibited only a dull, persistent ache rather than the sharp twinge he had experienced at the beginning of the session. In fact, as he stood upon both legs, flat-footed, he found the flexibility of his ankle and knee to be much more pliant now.

Not sure to believe it, yet unable to deny the truth of it right in front of him, Baze gaped at the therapist. "Thank you. That . . . actually helped."

"I am pleased to hear it, Basil. That is a good sign." Sebastian pressed a gentle fist against Baze's chest. "If it is to continue working, we must be consistent. I expect you back here at the same time tomorrow."

Baze sighed. So much for spending early mornings in the company of his new bride. Still, he supposed they had a lifetime to spend in one another's company. He needed this. Adelynn would have to understand.

"Now, I have one more thing before you depart." Sebastian waded to the edge of the pool and picked up a glass bottle with a cork stopper. A dark liquid sloshed within as he held it out to Baze.

Baze accepted the bottle and cradled it in his open palm. "What's this?"

"I had a local toxicologist concoct it for you. You might have met him—Charles Caine. He is employed by the Bath Police but often works as a toxicologist for hire in his time off." Sebastian tapped the glass with a finger. "You will take this tincture twice a day in lieu of your current prescription. It is a weakened dose of opium that will help you wean off of your current regimen so you are no longer dependent upon it."

Baze stared at the tantalizing liquid within, tightening his hand around it in obstinance.

Sebastian cleared his throat. "Trust me, young man. You don't want to tempt fate with opiates. I have seen many a good man succumb to them. You wouldn't want to leave your pretty new bride a widow."

Leave Adelynn alone in this world? No, Baze had no intention of doing so, but he would also do whatever was necessary to bring himself healing. "If you can promise that your treatment will take my pain away, then I will commit to coming off my medication."

Sebastian squeezed Baze's upper arm, his sympathetic gaze unwavering. "Just remember what we discussed about expectations and outcomes."

Chapter Thirteen

WHEN THE TIME FINALLY CAME FOR my rendezvous with the mysterious Katherine Quinn, I donned an elegant tea gown, its pale fabric light enough for leisure but complex enough so that I could stand confidently before such a commanding presence as Miss Quinn's.

On my way past the front desk, Mr. Everett glanced up from an open newspaper. He folded it shut and flashed a look that encouraged me to slow. "Do you have grand plans on such a lovely day, Mrs. Ford?"

I swung toward him with a smile. "I'm about to have a sit-down at the famous Sally Lunn's. Anything on the menu you might recommend?"

He tapped a knuckle to his chin. "You certainly can't go wrong with a fresh-baked bun." His eyes drifted to the staircase, then fell back to me. "Is Mr. Ford not joining you?"

"No, he had other business to attend to I'm afraid." I tilted my head. "Why?"

Mr. Everett's mustache stretched as his mouth flattened, but he quickly brightened and shook out the newspaper. "No reason. I hope you enjoy your afternoon, Mrs. Ford."

I remained rooted to the spot, examining his face, alerted by the unusual agitation in his demeanor. Faint concern painted his brow, and as he turned the newspaper, I caught a glimpse of an image depicting the dead woman from the other night. Targeting him with an intent but soft stare, I eased up to the counter and placed my arms upon it, one on top of the other. "Do you have something you wish to tell me, Mr. Everett?"

He met my gaze, lips parted, but hesitated.

"I have experienced much in the last year, Mr. Everett," I said, hoping to lower his defenses. "I've heard much. Seen much. So I assure you, whatever you have to say will bring no more shock than I have already faced."

Glancing about, Mr. Everett laid the newspaper flat, folded his hands, and leaned against the counter, closing the distance between us and creating a semi-private space. "I am merely concerned about the events of the other night. That a murderer was able to sneak under my own roof disturbs me deeply. My staff is now on high alert, so we should be able to thwart any further attempts, but out there . . ." He flashed his eyes toward the door. "You'll have no protection, Mrs. Ford, especially if you plan to explore on your own without the company of your husband. I fear that you might stumble into trouble."

The knowledge that Mr. Everett stood as a diligent sentinel to keep his guests safe and that he cared enough to warn me of potential danger gave me comfort. However, he didn't know Baze and I had already determined that we would investigate the crime at hand, and he certainly didn't know this wasn't our first brush with death—and would likely not be the last.

Though perhaps not the most proper gesture, I rested my hand atop Mr. Everett's before I could consider the implications, but the move seemed to relax his shoulders as I leaned even closer, his crisp, clean scent a calming aura. "I am touched by your concern, Mr. Everett. Truly. I promise to keep my guard up and not to drink from any mysterious teacups."

Mr. Everett chewed the edge of his mustache, then nodded. "I merely ask that you be vigilant. If you see anything out of the ordinary, don't hesitate to call for me."

I smiled and stepped back. "Thank you."

As I left the Empire Hotel and made my way to the famous Sally Lunn's, I prayed that Mr. Everett wouldn't involve himself too much. It warmed my heart that he would extend such care to a stranger, but becoming entangled in a murderous plot was something I didn't wish on anyone. I shuddered to think what might happen to him should he meddle too deeply. Still, it bolstered my confidence knowing that he kept watch.

Tucked away in an unassuming side street, a green-striped awning marked the entrance of Sally Lunn's. A wide bay window filled with plump pastries and pies protruded from the tea shop's stone façade. With my mouth watering, I pushed through the shop door, setting off a pleasant chime near the top corner, and found my nostrils stuffed by the tantalizing scents of the fresh-baked goods and boiled fruit.

Inside, I glanced about the area, taking note of the counter overflowing with additional pastries, as well as several chairs and tables scattered about. Ladies, in their opulent hats and tea dresses, occupied several of the seats and spoke in muted tones, which filled the space with a pleasant din of conversation, enough to potentially mask any sensitive information that might pass between Katherine and me.

A flash of white and red caught my eye amidst the sunny tones of the bakery. Garbed in a bright gown and matching hat, her hair flaming in stark contrast, Katherine Quinn lounged at a table tucked in a corner a far distance from the other patrons.

When Katherine noticed my approach, she jumped up, opened her arms, and wrapped me in a hearty embrace, as though we had been lifelong friends.

I tensed, unsure how to repay such a candid display—and wondering whether I should.

"So good of you to come, angel." She tugged me toward the table. "I've already put in an order, if you don't mind. A classic Earl Grey and one of Sally's famous buns and tea spread for each of us."

Once seated, I laid my hands in my lap and studied Katherine, attempting to read her, but her face appeared a blank canvas.

Katherine sipped from her tea, already half empty, then reclined with a quirked grin, a mischievous sparkle in her emerald eyes. "I'm simply dying to know. Have you received any other tips of my demise?"

Sensing her playfulness, I decided to have a go with my own bold statement. "No, but I'm pleased to see you made it through the night with such a large target on your back."

She chuckled. "Indeed."

A petite woman interrupted and set before us a delectable meal of egg sandwiches, sponge cakes, and two golden-brown buns. "Enjoy, dears."

Katherine wasted no time in lifting a bun to her lips and taking a large, unladylike mouthful. Her eyes fluttered shut, and a pleased moan purred in her throat as she chewed and swallowed. "These are not at all friendly to my figure, but, good heavens, how could I deny a chance for such a transcendent experience?"

Spurred by the fear of missing out, I lifted the lightweight bread and sank my teeth into it. Its fluffy texture melted in response, a flavor of honey and wheat singing in harmony on my tongue, and I found myself inhaling a second bite before I'd even swallowed the first.

Katherine laughed, took several more chomps, and washed it down with a long sip of tea.

Clearing my throat, I returned the uneaten portion of my bun to the plate. As much as I enjoyed the amiable break from reality, we could dance around the topic all day long if given the chance. Enough pleasantries. I needed to address the conflict at hand.

I folded my fingers and placed my wrists on the table. "Miss Quinn, I—"

"We're too close for such formalities." She dabbed her mouth with a cloth serviette. "Katherine, please."

"Katherine. I'm not sure how best to broach the subject, so I'll get right to it, if that's quite all right." I took a breath to center myself. "I believe your life to be in danger. The police concluded that the water you nearly drank yesterday was indeed poisoned. Considering that a few days prior, another woman died by way of poisoning, I need to find out whether the two instances are related."

"I think we're getting ahead of ourselves." Katherine popped the final remnants of her bun into her mouth, chewed slowly, then swallowed. "First, I need to know *how* you knew my drink was poisoned before the police knew . . . before anyone knew."

I'd expected the question to come up—but perhaps not this early in the conversation. Either way, now it was time to see if the excuse I'd concocted would be enough to quell her curiosity. "After the first woman died, my husband connected with the Bath Police, and they uncovered the possibility of another planned poisoning, this time at the Roman Baths. It wasn't hard to put two and two together. I simply happened to be at the right place at the right time."

Katherine clinked her silver spoon on the side of her teacup and narrowed her eyes. "You're trying so hard to conjure such an elaborate excuse, angel. Wouldn't it be much easier to say you witnessed my death in one of your visions?"

Shock broadsided me. Had I not been supported by my chair's backrest, I would have toppled over. Of all the scenarios I had pictured in my head to prepare for, this was not one of them.

Breath shallow, I lowered my voice. "How could you possibly know about my—"

"I've been around for a long time. Worked as a journalist at one point as well. I know how to investigate and gather details." She leaned forward. "I always keep myself educated about crime across the country, especially when it's involving such a high-profile case as the one you were unfortunate enough to find yourself a part of last year."

I mirrored her concentrated stance, unsure whether the focus of our conversation worried me . . . or aggravated me. "Knowledge of my visions was never advertised or made known to the public. How did you hear of it?"

One of her shoulders came up in a half-shrug. "I have many sources with many secrets."

"Who was your source?"

"I prefer to keep that confidential. They're trusting me with their identity. I couldn't possibly betray their anonymity, you understand."

I picked up a slice of sponge cake and bit off a chunk to give myself time to ponder. Of the people who knew my secret, who could she have possibly coerced into relinquishing that information? Bennett and Cornelius were dead. Finn had been home in Ireland for many months now. And Baze, Emily, and Superintendent Whelan wouldn't dare divulge such information.

Of course, I did keep record of everything that had happened in my diary—in great detail—but hardly anyone knew of it except those I trusted, and it was tucked away safely in a drawer in my new home. Unless Katherine had somehow gotten her hands on it.

Another more sinister notion crawled into my thoughts. What if she had known Cornelius before his destruction? If that were the case, had she been working against him . . . or for him? Either way, it could explain why she was being targeted.

I closed my eyes briefly, tuning out the sounds of the café and homing in on the atmosphere surrounding Katherine and I—the faint scent of our tea, the warm rays spilling onto us from the window. I burrowed within myself and searched for any hint of unease or premonition as I had often sensed in Cornelius's presence, but I felt nothing. Not even a whisper of a chill.

Still, did that disprove the possibility of a connection between Katherine and Cornelius?

Palms clammy, I returned the remnants of the cake to my plate and swiped my hands on my serviette. "The only people, supposedly, who know of my gift are those whom I trust. So whoever told you about my visions either betrayed my confidence or isn't a person I know." I rested my elbows upon the table, laced my fingers, and set my chin on them. "The information you know is delicate . . . dangerous. Perhaps your source is the one who is targeting you."

"Impossible. I vet my sources carefully. They wouldn't dare turn on me." She waved her hand in the air. "Do we need to dwell on this, angel? The event is passed. I am alive and well. It won't be long before I leave Bath behind me."

I raised my eyebrows. "You're leaving? So soon?"

"As I told you once before, I'm a drifter. I make a point not to dwell in one place for too long lest I be followed by unsavory characters."

Tapping a foot on the floor, I studied Katherine's dismissive demeanor. How could she act so blasé about an attempt on her life? Sure, she might plan to leave the city, but that didn't mean the person targeting her couldn't follow her and try again in the next place she settled. No. We needed to solve this here and now.

I unlaced my fingers and pressed my hands flat on the table, leveling my gaze at her. "Because you seem to already be so familiar with my gift, then I will come right out with it. Your death was the sixth time I've witnessed someone die in a vision. I remember them all—down to the tiniest horrible detail—and they all have one thing in common. All of them are dead . . . all of them except for you, of course. That's never happened before, so I believe that the danger has not yet passed."

Her hands encircled her teacup and lifted it to her lips. After a drawn-out sip, she said, "Then what do you propose we do?"

"If you are so certain that your sources are trustworthy, then we need to consider alternatives. Such as close acquaintances. Family. A spouse."

I glanced at her left hand still cradling the teacup. It bore no adornment. On her right hand, however—and on the fourth finger no less—shone a simple silver band in the shape of a claddagh. Two hands grasped a heart topped with a crown, the symbols of friendship, love, and loyalty. The ring encircled her finger upside down, its crown pointed toward her. From what I remembered of Irish traditions, that placement indicated that her heart was taken—but in what capacity?

Noticing the direction of my pointed stare, Katherine released the teacup, snatched her hands off the table, and tucked them into her lap. For a moment, her eyes hardened, and an invisible barrier shivered between us. Then she raised her right hand and gazed at the ring, features softening. "I was married once. Or perhaps I still am . . ." Her words drifted away.

My nose tingled with emotion, tears pricking my eyes, as I recognized the pinched sorrow in her face, the same sorrow that Emily tried to conceal whenever she thought or spoke of Bennett.

Katherine had lost her love—whether by death or desertion, I wasn't sure.

Yet, one more detail transformed my empathy into apprehension— that the ring she wore came from the mystical green shores of Ireland. The claddagh dated back centuries, exchanged across the land as a sign of love and devotion between a man and a woman. Quinn was an Irish name, but her accent didn't betray any hints of that nationality. Of course, Cornelius had fooled me with his own fake accent, but he hadn't been able to stop certain inflections from bleeding through. Hers sounded complete and genuine.

So, could her husband have been an Irishman? If so—and if he yet lived—could he be the one behind the attack?

The air grew thick in my throat as I faced the implications. Not wanting to pry into a sensitive topic but determined to gain answers, I resolved to push forward. "Katherine," I said with a cool, even tone. "Cornelius concocted his plot out of revenge for his father's death, for what he deemed to be the corruption of Ireland, and he did it all under the guise of working for the Irish Republican Brotherhood. Cornelius may be gone, but the conflict across our two lands continues. My visions were connected to Cornelius and, therefore, Ireland." I tilted my head toward her ring and lowered my voice. "Your heart clearly belongs to that land in some way. Were you involved with Cornelius?"

Katherine's eyes flashed. "I didn't help him carry out those crimes if that's what you're insinuating." She spun the ring around her finger.

It was an answer but not a satisfying one. Rather, she'd effectively dodged the question. I pressed my lips shut and held her in a determined stare, hoping my quiet would coax more out of her, despite my own rising unease.

Yet, as the silence stretched on, Katherine's full lips tilted in a knowing smile. "Oh, brown eyes taught you well, angel. That technique would have worked on anyone else, so I credit you for trying." She lifted her teacup and gulped down the rest of the sweet drink. Smacking her lips, she swiveled in her chair. "However, I'm afraid that is all I can give you. If I reveal too much, it will put everything I've worked for in jeopardy."

Frustration mounting, I curled my hands into fists. "If you would tell me everything, my husband and I could help you. We stopped Cornelius, and we can stop whoever is after you. You don't need to face this alone."

Katherine halted, eyeing me with a look of doubt. Then she shook her head and stood. Her voice grew deep. "Cornelius Marx was a mere nuisance compared to what is occurring here." She placed one hand on the table and leaned over me. "Listen carefully, angel, for I say this with love. I really do. You and brown eyes need to leave Bath. Don't get any more involved in this than you already are, for if you delve deeper into this tangled web, it'll do far more than leave you two with persistent nightmares and a bum leg."

I gaped, a furious dislike for this woman beginning to rake at my insides. She spoke as though she knew me, knew what I'd been through, but no one could ever know such things, not even Baze, as much as he tried to understand. I had witnessed death after death but had been unable to prevent them. I had endured the guilt of being seduced and betrayed by Cornelius. And I had fought to keep control of my mind every night since the day I'd watched him die.

So, if I wanted to stay and investigate, so help me God, I would.

"We're on holiday." I popped to my feet and angled into her face. "Whether we stay or leave is no concern of yours."

To Katherine's credit, she didn't tilt away—didn't even flinch. Rather, she lifted her chin. "I am sorry that you've had to be involved in this. I truly am. But go home. Forget about Bath. Forget what you've witnessed here. Don't call down more misfortune upon yourself. Could you really allow yourself to go through all of that heartache over again—allow your husband to? Has he not been through enough?"

•

Katherine stepped back and swished out her skirt. "I have tarried far too long. It's time I left." Dipping her head, she bent in a curtsy. "It has been a pleasure, Mrs. Adelynn Ford. I owe you my life. Perhaps I'll be repaying the favor someday."

With a flourish of her hand, she turned.

I whirled after her, shouting, "Why invite me here if you're just going to leave?"

The only thing my outburst accomplished was to draw the perturbed stares of every patron as Katherine Quinn breezed from the shop. With a huff, I spun and dropped back into my seat, muscles quivering, torn between heeding her words and obstinately giving chase. Annoyance tightened my chest. If Bath was so dangerous, then why wouldn't she divulge anything about it? Withholding information could only put us in more danger. I folded my arms, anger flaring the more I thought of it. If Katherine Quinn thought she was clever, with her secrets and solo investigating, then she didn't know me. She was about to meet her equal.

Chapter Fourteen

THE AROMA OF FRESHLY BAKED BREAD warmed Emily from the inside out as she arranged pastries neatly within an empty basket. She glanced at Basil Allan, who sat on the other side of the arch leading to the living room and entertained himself with plain wooden blocks.

Fwip. A soft sound emitted from the direction of the front door. The morning post.

Emily's stomach leapt into her throat. Then she chided herself—no sense getting her hopes up. Barely enough time had passed for her letter to reach Finn, let alone for a return letter to reach her. Nevertheless, her hands quivered in anticipation as she squeezed past Basil Allan, snatched up the letters that lay scattered at the base of the door, and shuffled through the stack. When she sifted through to the last envelope and found no instance of Finn's name, her hopes fell.

She shook her head, passed back into the kitchen, and tossed the letters upon the newly repaired table. *Silly. Just silly. Who's to say he'll even write back?*

Swallowing a surge of emotion, Emily retrieved the basket she'd filled and turned to Basil Allan. She heaved a sigh and scooped him up, then bounced him in her arms. "What do you say, love? Shall we go to see that Daddy's colleagues are fed?"

Basil Allan giggled and touched her face, his bright hazel eyes—Bennett's eyes—alight with curiosity.

A brief cab ride left Emily at the steps of New Scotland Yard. She blinked against raindrops, shifted Basil Allan up her hip, and pushed through the heavy doors. As she emerged into the main area, Superintendent Whelan, Sergeant Andrews, and another officer came into view near Whelan's office. Gesturing wildly with his hands, Whelan appeared to be in the midst of giving orders. Though not close enough to hear the conversation, Emily caught pieces of it: break-in . . . door ajar . . . investigate. And when Whelan listed the address, Emily's ears perked.

Sergeant Andrews reacted as well, expression turning from concern to surprise. "You sure that's the place, sir? Isn't that—"

"Baze and Adelynn's new home," Emily found herself interrupting, trying to connect the pieces of what she had overheard. The three men spun and stared at her. She set the basket down on the nearest desk and faced them. "What's happened?"

"Nothing to concern yourself with." Whelan tugged up his trousers. "We've got it handled."

"Is it true, though? Did someone break into their home?"

Whelan half-closed one eye and stroked his mutton chops as though debating whether to give her the details. Finally, his lips puckered, and he nodded. "Aye. A neighbor reported it. Said they saw someone sneaking in and that the door had been left open."

Emily frowned and passed Basil Allan to her other arm. "Why would someone do that? Their possessions haven't yet been completely moved in."

"That's what we intend to find out." Whelan gave a reassuring smile. "Not to worry."

Before she could fully think through her words—and perhaps channeling a dash of Adelynn's courage—she said, "I'd like to come with you." The trio of men all but gaped at her. Urged by the notion of experiencing a thrill, she continued, "I have visited their new home on several occasions. I even helped Adelynn choose drapes for one of the rooms and arranged the furniture. I may be able to detect if anything is amiss."

Sergeant Andrews expanded his chest and leveled a stare at her. "There may still be unsavory characters lurking about. We can't put you in harm's way."

Emily rocked Basil Allan, his heavy head now resting on her shoulder. Sergeant Andrews spoke truth. She couldn't put herself in danger—for Basil Allan's sake. Of course, Baze and Adelynn likely wouldn't hesitate to raise him as their own if something ever happened to her, but she refused to allow her son to lose both parents, and she would fight with everything she had to make sure that didn't happen.

Still . . . if someone had broken into their residence, she needed to find out why—or their lives could be in danger. After Cornelius's death, the police had tried to round up all of the remaining theater staff, but some had never turned up. Hadn't she heard Whelan mention the IRB several days ago? Who was to say they weren't still out there, plotting revenge upon Baze and Adelynn for their role in Cornelius's death?

"I'll tell you what." Emily patted her son's back. "I need to find someone to watch Basil Allan. That should give you and your men time enough to check the premises and make sure no one is still inside. I shall join you when you deem it safe."

Sergeant Andrews clenched his jaw and looked to the superintendent. "Sir, this is ridiculous. We can't let her—"

Whelan thrust up his hand and silenced the sergeant. He lowered his chin, regarding Emily with a serious yet amused expression. "Having your peepers on the scene would certainly be helpful." The sergeant made to argue, but again, Whelan interrupted, eyes still on Emily. "*However*, if we find any indication that trouble may be afoot, you are to go nowhere near that place. Am I understood?"

Though Emily didn't answer to Whelan, she still feared what may happen should she disobey. She nodded. "Yes, sir."

Whelan grunted and held out his hands. "Good. Now, give us the lad. I want a look at 'im before you whisk him away."

Emily chuckled and passed Basil Allan to the superintendent, the toddler dwarfed in the man's large embrace. For such a hardened officer, Richard Whelan became quite the amiable teddy bear when in the company of children, likely due to the extensive time he spent with his own two grandchildren.

From the corner of her eye, Emily noticed Sergeant Andrews scowling in her direction. It warmed her heart that he sought to look out for her safety, but she refused to be swayed. She trusted the police—and she trusted that they would keep her out of danger.

After slipping back home to gather Basil Allan's things, Emily hailed a cab and directed it toward the Fords' sprawling estate. Coincidentally, it shared a garden with Adelynn's former home, where her mother yet resided, albeit alone after the death of Thomas Spencer two years ago. Apparently, Baze, Adelynn, and Bennett had made great use of the path winding between the homes, both for entertainment and dastardly acts—or so Emily had been told. She was fortunate that Baze and Adelynn had known Bennett in their adolescence, else Emily would no longer have access to such precious memories.

The cab rounded the circular drive and dropped her at the elaborate front doors. She braced herself, clinging to her son with one arm as she supported her basket of items in the other. How would the Fords react to her showing up unannounced—and to ask such a considerable favor? Mrs. Ford might be more receptive, but Mr. Ford . . .

Emily hadn't witnessed his wrath first-hand, but she'd been privy to his scheme to force Adelynn into a marriage with Baze, as if they wouldn't naturally have followed such a course anyway. His deception and manipulation had made the situation unbearable and had nearly driven Adelynn and Baze apart. After all that, they'd come to find that his actions had been spurred by Cornelius himself—the blackmail just another means by which he was able to infiltrate and poison their lives.

But now that Cornelius no longer pulled the strings, Adelynn and Baze had married, and they'd taken back their independence. What was Mr. Ford like now? Resentful? Bitter? Or had he begun to soften his heart toward his son?

Unable to stall any longer, Emily knocked on the doors. She waited but a moment until the butler answered, his eyes questioning and face stoic. "How may I help you, ma'am?"

Emily cleared her throat. "Emily Bennett here to see Mrs. Ford."

"Do you have an appointment?"

"No, sir." She tightened her hold on Basil Allan, hoping that the sight of a mother and son blanketed by rain would let down his guard.

The butler pressed his lips together but held the door open and allowed them to pass inside. "Wait here, Mrs. Bennett."

Emily nodded and rooted herself to the spot. As the butler quit the room, it grew quiet, aside from the ticking of a large grandfather clock at the end of the long hall. Emily closed her eyes, remembering what she'd overheard Richard Whelan telling another officer, that they had run into more members of the Irish Republican Brotherhood. It was possible that this break-in had been committed by an inconsequential robber simply looking for money or expensive goods. Emily prayed that was the case . . . but she couldn't shake the nagging feeling that this was something more.

When the butler returned, he beckoned her to follow and led her into the sitting room. Mrs. Ford met them at the entrance and surrounded Emily's shoulders with a gentle embrace. "This is quite unexpected, but I'm so delighted that you've come."

Arms aching, Emily gave a weak smile. "I hope I'm not intruding."

"Oh, no, dear. No." The woman dismissed the butler and ushered Emily to the couch. "You are welcome any time."

As Emily sat beside Mrs. Ford, Basil Allan wriggled and kicked his little but strong legs into her stomach. "All right, enough." She turned him loose on the extravagant rug. He rolled onto his back and began playing with his feet.

Emily sighed. "Thank you for seeing me, Mrs. Ford. I realize this is quite the impromptu visit."

"I regard you as family." Mrs. Ford patted Emily's leg. "And please, I would like it if you would call me Frances."

Emily's heart warmed at the affection reflected in the older woman's eyes. "Thank you."

Frances tilted her head, and her jeweled earrings caught a glint of light from a nearby lamp. "How may I help you, dear? I assume this is more than a simple social call."

Unsure of the best approach, Emily recited several words in her head before deciding direct was best. "I need to help Superintendent Whelan with something, but I'm afraid I can't take my son with me. I was wondering if you might watch him while I'm away."

"I would be delighted and honored." Frances's green eyes brightened, but then she frowned. "Do you not have to supply his feedings?"

Emily's stomach knotted, but she tried to keep her features indifferent. "Oh, the little nipper decided about six months ago that he wasn't too keen on breastfeeding." Trying to hide the building tears, Emily tipped her head toward her bag. "I brought his formula along, as well as everything else you should need."

Frances's frail hand covered Emily's, encouraging her to lift her gaze. "There is so much pressure that we women feel from the society at large—not to mention the pressure we put on ourselves—but we can't do it all." She smiled toward Basil Allan, who now explored the fringe at the rug's edge. "I wasn't allowed to nurse my own Basil after he was born, you know. I had been relegated to bed rest throughout the entire pregnancy because of my age, and Mr. Ford thought it best not to take any unnecessary risks. So, Basil was fed by a wet nurse." Her smile wilted. "I used to wish so deeply that I could have been the one to do it, to savor the moment when a mother bonds with her baby, but it mattered little in the end. All that concerned me was that he was healthy and nourished."

The coils in Emily's stomach loosened ever so slightly, knowing that Baze had been raised in such a way and still had grown into the amazing man that he was.

"Speaking of my son reminds me of your precious husband." Frances chuckled. "He was quite the little spitfire in his youth. And just a scrawny thing. Oh, but I don't want to upset you."

"No!" Emily blurted, grasping the woman's hand as though trying to cling to any memory of her husband that she could. Then, quieter, she said, "No, I don't mind. I'd like to hear more."

Frances's lips spread in understanding, and she continued. "Basil was barely two years old when the Bennett family came to us for assistance. I don't have to tell you that they were in the midst of a nasty scandal, and as a result, young Bennett's home life was in shambles, poor thing. So while they attempted to get everything sorted, he often stayed with us. Oh, it had been so long since I'd had boys of the same ages under one roof. My other sons were grown and gone, so Bennett and Basil became like brothers. They were utterly inseparable, whether they were playing quietly or getting up to mischief."

A mix of heartache and pride threatened to spill out in a deluge of tears. With a bite of her lip, Emily managed to keep it restrained—but only just. "Thank you, Frances. You've no idea what your words mean to me. Now shall we . . ."

She turned toward her son, only to find the carpet empty. Panic gripped her, and her eyes hooked on the open door leading to Mr. Ford's study. Stomach in her throat, Emily lurched from the couch and darted into the room.

Mr. Ford stood in the center of the room with Basil Allan held in his arms.

Emily stopped short, muscles locking in place. The look of a babbling toddler in the arms of a stoic businessman struck Emily as unsettling. The contrast of her son's mussed hair and wrinkled clothing and Mr. Ford's groomed appearance further declared the stark difference between the two.

"Mr. Ford." She gasped. "I'm terribly sorry. I wasn't watching. He's gotten so fast and—"

"It's quite all right, Mrs. Bennett." Mr. Ford gazed at Basil Allan as he spoke, caressing the child's pudgy cheeks with his finger. "He is a fine boy. You are raising him well, despite the circumstances. I have no doubt he will grow to be an outstanding young man."

Still tense, Emily wet her lips. "Thank you."

She looked from her son to Mr. Ford, unsure how to proceed, but she knew she must tread carefully. Bennett hadn't spoken too deeply about his time spent with the Fords. After his illegitimate birth, his mother and her family had been wrapped in disgrace, left with nothing but the air in their lungs. The Fords, having previously developed a strong relationship with the family, quickly stepped in. To protect Bennett from the toxic environment, they had allowed him to live with them for a time. Meanwhile, they had managed to flush out Bennett's scoundrel of a father and coerced him to admit to forcing himself upon Bennett's mother—whether true or not—and thus restored honor to the Bennett name. Yet, the damage had been done.

Years later, after Bennett had returned to living with his mother, his father began slinking back every now and again to offer up empty promises of marriage. Unfortunately, it drove his mother straight to the bottle and led her to an untimely death.

Still, knowing the lengths Mr. Ford went to fight for Bennett and his family, Emily couldn't reconcile the honorable man who had risked his own reputation for people who weren't even blood relatives with the man standing before her now, who viewed his own son as nothing more than a means of improving his status. It had only been after the fact that Emily learned the full extent of what Mr. Ford had put Adelynn and Baze through . . . and what he still tried to press upon them from afar. Had Mr. Ford learned nothing?

But when it came to Basil Allan, Emily was determined not to let Mr. Ford smooth-talk or intimidate his way into her son's life. Basil Allan was *her* son—hers and Bennett's—and she would raise him as she saw fit.

Finding her voice, Emily managed, "I apologize again, Mr. Ford. We should—"

"It won't be long now before Basil produces his own son." As though not hearing her, Mr. Ford rocked the child slightly, his usually sharp and steely eyes now soft and amused. "His son and yours will grow up together. They'll have access to everything I didn't have.

Influence. Money." His voice fell in pitch. "Food on the table. A consistent place to lay their heads."

The words struck Emily, and despite all that she knew of Mr. Ford's recent actions—his manipulative nature, his callous emotions—empathy spread through her heart. Perhaps the compassionate man who had once helped her husband was still inside that apathetic shell somewhere, but was his façade too hardened to break through? Baze and Adelynn had tried and failed, but maybe cracks were beginning to form.

"Ah, forgive me." Mr. Ford sidled toward Emily and held out her son. "I have work I must finish. Thank you for bringing him by."

She accepted Basil Allan and propped him against her shoulder. "Mrs. Ford has agreed to watch him for me while I attend to personal matters, so thank you for opening your home."

"Oh, of course. It is my pleasure."

They exchanged tight-lipped smiles and turned, Mr. Ford to his desk and Emily to the door. As she reached for it, her heart squeezed with conviction. What if she could do something to help soften his shell, to give Baze a better chance of reconciling their relationship?

She turned back. "Mr. Ford, if I may?"

Already behind the desk, he halted and remained standing. His shoulders stiffened as his eyebrows rose expectantly.

"Baze is one of the finest men I know," she said before she could stop herself. "He is adept at his job. His peers respect him. He is an honorable man, and I have no doubt he will be the best husband." Mr. Ford's jaw shifted, but Emily plowed ahead. "I don't know by which standards you judge a person's worth or success, but I can assure you, Baze is one of the most successful and worthy men I have the pleasure of knowing. You were proud of the man my husband became after you helped to restore his name. So you should be equally proud of your own son—if not more so."

Emily pressed her lips shut, only now realizing the consequences her words could bring, having spoken so boldly. She didn't believe he would unleash wrath upon her, but what if he took it out on Baze? What if she had made the situation worse? Pulse pounding, she hugged Basil Allan tight against herself.

Mr. Ford sat slowly, back rigid and upright. He focused on the organized papers before him and said, "I have work to attend to, Mrs. Bennett, if you don't mind."

Tears pricking her eyes, Emily spun and hurried from the room. *Foolish. I'm so foolish.* The rift between Baze and his father was a deep chasm that couldn't be solved with a well-meaning lecture. No, it would take so much more, and it would take things that Emily did not have.

When the cab pulled up to Adelynn and Baze's home, Sergeant Andrews met Emily with an extended umbrella to shield her from the steady stream of rain. Thunder rumbled above.

As the cab pulled away, Emily tried to take enough shelter beneath the umbrella to block the rain while not drawing too close to him. Fortunately, he held the protection above her head, exposing his broad shoulders to the elements. The humid air around them heightened the scent of his stark cologne, dizzying her thoughts.

Yet, his usually pleasant demeanor seemed hesitant, aloof even. Did he still disapprove of her interfering with the case? Good. Perhaps that would put him off enough for him to drop his hopeful thoughts of courtship.

They made their way up the walkway in silence, and Sergeant Andrews propped the front door open for her. Electric lights shone from within, but the space sat empty and hollow, not yet occupied. In comparison to the Spencer and Ford estates, Baze and Adelynn's new home was modest, yet opulent, only requiring a small staff. Though they had yet to live in it, all of their effects—from furniture and paintings to draperies and rugs—had been placed immaculately so that they could return from holiday and begin their new life together straightaway.

Emily turned to Sergeant Andrews as he furled the umbrella and leaned it against the wall behind the door. "What did your men discover when they searched the home?"

He shrugged and glanced down the foyer. "Nothing. Other than the front door hanging ajar."

"Did you find fingerprints on the front doorknob or within the house?"

"No. The perpetrator knew what he was doing."

Emily sighed. "Well, I helped organize and decorate this home, so if there's something out of place, I'll be able to spot it."

Keeping his gaze fixed down the hall, Sergeant Andrews grunted but didn't speak.

Pursing her lips, Emily entered the formal dining room to the left of the foyer. Sergeant Andrews likely didn't know that she'd overheard Whelan discussing with another officer that they believed the Irish Republican Brotherhood to have infiltrated the city again. Emily didn't yet have proof of anything, but like Bennett, she didn't believe in coincidences, so there had to be a reason why someone had broken into Adelynn's home at the same time that the IRB returned.

Sergeant Andrews followed Emily in silence as she crept from room to room. Every chair appeared in perfect order, positioned the same as when she'd last visited the home. In the sitting room, each fluffed pillow and rug tassel lay untouched. The grand piano gleamed in the corner, its bench, fallboard, and lid unmoved. Items upon the fireplace mantle and side tables seemed to be in order. So far, nothing raised her alarms.

She made her way to the study and again found everything untouched as one might expect of a couple on holiday. The sergeant's heavy footsteps echoed in the compact, quiet space. Emily cast him a glance. "Please don't feel obligated to escort me through the house. I know my way."

"I don't mind." Sweat on his brow glistened in the dim light. "I prefer to keep you in my sight."

The words sounded earnest, not at all as playful as they could have been construed. That he wanted to keep watch for her protection was clear, but could there be something more to it?

She brushed her fingers along the shelf of a large bookcase. "Are you worried the perpetrator is still here?"

Sergeant Andrews's brow crinkled in a frown, and he made eye contact for the first time since they entered the house. "No. I trust that our men were thorough. I simply need to ensure you don't muck anything up. This is still an active crime scene, after all."

The barb in his words pinched her chest. What had set him on edge? Was he cross about her hesitancy of a courtship between them? Or was this simply the behavior he adapted while working a case?

Choosing not to press the issue, Emily made her way to the master bedroom. Rain thrummed hard on the roof overhead, and the lights flickered as a clap of thunder sounded. In her peripheral vision, she noticed Sergeant Andrews flinch, then quickly try to appear undaunted. Emily bit back a facetious comment and instead scanned the room, noting the unwrinkled comforter on the large bed, then examined each item in turn—the lavish vanity, the closed wardrobe, the full-length mirror, the matching nightstands, the—

Emily's eyes darted back to Adelynn's nightstand, to the top drawer. A fold of fabric stuck out from the corner. Adelynn and Baze had yet to use the room, so how could such a thing fall out of place? Senses on alert, Emily approached it and edged the drawer out. The fabric belonged to an ornate handkerchief adorned with the initials B. A. F.—Basil Alistair Ford. Emily recognized it as the handkerchief that Adelynn had swiped from Baze long ago and now used to wrap her diary when not in use.

Emily tugged the handkerchief, and it fell open—empty. She frowned, noticing a large ink smudge on the handkerchief's otherwise pure white linen. Though it lay next to a pen and inkwell, Adelynn prized the handkerchief and would never have allowed the ink to contaminate it in such a manner. And why had Adelynn taken her diary without its makeshift cover?

Or had the robber taken it? If that were the case, why her diary? Of all the things a burglar could steal, why that? Emily hadn't read Adelynn's diary—they were kindred friends, but it contained Adelynn's most intimate reflections. Adelynn poured everything into that diary and had likely recorded each private detail about what she had experienced in her confrontation with Cornelius—and about her visions. What if the perpetrator was involved with Cornelius and wanted to learn more . . . wanted to get revenge?

"Did you find something?" Sergeant Andrews's imposing presence came up behind her, his clean scent enveloping her.

Emily glanced back at him, nearly swayed by his eager expression, but something stayed her tongue. She didn't feel comfortable confiding in the sergeant. Not yet. No, she should take this to Superintendent Whelan. Now that Bennett was gone, Whelan was the only man outside of Baze that she truly trusted.

Emily shook her head and slid the door shut. "I thought I had spotted something, but it appears I was mistaken."

Sergeant Andrews sighed, and his shoulders relaxed. "Then we should try to—"

Thunder erupted. Windows rattled. The lights sputtered and went out, plunging them into darkness. Emily fumbled through Adelynn's nightstand and found matches, thankful she had yet opted to use an oil lamp as opposed to an electric light source. Once the lamp glowed to life, Emily turned, forming a quip about the storm.

But Sergeant Andrews no longer stood behind her. He had disappeared.

Emily took a step, about to shout his name, but a hunkered form on the floor beside the bed caught her eye. Sergeant Andrews sat curled against it, eyes squeezed shut. His chest heaved, and the dim light accentuated the pale sheen of his face.

Quietly, Emily tiptoed and knelt beside him. In the smallest of whispers, she said, "Rees?"

He started. His eyes flew open and fixed on her, then quickly darted to the floor between his feet. Working his jaw, he swallowed and murmured, "I'm sorry that you had to witness such an episode, Emily."

Ignoring their instinctual use of each other's Christian names, she shook her head and offered a gentle smile, one that she often gave Basil Allan when he became upset. "It's just a bit of thunder. We all get startled from time to time. No harm done, eh?" She had hoped her light tone would diffuse the tension, but the sergeant's countenance only turned grimmer.

He gave a slow shake of his head, scraping his thumbnail over his bottom lip. "Ever since that night—ever since my squad and I escorted Miss Spencer into the Empress Theatre—I'm often panic-stricken by darkness and sudden loud noises."

Emily clutched her hand to her heart as she absorbed his vulnerable admission. In her silence, he continued, voice quiet and contemplative, as though he now spoke to himself.

"We were supposed to protect her that night. There were so many of us. Two squads. She should have been safe. But we were foolish, arrogant, to think we could protect her from that man—from that power. The lights went out, and in a panic, some of the men opened fire. I pulled Miss Spencer to the floor and tried to shield her." He stared at his open palms, flexing his fingers as though trying to grip the air. "I had her. I had her safe in my grasp . . . but something struck me from behind. When I awoke several hours later and learned that madman had stolen her right out from under me . . ." Tears sparkled in his eyes. "Sometimes I can still hear the gunshots . . . can feel his touch on my mind."

Compassion and understanding swirled within Emily. Had he carried such remorse and fear this whole time? She felt guilty that it hadn't occurred to her that Adelynn and Baze weren't the only people who felt the lasting effects of that night. If Sergeant Andrews felt this so deeply, how many others also harbored such raw emotions?

She laid a gentle hand on his arm. "You did everything you could do. It's not your fault. Adelynn is . . . well, Adelynn. Heaven and Earth couldn't have stopped her from charging into that theater, even if she had to go alone. She knew what she was walking into, and she doesn't blame you—no one does."

The sergeant blinked and pulled from her touch. He scrubbed his hands down his face, leaving his expression hard and detached. "I apologize. I shouldn't have shared that. You shouldn't have to carry my burdens." He struggled to his feet. "It won't happen again."

Chapter Fifteen

I WAITED ABOUT A QUARTER OF an hour after Baze departed for his early morning physiotherapy session before I ventured out as well—with the intention of finding Miss Katherine Quinn. Our previous conservation had left me unsatisfied and with more questions than I had answers. I needed to find these answers before she became a target once more. She only drew breath today because I'd been close enough in proximity to get to her in time. But if someone targeted her again, I feared that they would succeed.

Inspired by Katherine's red-headed feistiness, I donned a crimson walking suit with ornate black embroidery swirling down the bodice and the sleeves and peeking out from skirt's bottom layer. To complete the look, I fastened a black small-brimmed hat with red and white feathers atop my head. Though Katherine's obstinance ground my bones in annoyance, I admired her tenacity . . . and perhaps saw a bit of myself in her. As such, I knew how to combat her.

Chest swelling with determination, I glided down the stairs into the lobby. Last year, my visions had been nothing but a curse, taunting me, showing me the moments before a person's death but leaving me without enough time to do anything about it. Now, I'd been able to make a difference, to save a life. It wasn't much, but it helped to lift some of the guilt I'd been shouldering, both in my heart and in the subconscious thoughts that plagued my dreams.

Mr. Everett beamed as I approached. "Good morning, Mrs. Ford. How are you this fine day?"

"I am well, thank you." I stopped at the desk and folded my arms upon it. "Actually, I was hoping you might be able to locate someone.

You seem to have such a comprehensive handle on the pulse of this city."

Mr. Everett laced his fingers atop the counter. "I can certainly try."

Before continuing, I took a quick moment to burrow deep inside my mind and assess my intuition. I stared into his eyes, a light gray, and noted the calm beating of my heart and dormant senses. No alarm. No detection of any malignant forces at work. From what I could tell, he acted under no one else's influence but his own.

Satisfied, I traced a finger along the edge of his open newspaper. "I'm looking for someone. Her name is Katherine Quinn, and I was hoping you might know her whereabouts."

Mr. Everett stroked his neatly trimmed mustache. "If I am recalling the correct person, she is a relative newcomer to Bath. An enigma of sorts. But I believe she likes to take her morning tea, usually over a game of solitaire, at a place called the Bath Bun Tea Shoppe, just a short jaunt from the Bath Abbey and spa."

I raised my eyebrows. "So much detail."

"Well, as you said, I have my hand upon the pulse of the city." He pressed his palm flat on the newspaper and winked. "I must live up to such claims, mustn't I?"

"Indeed. Thank you, Mr. Everett. You have been most helpful."

"It was my pleasure. I hope you find the answers you seek."

The comment gave me pause, but I managed to turn, hiding any revealing facial expressions. I hadn't mentioned to him the reason why I sought her. So either he was especially perceptive or there was more to it. Even though I didn't sense any of the darkness Cornelius had used to control people, that didn't mean Mr. Everett wasn't involved somehow.

Outside, the crisp spring air invigorated my steps as I hastened along the ancient pavement leading toward the Bath Abbey towering in the distance. A lyrical melody drifted along the cool breeze. As I drew closer to the magnificent structure, I spotted a man swaying near the abbey fountain, a violin tucked under his chin. Recognition of the song drew me to a halt, guilt and inadequacy bubbling up as the music enveloped me. "Be Thou My Vision." Silently, I recited the lyrics in time with the melody.

"Be thou my vision, O Lord of my heart. Naught be all else to me, save that thou art."

Tears prickled behind my closed eyelids as I recounted the next words.

"Thou my best thought, by day or by night. Waking or sleeping, thy presence thy light."

My throat tightened. God's light had seemed elusive of late. No matter how much I prayed or how hard I attempted not to dwell on events of the past, the nightmares continued—both in waking and in sleeping. They forced me to relive that last moment with Cornelius as he had accepted his fate, rejected redemption, and perished by Baze's hand . . . and perhaps, in part, by my own as well.

As I watched the violinist, his brows drawn and left-hand fingers darting over the strings, my vision grew hazy. A new man stepped out from behind the musician.

Cornelius.

The world around us froze. His ice-blue eyes glinted in sadness and resolve. Just as I shook my head, a gunshot erupted behind me. I yelped, hugging myself. The bullet struck Cornelius. He stumbled back, hands clutching at his chest, then collapsed.

"Miss?"

The voice was Cornelius's, but his mouth didn't move. I trembled as I stared at his body, blood seeping from beneath him. His destruction could have been prevented, could have resulted in a different outcome. I should have done more to wade through the darkness that bound him in resignation. But I had failed—failed Cornelius, failed myself . . . failed God.

"Miss?" The voice shifted, and the music came to an abrupt stop. "Miss, you okay?"

I blinked. The scene flashed. Cornelius and the blood disappeared, and the violinist stepped into my sight line where the magician had been, his instrument tucked under one arm and brows drawn in concern.

Shaking my head, I waved my hands. "Yes, yes, I'm well, sir. Thank you. I was simply transfixed by your music." With shaky hands, I dug through my reticule, retrieved a few coins, and tossed them into his open violin case. Then, ducking my head, I hurried away.

The more distance I put between the violinist and me, the more my erratic heart calmed. His music resumed, but my thoughts dwelled on the song that had conjured such a reaction in me. Waking or sleeping, I couldn't escape the guilt, couldn't stop reliving that moment when Cornelius rejected my pleas, when he had taken his last breath.

About a block behind the Abbey, down a cramped street, an array of storefronts brightened the path ahead with colorful awnings and doors. Vining plants of all sorts trailed along the Bath stone walls, and wrought iron tables and chairs here and there gave off an inviting aura.

Halfway through the street, I noticed a large window with white trim and bright gold letters reading, "The Bath Bun." Exactly as Mr. Everett had predicted, Katherine Quinn lounged at one of the distant outdoor tables. Her hands moved quickly, flipping weathered cards between her fingers and advancing a game of solitaire. A cup of tea, a plate with a scone, and a dish of clotted cream sat next to it, all untouched.

I put on a pleasant smile, held my posture erect, and approached. "Fancy meeting you here."

Katherine glanced up but stayed intent upon her game. "Good morning, angel. Have a seat. I'm about to win."

True to her word, as I sat opposite her, she deposited the last card in the top row and clapped her hands. "That makes three." She collected the deck and began shuffling with a precision that reminded me of the finesse Finn had exhibited in his own card tricks.

"I've been looking for you, Katherine," I said, tucking one foot behind the other.

"Why look for me when you have handsome brown eyes to

entertain you?" She smirked. "Were I in your shoes, I would spend every moment—"

"There are more pressing things we have to address," I interrupted, heat prickling my skin. "You left in a rush the last time we crossed paths. I still have many questions, and I'm not certain you're out of danger."

"You needn't worry about me, angel. Go back to your husband. Go back to London, as I told you before." She began dealing a new game of solitaire.

"I can't." I lowered my voice as I thought of each of Cornelius's victims—how I hadn't been able to help them. This time needed to be different. "I'm not doing it only for you."

Katherine paused mid-deal and studied me. Then the corners of her mouth deepened as she picked up the cards and shuffled again. "Going after what you want. I like it. You remind me of myself in my younger days." Her eyes gleamed. "But I don't give away my backstory for free. You must give me something in return."

I lifted my chin. "What do you want?"

With a widening smile, she stopped shuffling, dealt me one card faceup—an ace—and then placed one facedown before herself. "A wager."

It took me a moment to realize what she was proposing. "Gambling?"

She snorted. "The fact that you immediately knew the game suggests you've participated before without question. I'm not asking you to bet money—but rather, answers. If you win, you may ask one question and receive one answer. But if I win, then I may do the same to you. What do you say?"

Katherine spoke truth. It hadn't taken much to recognize the telltale game of blackjack thanks to Baze's influence. Ever curious of his father's social dalliances at the gambling table, Baze soon learned how to win a good wager himself, and he'd enthusiastically roped Bennett and I into his games. Back then, we had bet with small coins and trinkets. Unsurprisingly, considering his interest in mathematics, Baze had won handily nearly every time. But that didn't mean I wasn't confident I could best Katherine.

Suppressing a grin, I tapped the table. "Deal me another."

Katherine grinned. "Excellent." She flipped a new card onto my ace. A two.

I tapped again and received a seven, which brought me to a total of twenty, so I waved my hand. It was as close as I could get to the needed twenty-one.

Katherine revealed her card to be a king. She flipped a three, then a six, bringing her to nineteen. "A deal's a deal, and I am a woman of my word," she said as she scooped up the cards. "What burning questions lie upon your heart?"

Now that the opportunity to question her presented itself, I took a quick moment to gather my thoughts, sorting through the most important inquiries. "From what I have concluded, you live quite the nomadic lifestyle, but where are you really from?"

Her right shoulder came up. "I don't believe I'm from anywhere."

"Nonsense. Everyone is from somewhere."

"Well, we can get technical if you prefer. I was born in York to an English mother and an Irish father, but we never stayed in one place for too long. I've lived in England. I've lived in Ireland. I've lived in Scotland. Never in one place for too long. I'm a drifter, as you stated. I go where the wind blows."

I nodded. An Irish father. That explained her ambiguous accent—not quite English but not quite any other accent of the British Isles. Not to mention her flaming red hair and surname. Her Irish connection stoked my suspicions. If another person had indeed been aiding Cornelius, they could be the one targeting her . . . or *she* could be the accomplice. Obviously, not everyone of Irish heritage was caught up in Cornelius's schemes, but the coincidence was hard to ignore—because of all the wise counsel I took from Bennett, there was no such thing as coincidence.

Katherine dealt a new round. I received a three, so I tapped the table and got a seven. One more tap—a five. With a total of fifteen, the odds could go either way, but I decided to shake my head.

"Bold choice." Katherine flipped her card—a five. Then another five. And finally, an ace, which left her with a total of exactly twenty-one. She grinned. "A shame it didn't pay off." She picked up the cards and leveled her emerald stare at me. "Why do you blame yourself for what happened in London last year?"

Startling tears leapt to my eyes. Words stuck in my throat. The emotions from earlier came barreling up against the barricade that I'd fought to keep reinforced. "That question is incredibly personal."

Katherine nipped from her teacup and swallowed with pursed lips. "It's the name of the game, angel. You agreed."

I resisted the urge to make a face but resigned myself to the duel to which I'd committed. Forcing words past the emotional barrier, I whispered, "Because I was there. I should have been able to stop him. I told him to surrender . . ."

"Hmm." Seemingly unfazed by my vulnerable confession, Katherine dealt the next hand.

I emerged victorious this time and jumped straight into my next question. "Did you know Cornelius Marx?"

She tilted her head, a faint smile upon her lips. "I did."

Alarm bells clanged in my head. Unsure how to process the information, I blurted, "How did you know him?"

"Ah, ah, ah. One question at a time."

"But that was hardly an answer."

"Then learn to ask better questions."

As I muddled through the information, wondering how she possibly could have known Cornelius and what that connection meant when considered along with the case of the poisoned woman, Katherine took the next game with ease.

Grinning, she propped her chin on her upraised hand. "Since we're on the topic, the gossip columnists in London did their fair share of speculating, noting that you spent quite a lot of time at the Empress Theatre . . . with Cornelius Marx. Even had your engagement to brown eyes called off. The papers said it was Alistair Ford's doing, but I wonder if it was something more." Her sleek eyebrows elevated slightly as her voice lowered. "Did you love Cornelius?"

I closed my eyes, and the sensation of that man's kiss prickled on my lips. He'd manipulated and seduced me. Yet, what had my true feelings been before I learned the truth? My heart had been wandering down the oblivious path toward love—that I didn't deny—but had it ever arrived?

No. I had told Baze, adamantly, that I didn't love Cornelius, and that statement remained true.

Opening my eyes, I took a solid, reassuring breath. "No, I didn't."

"How curious," Katherine murmured as she began the next game, which she won in short order. Her expression fell a tick as she watched her shuffling hands. "How many times does Cornelius visit you in your nightmares or your waking moments?"

More emotion gripped my chest. I flared my nostrils and shoved his image out of my mind. "Do you have legitimate questions, or are you deliberately trying to get a rise out of me?"

"These *are* legitimate questions, angel." She met my eyes. "Answer me."

I tensed. "I see him nearly every day . . . and every night."

She nodded. As she shuffled, she mumbled almost imperceptibly, "As I thought."

Like before, Katherine progressed the game too quickly to allow me to percolate on the words we'd exchanged. This time, I emerged the victor and finally earned the opportunity to ask, "How did you know Cornelius?"

She smiled. "I met him in Ireland when he still went by his Christian name of Ciaran O'Connor."

The admission twisted my stomach. "Then do you—"

"My, my, you don't like to follow rules, do you?"

I slapped my palm on the table, rattling her teacup and splashing some of the liquid onto the ground. "Enough of the game. This is too serious. Lives are on the line. Tell me how you're connected to Cornelius. Do that and I might be able to help you uncover the person who's been hunting you."

Katherine sniffed, her expression hardening. She began collecting the cards. "We're done here."

"No!" I grabbed her wrist, but when we touched, an electric shock snapped between our skin. I yelped and yanked my hands back. The energy that had passed between us brought my mind back to the first time I had met Cornelius at my and Baze's engagement gala, when our connection had first formed and catapulted me into his dark world of visions and murder. Was she—

"I don't need your help." Though her cheeks had flushed, Katherine's features didn't betray any surprise or concern. "I've survived on my own for a long time, so there's no need for me to change my ways now." She dropped the deck into her reticule and fastened it with a flourish. "Besides, I have tickets for an afternoon train. Soon, I shall leave Bath behind and move on to new adventures, so you won't have to give me another thought." She stood and poked my forehead. "You have enough going on up here without adding my own burdens on top."

As she strode away, I spun and called, "But you aren't a burden."

She halted, her brows low and mouth twisted in a grimace. "Try being a little more selfish every once in a while. Even guardian angels need to focus on refilling their own cup from time to time so they can continue providing liberation for those who need it." Her soles scraped as she twirled around. "Focus on yourself, angel, and banish me from your mind."

Chapter Sixteen

EXHAUSTION AND FRUSTRATION SNAPPED AT MY heels as I trekked back to the Empire Hotel. The intense wordplay with Katherine had left me mentally drained and, again, with more questions than answers. Pushing through the doors with my hip, I brushed my thumb over my fingertips, reliving the startling jolt that had passed between us. What did it all mean? She'd known Cornelius. She'd met him in Ireland when he still went by Ciaran. Did that connection have anything to do with the attempt on her life . . . or with Cornelius's power of manipulation?

"Mrs. Ford! Excellent timing." Mr. Everett's cheerful voice broke me out of my reverie. "I have something for you."

I drew up beside the counter, blinking wearily. "What is it?"

"Mr. Ford swung by perhaps half an hour ago. He left this for you." Mr. Everett held out a sealed envelope.

Maintaining silence, I nodded my thanks and continued to our room before breaking the seal. Curiosity, and perhaps a touch of hesitation, piqued as I unfurled a short letter written in Baze's hand. At the top, his salutation consisted of a sweet, simple "Al." I read on.

When we first embarked on this holiday, I had hoped that we could relax and use this time to grow ever closer, but as you know, events have taken a disturbing turn. Though I do not have the power to erase what has happened, I can try to salvage moments and memories that we might still create together. I have decided to take the afternoon away from my investigation and would be delighted if you would grace me with your presence at the Royal Victoria Park at two o'clock for a

picnic catered by yours truly.
    Love, Baze

    P.S. I can already hear the arguments forming in your mind, so I shall cut your protests off at the pass. The investigation can wait. Our marriage is far more important to me. Don't make me come find you.

If I hadn't been absolutely sure this was Baze's handwriting—his penmanship left much to be desired yet only endeared him further in my heart—I'd have been convinced the killer at large was attempting to lure me to that location. But this appeared to be Baze's doing and Baze's alone.

What had gotten into him? As much as I knew he loved me, elaborately planned surprises were not his preferred method of showing affection—especially when he already had precious little time to devote to the investigation.

Exactly as he had predicted in the letter, excuses began rising, urging me to seek him out for the solitary purpose of leading him back to the case at hand. But he was also correct. If we didn't take time to pause and focus on one another, we risked drifting apart even though our life together had barely begun.

Two o'clock. That gave me ample time to change into something more comfortable and tidy the room a bit. Of the things Baze and I were discovering about one another, one was that I tended toward a neat home while he was rarely bothered by a little clutter.

With a huff, I busied myself about the area, fluffing the pillows on the bed, organizing the flowers on the coffee table, and straightening Baze's shirts in his wardrobe. As I passed the cabinet in the hall, my hip bumped the corner. One of the small doors popped open. A gleaming bottle within caught my eye and caused me to backtrack. *Where did that come from? That's not the same bottle he had before.*

With gentle fingers, I withdrew the glass vessel, uncorked the top, and sniffed. A strong vapor stung the inside of my nose and forced out several coughs as it crammed down my throat. Laudanum . . . or something of that nature. And it smelled strong.

Quickly, I put it back in its place and shut the door. Baze had said he was taking it for his leg, but how much did he need? Hadn't Frederick instructed him to start weaning off?

Trying to ignore my discovery, I readied myself for the picnic, twisting my hair into a loose design and donning a light, breathable tea dress made of a blue cotton fabric. I'd timed it nearly perfectly, as the clock showed a quarter to two right as I finished dressing.

Mr. Everett called a driver to take me to Royal Victoria Park. Walking would have taken me a good twenty minutes, providing I didn't get lost along the way, but by motorcar, I arrived in barely five. He dropped me at the gravel avenue that ran through the middle of the park. Miscellaneous notes from a string quartet tuning their instruments drifted up from the bandstand at the base of the hill. Rising in the distance at the top of the slope, the grand architecture of the Royal Crescent loomed in the background, its stone Georgian exterior exuding wealth and decorum. We'd considered staying in one of the thirty opulent homes that comprised the half-moon structure, but they'd been fully booked.

Locating Baze's chosen spot farther up the hill in the direction of the crescent, I lifted my skirt and trudged up the incline.

Hands clasped before him, Baze stood at ease and gazed out across the park. When he noticed my approach, he brightened, touched a hand to his chest, tucked the other behind his back, and bowed. "I am delighted you've chosen to join me, madam." He lifted my hand and brought it to his lips for a brief kiss. "It is my pleasure to host you this afternoon."

Jaw slack, I surveyed the blanket at his feet strewn with fresh-cut watermelon, cucumber sandwiches, jam tarts, plump strawberries, and chilled lemonade. "Look at all this," I breathed. "Whatever compelled you to do such a thing?"

"Can't a man treat his wife to a delectable lunch?" He grinned, cheeks rosy.

"Of course, but—"

"You must be famished. Come. Sit." Supporting my hand, he guided me onto the blanket and helped me lower to the ground, then took his own spot across from me. He busied himself adding food to a porcelain plate.

I laid a hand on his wrist, halting him. "Baze, really, what is this?"

He let the plate sink into his lap, his cheery countenance falling a touch. "I knew it would be difficult to distract you from all that's been happening . . . but I wanted to try."

Warmth and love spiraled through me. I slipped my hand into his. "I appreciate your thoughtfulness, but you know we can't ignore this for long. I was able to save a woman's life, and we have a chance to solve this before anyone else falls victim."

The light in his eyes dimmed further. He cleared his throat and pulled from my touch. "Watermelon or strawberries?"

I tilted my head. "Both."

"Brilliant choice."

His attempts to avoid the subject weren't lost on me, but I permitted him a moment of reprieve, watching him fix our plates and pour a refreshing splash of lemonade. As we ate quietly, the quartet began to serenade the park patrons with a lively ragtime piece, and it didn't take long for the music to loosen my muscles and allow me to give my full attention to Baze and his sweet gesture. I swayed to the tune, and when I caught Baze doing the same, we shared a lighthearted laugh.

The food satiated my rumbling stomach, and my corset soon felt tight around my midsection. In between nibbles of jam tart, I asked, "How goes your time with the physiotherapist?"

Baze swallowed a mouthful of his sandwich and smiled. "Excellent, actually. We've been focusing on the hydrotherapy, and I think the water is helping."

"Not because of the water's healing powers, of course."

"Why not? We've seen stranger things . . . much stranger." He shrugged. "Or perhaps it's a combination of all three—the water, the therapist, and the Almighty."

I bit my lip, wanting to add a fourth item to that list—his laudanum—but I didn't quite know how Baze felt about the drug and opted to proceed carefully. Frederick had warned of the opium's addictive properties, and once addicted, a person couldn't simply quit at a moment's notice. How could I know if Baze only used it as needed to manage the pain or if he were truly addicted?

Before I could form the right words, Baze reclined and propped himself on his arms. "What sort of trouble did you get into today while I was out?"

I popped the rest of the tart in my mouth, chewed slowly, and swallowed. "I found our Miss Katherine Quinn and challenged her to a game of blackjack in exchange for answers."

A short laugh rumbled in Baze's chest. "Well, why would you go and do such a thing? We both know you're rubbish at blackjack. Did you even get anything out of her?"

"Yes, I did, thank you very much." I drove a light fist into his arm.

Even though delving into the topic of Katherine Quinn would steer our conversation back to the case, I decided to forge ahead anyway, despite Baze's earlier objections. His face grew solemn as I spoke, but I pressed on, recounting everything Katherine had admitted to me . . . and eventually divulged her acquaintance with Cornelius.

"Baze, what if that's our connection? What if she has the same abilities that Cornelius had?" I lowered my voice. "What if she's actually the one behind all of this?"

Baze chewed pensively and took a long draw from his lemonade. He smacked his lips and sighed. "I suppose it's possible. Shouldn't you ought to know? You always sensed evil around Cornelius. Have you felt anything of the sort around Miss Quinn?"

"No, nothing has raised my alarms. Then again, I didn't detect Cornelius's powers right away either."

"True." He looked into his glass and swished the liquid around. "It took you a good while to see through his charms."

Whether he meant the statement as a deliberate jab or an innocent aside, it stung nonetheless. I swiped my hands together and said under my breath, "Anything new to report from the chief inspector?"

Baze shifted his jaw. "We're working with a toxicologist, Charles Caine, and he said cyanide salts killed the woman at the hotel. It appears to be the same substance found in the fountain at the Pump Room. Could be the same killer."

"Any ideas for a motive?"

"No, we don't have enough to ascertain that right now."

I stared at the quartet in the distance as I pondered aloud. "Last time, all of the victims were connected to me in some capacity. If this is indeed linked to Cornelius, then I'm not the target this time, because I don't know either of the women." I brushed a strand of fringe out of my eyes. "I think Katherine is the key to unlocking this mystery."

The music transitioned into a timely waltz. Baze set his glass down, rubbed his palms on his thighs, struggled to his feet, and reached out an open palm. "Dance with me."

I stared at his proffered hand. "What?"

"Dance with me. It's been ages since I've had the chance."

I glanced around, noting other happy couples and families enjoying similar luncheon spreads across the luscious green lawn, then narrowed my eyes at him. "I thought we agreed to no more public affection."

"Well, maybe I've changed my mind." He bent, scooped up my hands, and pulled me to my feet. Before I could protest, he swept me straight into rhythmic steps in time with the music, his sturdy arms holding me in the proper rigid form of the waltz.

I tensed, held my breath, but he stepped confidently with smooth, uninterrupted movements as though his leg injury had never happened. Maybe his leg was healing after all.

Head spinning with elation, I allowed myself to relax into him and followed his lead to the flow of the music. We spun, swayed, and twirled, and I found myself giggling uncontrollably. Despite my highborn status, I didn't have as many opportunities to dance as one might expect. How long had it been? The last time I'd danced so freely—

Cornelius flashed in my mind's eye, yanking me back to our dance in the Irish pub, when I'd been overwhelmed by his intoxicating control, dizzied by my wayward desire . . .

No, stop!

I wound a tight arm around Baze's neck, pressed against him, and forced myself to concentrate solely on his presence. Cornelius no longer held any sway upon me, no longer dictated my thoughts and feelings. *Lord, cleanse my mind. Please.*

My hold seemed to spur something in Baze, and he bent forward, dipped me low, and planted a firm kiss on my lips. When we parted, I gaped up at him, aware of people's judgmental eyes upon us. "Basil Ford, what's gotten into you?"

He grinned and pulled me back up to a stand, his face reddening. "I'm so utterly in love with you, Al, and I want the world to know."

Placing a hand on his chest, I smiled but fought to keep from rolling my eyes. "Well, aren't you romantic."

Chuckling, he wrapped his arms snugly about my waist, lifted, and spun me. I squealed as my stomach flipped and my vision spun. Sunlight flashed. Scenery blurred. After several rotations, my feet touched the ground, and the earth ceased its rotation.

But I no longer reclined in Baze's arms.

Now, I found myself positioned at the base of the hill among a group of spectators watching the musicians' performance. I tried to move, but my body seemed frozen in place. Chills raised gooseflesh on my arms as my gaze locked on one of the violinists. Sweat poured down his face, and his fingers trembled. The bow bounced on the strings, but judging from the concerned looks of his fellow musicians, the movement wasn't intentional.

Then, he yelled and threw his instrument on the ground. *Crack.*

Strings snapped. The violin splintered. Hands gripping his throat, the violinist stumbled about, and his skin flushed to a deep red.

The image faded to darkness, and when I came to, I lay on my back, staring up at the sky. Baze leaned over me, his face drained of all color. "What did you see?"

I quivered, gasping in air. "The quartet. Hurry."

The music hiccupped. Halted. A murmur swept through the crowd—then a scream.

Chapter Seventeen

AFTER LEAVING ADELYNN SAFE IN THEIR room and ordering her to stay put despite her remonstrations, Baze hurried to the police station where he joined Detective Chief Inspector Whitaker and the toxicologist. He battled an inner war against simmering anger and resentment—knowing that, try as he might, he couldn't escape the danger infecting the city of Bath.

"His name was Edwin Davis," Whitaker said as they waited for Caine to examine the samples in his microscope. "He's been a musician here in Bath for nearly fifteen years. He often performed for the most exclusive of events with the rest of his quartet but took to the streets to busk when otherwise disengaged."

Fingers wobbling, Baze shook out his hand and tried to focus on what the chief inspector was saying. The effects of the opium tincture he'd ingested mere hours earlier were starting to wear off—disturbingly faster than last time—and his leg had begun to throb. Yes, the physiotherapist had said it was a weakened prescription, but Baze hadn't anticipated it to be *that* weak. He'd have to take another dose soon before his body devolved into a quivering mess.

"His fellow musicians are here waiting to give their testimony," Whitaker continued. "Would you like to accompany me?"

"Of course."

Caine cleared his throat. "Before you do that, Chief Inspector, you may want to know what killed this man."

"Indeed." Whitaker approached Caine's table where he had the violinist's instrument disassembled next to him—the bridge removed, the strings unwound, and the neck severed from the body. A white dust coated the fingerboard.

Drawing closer, Baze noticed the same snowy powder clinging to the coiled strings.

"That substance you're seeing is called rosin." Caine grabbed a tiny chunk of a solid amber-colored material and held it aloft. "This is what it looks like before application. String players must coat the bow hair with the rosin in order for it to grip the strings and produce sound."

"Is it common for them to use so much?" Baze reached for the fingerboard to get a closer look.

"No, because that isn't rosin." Caine shook his head. "That's sodium cyanide."

Baze yanked his hand back.

"It appears someone infused this block of rosin with cyanide so that when Mr. Davis drew his bow across it, the cyanide would bury deep into the horsehairs. As he played, the bow movement across the strings caused particles to become airborne, and because the violin rests so close to the musician's face, he inhaled copious amounts as the performance progressed."

Whitaker shifted his weight, placed his hands on his hips, and cursed under his breath.

Caine snatched up a rag, wrapped it over his hand, and lifted the body of the violin. Though the wood exterior had been fractured, it retained its shape. As Caine studied it, he turned it over, then sideways. A hollow *thunk* came from within.

Ears perked, Baze gestured to the instrument. "What was that noise?"

The toxicologist shrugged. "Something loose on the inside, perhaps."

Baze frowned. "An expensive instrument like that shouldn't have anything loose."

Caine shook the violin. Something thwacked inside the hollow interior, this time louder and more distinct. While Baze and Whitaker looked on, Caine brought his desk light closer and peered through one of the f-holes. He grunted. "I can't quite make it out, but there is indeed something inside."

Baze eyed the thin holes. "Do you think you can get it out?"

With a grimace, Caine fished around on his table and came up with a long, sharp tool resembling a letter opener. Before Baze could object, Caine turned the violin on its side, rammed the instrument under the top plate, and wrenched. The violin split apart with a sickening *crunch*.

Baze closed his eyes briefly, lamenting the destruction of such an exquisite piece.

As though reading his thoughts, Caine said in a monotone, "It was already damaged, Inspector. Surely bringing a dead man's killer to justice is more important that preserving a broken violin."

To that, Baze couldn't argue.

Now that the violin's innards lay exposed, it allowed them to fully search inside the hollow base. Baze spotted a small, folded scrap of paper lying beside the sound post, but Caine snatched it up before Baze could.

Caine took his time unfolding it. He scanned the note, then handed it to Whitaker. Baze leaned over to look and read it silently: *You escaped once. Never Again.*

Baze's stomach turned. Like the first note, this one also addressed someone directly. Was it speaking to the victim . . . or someone else?

"Do you wager that capital A is significant?" Whitaker tapped the paper. "First a capital K. Now this? Surely they're connected."

In Cornelius Marx's own gruesome note left on Sergeant Peter Moseley's body, he had intentionally capitalized a letter in order to lead them to the next clue left in place of one of the sergeant's eyes. There was nothing to suggest to Baze that this situation wasn't exactly the same. But what could it mean? K and A.

"What do you make of it, Caine?" Whitaker directed the conversation toward the toxicologist.

Rigid, Caine chewed the end of a pen. "A rich woman. A violinist.

Cyanide poisoning. Tell me, Chief Inspector, what does that correlation conjure in your mind?"

Curiosity aroused, Baze looked to Whitaker. The chief inspector pondered, stroking his beard. Then, as though realization had struck, his fingers froze and his face paled.

Caine nodded in confirmation.

"What?" Baze urged. "What is it?"

"This has happened before," Whitaker murmured. "Fifteen years ago, Bath fell prey to its own serial killer. He used cyanide as his poison of choice. The first victim was a woman of great wealth. The second was a cellist . . ." His voice grew quieter. "The man was never caught."

Palms clammy, Baze absorbed the words. Nearly identical killings. A murderer still at large. Either this was a large coincidence . . . or the man was back.

Then where did Katherine Quinn fit into this? The water she nearly drank had been tainted with the same poison that killed the current victims, but did that mean the same perpetrator hunted her as well?

Whitaker jutted his chin at the toxicologist. "What do you think? Is this the same man?"

"Hard to be sure," Caine said, distractedly sliding the photograph of his young son toward himself. "The killer last time was meticulous. Detail-oriented. The fact that our second victim is a violinist and not a cellist casts shadows of doubt. But I'll try to isolate the cyanide and see if it's the same composition as the last poison. That should give us a start."

"Let me know as soon as you find something." Whitaker grimaced. "I'm sorry, Caine."

Gaze unfocused, the toxicologist flattened his hand over the photograph and gave a small nod.

Whitaker nudged Baze's arm. "Come. Let's leave him to it." The chief inspector headed from the room with Baze in tow, and when they'd passed into the hall, Whitaker halted near the closed door and exhaled. "I never thought I'd come face-to-face with a serial killer, but here we are."

Baze folded his arms, if only to mask the heightened trembling in his hands. An ache began to squeeze his head. "Were you not on the force last time?"

A humorless smile spread Whitaker's beard. "I was the greenest of rookies last time and barely knew what was going on by the time the killer's reign of terror ended. Caine, however, was fully immersed in the chase . . ." Whitaker picked at one of his thumbnails. "What do you know of Caine's son, Inspector Ford?"

Baze tried to make the large leap from the serial killer to Caine's son. "From what I've gathered, he perished prematurely, but I'm not sure how."

Whitaker's throat rippled in a slow swallow. "Fifteen years ago, the boy, Isaac Caine, was the killer's last victim."

Memories of Bennett's cold form lying upon the mortuary table nearly punched the air from Baze's lungs. To have lost someone so close, to realize there was nothing he could have done to prevent that loss, made each additional breath that much more guilt-ridden. He could barely fathom what it must be like to lose a son in that manner.

"That's terrible."

"Indeed, it was. Caine was a talented toxicologist before the event, but after Isaac's death, he threw himself deep into his work, almost to the point of collapse. His marriage deteriorated, his health declined, but the killer never emerged again, disappearing like an apparition into thin air. It drove Caine to the brink of madness. He grew resigned over time, accepting that he would never achieve the justice he longed for." Whitaker sighed. "I can't image what this new development is doing to his psyche."

Emotion clawed its way up Baze's throat, but he pushed it down. "How many victims were there last time?"

"Four in total."

"Did the killer leave notes then too?"

"No, that's a new detail." Whitaker knocked a knuckle against Baze's chest. "Listen, with what little evidence we have at our disposal, this case could go one of two ways. Either the similarities to the cold case of yesteryear are mere coincidences or they're being committed by the same man and will continue to follow the same pattern."

Baze tried to follow the chief inspector's reasoning, tried to factor in Isaac Caine's murder, but he didn't allow himself to complete the calculation. The mere idea of it made him sick. His finger came up to stroke his nose as he murmured, "Then we need to move faster."

And he would start with Miss Katherine Quinn.

I had just settled onto the sofa to rest, an arm draped over my eyes to block out the light that inflamed my headache, when Baze came stumbling into the room. Temples throbbing, I rolled into a sitting position, determined not to let the affliction stop me from hearing what he might have to say. Before I could stand, he sank next to me and dropped his face into his hands.

Wordlessly, I massaged the rock-hard space between his shoulder blades until I felt the muscles ripple and relax. "What did you learn?" I whispered.

With one last scrub down his flushed face, he laced his fingers and rested his elbows upon his knees. "This is getting more and more complicated by the moment, Al."

A pronounced tremble in his hands sparked my alarm. Fear? Or something else? I slid my fingers over the top of his and held them still. "You're shaking."

"It's nothing." He pulled away, straightened his spine, and attempted a smile that fell flat.

"Then tell me what happened." I coaxed him with my eyes, intent, insistent.

Finally, a jumble of words spilled from his mouth, and he explained every detail that he had learned so far. According to the toxicologist, Charles Caine, the killer had infused the violin's rosin with cyanide and left a note within the instrument. Chief Inspector Whitaker and Caine had pointed out striking similarities between this case and one from fifteen years ago, but it was unclear whether the two were connected. Still, Caine had taken a vested interest in solving the case, as his son had been the final victim in the previous rash of murders—and the killer had never been caught.

"I actually need your help." Baze bobbed his leg, and sweat beads sparkled on his forehead. "I'm looking for Katherine Quinn."

For a moment, I narrowed my eyes at him, bracing against the irritation I felt radiating from his jittery frame. It spurred my own impatience. "Why do you need her?"

"I'm not sure yet, but her name has come up far too often for me to believe she's merely a bystander. Besides, you said it yourself. She knew Cornelius Marx. She could be the key to all of this."

Yes, I harbored my own suspicions toward Katherine, but the scales of indecision still teetered in the middle. I'd only begun to scratch the surface of what lay below her unyielding exterior. She could be the mastermind, or she could be an innocent victim. During our last meeting, that final fleeting glance she'd given me hadn't resembled the look of a conniving criminal. No, the fire in her eyes, the chaos in her face, had likened her to a caged animal awaiting an unknown fate.

Not that any of that mattered anymore.

"I'm afraid we may be too late," I said. "She mentioned that she had secured tickets for an afternoon train. She has likely already departed."

Profanity sprang from Baze's lips as he kicked at the coffee table.

A gasp burst from my mouth as the table's contents scattered and glass cracked. Annoyed by the destruction and that he'd startled me so abruptly, I seized his arm as though to restrain him and felt the muscles quivering beneath his sleeve. "What has gotten into you?" I snapped. "Earlier, you were overly ecstatic in the park, and now you're completely the opposite. You're not acting like yourself."

"I said it's nothing." He tore from me and vaulted to his feet. Steps uneven, he clomped across the room to the cabinet, retrieved the vial I'd found earlier, and clutched it to his chest.

When he wrenched open the door to our room, I shouted, "Wait, where are you—"

The door slammed. The walls shook.

Anger thundered inside my head. Why wouldn't he talk to me? At the start of our marriage, we had agreed to share everything with one another. We had agreed not to keep secrets. Had I ever given him reason to think I would judge him for his struggles were he to confide in me?

I glanced at the telephone sitting on a nearby table. Either I could allow my suspicions to percolate, or I could go straight to an expert. *Very well, Baze, if you want to carry this on your own, then I will seek help for you on* my *own.*

I crossed to the telephone and lifted the receiver to my ear. The operator came on, and I relayed the name and location. My pulse quickened as I waited for Frederick Ford to come on the other line. Baze wouldn't like this—would probably consider it sneaking around behind his back—but I couldn't bear to see him suffer like this, especially when he refused to admit there was a problem in the first place. What choice had he given me?

"Adelynn?" Frederick's deep voice rumbled in my ear. "To what do I owe the call? I thought you were on holiday."

"I am . . . we are," I stammered quietly, then gripped the receiver tight. "Frederick, I need your help. It's Baze."

"What about him?" Concern tinged Frederick's voice.

"He's been taking opium for his pain since his surgery, but you were helping him wean off, correct?"

"Yes."

"Well, I think . . . I think he's taking more than he should."

A pause. "Why do you think that?"

"He's been acting strangely. I've caught him taking a new tincture I've never seen before, and the more time that passes between doses, the more irritable he grows. Yet, at other times, he's borderline euphoric."

"How is his leg?"

"It seems that it's improving. He walks as though the injury never happened."

Frederick expelled a short sigh.

My breath grew shallow. "Frederick, what's happening to him?

"I don't want to use conjecture without examining him myself, and I don't wish to scare you, but it sounds like he is developing an opium dependency. If he has indeed begun taking more, then that's of grave concern. The more a man takes, the more he becomes resistant to it, which forces him to take more still in order to feel the same effects. As a result, he becomes fully dependent upon it. It is what I was hoping to avoid by lowering his dose."

I closed my eyes, chafing at the possibility that Baze may be in the evil grip of that drug. "So what do I do?"

"Listen to me carefully, Adelynn. Allow him to continue as usual, but I need you to keep an eye on his behavior. Monitor the symptoms." Frederick's tone grew calm, collected. "Don't push him. Someone under the influence can be unpredictable. If he worsens, contact me immediately."

After I hung up the receiver, I covered my mouth with a hand to hold in building emotion. Last year, Cornelius had taken Baze's mind captive, and now, opium was doing the same. But this time, it was worse. The opium actually removed the pain that had assaulted him every minute of every day since his injury—but it was false hope. The injury remained. The drug merely hid the trauma. And to take away the opium would be to take away Baze's hope. Could I bring myself to do that? *Lord, what do I do? How do I proceed from here without crushing his spirit or creating a divide between us?*

Chapter Eighteen

I SKIRTED THROUGH THE BUSTLING STATION, the afternoon train about to depart. Steam poured from beneath the locomotive, warming my arms and rustling the thin skirt about my legs. I tipped my head as a conductor passed and hopped into an open door. As I strolled down the platform, I glanced at each oblivious passenger through the hazy windows.

A sharp crying drew my attention to a young woman and her child. The little boy resisted his mother's attempts to pull him toward the train. Thick tears streamed down his ruddy cheeks. He heaved in and out. "I d-don't want to. I'm s-scared."

"I know you're scared, but we have to go. The train will leave without us." Desperation laced her light voice.

Amused at the boy's misplaced fear, I smiled to myself. Oh, to be afraid of something so inconsequential when the world positively teemed with true terrors.

I turned away from the scene, seeking out the train number listed on my ticket. The moment I located it at the end of the platform, a man's distant, familiar voice cut through the crowd.

"Excuse me."

Every instinct to run flared, but I rotated on disobedient feet and speared my gaze toward the boy and his mother.

Sully knelt in front of the boy, forearms rested on his propped knee. "What's got you in such a state, lad?"

The boy hiccupped a sob and wiped a large glob of mucus from his nose with a sleeve. "I-I'm scared."

"You're scared?" Sully raised his brows. "Whatever for?"

His cries lessened a touch, and he rubbed one of his eyes. "It's noisy. And big."

Sully glanced at the mother—and then, for a fleeting moment, his gaze darted to mine. A smile that held deeper meaning than what the mother would recognize wrinkled the skin by his eyes as he focused on the boy. "I have just the thing for you now." He fished into his trouser pocket and extracted a shilling and held it up. "This is a special coin, lad. Blessed by the fairies in Ireland, it is. I carry it with me, and whenever I'm scared, it fills me with courage."

With halted cries, the boy made a grab for it, but just as his pudgy fingers touched it, Sully twisted his hand, flicked the coin away, and made a show of his empty palms. "Oh dear," he said in exaggerated distress. "It appears I've dropped it. Those fairies be tryin' to hide it from me." They searched the ground a moment. Then Sully widened his eyes at the child. "Hold on. What's this? It appears the fairies have hidden something in your ear." Before the boy could recoil, Sully reached behind the boy's ear and flipped the coin back between his fingers. "Look what I've found on you." Sully held it up for him to see.

Alarmed, the boy clapped a hand over his ear and wiggled the tip of his finger into it.

Sully chuckled and held it out to him. "It appears me fairies be wantin' you to have it." The boy accepted it gingerly and gaped at it in awe. Sully tapped the boy's nose. "Remember, whoever be holdin' the coin must have courage in him. Understand?"

The boy nodded, still examining the shilling.

"That means you can't fear the train anymore, aye?"

Drying his eyes, the boy nodded again, this time more confidently, and said, "Yes, sir."

"Good lad." Sully ruffled his hair and stood. He tipped his herringbone flat cap at the mother as she mouthed, "Thank you," and tugged her son onto the train without so much as a whimper from the child's mouth.

Then Sully's eyes locked on me.

I froze, holding my breath, as he moseyed my way and stopped a few feet before me, hands relaxed in his pockets.

Jutting my chin, I scoffed. "Really? Cozying up to children? Isn't that beneath you?"

"Children are a gift to be cherished, sure." He shrugged. "You once thought like I did, Kate. Once wanted your own . . . our own."

My nickname sounded sweet yet cynical on his tongue, covering me in gooseflesh. I folded my arms tight. "That was many years ago."

Sully's gaze traced over my face, slowly, painstakingly, before drifting to the train behind me. His thick lashes fluttered in an almost imperceptible blink. "You're leavin' then."

What ran through his mind as he considered the thought? Relief? Sorrow? As if he had a right to feel anything toward me anymore.

"I told you I would. You shouldn't be shocked."

Hands still slotted in his pockets, he closed the gap between us and leaned his mouth to my ear. "I will say this once and only once, Kate. If you leave the city, Adelynn Ford will die."

The train fired a spray of steam. I flinched but managed to keep my muscles firm. "You wouldn't dare," I said through my teeth.

His lips tickled my ear, and I shuddered. "You know of what I'm capable. If it will take a sacrificial lamb to stop you, then so be it. I can't be lettin' you go. You're too dangerous."

Though the train's warm vapor flared around us, flurries of cold air swirled at our feet. Awakening my practiced mind, I pushed out against his own, gently at first, then stronger, trying to coax him to step away.

As though feeling the pressure on his thoughts, he tilted back and narrowed his eyes.

Annoyed that he'd resisted me, I smirked to hide my emotions. "Well, I think you're bluffing. What else would be keeping you from offing me right here and now?"

He cocked his head with another shrug and backed up a few steps. "Believe what you wish, mo ghrá.*" He continued edging away, eyes never leaving mine. "But either she leaves the city alive—or you do. It's your choice."*

Chapter Nineteen

A CRACK OF THUNDER WOKE BASIL Allan in the early hours of morning. Emily rolled out of bed, sleep still tugging at her eyelids. She rocked him, held him tightly to her bosom. "There now, love. It's all right. You're all right." Gradually, Basil Allan's cries lessened along with the storm.

Emily lit an oil lamp and slumped into the rocking chair in the corner of the room. Weariness weighed her muscles, and Basil Allan's dense form atop her chest hindered her lungs. Toeing the floor to rock the chair slightly, she peered about the room with half-lidded eyes. Eventually, her gaze fell upon the dresser and dragged to the framed photograph of Bennett. She stared into his eyes, and he stared back, stone-faced, posture erect and professional in his uniform. A single tear welled and escaped down her cheek.

I miss you. I miss you so much . . .

As loneliness threatened to devour her, her thoughts yanked to Sergeant Rees Andrews. A good man, an honorable man, but not the man for her. Though he had offered courtship—and thus a potential marriage—Emily couldn't bring herself to say yes when her heart had closed itself off to him, even though the pain of living the rest of her life without a partner seemed too great to bear.

Musings about Sergeant Andrews led her mind to the break-in at Adelynn and Baze's residence. The sergeant had clearly hated the fact that she'd accompanied him to have a look around, but what else should she have done?

Emily's eyes stung as she attempted to hold the gaze of her husband's photograph. "What would you do, Bennett?" she whispered.

His image blurred. He would have spent every waking moment he could trying to solve the mystery, to keep his friends safe—but Emily couldn't do that. She had Basil Allan to care for. He was her priority, and she would protect him with her life if she had to.

Another tear found its way down her face. Basil Allan emitted a groan from the back of his throat and snuggled deep against her chest. Pressing her lips shut to keep her cries locked within, she closed her eyes and allowed her body to shake in silent sobs.

Lord, how do I keep going? How do I find the strength to get up every day and be the mother my son needs me to be? How do I stop feeling useless . . . feeling lonely? How do I continue without him? Without Bennett? Without . . .

They were all questions she'd asked a thousand times before—all questions to which she had yet to receive an answer.

Sleep nipped at the edges of her perception. Her eyelids grew heavy. The rocking of the chair slowed. What was stopping her from simply locking the door and never emerging into public again? What more was there for her out there? *Why should I keep going, Lord?*

A distant metallic clink sounded from the front door. Emily's body jolted back from unconsciousness, her ears tuned to the sound. The mail slot? Had she dozed so long that the morning post had arrived?

With small, careful movements, Emily rose and laid Basil Allan inside his crib. He didn't stir, still sleeping soundly. Emily padded out of the room and to the front door, her nightgown swishing about her ankles. Sure enough, the post lay scattered on the floor.

Emily dropped to her haunches, settled cross-legged on the carpet, and collected the letters. Squinting in the dim light, she sorted through them, tossed each one aside . . . until she came across a familiar postmark that sent her heart racing. Finn O'Brien.

Had he received her correspondence? No, there couldn't have been enough time for him to post a reply. So then, what could this letter hold within?

After tearing into it, she extracted the crude paper, marked with

Finn's light, delicate hand, and eagerly absorbed the words as though they contained precious lifeblood.

Dear Emily,

I imagine that you are curious as to the reason for this second letter so soon after my first. In truth, I found my thoughts constantly drifting back to you. Perhaps it is my own yearning that is prompting such thoughts, or maybe it is the coaxing of a more divine power. I admit I have much to learn by way of discerning the Spirit's voice, so as of yet, it is impossible for me to tell between the two.

You and I are a lot alike, I think. We are spectators. We prefer to remain in the background, never causing much of a ruckus, but in that, we tend to retreat too far, so far that we fall out of sight of others. Sometimes, it is unintentional, but sometimes, we like it better that way.

Forgive my boldness, but I cannot imagine the extent of your retreat. When I returned to Liscannor, I lost myself in rebuilding my parents' home. I did not speak to anyone. I did not allow anyone in.

Do not do what I did, Emily. Do not cut off the people who love you. For your sake and your son's, get out there. Find something to give you purpose. Whatever that may be. Find it. Then go after it.

I shall be thinking about you. Praying too. We have been given a great gift, and it pains me to think that if you remain locked within, I might never see you again. Because I do hope I shall see you again someday.

However, I have begun to doubt that it will ever be possible. The effects of Ciaran's misdeeds have followed me here to Ireland. There is so much more to his story than what happened to us in London last year. He was involved in something much deeper, and I fear that he set a series of terrible events in motion that cannot be undone, events that would threaten your very life should we ever cross paths again.

All that to say, be vigilant. Allow the events of the past to become just that—the past. Because once you involve yourself, there is no going back, and I do not wish that for you. I wish that my and Ciaran's lives will never affect yours again.

I apologize for my rambling. Perhaps I simply do not want this letter to end. Now that I have reached out to you, now that I have opened this door, I do not want to shut it. But I must. For now. I have said what needed to be said. Stay safe, Emily.

Sincerely,

Finn O'Brien.

Emily clutched the letter to her chest, tears spilling down her cheeks, a spiral of anger and awe filling her. In this moment, they had not been the words she wanted to hear, but they were the words she *needed* to hear. Even as she chafed against them, she knew they spoke life into her.

Clambering to her feet, she tossed on a shawl, shoved through the front door, and snuck out to the edge of the landing. The morning sun peeked over the tops of the distant buildings. Its rays caressed her feet and gradually lifted to her knees, then her thighs. Warmth banished the chill in her bones. In a daze, she gazed at the sunrise, mouth agape, Finn's letter held securely in her hands. Continuing its slow, deliberate trek into the sky, the sun embraced her in its warmth until it finally kissed her face. She squinted against the brightness, took in a shuddering breath as birds and the bustle of the city began.

"Okay, Lord," she whispered. "I'll try. I can't promise I'll keep it together the whole time, but . . . I'll try."

Chapter Twenty

DARKNESS YET CLUNG TO THE SKY when I felt Baze shift. The bed shuddered, then grew still. Quiet footfalls whispered toward the wardrobe. I lay motionless, listening to his clothes rustling—the sound like a roar amidst the deep silence. My exhausted muscles begged me to close my eyes and succumb to a restorative slumber, nightmares having kept me awake most of the night. Overcoming the impulse, I chose to roll over and face Baze.

"Where are you going?" I murmured, voice muted with fatigue.

His fingers scrambled up the front of his shirt, fastening the buttons as they went. "I have another early session with the therapist."

I sat up, keeping my arms bundled beneath the covers to trap the warmth within. Still on edge from the tension caused during our row the evening before, I asked, "May I accompany you?"

He shrugged into his coat and shook it into place. "Why? I imagine it would be quite dull for a spectator."

"Not to watch. I feel terrible for yesterday, and I simply don't want you to leave before we've had a chance to talk. Once we arrive, I'll retreat to the ladies' bath so you can complete your session in privacy." I drew my legs upward and rested my chin upon my knees, then batted my eyelashes. "Please."

After a long, noiseless moment, Baze's eyes gleamed soft in the shadows. "Up with you then." He fished out his pocket watch and clicked it open. "If you can be ready in ten minutes, you can come."

Spurred by the challenge, I kicked off the covers and raced to my wardrobe. A gentle chuckle from Baze only increased my urgency. With years of muscle memory directing my hands, I threw on each layer—the combinations, the corset, the corset cover, and finally the gown—all within a couple of minutes. To finish, I tossed my hair into an updo and hid the crude handiwork beneath a hat. Triumphant, I planted myself before Baze, hands on hips and lungs heaving for breath.

Stashing his watch, he rolled his eyes. "You were lucky."

"I reject that statement." I slipped my arm through his and steered us toward the door. "Luck had nothing to do with it."

Already at his post despite the early hour, Mr. Everett looked up from his newspaper and gave a polite acknowledgement as we crossed through the lobby. Without stopping, we stepped into the cool dawn air. Though the stars had begun to fade and a light turquoise spread up from the horizon, the rows of street lamps still burned bright.

Baze led us in the direction of the Roman Baths, gait smooth, as though his injury were merely a small nuisance.

An accusation fueled by the events of yesterday leapt to the tip of my tongue, but I clamped it down. He had made it clear that he wasn't ready to explain himself, so I resolved, reluctantly, to allow him the time and distance needed to gather his thoughts. Instead, I drew tight against his side until our hips brushed together and whispered, "I'm sorry for what I said yesterday. I can't imagine the pain you've been going through, but I want you to know you don't have to carry it alone."

I had hoped my admission might help to lower whatever defenses he refused to abandon, but he simply responded with, "I'm sorry too."

Biting back my disappointment, I leaned my head against his shoulder, unconcerned that it bent the rim of my hat, and tried a different approach. "I've missed you."

He matched my hushed tone. "I'm right here."

"But your mind has been far away."

His arm tightened around mine. "And what about you?"

Bristling that he'd directed the attention at me, I straightened. "What about me?"

"You've been just as distant—if not more so. You may think you're hiding it well, Al, but don't forget that I sleep beside you every night now. Your nightmares are getting worse." Annoyance coated his next exhale. "I thought you'd broken free of him. How can his hold on you still be this strong?"

I frowned at the passing shops, fortifying my own defenses. "The mind is no different than the body. They both need time to heal."

Bodies rigid, we fell silent as we crossed the street toward Bath Abbey, the emotional chasm widening between us. Somehow, despite being closer than we had ever been, our minds had drifted apart as we tried to conquer our demons on our own. That's all we'd known how to do before now—to shoulder our burdens without involving others. Breaking such a habit and learning to fully rely on one another would take time and incredible effort . . . and thus far, we were doing a rubbish job of it.

The physiotherapist, Sebastian Cutler, awaited Baze inside the spa entrance. Baze made to follow him to the men's bath, but I tugged him back. "I love you," I murmured and rose toward his lips.

Baze angled his face to avoid my attempt and pecked a light kiss to my cheekbone. "I love you too." His rapid retreat left the atmosphere around me cold and empty.

Heart lamenting at the intentional slight, I wandered through the silent hall and into the vacant women's area. Despite the humidity curling tiny wisps of hair about my face, I shivered as I undressed. The stone pillars, the dim light, and the eerie echoes tainted the typically relaxing ambience. Thankfully, however, the Almighty had already helped me overcome the most malevolent of forces. Anything less than that was mere child's play.

Flickering torches on each pillar in the bath area punctuated the dawn's shadows with warm illumination. The moment my toes touched the heated, bubbling bath water, a rush of tension drained from me. I tumbled forward and submerged myself fully in the soothing liquid. There, suspended in the pool without gravity anchoring my weary limbs to the ground, I reveled in the calmness, trying to keep my mind clear as it fought to fixate on the conflict at hand.

Finally, my thoughts diverted to Katherine. Had she made it out of the city and to her next destination? What did she hope to find there? Why would she choose to leave when I had already helped her once? This only assured that I wouldn't be there to help her again.

Her life is not yours to keep. It's God's.

I broke the surface for air, tipped my head back against the rough wall, and shut my eyes.

Then why do I have these visions if not to help? Should I merely sit back and let them happen without action?

A faint crackle, like the sound of a pebble scattering on the ground, perked my ears. I lifted my head and scanned the area. Mist rising from the pool made it difficult to see past the pillars lining the area. After spending several minutes on alert, listening, looking, I relaxed. Perhaps it had been something on the roof—an animal or a bird.

Sinking down to my chin, I glanced toward the entrance. My stubbornness for independence went to war with my desire for safety. Either I could remain and continue my session of relaxation, or I could seek out Baze and the therapist . . . just in case.

With a sigh, I stood up straight.

Rocks scraped. Footsteps pounded behind me.

I gasped and whirled, caught sight of a figure leaping in midair.

Splash!

Fingers rooted into my hair. They ripped my head sideways and yanked me under. Water absorbed my scream and flooded my lungs, burning, suffocating. I flailed, precious oxygen escaping in another shout, but the hands trapping me subsurface seemed solid as pavement. Oblivion closed in.

"Excellent, Basil. That was a productive session." Sebastian hovered a guiding hand over Baze's back as they broke from the pool and headed for the dressing area.

Toweling his chest, Baze tested his leg. The exercises had resulted in dull soreness, but the combination of stretches and the laudanum helped to take the edge off.

"Be careful." Sebastian eyed Baze's feet. "Don't inundate it with too much weight too soon. That could erase all of the work we've put into it."

Baze grimaced. "Even if it feels fine?"

"Even then."

Baze worked his jaw but altered his posture to put more bearing on his healthy leg, if only to appease the therapist. "By the way, I'm running out of that tincture you created. You wouldn't happen to have another ready for me, would you?"

Sebastian swiped the towel over his ear and narrowed his eyes. "You're going through that rather quickly. Perhaps I need to have Charles adjust the dose. How often are you taking it?"

"Only when the pain begins to return." Not a lie—but also not the complete truth. Baze couldn't help but feel a twinge of guilt when he thought about the pointed words Adelynn had directed toward him regarding his opium use. He wasn't sure how to best explain it to her in a way she would understand, not when she was battling her own demons.

At that, Baze clenched a hand into a fist. Cornelius was dead. They were long past the ordeal, married even, and yet, the man still plagued her. Nauseous, he pictured Adelynn kissing Cornelius—an event he had imagined countless times since her confession of the intimate incident. She had said she didn't love Cornelius, but when she continued to have thoughts and dreams about him, what was Baze supposed to think? Forgive her, yes. He had already done that. But forget? That was proving harder than anticipated.

A noise rumbled in the therapist's throat. He gestured toward a stone bench. "Sit down."

Apprehension flared, but Baze did as he was commanded and braced for what the therapist might direct toward him.

Sebastian tossed aside the towel and faced Baze. "You are far too young to have such deep creases in your brow. I am doing what I can to alleviate this burden you carry, but I must admit, I have not done *all* that I can." He raised his bushy eyebrows. "May I pray for you?"

The request caught Baze off guard. He had tried to maintain his own spirit of prayer since he'd seen its effects deliver them from evil, but hearing another person so willingly offer it hit Baze square in the chest and disarmed every resistance he might call up. Unsure what to say, he merely nodded.

Sebastian stepped closer and rested a heavy, heartening hand upon Baze's head. "Almighty Father, your beloved child is hurting. I know not what divine plan you have for him, but walk this journey with him. Uphold him. Strengthen him. And if it be your will, summon a miracle, binding his bone and muscle so that his leg may be made anew. However, if you have other plans, soften his heart, mold it, so that he might release this anger and may embrace your mercy and grace."

Realizing that tears dripped down his cheeks, Baze cast his face downward, embarrassed, aggravated—yet overcome with gratitude. He relaxed his muscles, carefully opening his heart to the therapist's entreaty, and allowed himself to hope. Hope for healing. Hope for reconciliation. *Please, let it be so . . .*

Sebastian's hand grew heavier, compressing Baze's body in security and encouragement—something Baze imagined a benevolent father might do to his son. Then the therapist lifted his hand away and, with it, seemed to remove fragments of Baze's worry.

"Patrons will arrive soon. We should get on about the day."

Baze cleared his throat and smeared his tears with the inside of his wrist. "Thank you," he whispered, finally meeting the therapist's eyes. Sebastian smiled warmly and winked.

Outside, the cool, crisp air awakened Baze's senses. Though the city remained the same, with the same buskers and crowds milling about, something in Baze felt different. Renewed. Determined. Suddenly, all he longed to do was locate Adelynn and speak to her. She deserved honesty, and it was time he—

A woman's shrill yell erupted in the distance.

Baze and Sebastian whirled to the noise.

Skirts flashed as a woman sprinted past Bath Abbey and headed directly toward them. She shouted again, her words ringing clear. "Basil Ford!" Her foot kicked up pebbles. She stumbled, then righted herself. "Your wife. Hurry!"

Paralyzed in confusion, Baze frowned, and recognition sparked. Katherine Quinn? But Adelynn said she left the city. What was she—

"Stop standing there!" She thrust a finger toward the baths behind him. "She's in danger. *Move!*"

Seeing the whites of her eyes and the terror written on her features finally prompted action. Baze spun and ran. He endured the explosion of pain in his leg as he flew through the halls and burst into the women's area.

A motionless figure drifted facedown on the surface. Hair billowed out around her like a gruesome halo.

Baze launched himself into the pool feet first. He wrenched Adelynn over. Her head drooped, and her blue lips parted. *Please, God, no. Don't take her. Don't take her from me.* His breaths became ragged as he hoisted her sodden body over the edge of the bath with all the strength he could muster. Her limbs flopped lifelessly as he dragged her onto the uneven floor.

Frederick's words from so long ago came crashing back. *"Artificial respiration is the only technique that has had any success in saving a drowning person . . ."*

Baze grabbed Adelynn's face, tilted her chin up, and covered her mouth with his. As he forced air into her lungs, he watched her chest rise and fall, rise and fall. "Please," he whispered between breaths. "Please." Bitter minerals from the bath water and the salt of his tears assailed his tongue, but he continued.

Seconds raced by. Minutes. Perhaps hours.

Then a gurgle from the back of Adelynn's throat preceded a gush of water. He thrust her head to the side so she could spew the cursed liquid. Coughs racked her delicate frame. Her body convulsed, gasping for air.

"Oh, thank God." Baze lifted her torso into his lap and clutched her to his chest. She trembled, still clearing water from her lungs, hiccupping and sputtering between sobs. His own tears flowed freely. "You're okay. I've got you. I've got you."

"I've called the authorities. They should arrive shortly," came Sebastian's distant voice, warped as though part of a cruel dream.

Words failed Baze. He clung to Adelynn, refusing to let her go. They trembled together as he lowered his head against hers, and when two medical officers and a constable came loping into the bath area, they had to pry Baze's arms away in order to attend to her.

Numb, Baze remained seated on the saturated ground and watched them take his wife away. He shivered uncontrollably, his soaked clothes cooling on his damp skin. Thoughts in a haze, he looked to Sebastian—then noticed Katherine Quinn lingering nearby. Fear still pulsed behind her eyes, and her fiery hair stuck out around her flushed cheeks.

"You knew," he breathed, the only words he could muster. "You knew."

"Yes, and it's a good thing too." She sucked in a sharp breath. "You shouldn't let her wander off on her own, brown eyes. It's fortunate you stayed close at the very least."

Heat built under his collar. He scrambled to his feet and stumbled toward her. Raising a trembling hand, he gestured at the nearby constable, then back to her. "Arrest this woman."

"Arrest me?" Miss Quinn's eyes blazed. "Whatever for?"

"If you knew Adelynn was in danger, why didn't you attempt to rescue her yourself?" he bit out. "Unless *you* were the one who *put* her life in danger."

"How dare you!" Miss Quinn's face reddened. "I had just departed from the train station when I ran up to you. It was faster for me to enlist your help than to—"

"I don't want to hear your lies." Baze snatched the handcuffs from the constable's belt, caught up her hands in his, and secured her wrists together.

She fought against the restraints. "I saved your wife's life. You're making a mistake."

Baze gave her a rough shake and forced her toward the exit. "We shall see."

Chapter Twenty-One

A GREAT WEIGHT PRESSED UPON MY chest. Suffocating. Dark. Artificial scents of antiseptic and metal curled my nose. Low, indistinguishable sounds resembling muffled voices whispered all around me. Yet, there in the distance, a pinprick of light beckoned. I clawed at invisible walls, trying everything to reach the illumination. It grew brighter and brighter, and all at once, consciousness rushed up to meet me.

I peeled my heavy eyelids open. White walls surrounded me, and a white sheet lay draped over me, rising and falling with each of my ragged breaths. My gaze darted about the dimly lit room, then fell to my side. Baze sat bent over the edge of my bed with his head resting on his forearm and his other hand grasping mine. I twitched my fingers, unable to force any larger movement.

Baze's head jerked up. With eyes tired but alert, he studied every inch of my face. Slowly, that familiar crease in his brow faded as he expelled a long burst of air.

Memories of the event eluded me but offered torturous flashes—water splashing, hair ripping, chest flooding. Eager to fill in the missing pieces, I lifted my chin and croaked out, "What hap—"

My throat burned and sent me into a lung-prickling cough. I cringed as I settled back into the bed and waited for the pain to subside.

"Easy," Baze said softly and smoothed the hair away from my forehead. "There was an accident in the baths. You nearly . . ." Muscles popped in his jaw. "I managed to get to you in time."

The sentiment threatened to provoke tears, but my body rebelled, far too weary for such a display.

"Al"—he squeezed my hand—"do you think you'll be able to answer questions from the chief inspector? The more time that passes, the more your memories are going to grow faint."

Only after absorbing his comment did I notice Detective Chief Inspector Whitaker sitting on a chair in the far corner of the room, back arched and arms upon his knees. My attention seemed to signal him, and he rose and approached the end of the bed.

"If this will be too much, we don't have to do this right now," Baze said. "I don't want you to strain yourself. If you're not—"

"No." My voice cracked. "No, I want to."

Chief Inspector Whitaker nodded and touched a hand to the bed's metal frame. "Why don't you start by telling us what you remember."

I swallowed, my throat feeling simultaneously dry and coated in mucus. "I was in the bath . . . alone." Speaking proved more laborious than I'd anticipated, but I tensed and forged ahead. "I heard something, a bird or pebble . . . thought nothing of it. I decided to . . . I tried to leave, but . . . there were footsteps. Then a splash behind me." My breath caught as phantom pain tore across my skull. "Something grabbed my hair. Pulled me under. Held me there. I tried . . . tried to . . ."

"It's all right. Take your time." Chief Inspector Whitaker's quiet voice soothed my nerves. "Can you remember any specific details? The sound of the footsteps?"

I fought to drag the recollections to the surface. "They were fast . . . long."

"What about the splash? How big was it?"

"I don't know." Tears welled, and my lungs heaved, constricting yet begging for air.

"Take a deep breath," Chief Inspector Whitaker instructed gently. "The danger has passed. You've nothing to fear."

Gulping, I did as I was told.

"This is my fault." Baze stroked the bridge of his nose. "I should never have left you alone."

"Stop," I rasped and yanked on his hand. "You saved my life." A thought occurred to me. "But . . . how did you know . . ."

"The infamous Katherine Quinn." Baze gripped my hand a little too tightly. "She came running up to the baths, shouting like a madwoman. She said you were in danger."

What was she still doing in Bath? Hadn't she left?

A sheen of sweat appeared on Baze's face as he continued recounting. "I don't know if I've ever run faster than in that moment. When I found you floating in the water, I feared you were already dead." He paused to swallow, then said, "Thank God above that Frederick taught me mouth-to-mouth resuscitation when I was a boy."

Gratitude overwhelmed me—gratitude that he had sprung to such action for my sake, gratitude that he had arrived in time to save my life.

I tugged my hand from his and stroked his jaw, and despite the heavy ache in my chest, mirth relaxed my features. "Mouth to mouth?" I tapped his lips with my index finger. "Another . . . public display?"

Baze caught my hand and secured it against the bed, screwing his face up as though to say, "*Really?*"

A snort, then a chuckle emanated from the chief inspector's direction. Crow's feet spread beside his eyes. "You're resilient, I'll give you that, Mrs. Ford."

I offered a weak smile. "Call me Adelynn."

He hesitated, then tipped his head. "I would give you the option of using my Christian name as well, but something tells me that you would just as soon do so without permission."

"Indeed." I cleared my throat and swallowed, trying to relieve the raw flesh. "Where is Katherine?"

The chief inspector—Sydney—opened his mouth, but Baze jumped in. "We have her at police headquarters waiting to give her statement." A telling look passed between the two men.

I narrowed my eyes. "What aren't you saying?"

They remained silent until Baze dropped his gaze. "We've arrested her as a suspect in your attack."

The words didn't quite sink in right away—surely he had

misspoken—but when his rigid demeanor indicated his seriousness, I shot straight up. "You did what? Why—" Fire built in my throat, and coughs racked my chest.

Baze coaxed me back against the pillow and held me in place. "She was already a suspect before this," he murmured. "You yourself had doubts about her. This will help us expose any secrets she may have."

Breathing deeply, I clenched and unclenched my fists to calm my rising emotions. The action left my lungs fatigued. Baze spoke truth. Could I truly fault them when I harbored my own suspicions, unsure how her connection to Cornelius related to the case at hand?

Tilting my head back against the pillow, I gave Baze a pointed stare. "Will you . . . tell me what you learn?"

"We'll share what we can," the chief inspector jumped in. "But I don't want you any more involved than you have to be. Your assignment is to rest, recover, and stay safe. Your husband and I are handling this. Understood?"

Despite the furious stubbornness within me, I nodded. "Understood."

Even though Adelynn had been returned to their room to rest—the doctor having determined her well enough for discharge—Baze felt guilty for leaving her. After all, hadn't his absence made way for her attack in the first place? Not to mention, he couldn't completely trust that she would stay put, even with Mr. Everett defending the front doors. However, rather than remain with her to stand guard, Baze had chosen to accompany Detective Chief Inspector Whitaker to interrogate Miss Quinn.

Before entering the room that held the enigmatic woman, Whitaker leaned close and nudged Baze's chest. "Let me ask the questions."

Though he wanted to protest, Baze bit his tongue and nodded.

Inside the room, positioned behind a single table, Miss Quinn targeted them with an unblinking stare. A deck of cards blurred and buzzed in her hands as she shuffled expertly.

Baze hesitated, Miss Quinn's actions drawing his mind back to when he and Bennett had interrogated Cornelius Marx and Finn Kelly. Hadn't Adelynn said that Miss Quinn knew Cornelius?

"So good of you to join me, gentlemen." She shrugged one shoulder. "Let's try to keep this quick, shall we?"

Whitaker smiled as he and Baze took their seats. "I appreciate your candor, Miss Quinn. If you wish to conclude quickly, then surely you are prepared to cooperate fully."

Quirking her bright-red lips, she gathered up the deck and smacked it on the table before her, then folded her hands beside it. "I had nothing to do with Mrs. Ford's attack or the recent murders. I was actually out of town until this morning. My fellow train passengers and service crewmen will be able to corroborate my story."

"Thank you, Miss Quinn. We'll be sure to follow up with them." Whitaker withdrew his notepad and wrote a few sentences. "So, tell me, why were you leaving the city in the first place?"

"I was the target of an attempted poisoning. You can't blame me for wanting to escape death."

"No, of course not. But if that's the case, then why did you return?"

She smirked as though picking up his underlying meaning. "I had unfinished business that couldn't wait."

"What business is that?"

"I should like to keep that to myself, if you don't mind."

Whitaker sighed. "Miss Quinn, may I remind you that the more you cooperate, the sooner we can have you on your way."

"Ask the right questions and I'd be happy to oblige." Smirk widening, she batted her thick eyelashes.

Baze scrutinized Miss Quinn—her relaxed posture, her smug expression, her inscrutable eyes—trying to detect any crack in her armor. She flaunted a façade of confidence and control, but was that truly how she felt deep down? Or was she putting on a clever mask to throw them off her scent?

"What do you know of the two recent victims?" Whitaker leaned forward. "Mary Sands and Edwin Davis."

Miss Quinn matched his movement. "I am afraid I was never acquainted."

"Is that so? Surely someone of your background, a former journalist I'm told, would ensure that she was well educated on the happenings of her current location."

"I have not been in Bath long, and I was not planning to stay long, so I did not set out to mingle with the locals." She cocked a trim eyebrow. "Again, such questions are going to lead you nowhere."

"Then let's try this." Whitaker placed his pen on the table and nudged it parallel with the notepad. "Do you have any idea why you were targeted? Or who might have wanted to kill you?"

"I have made many enemies through the years. So the real question is, which one wants to kill me at the moment?"

"Do you have any indication of who it might be?"

Baze crossed his arms. The woman was adept at avoiding direct inquiries. He simply couldn't tell if she did it on account of nervousness or guilt.

"Miss Quinn, I am not sure if you're aware, but the poison used in the attempt on your life was the same substance used to kill Mrs. Sands and Mr. Davis."

"How curious." Miss Quinn reached for her deck of cards and began flicking through it.

"It is even curiouser that the two of them are dead and you still live." Whitaker's voice grew low and sharp. "Did you plant the poison to make it look as though you are a victim and not a killer?"

Miss Quinn placed a hand on her chest in mock incredulity. "How dare you suggest such a thing."

Unflinching, Whitaker locked her in his stern gaze. "Did you?"

Her cheeks grew a rosy tint that clashed with her red hair. "If I had the motive to kill those people and were clever enough to think of such a thing, then why would I risk my own life to prove my innocence? I didn't know Adelynn Ford before that incident, so you tell me. How could I have orchestrated her intervention?"

Whitaker's eyes flashed. "Perhaps you had arranged for another distraction and Mrs. Ford merely happened to get in the way."

"That's absurd!" Miss Quinn slapped the table with her palm. "I am innocent, and I stand by that."

Unperturbed, Whitaker said, "Miss Quinn, if you weren't involved, then how did you know Mrs. Ford was in danger today? You said yourself that you had just returned from out of town."

For the first time since the interrogation began, a look of indecision darkened Miss Quinn's features. Her eyes dashed to Baze. "I knew because Adelynn and I are the same."

Baze's skin prickled. The same? Did she mean . . .

Whitaker frowned. "Can you elaborate what you mean by—"

Baze stood abruptly, chair screeching. "Chief Inspector, a word please." Without waiting for confirmation, Baze stumbled from the room on weakened knees. He supported himself against the wall, thoughts racing. Like Adelynn? Was it possible? Could Miss Quinn be referring to Adelynn's gift? Or was she merely alluding to something simpler, something less supernatural?

Whitaker's hand fell on Baze's shoulder. "What was all that about?"

"I'm sorry for the outburst, sir."

"That means something to you, doesn't it? Her comment that she and your wife are the same."

"I have a hunch, but I can't be sure yet," Baze said carefully so as not to reveal too much. "I think I need to bring Adelynn into this. May we question Miss Quinn alone?"

Whitaker's eyes narrowed as he folded his arms. "I permitted your involvement, Inspector, lest you forget. Now you wish to continue *my* investigation alone?"

"I know." Baze managed to straighten, the faint sensation fading. "But I need to do this. If Miss Quinn's words mean what I think they do, then these murders may be more connected to the crimes in London than we first realized."

The superior officer stared long and hard, though not unkindly or maliciously—rather, with an air of uncertainty. Whitaker shook his head. "I will allow you and your wife to speak to her, but I will be present. This is my case and my jurisdiction, so either you investigate with me or you don't investigate at all. Is that clear?"

Debating whether to stand his ground or give in to the chief inspector's orders, Baze clenched his jaw. Yet, years of training and submission to superior officers prompted Baze to respond, "Yes, sir."

Could they tell Whitaker the truth? The *full* truth? Baze had developed a deep respect for the man, such that it had grown into trust, but Baze knew firsthand how difficult it was to accept such a notion, that people could see visions of the future. How would Whitaker react to such news? And would he banish them from the city upon suspicions of madness?

Well, whether they liked it or not, secrets were about to become exposed.

Chapter Twenty-Two

DEEP IN THE DEPTHS OF SLEEP, I couldn't escape the clutches of the water. It forced its way into my nose, my mouth, my lungs. The hand in my hair twisted, craning my neck, keeping me submerged. I gasped for air but only inhaled more of the smothering liquid. *I'm going to die. This is how I die. Lord God, what do I do?*

The hand released my hair and gripped my shoulder. "Adelynn."

I fought, kicking, thrashing. *No, let go.*

The fingers shook me gently. "Adelynn, wake up."

My eyes flew open to darkness. Baze's face, barely visible in the dim light, hovered over me. The memories came flooding back. I'd left the hospital. Baze had gone to question Katherine. I had crawled into bed, hoping to sleep off the trauma—a task that proved nearly impossible when the torment saw fit to pursue me into the unconscious realm.

"I didn't mean to startle you," he whispered.

"Why are you here?" I mumbled. "What happened to Katherine?"

"She's exactly why I'm here." He rubbed my shoulder. "She admitted something to us that I think you need to hear."

I propped myself up on an elbow. "What did she say?"

His voice grew deeper, quieter, and for a long moment, I feared he wouldn't answer. But finally, he said, "That you and she are the same."

I blinked, absorbing the words. They could have any number of interpretations, so what did she mean by such a cryptic remark?

But deep within my heart, I already knew the answer.

I sat up fully. "Take me to her."

The moment I stepped foot within the precinct's interrogation room—trailed closely by Baze and Sydney—Katherine and I locked eyes. We stiffened, holding one another in a fixed stare, neither moving, neither daring to breathe. Suspicion passed between us, followed by understanding and then, strangely, relief.

"I'm pleased to see you standing on two solid feet, angel," she said lightly and tapped the top of her deck of cards positioned before her. "That incident in the baths could very well have ended poorly."

Ignoring her well wishes, I murmured, "What did you mean?" My voice still rasped and burned from what I'd endured. "What did you mean that we're the same?"

"I meant exactly what I said. We're the same in nearly every way." Rigid, Katherine's skin seemed made of stone. "Because I, too, can see visions of the future."

A surge of gooseflesh raced across my arms and up my scalp. *I'm not the only one.*

Katherine severed our optic connection and looked down at her hands. "I had planned to leave the city exactly as I told you. I'd already made it out into the countryside when I saw you die. We couldn't have that." Her tone crackled with ice. "So I came back, hoping, praying, that I would make it in time." She pierced me with another stare. "Clearly I was successful."

Baze's arm came around my shoulders and coaxed me into a chair. I barely noticed him take the adjacent seat as I leaned forward, intent, as though I could pry an explanation out of her simply through my eyes. "How did you get like this . . . like me?"

Katherine glanced at the men—Baze sat with bated breath while Sydney scuffed his shoe on the floor, his face white and brows drawn—before she said, "I don't exactly know how. Much like you, I presume, it caught me unawares. One moment I was out for a cheery jaunt in the beautiful Irish landscape and in the next, I was witnessing a man die right before my eyes."

"Who?" I scooted to the edge of my chair. "Who was the victim?"

"A local orphan keeper, one who had a nasty reputation for being strict—abusive even—to the waifs he took in."

"But who was your vision connected to? Mine were linked to—"

"Yes, I know. Cornelius Marx—or Ciaran as I knew him."

The skin on the back of my neck prickled. My face must have revealed my astonishment, as Katherine chuckled. "Oh, you wanted me to go back to the *very* beginning." She snatched up the deck of cards. "Strap in then."

Seeming unfazed by our intense attention, Katherine began shuffling aimlessly as she spoke. "Being that my father was Irish, there was a time when my family traveled between England and Ireland several times a year. I soon decided to seek apprenticeship as a journalist in Dublin and made my permanent residence there." Her expression grew melancholy. "I fell madly in love with a young musician turned magician, ran off and united with him in blissful matrimony, and embraced a nomadic lifestyle. We explored every hidden castle ruin and mysterious fairy fort, but our visit to the west coast proved the most life-changing. It's where we stumbled upon two teenage urchins living on the street—Ciaran and Finn."

I pictured the two young boys, dirt-covered and starving, with no one to whom they could turn, unable to enjoy a normal childhood and forced to grow up far too quickly due to the deaths of their parents.

"We took the boys under our wing, having always wanted children of our own—a possibility that wasn't in the cards for us. The more heartache we uncovered across the land, the more dishonesty we discovered woven into the very fabric of the government, the more distant my husband became. Until I realized that he had a gift . . . a terrible gift. The ability to control people and make them carry out his wishes. And somehow, I could see visions of each of his victims.

"During our travels, my husband began teaching the boys sleight of hand and the trade of a magician, and I picked up skills along the way." Katherine flipped several cards with a flourish. "The boys were innocent, impressionable, their minds wide open to anything he had to pour into them. Finn was bright but reserved. He caught on quickly but was somehow resistant to any underhanded tricks that were taught to him. Unfortunately, the same couldn't be said for Ciaran. He latched onto my husband's every word, hellbent on avenging his father in any way he could, until my husband decided it was time to teach him the secrets of his dark gift.

"As the boys grew, they became skilled illusionists, and we traveled across the land, performing shows together, just the four of us." Tears sparkled in her eyes. "Though less than ten years separate us in age, I loved those boys like my own. So when they made the decision to go to England with the cruel intentions of infiltrating it from within, my heart shattered. I don't think Finn wanted to go, but he was too loyal, too naïve, and Ciaran was able to easily manipulate him into following like an abused dog on a chain.

"I hoped—prayed—that Ciaran wouldn't carry out what I knew he would, but my husband's influence was too strong, Ciaran's lust for revenge too deep. When I read the report of the first murder . . ." Katherine's hands trembled, and several cards spilled out of her palms.

"Why didn't you come then?" Baze rammed a fist onto the table. "If you knew what he was doing, why didn't you try to stop him? Some of his victims could still be alive today."

Katherine blinked at him. "My heart breaks for the loss you endured. Truly. However, my choices were not as black and white as you might think. When Ciaran began murdering in London, my husband was wreaking havoc of his own in Ireland. I found that I could use my abilities, my own premonitions, to foil him at every turn. Whether I chose to intervene in Ireland or England, people would have died. I was doomed no matter my decision."

"Who's your husband?" Baze snapped.

"A magician. A trickster. A nationalist."

"No, give me a name."

"Names are powerful, brown eyes." She smiled forlornly. "I do not wish to burden you with such a thing. It's better that you never cross paths with him." Before Baze could protest, she straightened her spine and continued. "I think I was growing close to exposing his plan, but then he realized what I was doing. That's when he began hunting me, chasing me into hiding. I've had to keep moving ever since, never staying in the same place for too long." Her eyes grew glossy. "Yet, here I am, trapped in Bath, and it appears he has determined that this will be my final resting place."

"He put his plans on hold just to come after you, did he?" Baze asked.

"Not just. His abilities are strong, far-reaching. I don't know how, but once he's forced his way into someone's mind, he's able to keep part of it bound to himself, accessing it when it suits him. Distance doesn't seem to hinder his abilities anymore. Which is why I need to stop him as quickly as I can." Tears pooled in her eyes but didn't fall. "Unfortunately, it appears that he'll also stop at nothing to put an end to *me*. He's determined to keep me here in Bath until he's finished, and he doesn't care who he has to use as collateral to force my compliance." She nodded at me. "I am sorry we had to involve you in this."

I searched for words, fingers numb and head spinning with everything she had divulged over the past several minutes. In my hesitation, Baze jumped in, his voice shaking with emotion. "We were involved after Cornelius murdered the very first person in London a year ago. We were involved when he took Bennett's life from us. We were involved when he targeted Adelynn and chose to take control of me. So we're *involved*, Miss Quinn, and your apologies can't reverse that."

She shuffled the cards and clacked them onto the table to flatten them. "Then it's best that I leave. Lure him away from here. That's the only chance you two have of escaping with your lives."

"You can't!" I blurted, shooting to my feet. The others started in shock, but I planted my palms on the table and lanced Katherine with a glare. "Like Baze said, we're involved, and that means we have to help you make sure your husband doesn't succeed. He was the reason

Cornelius was able to create such chaos, so if we can do something to ensure he never harms anyone else, never compels anyone else to do what Cornelius did, then we'll do it."

Katherine laughed, the sound echoing boisterously in the small space despite the tense atmosphere. "Oh, angel, your heart's in the right place, but you're no match for him."

"We defeated Cornelius," I said, chest swelling with the remembered power of light that had flowed through me on that day. "This man will be no different."

Baze grasped my wrist and pulled me back into my seat before scrutinizing Katherine with a mistrustful curl of his lip. "How do we know you're not actually helping him? How do we know you're not simply telling us this to earn our trust?"

"I suppose you don't, brown eyes." Katherine shrugged. "Not unless you accept my word as truth. Which, judging by your tendency to doubt without concrete proof, is likely not sufficient for you."

I twisted my hands in my lap. All of my being wanted to believe her, but the guilt and embarrassment of my believing Cornelius's ruse ran too deep, hurt too viscerally. If she was truly innocent, what could I do to help her prove her innocence?

"Tell me what happens when you experience a vision."

Baze groaned. "Adelynn, we don't have time for—"

"Trust me." I flashed him a severe look before focusing on Katherine.

Hands continuing to shuffle as though acting autonomously, Katherine closed her eyes. "My very consciousness seems to leave my body and enter that of someone else's, my husband's usually, though I have also managed to embody the people under his influence. I can see through his eyes, and I believe that he knows exactly when I'm watching, though we cannot communicate through the connection— yet, anyway. There was once a time when all I could do was watch, unable to help the victim as they met their untimely end. But by the Lord's provision, as my own abilities have grown, I have been able to summon visions almost at will and thus have been able to spare the lives of several people—yours included."

I brightened at her words, hope springing in me. "How have you been able to resist the darkness that attacks and tries to control you?"

"I'm stubborn, as I'm sure you can surmise." Katherine snorted. "Submitting is not in my nature. Though I would love nothing more than to credit my own willpower for my resistance, I know that it had nothing to do with me. My relationship with the Almighty has been rocky of late, but I know better than to attribute the power to anyone but Him."

Warmth filled my belly, and a deep kinship toward Katherine began to work its way through me. Everything she described, down to the protecting power of the Almighty, was exactly as I had experienced. If that wasn't proof of her sincerity, I didn't know what was. Folding my arms, I rotated toward Baze, but suspicion still lingered on his features. Oh, that he could stop hardening his heart for one moment.

For the first time since we'd entered into dialogue with Katherine, Sydney shifted. To his credit, he'd listened to the entire exchange in silence, face slack so as not to betray any emotions bending one way or the other. What did he think about all this? Baze, God love him, had taken his sweet time accepting that my visions were real. Would Sydney also resist the revelation?

The chief inspector cleared his throat and placed relaxed hands on his hips. "So, where does this leave us, Miss Quinn?"

She cocked an eyebrow. "You tell me, Sherlock."

"If your husband is as dangerous as you say, then he's our top priority. As is keeping you safe. We'll assign you police protection for the time being."

Katherine smiled. "You're sweet, but if he wants me dead, then no amount of human intervention will stop him."

Sydney pondered a moment. "Then we need to apprehend him before he can get the chance to strike again. Can you lead us to him?"

"I wish I could, but he's like the wind. Always moving, always shifting. If he does not want to be found, then no one can."

"Then perhaps we can lure him out."

"It's a lovely thought, but he would not fall for such a ruse."

Frustration growing in Sydney's voice, he massaged his beard. "Then what do you propose we do, Miss Quinn?"

"Focus on the case at hand. The two poisonings. All that matters at the present is your duty to protect the people of Bath. Solve those murders and you'll do just that. Don't worry your little blond head about me, Sherlock."

As Sydney chewed on his fingernail, I caught a glimpse of Baze leaning back in his chair, eyes closed, finger stroking the bridge of his nose.

Sydney sighed. "This is enough for today. I need time to sort through my notes and collect my thoughts. Thank you for your cooperation, Miss Quinn. It has been most . . . enlightening."

"My pleasure." She collected her deck of cards and stashed it away. "Not that it will be much help."

"Do you have somewhere to stay in the meantime? I'd like to remain in communication. I fear we've only tapped the surface of the knowledge you may have regarding the murders."

"Stay with us," I said before I could think better of it.

"Oh, no, you wouldn't want me intruding upon your lover's den." She winked and flashed her eyes in Baze's direction.

I bristled. "At least stay at the Empire Hotel. I'm sure Mr. Everett could find you a room."

"Don't worry about me. My lodgings are hidden and private. Plus, I have my own methods of remaining undetected. They have been enough to keep me out of harm's way."

"So far," I muttered.

"I'm aware of the risks, but I'm also aware of the risks you would take on for sheltering me. It's best to keep his eyes fixed on me and me alone. I don't want to see him keep using you as a conduit to get to me."

"She's right." Baze placed a firm hand on my arm, finality in his words.

I huffed, not liking the answer, but I knew Baze was prepared to put up a righteous fight were I to object.

"See. He's a smart lad." Katherine hopped to her feet and nodded to us. "It has been a right treat, but I'm afraid I must be off." She grinned at Sydney. "Would you see us out, Sherlock? We're done here."

Chapter Twenty-Three

AS WE EMERGED FROM POLICE HEADQUARTERS, I loitered, waiting to see what Katherine would do. Glowing with warm purples, oranges, and yellows, the eventide sky cast a faint halo across Katherine's back but darkened her face with shadows. With a shuddering inhale, she looped her reticule over her wrist and stepped off the pavement into the street. "Until we meet again, angel."

"So that's it then?" I planted my hands on my hips. "You're going to leave just like that?"

"What more would you have me do?" she called back over her shoulder without slowing.

I hesitated, searching for the right words. "We're the same. You said it yourself. Doesn't that mean anything to you? We could lean on one another, face these terrors together."

Katherine shot back up on the pavement and angled her face inches from mine, eyes edged with ice. "The fact that we have the same abilities does not mean we are friends. I have survived this long without needing to rely on anyone. Partners are a liability. They open the door to unnecessary danger and betrayal. It's best not to get attached. It's easier that way." She turned and retreated.

I took a determined step to follow, but Baze caught my arm and held me back. "Let her go, Al," he said softly.

Battling against his hold, I fisted my hands into my skirt and shouted, "So you always take the easy road, then?"

"It's what I do, angel." She waved a hand. "May the road rise up to meet you."

Shock and disbelief coursed through me as I watched her march in the direction of Bath Abbey. My mind whirled. Dizziness weakened my knees. I wasn't alone, wasn't the only one who experienced visions. I had finally found someone who truly understood what I felt each time I watched someone die—but now that person wanted nothing to do with me. As much as I tried to steel my emotions, I couldn't escape the barb of her cold shoulder.

Baze proffered his arm, looking at me with expectant, heavy-lidded eyes. "Shall we turn in for the night?"

I considered his request, my body aching to crawl into bed and stay there for a good while, but I couldn't allow Katherine to disappear, not when she might slip away and never return now that we had flushed her out of hiding and exposed her secrets.

I shook my head. "I have to go after her."

He turned back my way. "I'll come with you."

"No, this is something I have to do alone."

"You think I'm going to let you run around after dark by yourself after someone has made an attempt on your life?" He gave a bitter laugh. "Have you learned nothing by now?"

"Please, Baze. I have so much more to ask her." Urgency heightening my pulse, I watched her figure grow small and distant.

"Then you can talk to her with me. I'm not going to allow anything to happen to you."

"Nothing's going to happen. I'll be with Katherine."

"That's not reassuring. She *also* has a target on her back."

I groaned. Katherine had made it to the fountain by the abbey. "I'm losing her."

Baze closed the distance between us and caught my hand in his. "Then we'd best hurry."

Yanking free, I stepped away from him and snapped, "You can't run. You'll only slow me down."

Baze's lips parted, his face flushing.

Ice ran through my veins as I realized the knife my words contained, but I didn't have time to rectify them. If I lost Katherine, then all of the answers I sought would be lost with her.

I swiveled and jogged away from Baze. As Katherine disappeared around the side of the abbey, heading toward the baths, I quickened my pace, yet tried to use soft footfalls to keep my heels from clicking too loudly on the pavement. Already feeling the strain in my chest, I fought to breathe deeply against the confines of my corset.

When I rounded the corner, I searched frantically for Katherine. She had set off at a good clip toward the baths. Now, with her in my sights, I slowed my pace to keep my distance. She walked briskly, head held high, gaze straight ahead. I ducked through the crowd and tried to ignore the fanciful storefront window displays.

After she'd gone a good ways, she veered left around another corner. I hastened until I rounded the same corner and entered a pedestrian street brimming with suits and skirts. Katherine's feathered hat bobbed above the sea of people until it disappeared from view.

Stomach lurching, I rushed forward, noting the pillared bridge leading to the baths on my left. Where had she gone?

I veered closer to the columns as I searched the area for any sign of her. How could I have lost her so suddenly? She had been right—

Katherine stepped out from behind a pillar directly before me.

A squeal caught in my throat as I skidded to a halt.

Indignation flared in her green eyes. "Why are you following me?"

"I'm not—"

"I know when I'm being followed. You were practically blaring your presence to the entire assembly." She sighed. "Clearly, brown eyes hasn't taught you the art of tailing someone. So I'll ask you again, why are you following me?"

Composing myself, I folded my arms. "Because I still have questions."

"Angel, I'm as baffled by all this as you. I don't know that I can reveal anything you don't already know."

"But you've had your gift for years longer than I've had mine. I want to hear more about your experience. You don't have to have answers. Please." As I spoke, the hard edges of Katherine's expression softened, so I took that as encouragement and kept driving forward. "I've been all alone in this."

"Oh, but you're not alone. You've got your husband. Confide in him. That's how it should be."

She started to turn, but I clutched her sleeve and spun her back. "He can't understand the way you can. Please, Katherine. Give me one half hour. Then I'll leave you alone." I tried to keep the pleading from my voice while also trying to portray a tone of urgency. If she refused, I'd be forced to continue struggling through my uncertainties and doubts.

Katherine's features sobered. "I can't take away the conflict you feel."

"I know." I swallowed, gripping her arm tighter. "But you could listen."

She stared with her piercing, judgment-filled gaze, then finally heaved a large, grumbling sigh. She wrenched from my grasp before snatching up my hand, whirling, and yanking me into a brisk walk. "You must tell no one where I'm staying. Do you understand?"

"Of course." My feet quickened, spurred by the prospect of achieving some relief.

"And if you don't find what you seek, you will stop trying to contact me."

"Very well."

Katherine tugged me down a narrow side street, its tall Bath stone walls blocking out the last light of the evening sun. As I tried orienting myself, she charged to the right and down another little street. She slowed near an inset in the wall, hiding blue double doors that extended upward in a peaked arch. I managed to catch a glimpse of a plaque above the door reading "St. Catherine's Hospital." Despite the circumstances, I snorted. Was it clichéd or was it clever?

We crossed the threshold, passed through a short tunnel, and emerged into a small but quaint rectangular courtyard. An old well sat directly before us. Dark stone pavers covered most of the ground except for where a number of flower beds teemed with colorful plants. Bushes lined the walls, with several doors dispersed in between.

Still grasping my hand, Katherine headed toward the door tucked in the right-hand corner. She dug through the reticule at her hip, extracted a key, and unlocked the door. "Hurry now."

The inside of the small, modest flat was plain and unadorned—not at all matching her vibrant personality. The bare white walls injected a chill into the space. Katherine dumped her reticule on the little square table interposed by two chairs and collapsed into one of them. She unpinned her hat and hung it on a hook on the wall. Giving her scalp a good scratch, she raised her eyebrows. "Well? Are you going to join me or not?"

"Oh, of course." I pulled out the second chair with a screech and sat down.

"Ask your questions then." Her mouth hardened in a straight line.

Unflinching, I stared back at her. The life she had lived—the hardships, the loneliness—shone in her eyes. I didn't know what it would take to crack that, but I wanted to try. After all, she had come back after learning I was in danger, so she wasn't all that her pitiless exterior made her out to be.

I folded my arms upon the table. "Tell me about your life in Ireland, with Finn and Cornelius."

She grunted with mirth. "I thought you wanted to know about your visions."

"I'm getting to that. First, I want to know about you."

Katherine maintained the hardened expression while studying her pristine fingernails. "I loved my life in Ireland," she said quietly. "There's a certain magical quality about that land. Mysterious. Full of lore and legend. It doesn't take long before you find yourself entranced by the emerald green countryside. I was young when I moved there, younger even than you. Maybe if I hadn't been so naïve, I wouldn't have fallen so haphazardly in love with a rapscallion." She smirked.

"Sully was a handsome Irishman with an attractive accent, nearly ten years my senior, and I was a lovesick girl."

Sully. It wasn't a full name, but it was a start, one that indicated Katherine might be open to revealing more than she had initially intended.

"We traveled all across the land together, exploring ruins and cities. Sharing a penchant for risk and adventure, we also ventured into several ringforts and camped under fairy trees, simply to tempt fate." Her lips curved upward. "When we adopted those boys, it felt as though we had become a complete family. All for naught now."

I softened my stare. "Do you still love him?"

Her gaze grew distant. "When you love that deeply, there is no breaking it. Ever since his betrayal, love and hate have tumbled together in conflict within my heart." Her lip curled and quivered. "That's why I have to stop him. It's the only way to end my suffering."

Cornelius's fateful gunshot reverberated in my head. I forced my eyes to stay open so as not to relive the scene once more. "How do you plan to stop him? Will you try to turn him toward repentance and redemption? Or will you . . ."

"I will do what is necessary," she stated in a monotone.

Despite my best efforts, the images of Cornelius's demise entered my mind again. I tensed, perturbed that I had allowed it to creep in. "I tried to save Cornelius. I tried to convince him to give up his twisted scheme and turn himself in." My throat squeezed. "But he refused, and he died for it."

Katherine cocked her head. "Ciaran murdered your friend—along with several others—and ordered the death of your father. Yet you seem saddened by his death. Why?"

I frowned. "I don't take pleasure in the loss of life—the loss of a soul. Would you not be grief-stricken if Sully died?"

"Two things may be true at once. That I love him does not mean he does not deserve death. Would I grieve? Of course. Would I be relieved? Most assuredly."

"But you have a chance to save him." I rolled my shoulders back. "Cornelius came so close, but he chose not to accept redemption when it mattered most. I helped usher in an amazing transformation in Finn, so I thought I could do the same for Cornelius—but I failed."

Katherine puffed air at her hat's feather dangling over the table. "You need to let go of that pride, angel."

I dug my fingernails into my forearms. "I beg your pardon."

"Everything you said a second ago, that's your pride speaking." She leaned forward. "Be honest. Did you truly want to see him saved, or were you so besotted by Finn's conversion that you merely wanted the satisfaction of feeling that sensation again?"

My mouth dropped open, but no words came out, leaving me gaping like a dead fish. How dare she insinuate that I had wanted to save Cornelius for my satisfaction alone. My attempts to lead him to the light had nothing to do with me. I'd been trying to save his life, save his soul, so that he might experience the renewal of God's mercy.

But the more Katherine's words percolated, the more my stomach twisted. *Was* it pride?

Katherine laid a hand on my arm. "If there's one thing I have learned after all these years, it's that it's not up to us flawed human beings to save souls. We can be obedient if the Almighty chooses to use us as a catalyst for change, but we cannot take it personally if someone refuses. Just as we can't take credit for the opposite. *We* are not saving anyone."

As I absorbed her chiding words, she popped up, flitted to the kitchen, and set about filling a kettle and putting it on to boil. While she spooned tea leaves into a pot, she glanced toward the window. "You'd best ask me about those visions. It's getting dark out, and I don't want you wandering around here at night."

"Very well." I traced the dark curvy grain in the table with my gaze as words began tumbling out. "How did your visions begin? How long have you had them? Do they occur before or after the event happens, or is it a mix? You mentioned back at the police station that you've been able to control them somehow. What did you mean by that?"

A sharp whistle erupted from the kettle. Katherine laughed, poured the steaming liquid into the teapot, and left it to steep. "Slow down. Why don't you start with one."

I huffed. "How did your visions begin?"

Katherine turned her back to the cupboards and leaned against them, arms crossed. "I don't know if I can pinpoint an exact moment, but Sully and I explored several ancient places, many of which people have avoided for centuries on account of superstition. I can't say I believe in the Irish myths of fairies and otherworldly happenings, but all I know is I discovered my gift in Ireland—Sully and I both did."

"When do they occur? Can you truly control them?"

"When I first experienced the visions, I could only brace myself and bear them. They seemed to happen at random, with no rhyme or reason, but the more I experimented, the more I learned that I could begin to influence when they occurred. I grew accustomed to Sully's tendencies, and soon, whenever I sensed that he was about to entangle himself in a precarious position, I could reach out with my mind and commandeer his eyes."

"That's incredible." I deliberately had to force my mouth not to fall open. "Can you communicate with him when you do that?"

"Not with words"—she smirked—"but he has ways of letting me know that he's aware of my prying eyes." Satisfied that the tea had steeped long enough, she strained it into two teacups, added a helping of milk, and stirred in a dash of sugar. Then she carried them to the table and dropped into her chair.

Accepting the refreshment and inhaling the earthy bergamot scent of the Earl Grey, I asked, "If you can willfully put yourself in his mind, can he see through your eyes?"

"Not that I am aware, but if I linger in the vision for too long, I run the risk of his mind influencing my own. It's easy to allow the darkness to seep in if you open the door wide. It almost consumed me once. It's a miracle that I didn't buckle under it."

I thought back to all of my visions, of the darkness I could feel trying to penetrate my mind as though it were a tangible enemy, and how its effects had culminated in the intimate moment I shared with Cornelius. It wasn't hard to imagine that if we willingly created a link to it, the darkness would capitalize on any minute opportunity to take control.

Katherine held her cup to her lips, tapping a finger on its side, eyebrows drawn and pensive. After swallowing, she said, "You know, there was once a time when I could see through both Sully's and Ciaran's eyes—and sometimes even through the eyes of those they control. It takes a great deal of concentration, and you must be of sound mind. But . . . maybe *you* could see through Sully's as well." She furrowed her brow. "Hopefully you are never caught up in his dark endeavors, but should you find yourself in that position and need to gain the upper hand, you might consider attempting to conjure a vision through him at will."

Sipping slowly, I tried to imagine such a thing, seeing through someone else's eyes—not just Cornelius's. "Do you really think that would work?"

She shrugged. "I haven't the faintest idea, but it does appear that people with our gifts are connected to those with the opposite gifts. Therefore, I've determined that for every Sully and Ciaran in the world, there's someone like you and me."

I gulped too quickly, and the tea scalded my throat. My eyes watered, but I managed, "You think there are more people out there with these gifts?"

"There's no reason to believe otherwise."

I allowed myself to entertain that possibility, that there were others who also had our abilities. I shook my head. "That would mean there exists an unending cycle of good and evil. Someone commits an atrocity, we stop it, and it begins again?"

She set the cup into its saucer with a *clink*. "Isn't that what life is, angel? One goliath struggle between good and evil? Unfortunately, there will always be struggles in this life, whether seen or unseen."

I bit my lip, lowering my own teacup. "How do you deal with the nightmares?"

"Nightmares?"

"I see him—Cornelius." My vision blurred. "I relive the moment when he died over and over again. I can't escape it, no matter what I do."

Katherine's lips parted in empathy, her eyes sincere. "Oh, angel, you witnessed a man shot right in front of you. That's merely your mind's way of coping with such a tragedy."

"He appears in my waking hours too—and I experience more than the moment of his death. He materializes before me, speaks to me like a real person. It's almost as though he's . . . as though a part of him still dwells in my mind."

Katherine tipped her head back. "Well, I don't claim to be an expert on people's mental capacities, but we've already established that your mind is not normal."

I grimaced. "Following that logic, neither is yours."

"I am merely stating facts." She chuckled. "From the sound of it, your trauma is manifesting itself in the form of Ciaran. A specter of the real thing. You two were connected, but now your mind has lost its link to that darkness, toxic as it was." She sat back and squinted, turning her nose up. "It is a battle you will have to overcome on your own."

"I have already prayed about it," I protested. "God could remove these nightmares without lifting a finger, so why hadn't He?"

"Sometimes God answers prayer in a way we don't expect. Sometimes He merely equips us to take control of the problem." She lifted her teacup, pinky finger extended. "You have a gift. Next time you find yourself caught in a nightmare, use it."

"But it's just a nightmare. It's not real."

She tipped the cup to her lips, her brows rising above it. "Is it not?"

I fell back against the chair. Take control in a dream? Was that possible?

Katherine glanced at the window and tapped a fingernail on the table. "It's getting late."

"Are you saying I should leave?"

"I don't like the idea of your wandering around after dark, not when we know who lurks in the shadows. That's all."

I inclined my head and cracked a smile. "You know, for someone who was so hesitant to chat, you have revealed much. Thank you."

She swiped a finger around the rim of her cup. "If you're going to involve yourself in matters concerning Sully, I'd rather you were prepared."

"You'll let me help you, then?"

"No. I said *if*." Her eyes flashed. "Don't forget, if I make any moves he doesn't like, you'll suffer the consequences. In that regard, my hands are tied."

Flattening my palms on the table, I stared at her for a beat, then nodded and stood. "I suppose I'll go then." As I backed toward the door, Katherine got up and trailed me, arms crossed, shoulders hunched. Hand on the knob, I looked back. "Thank you for returning to the city. You didn't have to come back to save me, but you did."

Pursing her lips, Katherine sniffed and shrugged one shoulder. "I suppose our debts are squared away now."

I took that as acknowledgement of the weight of her deed and exited the flat. The cool evening air chilled my fingers and the tip of my nose. Shadows accentuated the small alcove of St. Catherine's Hospital, but once I exited through the tunnel, the moon's light reached the street and guided my way forward.

Confidence drove my footsteps, as did the awareness that I truly wasn't alone anymore. So much of what Katherine had said never occurred to me. That there could be even more people out there with our gift, that there was a chance I could actually control my visions, and that my pride might be tainting the way I went about my mission in this world.

With all the thoughts swirling in my mind, I barely paid attention to my walk back and only realized I'd reached the Empire Hotel when I saw the bright lights shining starkly through the rows of windows, beckoning me toward its warm interior.

Entering the hotel drew my mind to the room—and to Baze. I grew nauseous as I remembered the words I'd spoken to him in anger. Hurtful words.

Our suite was dark, save for a candle glow emitting from the bedroom. Inside, I searched the area and noticed the lump of Baze's form in the bed, his back to me. I glanced at the candle flickering on the side table. Despite my offense, he had still chosen to leave a light on for my return.

Trying to make small movements and rummage through the wardrobe quietly, I slipped from my dress and undergarments and into a nightgown. As I untangled my hair and draped it over my shoulder, I glanced at Baze. He still appeared to sleep soundly, breathing rhythmically.

Finally, I pushed back the covers of my side and slipped onto the bed, remaining upright. How could I sleep with this hanging over me?

I sat cross-legged and faced him. "Baze," I whispered. He remained motionless, so I tried again, this time brushing a hand over his shoulder.

"I'm sleeping," he mumbled, voice husky.

"No, you're not. If you were sleeping, you'd be snoring."

He rolled onto his back and peered out from half-lidded eyes. "I don't snore."

"You most certainly do." The hint of a smile teased my lips, but it dissolved when I remembered why I had awakened him. "I'm sorry for what I said earlier. It was cruel. I shouldn't have uttered those words."

"Then why did you?"

"I was upset. Anxious. I didn't want Katherine to get away, and I spoke in haste."

He closed his eyes and swallowed. "I'm doing all I can not to think less of myself because of my leg. I don't need you, of all people, looking down on me too."

"I'm not. I don't." I gripped his arm. "It was a foolish thing to say."

He peered up at me. "But it was true."

My nausea intensified. I scrambled to formulate heartfelt sentences, something that might reverse the damage that I had dealt, but I could only muster, "I'm sorry, Baze. So sorry. Do you think you could forgive me?"

His chest deflated in a deep sigh. "If it would make you feel better, then I'll forgive you."

The words didn't sound sincere, didn't resolve the guilt I felt. He was angry, hurt—and rightfully so. How could I further express my remorse so that he might truly forgive me?

"I *am* sorry," I whispered.

"As you've said." He rolled back onto his side, driving a concluding stake into our conversation. "Good night."

Chapter Twenty-Four

NIGHT OVERCAME THE GLOW OF EVENING, *smothering it with all-consuming darkness. Heart beginning to pound, I stumbled about the cramped one-room flat, having to use touch and the minimal moonlight peeking through the curtains to see. I couldn't risk lighting a candle, not now—not when Adelynn's visit had compromised my location.*

Thus far, I'd been able to evade him. My ability to ensure I wasn't followed, fortunately, far outweighed his ability to follow someone, but Adelynn had disrupted the careful routine I'd constructed. So it was only a matter of time before he flushed me out again, which was why I had to leave before he got the chance. Though, the fact I was trapped in Bath—unless I chose to value Adelynn's life beneath my own—would make this new endeavor more difficult.

A rustle and a crack sounded outside the window.

Nerves flaring, I slunk to it and peered around the curtain. A bird flitted through the bushes in front of my flat. I sighed, but the unease remained. The sooner I could flee this place, the sooner I could assemble the evidence I'd collected against him, which meant I could finally stop him and stop living life looking back over my shoulder.

Feeling my way around the flat, I collected my things and stuffed what few garments I owned into a small suitcase. Finally, I attached my reticule to my hip and gave my temporary lodging one final glance over. Then I faced the exit.

As I gripped the handle, a chill stopped me in my tracks. Malevolent tendrils of ice whispered beneath the doorframe and lapped at my feet. I stared, rejecting what my eyes were seeing and what my heart was sensing.

No. I was so close.

Unable to prolong the inevitable any longer, I eased the door open.

Sully stood before me. Moonlight swathed his shoulders and chiseled shadows into his angular face. "And where be you off to at such an ungodly hour?" His whisper sliced the silent darkness as though he'd shouted.

Somehow, despite the deafening alarm bells in my head, I remained rooted in place and maintained a neutral expression. I put on a false expression of pity. "Had I known you planned to come round, I'd have put the kettle on. Sorry to disappoint."

He took two steps across the threshold, and I took two steps back in response. His gaze drifted about the tiny space. "So this is where you've been hidin'."

"It's rather bland." I glanced about, feigning indifference. "But it has served its purpose. It's time I moved on."

Sully advanced several more steps and swung the door shut behind him. It banged, and I flinched. He slid his hands into his pockets, posture relaxed but resigned. "I hate that you feel the need to run from me, mo ghrá."

"Well, I hate that you feel the need to threaten my life." I smiled cynically.

"You don't have to do this now." His voice cracked. "If you would give up your misguided quest, we could go back to what we once were. Do you not miss our home? Do you not miss me?"

I bit the insides of my cheek until I tasted blood, fighting to keep control of my emotions and my facial expressions. "Those days are long dead, Sully. We can never have what we once did. You saw to that. To think otherwise would be naïve."

"Do not cast the blame on me when you are the one who first drove a stake between us."

"Because you were hurting people," I snapped. "How dare you call me *misguided when you have only caused more pain with your actions."*

"I've been doing what's necessary to save the innocent." His eyes hardened. "If it means that I must lay you to rest as well, then so be it."

His words cut the cord of control within me. A yell tore from my lips. I threw down my case and lunged at him, fists swinging. I struck his muscled chest, the solid surface bruising my hands.

Sully endured my blows for a long, frenzied moment—his wounded expression slowly morphing into wrath—until he finally lashed out, seized my wrists, and forced them together as though cuffed. "Tread carefully, Kate. A woman striking her husband is a punishable offense."

"You're no more my husband than I am your wife," I spat, struggling against his hold.

"You may wear that ring on the wrong hand, mo ghrá, *but it doesn't change the fact that we are yet legally bound." His teeth flashed. "Till death do us part."*

I whipped my hands down with such force that it yanked my wrists from his hold. It surprised him enough for me to grasp his own wrists and lift his hands to my neck. I molded his fingers around it and held them in place. "So do it then," I snarled, even as fear invaded my mind. "Rid yourself of me. Right now."

With a look of shock plastered on his face, he stood still, fingers limp around my neck.

"This is what you wanted." I stared into his eyes, challenging him to accept my twisted offer. "What are you waiting for?"

Sully's jaw muscles pulsed, and gradually, a look of hunger, of rage, darkened his expression. His fingers tightened, thumbs pressing into the flesh under my chin.

As he squeezed my airway, my survival instincts flared, followed by panic. He's going to do it. He's actually going to do it.

An involuntary whimper emerged from my throat. As though remembering himself, his features—and his fingers—quickly relaxed.

I gasped in air, then wheezed it out in a bitter laugh. "You're such a coward."

Sully thrust his fingers into my hair and compressed my head between his palms. "Is it cowardice to spare a life?" he whispered. "My affection for you is what stays my hand. Does that mean nothing?"

"Your words are empty when your actions have proven the opposite." I curled my lip. "You may not be able to take my life with your own hands, but nothing has stopped you from manipulating poor, innocent souls into attempting to poison me. So, whether you take my life indirectly or directly, my blood will be on your hands regardless."

Fire burned in Sully's eyes. His grip on my head grew tighter, almost unbearable, until I was convinced he would crush my skull. Then, abruptly, it loosened. Stepping closer, Sully bowed his forehead against mine. Strained moments crawled by until, little by little, our tension eased and our breathing became rhythmic.

"Kate," he murmured almost inaudibly.

It was a single word, but it was enough to reawaken the dormant longing within me, arousing memories of our time spent together all those years ago, of raising those boys, of performing sleight of hand in tandem, and of trusting one another with our very lives. I missed him. Missed the man he had once been—or at least, missed the man he had convinced me he was.

But he was a schemer. A liar. A murderer. Such a man didn't deserve love . . . much less my love. Yet, he still held my love captive.

Yearning drenched me as Sully's hand slipped around my waist.

No, I can't do this. I can't let him manipulate me again.

But the love in my heart defeated the logic in my mind . . . and I surrendered.

Chapter Twenty-Five

KATHERINE QUINN. ADELYNN FORD. WE WERE the same. The same gifts. The same affiliations. Dreams of Ireland bombarded me. I soared like a bird over the rolling green hills until I came to land at the grand Cliff of Moher. Faces swirled—Katherine's, Cornelius's, Finn's. And finally, a figure eclipsed in shadows emerged before me. Katherine's mysterious husband, the nameless one who could either be of no consequence or who could very well be the cause of all this.

"Adelynn."

The figure spoke. But . . . that wasn't a stranger. I knew that voice—calm, encouraging, with a hint of humor.

Slowly, the figure's face faded into view, revealing trim brown hair, a cheeky grin, and familiar spectacles.

I jerked from the dream with a start. Shock paralyzed my muscles. My breath came in shallow gasps. *Bennett.* Dates and time raced through my mind. Today was the day—the day that Bennett had lost his life a year ago. After all that had been happening with Katherine, I'd completely forgotten. A torrid mix of emotions ran wild in my heart.

Faint rustling sounds reached my ears. I shifted up to an elbow and noticed Baze perched on the side of the bed, neck bent, back hunched. I cleared my throat softly so as not to startle him. "Baze?"

He tensed ever so slightly. "Go back to sleep, Adelynn."

I bit my lip and grasped a fistful of the sheets. "Do you want to talk about it?"

With a heavy sigh, he shook his head. "No." Then he stood, snatched up his coat, and limped from the room. Soon, the outside door banged, declaring his departure.

Numb, I lay my head back on the pillow and tried to push down my feelings. No sense letting myself suffer them now, not when dawn had still to break. Yet, I could only doze, coming in and out of consciousness for what seemed like hours, nearly toppling over the edge until a physical jolt would yank me right back.

Finally, gritting my teeth, I rolled from the bed and bathed, taking my time to bask in the warmth and relaxation. Once I was dressed and ready, the sun had cast Bath in the cheery, rosy glow of morning. I took the stairs more quickly than I should have, but I wanted to sneak past Mr. Everett unnoticed. Absorbed in his daily newspaper, he seemed unaware enough for me to succeed, and I did, experiencing a rush of elation as I sensed the door close behind me without drawing his attention.

Though cool, the air held a tinge of warmth that caressed my cheeks and rustled the gown at my feet, nudging me across the way to Bath Abbey. Who knew if it was even open this early in the morning, but it was the only place that felt right in this moment. As I reached the door, I said a quick prayer and grasped the heavy iron handle. It moved freely.

Suddenly feeling outed as a trespasser in the quiet but massive space, I trod forward with care. My footsteps echoed in the empty chamber. Two rows of dark wooden pews stretched to the opposite end of the nave, perhaps two hundred feet long if I had to wager a guess. Directly before me, all the way on the far wall, sunlight streamed through a colossal stained-glass window and bathed the sanctuary in a medley of colors. The sides of the room, constructed of the yellowed Bath stone that I'd become so familiar with, sported small columns that rose to a vaulted ceiling and splayed out in ribbed semicircles resembling fans. I couldn't remember the name of the architecture. Baze would have known.

Clearing my mind and calming my heart, I dropped into one of the back pews. I clasped my trembling hands in my lap, twisted my ring around my finger, and bowed my head. What should I even pray for?

What could I possibly ask for when so much pain had already been endured? With silent meditation, I began with Emily, that she would find peace and meaning in her life once again, and then moved on to her son, that he would grow into an honorable man.

After that, I prayed for Baze. With the burden of his injury and Bennett's death, he had carried a great weight for far too long, so I prayed that his affliction might be taken from him and he wouldn't have to resort to medication simply to feel normal.

Finally, I decided to petition for myself, as uncomfortable as it felt. I squirmed as my heart cried out, pleading that I might find the peace of mind I truly sought and that I might be able to soften Katherine's heart.

When the well of words within me ran dry, I sat in silence, listening, waiting.

Muffled scuffs interrupted my reverie. I peeked through one eye. Dressed in the customary clerical black garb and high white collar, a tall reverend approached, hands linked before him as though he were lost in prayer. His kind eyes rested on me as he slid into the opposite side of my pew. He sighed and leaned back, pressing both hands on his knees. Then he tilted toward me and said in a light, clear voice, "What brings you here, child? It is quite early. I was under the belief that individuals of your age tend to retire late and thus rise late. Though, perhaps you are an exception."

Hands still clasped in my lap, I faced forward. "I lost a friend." Somehow, I spoke without faltering.

"Ah, my condolences." His thin face wrinkled in sympathy. "How long ago?"

"One year."

"And what do you hope to find within these walls?"

His question gave me pause. What *did* I seek? I ruminated on the query and eventually said, "To calm the storm in my heart and my mind."

The reverend nodded and stared ahead at the stained-glass

window. "Something tells me that there is more to this visit than your loss."

"Indeed."

He looked at me sideways. "How does one so young carry so great a burden?"

I shrugged. "I have seen much. Lost many. My life seems to have no shortage of adversity or hurt, but I suppose I can take comfort in the fact that God won't let me face more than I can handle."

"Oh, no, child. We will come face-to-face with many situations that are far too much for us to endure. That I can assure you."

I narrowed my eyes. "Are you trying to cheer me up? If so, that's not the way to do it."

A deep smile lit his face and shifted the sparse hair on his head. "I am trying to give you hope. It is true, we do not have the strength to face down our foes ourselves, but that is how it should be. Because God has the strength needed. He will face our enemies and our trials with us and deliver us into the hands of victory. It was the Apostle Paul who said that, while in Asia, he faced so much adversity that he despaired even of life." The reverend lifted a fervent fist. "But he chose not to trust in himself but rather to trust in the God who would yet deliver him."

Twisting my ring around and around my finger, I clenched and held my breath until my lungs begged for air. What the revered suggested warred with my previous beliefs. It was easier to accept that I would face hard situations but that God wouldn't allow them to be *too* hard—because then I could overcome them. What the reverend suggested, that we were inherently weak, proved difficult to reconcile within myself. I wasn't weak. In fact, I went out of my way to avoid appearing as such. Yet, the reverend's words suggested I was utterly helpless . . . without God.

I wish I could do it on my own. I wish I was strong enough.

Through the silence, a still small voice whispered, *You're not strong enough, and that's all right because I am—and I am with you.*

The reverend cleared his throat and extended a handkerchief. I blinked at it, stupefied, until I realized that tears dripped from my jaw. Embarrassed, I snatched it up, dried my face, and tried to quell the sobs. "Thank you for your words," I mumbled through hiccups. "I think . . . I think they were exactly what I needed to hear."

"I am pleased." Folding his hands, he gave an encouraging wink. "You may stay as long as you like or you may go if you need to. Whatever you choose to do, remember—God will be with you, whether you are inside or outside of these walls. Always."

Chapter Twenty-Six

STOWING A SMALL VIAL OF OPIUM in his pocket—just in case—Baze set out from the Empire Hotel on foot. A bold endeavor in his current state, he would admit. Mr. Everett had supplied him with directions to the Bath Abbey Cemetery, so now it was merely a matter of getting there without his leg giving out. At this hour, barely anyone milled about, but he did pass a hunched elderly gentleman ambling alone.

Baze crossed Pulteney Bridge without incident, and as he edged south along the River Avon, he watched the fishermen stationed above the weir, hoping to capitalize on the morning bite. Soon, he left the river behind, passed over a narrow canal, and turned farther south onto Prior Park Road. Straightaway, he found himself walking beside a lane of homes. He kept to the right-hand side, where a stone fence nearly the height of a man held back a steep hill. Heavy trees blocked out the morning sunlight and cast cool shadows on Baze's shoulders.

Pebbles crunched beneath his shoes, and he breathed in earthy scents of wet leaves and fresh flowers. He focused on the walk, keeping his mind clear and focusing solely on the task at hand. As the neighborhood drew to an end, he began feeling a strain in his calf and noted the slight upward slope of the pavement.

The sun broke above the trees and caused him to squint. Finally, as his leg began screaming, he paused and leaned against the stone wall to take the pressure off. He'd hoped to at least make it to the cemetery before having to use the tincture, but he wouldn't have the endurance to complete the journey if he didn't. After tilting it to his lips, he cursed under his breath as its sweeping effects took control of every muscle and toyed with his mind. He swayed a bit, bright euphoria pulling a chuckle out of him despite the solemnity of the occasion. At least he stayed conscious enough to remain on his feet.

Now filled with renewed energy—albeit a false energy—he continued the trek. Eventually, he came to the cemetery's ancient entrance. A chapel rose in the distance, and as he meandered through the various headstones and monuments, he admired the wide array of architecture represented on the grounds, everything from new-classical to Greek revival.

Baze allowed his gaze to drift along each of the names on the graves, not fully reading them—until he noticed the word "sergeant" and came to a halt in front of the white headstone, newer than many of its surrounding brethren.

Sergeant John Sutton. 1876–1899. A mere twenty-three summers.

"Wonder what got you," Baze whispered, his voice cracking after such an extended period of silence.

Though a stone bench was situated a few paces away, Baze squatted in front of the headstone and fell to his backside with a grunt. He sat with his knees propped up, supporting his forearms. "I came here on account of my partner. He's buried back in London, so you'll have to do. I hope you don't mind." Baze stared at the headstone as though it would answer him. Feeling silly, he breathed out a laugh and pensively rubbed the bridge of his nose with a knuckle.

"My mate died young too," he said, reluctant but propelled by the need to relieve the pressure building within. He hadn't talked to anyone about it in the last year, not even Adelynn. If he talked about it, then he'd have to deal with it. That would only invite pain. "We were investigating a case together when he was shot. The bullet did too much damage, and we found him too late. Didn't stand a chance. It infuriates me that the likes of Cornelius Marx took him out. Bennett was the better man in every way."

Baze's voice hitched, lowered. "I should have been there for you, but I wasn't. I gave up. If I had gone with you that night, Emily would still have her husband and Basil Allan wouldn't have to grow up fatherless. I'd wager you'd give me an earful about it if you were here now. Rightly so. I let you get killed."

Leaves crunched. "Do you really think so lowly of your friend?"

Baze spun to see Whitaker standing behind him, a bottle of whisky in one hand and two shot glasses in the other. The chief inspector raised his eyebrows and gestured toward Baze with the bottle. "I hope you don't mind the intrusion, but you seem to have discovered my partner's grave."

"This is your . . ." Baze read the inscription again, trying to connect the pieces. "Partner."

"He was, of course." Whitaker sat on the nearby bench, uncorked the bottle, and filled each glass. He lifted one toward Baze. When Baze hesitated, Whitaker chuckled. "Either you drink it or I'll have to pour it onto John's grave, and I don't think he's in the position to appreciate such a fine blend."

Baze heaved himself to his feet. "I suppose one or two couldn't hurt." He joined Whitaker on the bench, accepted the glass, and clinked it with the chief inspector's. Then they drank. As the liquid burned his throat and settled in his body, his head spun. He needed to take care not to mix too much of the spirit with the drug he'd just taken.

Baze breathed in through his nose, then blew a long, smooth exhale through his mouth. "What brings you all the way out here?"

"Visiting my partner. Today's the anniversary of our being assigned to work together. You?"

"Today's the anniversary of my partner's death."

"My condolences." Whitaker grasped Baze's shoulder with a firm hand and squeezed once. "I wish I could tell you it gets easier."

Baze glanced at the headstone. "What happened to yours?"

Whitaker heaved a deep sigh, leaned forward, and rested his forearms on his thighs. "He fell from Pulteney Bridge. Broke his neck. Died instantly."

Baze winced. "I'm sorry."

"Eejit had it coming. He was cocky. I always tried to tell him not to be the hero." He snorted. "Still, because of his actions that day leading up to his death, we were able to crack the case at hand. So when it came down to it, he *was* the hero." Whitaker shook his head at the grave.

Puzzled by the contrast between Whitaker's lighthearted tone and the slab resting before them, Baze cocked his head. "You seem rather unfazed by all this, having lost your partner."

"Unfazed isn't quite the proper word for it. Healed is more like it. It's been fifteen years, after all, so it's given me time to purge any negative emotions I ought not hang on to." He shrugged. "Besides, we'll be reunited someday. Of that, I have no doubt."

Baze looked at the bottom of his empty glass, watching the remnants of the amber liquid swirl around. If God willed it, he would also be reunited with Bennett. Why didn't that bring him comfort? Why couldn't he carry on with his life and honor the sacrifice that Bennett made? Why did he still harbor such deep feelings in his heart?

Whitaker topped off his own glass, then brandished the bottle and raised his eyebrows. Baze nodded and allowed him to fill his.

After emptying his glass over again, then pausing to absorb the effects, Whitaker thumped a fist on Baze's knee. "You don't really blame yourself for your partner's death, do you?"

Indecision tied Baze's tongue. A moment ago, he'd said he did, but did he really? Or was he just angry, looking for someone to blame? Rather than answer, Baze threw back his head and downed his whisky.

"Not a talkative bloke, are you?" A faint smile wrinkled the skin around Whitaker's eyes. "Well, I'll tell you what I think. Your friend chose to pursue that killer that night. He knew the outcome it could yield, but that didn't stop him from going out there anyway, did it? And if you had been with him, you very well may not be sitting here right now. What would that have accomplished, eh? You were spared for a reason, so pull yourself up. Living your life in perpetual guilt is a waste. Don't let his actions be in vain."

Baze lifted his face to the bright sky, tears prickling his eyes. *It seems I need healing in both body and soul. So heal me. Help me move forward.*

The chief inspector clapped Baze on the shoulder and stood. Sensing the visit over, Baze stood too, but upon straightening, blood rushed from his head, his mind whirled, and he stumbled back a step.

Whitaker eyed him as he collected the glass and held both in one palm. He turned toward the path and motioned for Baze to follow. When they'd gone several steps, Whitaker said, "What would your friend have to say about your addiction?"

Baze balked. "What? I'm not . . . I don't—"

"You can stammer all you want, but I know the signs. I've worked with Caine long enough to have picked up an eye for it." He smiled mirthlessly. "My question stands. What do you think Inspector Bennett would say to you if he were here?"

The answer popped immediately into Baze's mind. "He'd have no patience for it. Would likely give me a good lecture and drag me to a physician the first moment he could."

"Sounds like a good friend." Whitaker chuckled before sobering. "Then why are you letting yourself succumb to this?"

"It's . . . complicated." Baze shoved his hands into his pockets. "I've been seeing Sebastian Cutler, a physiotherapist who's been treating me with hydrotherapy in an attempt to rehabilitate my leg. He's been giving me a weaker opium dose to wean my body off of the drug, hopefully for good."

Whitaker's expression perked. "Sebastian Cutler, you say?"

"Yes, do you know him?"

"I know *of* him. He's an odd fellow. Bit of a recluse. I understand he was a standout physiotherapist back in the day. Caine often contributes his medical concoctions to the man for use with his patients."

"Anything I should be worried about?"

"Not unless you're worried about the therapist chattering you into oblivion."

"Oh, that I've already experienced."

They shared a laugh as they continued down the steep hill to the street below. Baze noticed Whitaker shortening his steps, likely to stay stride for stride with Baze, and he tried not to let it irk him. With the opium's effects already fading and the strain of the long walk to the cemetery resulting in sore muscles, he was doing all he could to maintain a steady pace.

Baze cleared his throat. "How are you holding up after yesterday's revelations? I know it can be a lot to take in, learning that such powers exist in this world."

Whitaker exhaled through his nose and shook his head. "On that, I need more time, I'm afraid. I'm unsure what to think at the moment. It's quite the claim."

About to spin up a defense of Adelynn, Baze thought better of it and stayed his tongue. Could he really petition for immediate acceptance when he himself had resisted for so long? No, Whitaker deserved to take the time he needed to reconcile everything in his own mind. So, instead, Baze simply said, "Thank you, Chief Inspector."

Whitaker cast him a sideways glance. "Whatever for?"

Baze gestured to the path, then back to the cemetery up the hill. "For all of this. You've given me much to ponder."

Whitaker halted—as did Baze. Eventually, he extended a hand. "Call me Sydney."

Baze took Whitaker's hand, and they clasped in a solid shake. "Likewise. Call me Baze."

Chapter Twenty-Seven

EMILY LEANED OVER THE PRAM AND adjusted the plush blanket around Basil Allan's chin. Though the sun shone bright and the summer heat had begun to seep into the temperature, she always worried that he wouldn't be warm enough. He smiled up at her and blew bubbles with the spit dribbling from his mouth. As she pushed the pram down the pavement, she returned his glee with an exaggerated smile, even as her heart pinched in anguish. No, she wouldn't let her son see her cry. Not today. It was not a mother's place to put that sort of burden on her child.

Emily filled her lungs with the fresh air and stretched her legs as she walked, flashing smiles and polite greetings at passersby even as her chest squeezed. At first, the people responded cheerfully, but upon seeing her mourning attire, their eyes grew sympathetic. She couldn't quite bring herself to abandon the black garb, but on this day, the one-year mark, she had finally allowed a little dash of color to return to her wardrobe—a vibrant blue cristella flower pinned to her bosom.

"I like it when you wear blue," Bennett had said on many occasions. "It brings out the color of your eyes."

Fighting a melancholy twinge of longing, Emily rounded the corner, habit propelling her legs along the familiar path. Basil Allan continued to gurgle comfortably as she passed the threshold into the lush green forest of St. James's Park. There, she found herself assuming a slower pace among other mothers with children and contented couples strolling leisurely by the lake. Swans and ducks paddled along its surface. The calm sounds of the water trickling, the wind whispering, and people murmuring lifted Emily into a state of calm as she pushed the pram past the beautiful Blue Bridge.

Finally, she came upon the willow tree—their willow tree. She halted the pram at the base of its wide trunk and set to work, fanning out a blanket and unpacking the picnic basket. The food consisted of tomato sandwiches on thick wheat bread, roasted chicken thighs, and strawberries and cream, admittedly an odd combination, but they had been Bennett's favorites. Lastly, she laid Basil Allan on a second blanket next to her and handed him a stuffed bear to keep him occupied.

Emily closed her eyes and reveled in the peaceful atmosphere. "Thank you for the beautiful weather. Thank you for this food. Thank you for my son. And thank you that I can draw breath on this day."

Upon opening her eyes, Emily took one last look about and noticed the familiar blue uniform of an officer. Though the man was walking away from her, those broad shoulders and slick brown hair were unmistakable. Sergeant Rees Andrews. Her stomach tightened. Had he seen her? Well, if he had, he'd had enough sense not to stop.

Forcing Sergeant Andrews out of her mind, Emily turned her attention to Basil Allan and began eating. "This is where your story begins, little one," she said between bites, allowing the flavor to awaken long-dormant recollections. "It was December. Bennett and I had been courting for several months, and he decided to take me ice skating here late one evening."

Suppressed memories flooded her, and she shivered at the remembrance of the frigid winter air. She and Bennett had taken to the ice while her chaperone, Mrs. Morris, watched their every move. The sounds of skate blades hissing across the ice and the occasional bout of laughter filled the night as Emily clung to his strong, proffered arm to keep herself standing, her legs unstable and unsure. After gliding by her side for a while, Bennett had whirled out in front of her and skated backward with ease, grasping her hands and pulling her along.

Her stomach fluttered as they picked up speed. She locked her knees and clung tightly to his hands. "W-what are you doing?"

"Having a little bit of fun." He laughed, eyes sparkling, hips twisting back and forth as he zigzagged his feet to pick up momentum.

Clad in a black overcoat, with his hair mussed and cheeks rosy, he had looked so handsome, but his charms could only distract her from their increasing momentum for so long.

"Stop!" she cried, ankles weakening.

Bennett gave a hearty belly laugh and swung her around. The motion carried them into a circle, and they slowly inched closer and closer until Emily finally lost her balance and toppled forward. She caught herself in his sturdy arms. They giggled and straightened but were quickly interrupted by a woman's sharp throat clearing.

From her position on solid ground, Mrs. Morris looked down her nose at them, appearing none too comfortable wrapped in her giant fur coat.

Blushing, Emily pushed away from Bennett and tried to stabilize her wobbly legs. "You know we can't act too familiar in public."

He gave a mock scoff and placed a hand on his chest. "Why, Miss Taylor, you are the one who thrust yourself upon me. I am the innocent party."

She swatted at him, but he nicked her mittened hand from the air and twirled her again. She squealed.

Emily smiled at the memory and finished one slice of the sandwich. Basil Allan watched her with wide eyes as though enthralled by the story, but she knew he didn't understand a word.

This was all for her.

"When we were utterly exhausted—well, I was, at least—we traded our skates for boots and strolled through the park, Mrs. Morris only a few paces behind. We stopped beneath this very tree, and that's when Bennett turned to me."

She closed her eyes and pictured the moment, her heart beating faster and aligning with the racing pulse of her past self as she watched Bennett fall to one knee. He peered up at her with his shining hazel eyes, so eager and so full of love.

"Will you marry me, Millie?" he had asked softly and opened a little velvet box to reveal a modest gold band with a single small diamond sparkling in the center.

Emily had covered her mouth with her mittens, positively paralyzed in shock. Sweat began to form as warmth emanated from her core, and she very nearly stripped right out of her coat. All she managed to do was nod vigorously and bounce on her toes.

The most joyous smile lit Bennett's features as he popped to his feet. He took her left hand and tugged off her mitten. Holding fierce eye contact, he stuck the mitten in his teeth, took out the ring, and slid it onto her finger—a perfect fit. Her stomach somersaulted and left her lightheaded.

Several skaters and bystanders on foot let out whoops and cheers. Even Mrs. Morris gave a few claps.

As Bennett replaced the mitten, he stepped closer, eyes intent on Emily's lips, but she lowered her head, all too aware of Mrs. Morris's fixed gaze upon them, ready to scold any show of affection. Instead, Emily stammered, "Look at you. You're a right mess." She reached up and plucked his spectacles off his nose, then cleaned the condensation from the glass.

He watched her with an amused expression and allowed her to perch them back on his nose. "Thank you, Miss Taylor."

"My pleasure, Mr. Bennett." Emily's cheeks flushed as she cast a glance at Mrs. Morris. A man and his dog had gotten the lead tangled about Mrs. Morris's feet, so for the moment, the older woman's attention seemed diverted from their betrothal. Perhaps she was distracted enough to—

Bennett grasped Emily's chin, angled her face toward him, and kissed her. He made good use of every precious second, channeling passion enough for a thousand kisses. Just as Emily leaned into him, surrendering fully, he brusquely severed their connection and took a step away from her. Cheeks a deep red, he glanced at the chaperone and straightened in triumph.

Head whirling from the experience, Emily bit her lip and fought against a grin—unsuccessfully. She playfully bumped his chest with her plush fist.

He snorted a laugh, winked, and flicked her nose with a knuckle.

A child's giddy squeal brought Emily back to the present. She closed her eyes and tried to hold onto the feel of Bennett's touch. She pressed a finger to her bottom lip and, for a moment, believed that he had been here in this moment, that she could still recall the taste of him—warm cinnamon and rum.

Basil Allan cooed, and Emily looked down, greeted by his shining eyes and gummy smile punctuated by four tiny teeth. She smiled back, tickled his exposed tummy, and tipped his nose with her knuckle as his father had always done to her. Keeping him entertained with silly expressions, Emily reached into the picnic basket and extracted a small cake that she'd baked the day before. Spice marble cake—once again, Bennett's favorite.

Rather than cut into it, she placed it aside and toyed with Basil Allan's foot. "Happy birthday, little one." Her throat tightened until she could barely draw breath. Tears pooled in her eyes as she whispered, "And happy birthday in heaven, my love."

How could one day hold so much grief and yet so much joy? For the rest of her life, this day would bring a torrent of memories, reminding her of how much she had lost but also of how much she had gained. She wasn't sure how to handle the feelings fighting for dominance. Which one should she allow to manifest? Perhaps both. Perhaps neither.

A flash of bright blue passed in her periphery, and Emily turned in time to see Sergeant Andrews steal by again. This time, Emily stared at his thick shoulders as he strode away, hands clasped at the small of his back. He glanced about as though oblivious to her presence. But this couldn't merely be a coincidence, could it?

Blinking away her tears, she maintained a close watch on him and aimlessly wiggled Basil Allan's toes. Sergeant Andrews continued his trek down the path, but when he'd gone about twenty paces more, he performed an about-face and came lumbering back her way. She suppressed a sigh. Most certainly not a coincidence.

Emily kept her eyes trained on him, but he cast his gaze everywhere but at her until he was so close that he couldn't resist peeking in her direction. When he did, she intensified her stare. His eyes darted away, and his jaw flexed, but finally, he relaxed his shoulders and approached.

"Beautiful day for a walk, isn't it?" she called as he walked up.

"I was merely out for a patrol." He scratched the back of his head. "I happened to notice you and . . . well, it isn't safe for a woman and a child to be out here alone. So, I thought—"

"You thought you'd hover in secret, protecting me from afar rather than stopping to give a simple greeting."

His brow wrinkled. "I wasn't aware you wanted me to greet you."

Emily clamped her mouth shut. He certainly had her there. She let her defenses drop and gave him a genuine smile. "I appreciate your care, Sergeant Andrews, I really do. Bennett would have been grateful to know I would be so well looked after in his absence."

Muscles in the sergeant's jaw pulsed as he lowered his gaze to Basil Allan. Upon seeing the child, he brightened and dropped to one knee. "And how are you, little man? Eh? You being good for your mum?" He tickled the toddler's round belly.

Basil Allan screeched and rolled side to side. Emily snickered at her son's cries of delight before her gaze drifted to Sergeant Andrews's large hand. Its massive expanse covered her son's whole torso, his thumb nearly the size of Basil Allan's foot. Her eyes wandered up the sergeant's wrist to his shirt cuff poking out from beneath the blue uniform sleeve. A dark splotch marred the white fabric.

Emily tsked and tugged on the sleeve. "Really, you would turn up in front of a seamstress with your wardrobe in such a state?"

He looked down at the sleeve, then covered the mark with his other hand. "Apologies. I can't seem to get it out, and I haven't had the time to purchase a new shirt."

"Leave it with me," she blurted, then chided herself. *I can't keep encouraging this.*

Sergeant Andrews blinked, eyes hazy and unsure. "Really?"

"Yes," she croaked out, not wanting to go back on her word. "Yes, I think I have just the thing to get that stain out."

He stared a moment longer, then smiled. "Thank you. I will." His voice went up a tick with a note of optimism. "Well, I'll leave you to it. I don't want to keep interrupting your time with your son." He hesitated, watching her, as though expecting her to invite him to stay, but she kept her mouth closed, already having said too much.

"Right then. Take care. I'll be round to drop this off later." He nodded and got to his feet. "Stay as long as you like. I'll be nearby—just in case."

As Emily watched him retreat, she sighed. Not only was she still in the midst of grieving, but she was also dancing around the advances of a man for whom she held no interest.

I can't keep doing this. Lord, what should I do? I want to find love again, but my heart isn't ready. I don't know if it will ever be ready. Besides, how could there be room enough for anyone else when I still love Bennett? Because I will always love him.

Chapter Twenty-Eight

WITH MY HEART LIFTED AND ENCOURAGED by the reverend's wisdom, I ventured back to the Empire Hotel. It was time I kept my pride in check, accepted that I was weak, and relied not on my own strength but on God's. That was the only way I would find true peace and receive the power to overcome the darkness that had settled over Bath . . . and to reconcile with Baze.

Easier said than done.

Upon entering the lobby, I felt the weight of Baze's absence even more heavily. Had he returned by now, or was he still off wandering by himself? To make the burden of remembering Bennett's death even worse, Baze likely still stung from the harsh words we'd exchanged. With the way events were unfolding, it seemed we would never get a chance to resolve this conflict between us.

At the counter, Mr. Everett hunched over an open newspaper—ever consistent. I drew closer and noticed others fanned out around him. Folding my arms atop the counter, I glanced at several headlines and realized that they all pertained to the recent poisonings. Why had he taken such an acute interest in this case? Was it mere curiosity, the desire to stay abreast of happenings in Bath, or was it something more?

Mr. Everett smiled and closed the paper before him, giving me his full attention. "How are you, Mrs. Ford?"

I took careful stock of my gut feelings. Was Mr. Everett someone I could fully trust? Thus far, he hadn't given me any reason not to, even when I had reached out with my mind in an attempt to flush out any underlying deception. If I didn't sense any darkness, could I be sure that I could trust *myself* in that regard?

Deciding to take a more conservative approach, I nodded at the newspaper. "What do you make of it?"

His shoulders drooped. "It is an atrocity, to be sure. We have been fortunate to enjoy relative peace in Bath, with the last crime of this nature occurring nearly fifteen years ago. It distresses me that we are having to endure this once again."

I perked up. "Were you here during those other crimes?"

"Yes, I was here. The Empire Hotel had yet to be built at that time, so I was working as a server in the Pump Room." He stroked his mustache. "I don't enjoy reliving these memories, but on one fateful night when I took the shift of a sick colleague, the murderer chose to make the Pump Room the location of his first kill." His eyes grew distant. "I didn't quite realize what was happening until the woman collapsed. It became a blur after that. Chaos. Confusion. I shall never forget it."

Shock hit me. Mr. Everett had witnessed the first murder fifteen years ago? Not only that, but he had also been present when the woman in my vision had died. Was that significant, or had he simply been unfortunate enough to be in the wrong place at the wrong time—twice?

"I imagine you know a lot about the previous murders." I softened my voice. "So, do you think this is the same killer as before?"

Mr. Everett let out a sound like a chuckle. "Oh, no. This isn't the same person."

I frowned, leaning closer. "You say that rather confidently. How can you know for sure when the police are not even sure themselves?"

"As you said, I am well-versed in the facts of the past case, and the details simply don't match between the two. Take the first two victims. Here, Mrs. Sands was killed with poisoned tea, but years ago, the first woman consumed poisoned coffee."

"So?" I shrugged. "Maybe the killer was simply working with what he had."

Mr. Everett shook his head. "The second person to die, the violinist, isn't quite the same either. The man who died last time was a cellist."

Not seeing the connection, I scrunched up my nose.

After stacking his newspapers in a neat pile, Mr. Everett bent toward me. "Whoever is committing these crimes is trying to emulate the previous killer, but they're getting details wrong, whether on purpose or by accident, I do not know. What I *do* know is that they are meant to mimic the crimes of the past." His voice lowered. "If that is indeed the case, then the question we must ask ourselves is this—is the individual copying the last killer out of admiration or out of spite? After all, the case was never solved last time, leaving questions unanswered and justice unfulfilled. Maybe our current killer is purely out for revenge, not against his victims, but against his predecessor."

I tapped the counter, studying his serious but sincere expression, and searched within, trying to detect any cracks in his demeanor. His story made sense. If it was the same killer as before, why would the man get such minute details wrong? It was entirely possible that someone else was purposefully changing things to draw someone out. After all, the killer could still walk among the citizens of Bath. In fact, he could be standing directly in front of me.

Emboldened, I tilted my head. "Don't you find it rather curious that on the night you happened to take a shift that wasn't yours, a woman wound up dead? And recently, you also happened to be in proximity when another woman met her fate, almost identical to the first."

"You are an astute observer, Mrs. Ford." Mr. Everett raised an eyebrow. "But answer me this—if a man committed a most heinous crime and then managed to escape the law and achieve freedom, why would that man remain in the very place that he terrorized, tempting fate with every second he remained?"

"I don't know. You tell me."

He smiled—a soft, kind smile that brightened his eyes. "I admire your tenacity, Mrs. Ford. I presume it is that same tenacity that allowed you to take down Cornelius Marx in London. I have no doubt you'll solve this one as well."

I nodded, still wary but, again, unable to sense anything that would indicate he was being misleading. A question formulated on the tip of my tongue, one I was almost afraid to ask, but I forged ahead. "Based on the series of events, who do you think will be the next person to die?"

"The third victim fifteen years ago was a stage performer, a ventriloquist to be exact, but considering today's altered details, I can only speculate." His lips flattened. "There is likely no way to accurately predict or prevent the next death."

Such a feat likely couldn't be achieved by mere conjecture, as Mr. Everett suggested, but if I could find a way to summon a vision in time—as Katherine had said—maybe we could strike first and put an end to this.

Chapter Twenty-Nine

FINALLY HAVING LULLED BASIL ALLAN TO sleep, Emily laid him in his crib, brushed a feathery curl from his forehead, and crept from the room. She left the door slightly ajar behind her. When she reached the kitchen, she set water on to boil and then lifted Sergeant Andrews's stained shirt to assess the damage.

He'd gotten into quite the kerfuffle. The ink marred a good portion of the cuff and had splattered up onto the sleeve, but it ended in an abrupt line, indicating that he may have been wearing a coat over the top when it occurred. With her own sleeves rolled up, Emily held the shirt above a basin and sprinkled the stain with chloride of lime. The chemical's odor stung her nose and turned her stomach as she retrieved the boiling water and scrubbed at the stain.

Soon, pigment began bleeding out of the fabric. As the ink clung to her skin and swirled in the bottom of the basin, sudden memories flashed before her eyes. An open drawer. Adelynn's diary. A tipped inkwell.

Emily gasped and dropped the shirt. It landed with a dull *squelch*.

Sergeant Andrews. It had been Sergeant Andrews. He was the one who had broken into the house, the one who had taken Adelynn's diary.

Sweat prickled Emily's skin, made worse by the steam rising from the boiling water. All this time, she had been in the presence of . . . of what? What did this make him? How could she assign a descriptor when she didn't even know his motive for taking the diary in the first place?

However, she *did* know one thing. He had lied. He had been standing right there, watching silently as she had investigated the house for clues that he already knew existed. If he had hidden that, what *else* was he hiding? What secrets did he keep buried within?

Emily's hands shook as she lifted the shirt and continued scrubbing at the condemning stain. Her thoughts raced. *What should I do?*

Thus far, he had treated her with nothing but respect and care, affection even, but what would happen if she confronted him? Wrongdoers went to great lengths to keep their misdeeds from becoming known, so what would he do to veil his own? Could he become dangerous? No, she couldn't risk confronting him on her own.

Emily had just hung the shirt to dry when Basil Allan's cries drew her away from her task. She took her time feeding and cuddling him, then set him on the living room floor within eyeshot. He babbled incoherently as he knocked two blocks together and held them up for Emily to see. She turned up a smile that quickly faded. The revelation of Sergeant Andrews's deceit had cast a heavy raincloud over her ability to enjoy the delight on her son's face.

Indecision burned a hole within her as she folded the now-clean shirt, but she needed to decide soon. Sergeant Andrews had said he would pick it up during his afternoon shift that brought him by her home. Should she merely pretend that all was well? If she ignored her newfound knowledge, there was no telling what else Sergeant Andrews would plan to do or how long he would keep up the ruse in front of her and his fellow officers. But if she revealed that she had discovered his secret, what then? What might he do? What might he do to *her*?

Basil Allan giggled, and a glob of spit dribbled down his chin. Emily laughed and wiped it away with a rag. His bright eyes shone up at her.

Her indecision turned into resolution.

Steeling her muscles, she crossed to the telephone and picked up the bell-shaped receiver, grateful that Baze and Adelynn had arranged for its installation. When Whelan's gruff voice boomed on the other line, her limbs nearly turned to mush in relief.

"Emily, this is quite the surprise. What can I do for you? Is everything all right?"

The admission caught on the tip of her tongue. Once she outed the sergeant, it would put in motion a series of events that she couldn't come back from. But she had to protect her son—above all else.

"No, everything's not all right," she finally said.

"Well, out with it then, missy, and I'll try to help as best I can."

"Do you remember that I found Adelynn's diary missing and a spilled inkwell within the drawer?"

"Yes . . ."

"Well, yesterday, Sergeant Andrews dropped off his shirt with me to be cleaned . . . because of an ink stain on the cuff."

Heavy air buffeted the mouthpiece on Whelan's end. "Do you realize what you're suggesting?"

"I do." She tried to keep her voice calm.

Whelan must have covered the mouthpiece when he shouted a muffled, "Andrews, get in here!" When his voice returned, he spoke slowly, even-toned. "Emily, do you have any other evidence to prove that he might have been the perpetrator?"

"No." Tears rushed to her eyes. "I know that such an accusation could ruin a man's life, but Sergeant Andrews has . . . taken an interest in me. He's been around my son. If there's any chance at all that he could be dangerous . . ."

"We'll look into it, Emily. You can rest assured."

Before relief had a chance to settle in her, another officer's voice reached her ears. "Sir?"

"What is it?" Whelan grunted.

"Andrews isn't here."

"Well, where's he gone?"

Emily white-knuckled the receiver, one of her worst fears staring her in the face. "He's coming here," she murmured.

"He's what?" Whelan snapped.

Trying to quell her rising anxiety, she said, "He was supposed to pick up the shirt today, but . . . Whelan, I don't want him here. Don't let him come here."

"All right. Hold tight. I'll send someone to—"

A knock rapped on the front door. Emily yelped and dropped the receiver. It clattered about until she wrangled it back into her hand by the cord and smashed it against her ear. "Whelan?"

"What in the blazes was that?"

Her breath a mere trickle, she said, "I think he's here."

"Don't open the door. We're on our way right now."

Another knock sounded. Emily peeked over her shoulder to see Andrews's face appear in the window. He squinted, then brightened as he noticed her.

Emily waved to acknowledge him but held up one finger to indicate that he needed to wait a moment. She could barely breathe. "He's seen me in the window. He knows I'm here."

"Don't do anything. I repeat, do not do anything."

"But he'll realized something's amiss if I don't answer."

"Emily—"

"How long will it take you to get here?"

Whelan swore and grumbled, "Why does no one ever listen to anything—fine. We can be there in minutes."

"Okay. I think I can stall him. Hurry."

She heard Whelan barking orders as she jammed the receiver onto its switch hook. A quick check on Basil Allan revealed that he still played contentedly on the floor. Every nerve fired red-hot. She sprinted into the master bedroom, still largely left untouched since the last time Bennett was there, and barged into his nightstand to the loaded pistol he had always kept nearby for any threat that might invade their home.

Fingers trembling, she grasped the gun's cold, unfamiliar grip and hid it in the folds of her skirt. Then she collected the sergeant's shirt, draped it over her arm, and poised herself at the door. She said a quick prayer for protection—and the right words to say to keep him composed—and swung the door wide.

Sergeant Andrews grinned, his cheery demeanor matching the afternoon sun that poured around him. Now, knowing the truth, she viewed him with a whole new perspective. She noticed the slight sag in his smile, the extra measure of rigidity in his shoulders, and the emotionless fog in his eyes. Had that all been there before this moment?

Heaving a breath, she pasted on a bright smile and held out the shirt. "Thank you for coming, Sergeant Andrews. I believe I was successful in restoring it to its former glory."

"Thank you." Sergeant Andrews held up the garment and ran his fingers along the cuff in question. "Incredible work. Truly. It's as though it were never stained in the first place."

She nodded at it. "H-how did you say it happened?" She fought off a wince. *Foolish!*

He studied her a moment, suddenly still. "An ink spill. A bad pen." Even standing on the landing several inches lower, his eye level was even with hers.

"Of course." She couldn't help but glance down the street, urging Whelan to hurry as she clenched the door handle in one hand, the gun in her other. *Calm down. Speak normally.*

The sergeant cleared his throat and tucked the shirt under his arm. "I'd best be off then. I'm sorry to have taken your time."

"You haven't," she blurted, her grip tightening on the gun. She had told Whelan she would stall, so stall she would. "I mean that to say, I'm not overly busy. You're welcome to some tea if you need refreshment before you finish your shift."

Brow furrowed, Sergeant Andrews half-closed one eye. "With all due respect, I thought you made it clear that you weren't interested. I don't want to overstep my boundaries."

Emily's defenses lowered ever so slightly. His resigned posture, his sad eyes—this wasn't a criminal standing before her. He was hurting somehow. In fact, his uncertain expression and his puppy dog eyes reminded her of Finn.

"Yes, I did say that. Thank you for the respect you've shown me. Now simply isn't a good time. You know . . ." She motioned down to her mourning dress. "But that doesn't mean I can't make a gesture of friendship."

After a long beat, Rees's features softened, and he stepped onto the top landing. "Thank you, I—"

Nerves unraveling, Emily's instincts jerked her back, away from him. She bit her lip and scolded herself, bracing for the windfall.

He froze, confusion etched on his face. "I'm sorry. I didn't mean—"

"No, no, it's not you." She waved her free hand but kept the gun pressed to her side. "I . . . I had a nightmare last night. That's all. It's put me a little on edge, I'm afraid."

His gaze drifted down to her gun-wielding arm—hopefully her skirt still hid the weapon—then jumped back to her face. "Is something wrong?" he asked slowly. "You're acting oddly."

"It's nothing. I—"

The screeching of tires preceded a car careening onto the street in the distance. Recognition piqued on Rees's face. He gaped at Emily, and she sensed his demeanor change.

She whipped out the gun.

He caught her wrist and twisted the gun from her hand. She yelped. As the car skidded to a halt, officers led by Whelan piled out. Rees wrapped his thick arm around Emily's neck, wrangled her in front of him, and pressed the gun to her head. She stifled a cry, hearing Basil Allan starting to fuss.

Whelan lifted his hands, brandishing his own gun. "Think about what you're doing, Andrews. You can still stop this before you get too deep. Let's talk about this."

Rees snarled. "Put down your gun, sir."

"You're welcome to go, son." Whelan kept his weapon aloft. "I just want the woman."

"This woman is the only thing that's keeping you from blowing my brains out, so if it's all the same to you, I'll be hanging on to her." His muscles flexed under her chin, and her nostrils filled with the ripe, bitter odor of sweat.

"Please, Rees." She felt ashamed by her quivering voice and her falling tears. "Don't do this."

"It's too late." He began backing through the open door, dragging her with him.

Whelan and the officers advanced a few steps. One of them hefted his gun, but Whelan was quick to grab it and yank it down. "Your aim's good but not that good," he snapped. "We hit her and Bennett would surge right through those pearly gates to give us an earful."

Anger flashing in his eyes, Whelan glared at Rees. "You hurt her, you hang."

The sergeant dragged Emily across the threshold and kicked the door shut. He shoved her in the direction of her son—who had devolved into a full meltdown—and wagged his head. "Shut him up."

Emily scooped Basil Allan into her arms and cradled him tight against her as Rees locked the door, then stomped to the kitchen. He returned carrying a chair and propped it under the door handle.

"Let me go," she growled, surprising herself with the ferocity of her voice. Even the sergeant's gait faltered a moment.

A look of sincere remorse shadowed his face. "I won't hurt you."

"How can I trust anything you say when you've been lying to me all this time? Why are you doing this? Why did you break into Adelynn's home?"

Rees paced in front of the door, scratching the back of his head with the gun. "I was trying to find a way to quiet the voices. So many voices."

"What voices?" Scalp prickling, Emily kept her gaze trained on him, thankful that Basil Allan was quieting.

"They . . . they did something to me that night, when I stormed the Empress Theatre." His frenzied yet hazy eyes locked on her, and it took all her power not to recoil. "I haven't stopped hearing voices, Emily. They're always whispering, trying to force me to do things I don't want to do. Horrible things. Things to people I care about."

Emily's mouth went dry. Voices? Could he be suffering from the same dark influence that had afflicted Finn last year? But how? Finn's manipulation had been Cornelius's doing, and he was no longer of this world . . . unless his power could linger even beyond the grave.

Rees massaged his forehead with unsteady fingers. "I thought maybe Mrs. Ford might have a way to stop it. She defeated him, didn't she? I thought her writings could help me."

"Why sneak around then? Why commit a crime when the solution was free and available to you?" Emily asked, even as the answer dawned on her. "There is no shame in asking for help. It's not a sign of weakness in the least."

He kept pacing, shoulders hunched, the gun still gripped in his hand. Ragged breaths crackled in his throat.

Whelan's rough voice filtered through the door. "Think about what you're doing, son. Don't do anything you'll regret."

"Shut up!" Rees pounded a fist on the door.

Emily tensed and clutched at her son. *God, give me the right words.* She calmed her voice and managed, "I know someone who was like you, Rees. He was tormented in the same way. He was also controlled by a strong voice in his head—but he escaped. He's free."

The sergeant wavered on his feet. "How?" The word cut sharp, desperate. "Tell me. Tell me how."

"The power of God set him free." She took a few tentative steps toward him. "It can do the same for you."

"But I . . . I'm not . . . I don't know how . . ." He bit his bottom lip as though chewing on something he wanted to say.

The phone erupted in a violent ring. Emily gasped and ducked while Rees aimed the gun in its direction. It rang again.

Emily and Rees made eye contact. "Don't answer it," he said. "Just let it ring."

Agonizing moments dragged by as the phone's clanging cut through the otherwise quiet home. Finally, after what seemed like a thousand rings, it fell silent.

The sergeant's shoulders relaxed, but he held the gun outstretched and locked his gaze upon it. A look of resignation wilted his features.

Fear speared Emily's heart. "Stop, Rees," she whispered. "Don't do anything rash. I can help you."

Sweat droplets seeped down the side of his face. "I don't know if anyone can—"

The phone sounded again.

As the sergeant swore and the ringing sliced through the air, Emily squeezed her eyes shut, praying that the chaos would end. Then, ever so slowly, the weight of purpose settled in the bottom of her heart. She wasn't sure how, but she knew that whoever waited on the other end of the telephone line was calling for a reason.

Resolute, Emily fixed her eyes on the sergeant. "It will keep ringing if I don't answer."

Indecision and fear wrestled on his face for a good while—so long that Emily feared the telephone would fall silent again. Then he nodded. Straightening, he marched toward the device and gestured with the gun to beckon her over.

Propping Basil Allan on her hip, she reached for the receiver.

Rees halted her briefly, eyes aflame but murky. "Not a word about any of this." The barrel of his weapon turned toward her head.

With an apprehensive nod, she pressed the receiver to her ear and bent to speak into the mouthpiece. "Hello?" She managed to keep the tension from her voice.

"*Shhh* . . ." Static buzzed.

She gripped it tighter to her ear as though to hear better. "Hello?"

"*Shhh* . . ." More static.

"I'm sorry. I'm afraid I can't make out what you're saying."

She strained her ears while keeping her eyes on the sergeant.

"*Shhh* . . . Em . . ." Gradually, a voice cut through the noise and grew clearer. "Emily? Are you there?"

"Yes, I'm here." Unsure she'd heard it correctly, she stared wide-eyed at the mouthpiece—faint familiarity causing hope to blossom within her.

"Emily, it's me . . . *Shhh* . . . Finn."

The world spun, and her body felt so weightless that she worried she might float straight up into the air. Myriad emotions clashed within her. Disbelief and elation pushed to the forefront, and she found herself gaping, all words lost to her.

"I had a feelin' I needed to reach you . . . *Shhh* . . . Are you well?"

Emily tried to picture Finn. Where was he right now? In a little Irish village somewhere in the countryside, perhaps, surrounded by green hills and abandoned castles. Then she visualized his face—bright blue eyes filled with delight, raven curls tousled about, and a dazzling smile. The scent of the flower he'd gifted her when they parted tickled her nose.

"Emily? . . . *Shhh* . . ."

"Yes." She squeezed the receiver. "I am . . . troubled. Afraid even."

"Don't be afraid." For the moment, his voice resounded clearly without static. "'Twas the strangest thing, sure. I felt a promptin' to tell you that there's hope. No matter what happens in this life. And you're never alone. Never. Remember that . . . *Shhh* . . ."

Emily leaned closer to the mouthpiece, her heart leaping. "Finn?"

"Em . . . *Shhh* . . ."

"Don't go!" Terror struck her.

"Emily, I'm . . . *Shhhhhh* . . ."

Finn's voice faded into a cacophony of static. The line went dead.

In a daze, Emily allowed the receiver to slip through her fingers and dangle over the edge by its cord.

Rees jutted his chin toward her and licked sweat from his top lip. "Who was that?"

Limbs trembling, Emily felt the terror from a moment ago transform into calm and spread throughout her body—from the tips of her toes to the top of her head. Jaw set, mind made up, she gently placed Basil Allan at her feet. He sat serenely, thumb in his mouth, peering up at her intently as though he sensed her shift to peace.

Then she turned toward Rees. Her face must have rattled him, for he stumbled back a few steps. She didn't let him get far, however, marching straight for him. He couldn't scramble away fast enough as she lifted on her tiptoes and took his face in her hands. His cheeks burned feverishly beneath her palms.

Lord, tell me what to say. Speak through me.

Emily opened her lips, and words spilled out. "There is hope, Rees—and freedom from the torment you feel. All you have to do is make an opening for the Almighty to work within you, open your heart to the belief that He can bring you out of darkness and into the light."

Wavering on his feet, Rees shuddered. Thick streams poured from his unblinking eyes and tumbled over Emily's hands. Yet, even as sorrow pinched his face, Emily detected something changing—in him, in the atmosphere. The air was beginning to warm, growing thick with electricity and energy. Emily's heart raced, and her lips threatened to pull into a smile.

Then, in one slow motion, he lifted the gun and offered it to her.

With deliberate movements, Emily first cleared the tears from his face and swiped her sodden palms on her skirt, then finally accepted the relinquished weapon. She made quick work of removing the bullets and allowing them to thump to the floor as Bennett had once taught her. A deep sigh rushed from her lungs.

Rees's wobbly legs brought him to his knees. Head lolling forward, he mumbled, "I'm sorry, Emily. I'm so sorry."

Emily eased a gentle hand through his hair, like a mother comforting her child. "Do not apologize, Rees. Your actions may have been misguided, but I believe God brought you here so that you might find the healing you need. And for that, I am thankful.

Chapter Thirty

I RECLINED ATOP MY BED, FULLY clothed, hands laced over my stomach, and eyes fixed on the ceiling. Though my body lay still, my mind careened through a tumultuous maze. It relived every event since we arrived in Bath, every pleasant memory, every troubling setback. Katherine. Mr. Everett. Baze. Sydney. Cornelius. Where did we go from here? *Was* there an answer at the end of all this? What would it take to find it?

A shiver rippled its way up my body, and with it, my thoughts homed in on something Katherine had mentioned in my last meeting with her. *"Hopefully you are never caught up in his dark endeavors, but should you find yourself in that position and need to gain the upper hand, you might consider attempting to conjure a vision through him at will."*

Could it truly be possible? Could I produce a vision on mere will alone?

Determined to discover the truth of it one way or another, I closed my eyes and focused on each inhale, each exhale, until my pulse slowed and my muscles loosened. Time crawled by. Tranquility wrapped around me. My fingers twitched. My body tingled. *Now?*

I centered my thoughts and pushed out with my mind. Physical sensations began to diminish. Images raced by in a blur as though I watched a motion picture. Then, one sole image separated from the rest and slowly consumed everything. Details materialized into view—a small auditorium, a red velvet seat cushion upon which I sat, well-dressed people filing through the aisle to my left, and a modest stage occupying the front of the space.

"How much longer?" a male voice whispered behind me.

My own mouth moved, but another man's voice came out. "Patience."

"You said he would have revealed himself by now. Nothing."

I tapped a fingernail on the wooden armrest. "Everythin' is still goin' accordin' to plan, provided you can keep up your end of this deal."

"She's proven difficult to find."

I smirked. "She's cunnin', sure, but I'm countin' on you. Don't let me down."

The man behind me grunted, and I heard a squeak and the groaning of wood, then retreating footsteps.

Fatigue dizzied my mind and dimmed the scene before me. How long could I hold on to this vision? Yet, why hold on any longer? What more was there to see?

My eyes narrowed as I—or rather, the person I embodied—sat rigid. He leaned to one side, resting an elbow on the armrest and stroking his chin. The air grew cold and dense. Then, his eyes widened a touch. "I wondered when you might test your limits," he whispered, his words barely audible. Who could he be talking to? No one sat anywhere near . . .

Realization dawned. The statement had been meant for me. He knew I was watching.

"I am impressed by your willpower," he continued in the same soft tone. "I presume Kate encouraged this experimentation?"

The sensation was like nothing I'd ever experienced before—conjuring my own vision and possessing another body and seemingly talking to myself. But without a mouth of my own, I couldn't respond. I could only linger and listen.

"You should be wary of her." He blinked slowly. "I can't imagine the relief you must feel, knowin' that you are not all alone in the world, so it pains me to be sayin' this. Kate is deceitful. She cares only for herself, and she will do anythin', say anythin', to ensure that she gets what she wants. Do not make the mistake of trustin' her."

I wanted to argue, to refute his claims, but I was a measly spectator, my mind barely keeping a hold on his while my body remained tethered back in my room.

Music suddenly swelled from the orchestra pit, the lights dimmed, and the audience quieted. When the thick stage curtains parted, they revealed a smartly dressed magician, his arms held aloft, an exaggerated smile plastered to his unblemished face. For a moment, the top hat, tailcoat, and dove perched on his shoulder nearly had me convinced that I was watching Finn performing at the Empress, but the curled mustache and baritone English accent shattered that illusion.

"Watch carefully now," my host whispered so that he could be heard over the magician's speech. "What you are about to witness is all Kate's doing. You'll see."

The magician circled a small wooden table topped with a lumpy sheet. He whisked the linen away to reveal a tumbler and a bottle of wine. With a mischievous grin, he poured himself a glass and took a swig. The audience rippled in laughter.

Then the magician grasped the dove from his shoulder and laid it on the table. He made quick work, rolling the dove in what looked like paper until all but its tailfeathers were visible, protruding from the bottom. Flourishing it in one hand, he made a show of it to the audience before pulling out a match, lighting it, and holding the flame under the tailfeathers. They caught, and the fire devoured the entire roll. The magician threw his hands apart. A few scraps of paper and feathers floated to the ground—the dove had vanished.

The audience gasped.

With a knowing smile, the magician gestured to the bottle. "Do not fear, ladies and gentlemen. Our feathered friend is well."

A red tinge began making its way up the magician's neck, and he covered a cough as he snatched up a cane, gripped the neck of the bottle, and whacked it. The glass shattered, and the pieces fell away to reveal a white dove within. But as the audience cheered, the magician's face twisted in confused agony. His hands flew to his throat as racking coughs overtook him, eyes bulging and face turning fully red. Horrified whispers filtered through the crowd as he bent forward, finally falling to his knees—then he collapsed.

Shock jolted me. I gasped, and my mind's link to the mysterious individual snapped. Thrust back into my own body, I tore my eyes open. Quick but heavy breaths cut through the silence. Everything I had witnessed mere seconds ago replayed in my mind's eye, over and over again. I had done it. I had managed to impose my will upon the enemy. This could change everything.

The blood drained from my face, and the elation of my supposed victory came crashing down when the reality of the situation sank in. I had watched another man die—the newest victim had been claimed.

Chapter Thirty-One

GUESTS POURED OUT OF THE THEATER Royal in droves. Fighting against the flow of the crowd proved a nearly unwinnable battle—with bodies jostling me from either side and shoes stomping my toes—but Baze surged out ahead, secured a firm grasp on my forearm, and cut a narrow path through the panicked exodus. A cloud of perfume and body odor smothered us and accompanied the frenzied people spilling into the street.

Inside the opulent foyer, Baze released his grip but threaded his arm around my shoulders. The warm, familiar scent of cedar and citrus wrapped as tightly around me as his embrace, but when we stepped into the empty auditorium, an icy chill infiltrated the comforting shroud. Gooseflesh rushed across my limbs. Flashes of the Empress Theater came crashing back as I took in the nearly identical space—complete with a vaulted ceiling, ornate designs, and a sea of red seats. And just like the Empress, darkness had taken root here too.

Knowing deep within what lay before us, I dragged my eyes across the seats, over Sydney and the officers congregated near the orchestra pit, and finally up to the stage. A lone, still figure lay upon it. Familiarity prodded my mind—that suit, the raven hair . . . *Cornelius?* The muscles in my neck tightened, and my mouth went dry. I squeezed my eyes shut. *No, he's not here. He's not. Stop it, Adelynn.* I peeked through one eye. As I'd suspected, Cornelius had disappeared.

Yet, relief remained at bay . . . for another man lay in his place.

Noticing our approach, Sydney excused himself from his men and met us part of the way. With shoulders held taught—whether out of formality or stress, I couldn't tell—he eyed me. "I'll come right out with it. I was skeptical about what you told me regarding your visions, Adelynn, but I've no other explanation for why you're here when I've only just learned of this myself. That serves as quite the compelling argument for your gift."

Baze gave my shoulder a squeeze.

As much as it bolstered my confidence to know that yet another person I trusted was aware of my gift, the reason for it soured my joy. "I wish it were under different circumstances."

He circled a finger toward the victim and tilted closer. "How much did you see?"

Focusing on the man, I allowed the recollections to filter back. "One moment he was performing his act, and in the next, he was on the floor. I assume it was poison—like the others."

"That aligns with what we've gathered so far from our preliminary examination, but we'll have Caine test it to be certain." Sydney dug a hand into his inner coat pocket and fished out a single card—a queen of hearts. "We found this on the magician's person. It doesn't match any of his existing decks, so we think it may have been planted." He tapped its surface. "There's also a message written here, exactly like the first two victims. It reads, 'Your time is nearly up,' and the T's been capitalized."

Baze furrowed his brow. "So we've had a K, an A, and now a T."

Clear discernment aligned the pieces of the puzzle in my head as I stared at the card. The queen's angular features and knowing smirk transfixed me. Framed within rounded, frayed corners, her weathered and smudged face betrayed years of use. With the familiarity of the card combined with the three capital letters intentionally left on each victim, I held no doubt about the identity of the person to whom the queen belonged.

I bit my tongue.

With a sideways glance, Baze nudged me between my shoulder blades. "What is it?"

Her name teetered at the tip of my tongue, but I held it back. Once it left my lips, I couldn't take it back. Saying the name could bring dire consequences I wasn't sure I was ready to face yet.

Baze pressed my shoulder to angle me toward him, and his intense eyes locked on me. "I know that look. You've thought of something."

Of all the times I wished he didn't have a direct window into my soul, now was one of them. However, she trusted me. I couldn't betray her confidence now, not when we'd—

"It's Katherine's, isn't it?" Baze's eyes widened as realization dawned on him.

Dash it all, Baze.

A fierce protectiveness bubbled up inside me as I yanked back from him. "She didn't do this." I gestured a hand at Sydney. "You already questioned her at length, and you let her go."

Confusion, then understanding, rippled across Sydney's expression. "We simply didn't have enough evidence to prove or disprove her involvement." Eyes stern but rimmed in sympathy, Sydney waved the card. "This is incredibly specific evidence that we can't ignore."

"Where is she, Al?" Baze asked, voice quiet but commanding.

"No. I know how this goes." I set my hands on my hips. "You'll bring her in, and because you don't have any other leads, you'll arrest her for good measure simply to feel like you accomplished something."

Jaw clenching, Baze looped an arm around my shoulders again and directed me away from the chief inspector. I dug my heels into the carpet, but he firmed his muscles and managed to tow me out of earshot. He whirled, face inches from mine. "Why are you protecting her?" he whispered through gritted teeth. "You barely know her."

I knocked his hand from my shoulder. "She didn't do this."

Baze sighed, rubbing the bridge of his nose. "Al, the fact that you two share a gift means nothing. You don't know anything about her true motives. She raised Cornelius. Did you forget that? Look how he turned out. You may know her gift, but you don't really know *her*."

"Yes, I do. She's scared. There's a madman trying to hunt her down. She's only trying to survive. If you bring her in, it'll make her more vulnerable than she already is."

Baze aimed two fingers at my face, then at his. "Look me in the eyes and tell me that you are absolutely certain Miss Quinn's hands are clean. One hundred percent. No doubts. Do that and I'll drop the matter."

Our eyes locked. I tried to withstand the scrutiny, but as it had done when we were children, and every time since, his expectant gaze utterly disarmed me. Fidgeting under my growing helplessness, I turned his words over in my head. Could I honestly say I knew the true intent of Katherine's motives? Could I trust that everything she had said was the truth? Cornelius had been her protégé, after all, and he had weaved an incredible tale of deception. Though I felt a connection to Katherine dwelling deep in my heart, skepticism had come to reside next to it.

Finally, Baze's stare snapped the last of my resolve. I closed my eyes and whispered, "St. Catherine's Hospital. The almshouse. That's the last place I saw her."

Nausea wrung my stomach during the entire drawn-out trip back to the hotel. I tried not to dwell on what I knew was occurring at that very moment—that policemen were storming the almshouse to take Katherine into custody. Yes, the presence of a card from her deck raised valid questions, but in my eyes, the likelihood that it had been planted was equally as high. *Please let it all be a misunderstanding.*

A mounting restlessness emanated from Baze as we retreated to the room. From the corner of my eyes, I noticed him favoring his leg—even more than he had the last several days. Coupled with his quivering hands, the behavior roused suspicion in me. Was he worried about the case? Or did he have something else on his mind?

The moment I latched the door, Baze turned on me, an accusing finger aimed at my nose. "What was that back there?"

I stopped short, jaw squared, hand still on the doorknob. "What was what?"

"Why do you have to be so difficult?" He slapped his hand on the panel beside my head with a blunt *thud*. "You know what I do. You know how important it is that we have all the information possible, but you impeded the investigation by withholding information and embarrassing me in front of the chief inspector. Don't you want this solved? Don't you want these deaths to stop?"

"Of course, I do." I crossed my arms, lifting on my toes to look at him eye to eye. "But Katherine is my friend, and I don't wish to break what little trust we've begun to build."

"That's not trust, Al. Trust works both ways, but what has she told you, eh? Not much by the sound of it." His warm breath buffeted my cheek. "Do you trust her more than me?"

"That's not fair." I dropped my voice low. "You know that's not true."

"Do I?" His brow crinkled in a frown. "If it wasn't true, you would have told us where she was straightaway."

"I simply don't believe in assuming the worst about a person. You should respect that."

Pain soured his expression. "And you should respect me enough to trust that I know what I'm doing."

"I *do*."

Pressing the heels of my hands into his chest, I tried to push him back, but he snatched up my wrists and glowered down at me. I opened my mouth, intent to continue the argument, when I realized that my arms trembled in his grasp—but I wasn't the one trembling. "Why are you shaking so violently?" I squinted. "What has gotten into you? What's wrong?"

He released me, stepped back, and rubbed his palms on his stomach. "Nothing." But the distractedness in his eyes implied otherwise.

Keeping his hands rooted to his trunk, he pivoted in a dizzy half-turn and stumbled toward the hall cabinet—the place he kept his medicine.

Righteous fury awakened in me, originating from my desire to see him well and to see him whole. Without pain. Without hindrance. But he couldn't achieve that with a deceitful drug, not when it was altering his very being and killing our marriage before it had barely begun to breathe.

I stomped in his wake, darted around him, and blocked the cabinet door with my body. "Enough of this."

He drew up short, wild rage swirling in his eyes. "Move, Adelynn."

"No, you need to stop." I braced my legs. "I don't like what this is doing to you. You're utterly reliant on that drug, and it's changing you. You're barely the same person any—"

"I said move." Baze seized my arms and shoved.

I stumbled backward. The cabinet's corner bit into my back, and my head smacked the wall. Pain fired through my spine and into my skull. Black spots impeded my vision. I grappled for anything to prevent myself from toppling to the floor and managed to dig my fingernails into the cabinet's wood.

Baze stood stock still, eyes wide with horror. His mouth barely moved as he murmured, "Adelynn . . . Adelynn, I didn't mean to." He reached toward me.

A cry escaped my lips as I scrambled away, anguished by the fear that gripped me. *He hurt me. Baze hurt me. I can't believe he did that.* Keeping him pinned under my frantic gaze, I edged along the wall until I was clear of him, then bolted for the exit, for escape.

"W-wait!" His voice broke. "I'm sorry."

I ignored his pleas and slammed the door behind me. Raw tears spurted, but I blinked rapidly to banish them. My head shrieked with pain. The place where it had struck the wall throbbed. All this time, a killer had been poisoning people throughout the city, but at the same time, right before my very eyes, my own husband had been succumbing to his own poison—and I hadn't even noticed. How could I have let this happen? How could I have been so blind?

Forgive me, Baze. Forgive me, Lord.

Fueled by resolve—and guilt—I charged toward the front desk.

Mr. Everett glanced up with a smile, but he quickly sobered and lowered his newspaper. "Whatever is the matter? You look affright."

Smacking my palms on the counter, I said, "I need to use your telephone."

Stunned to silence, Mr. Everett pointed me in the direction of the machine. I wasted no time in requesting a London connection, and the moment Frederick picked up, I blurted, "He's gotten worse."

Frederick didn't miss a beat. "What's happened?"

"He . . ." A sticky lump choked my words, tears springing anew.

I don't know if I can say it. I can't . . . but I have to.

My voice weakened into a whisper. "He hurt me."

There came a long pause. "Where are you right now?"

"Safe."

Another pause. "I'll be there immediately. Stay where you are. And stay away from him."

"I will."

When we hung up, I teetered, arms numb at my sides, and allowed everything to sink in. That wasn't Baze. I refused to believe it. That was the result of the horrible drug he was taking. All because of his leg. All because he'd come to save me from Cornelius.

"Mrs. Ford?"

I whirled.

Mr. Everett stood nearby, expression concerned. "Are you all right? Is there anything I can do?"

I debated whether to tell him about what had occurred but ultimately thought better of it. "The matter is being taken care of," I said curtly.

Still, I needed something to occupy me while I waited for Frederick to arrive, something to make good use of the couple of hours it would take for his drive from London to Bath. I couldn't return to the room—with the state in which I'd left Baze, that was out of the question—but I wanted to remain nearby in case he attempted to flee.

I filled my lungs and tried to lighten my expression. "Actually, there is something you could do."

"Name it."

"Provide a distraction."

Mr. Everett stroked his mustache. "What sort of distraction are you after?"

I tilted my head. "Do you still have those newspapers?"

As it turned out, Mr. Everett kept quite the extensive archive of newspapers behind the counter. Once again, a niggling thought made me wonder whether he was a mere hobbyist or if something more significant fueled his quest for knowledge.

Given the lateness of the hour, it proved quite easy to find an empty table in the darkened dining hall. Mr. Everett trailed me inside and laid the newspapers out before me. "Good luck," he murmured. "I shall be close by should inspiration strike."

As he turned, I called after him. "Oh, Mr. Everett?"

He looked back. "Yes?"

"If my husband appears in the lobby, would you fetch me?"

"Of course." He bowed and then retreated.

The hands of the large grandfather clock nearby meandered ever around and around as I shuffled through the newspapers and buried myself in the material. A baroness. A violinist. A magician. All poisoned with cyanide, which matched the nature of another string of murders from fifteen years ago. The man had never been caught.

So, was this the same man who had returned to wreak havoc upon Bath once again? Or was it someone new attempting to emulate the monster who came before? Provided the latter was the case, what was their motive?

Then there was Katherine. Someone had targeted her, tried to poison her too. On the surface, that incident appeared unrelated to the other three, but did she fit into this scheme somehow? For the moment, Baze believed her to be a guilty party in the murders, but was he correct? She seemed genuine by all accounts—in her confession, in her wariness, in her desire to preserve her life—but it could all be a ploy to misdirect us. What did I *really* know about her?

I snorted softly. A year ago, I hadn't thought to ask such questions, and the oversight had resulted in my being deceived. As much as I wanted to believe otherwise, my powers of discernment where people were involved left much to be desired.

Interest piqued as I came across an older newspaper, its curling pages yellowed and brittle. I pulled it to the top of the pile and looked at the date. 1899. A large, bold headline attracted my gaze: "Suspects identified in rash of poisonings."

Barely able to contain my eagerness, I devoured the words on the page. The police had suspected three individuals and had included mug shots of each of the two men and one woman. The first two names failed to arouse any familiarity, but when my eyes settled on the last name, recognition registered.

Joseph Everett.

Shock paralyzed me. Mistrusting my own eyes, I read it two times, then a third, and finally once more. Then I studied the photograph printed above it. The man sported an unkempt beard and long dark hair swept to the side. With an oval jaw, round nose, and prominent forehead, the man looked nothing like our own Cecil Everett of the Empire Hotel.

However, I'd experienced enough, endured enough, to know that occurrences like this were anything but coincidence, and my observations of late—his interest in city happenings, his obsession with the daily news—reinforced my conclusion.

Mr. Everett knew something about the current murders, and all this time, he had kept quiet.

Ire fueling my muscles, I surged to my feet and stomped into the lobby. As I set my sights on the front counter, a flash from the front door lit in my periphery, but I focused solely on the host, intent on digging for the truth.

Mr. Everett's eyebrows rose. "Did you find something?"

I struggled to contain the tremor in my voice. "Mr. Everett, I've come across—"

"Adelynn!"

Frederick's urgent voice derailed my mission, and when I turned to see him rushing in through the door, all the horrible events from earlier came rushing back. It seemed the distraction had done its job in taking my mind off of Baze, but now I couldn't escape reality any longer. My mind fought to convince my heart that questioning Mr. Everett about everything he knew was more important than seeing to my husband—and it lost the battle.

Mr. Everett could wait. Baze came first—would always come first.

"Never mind." I tapped my index finger on the counter. "I have to see to something, but I'll return soon to discuss my discovery."

I met Frederick halfway through the lobby and stopped before him. Large rain spots speckled his shoulders, and dark, heavy bags lined his weary green eyes. When he spoke, he used a careful, almost exasperated tone. "Where is he?"

My stomach clenched. "If he's where I left him, he's in our room."

"Take me to him."

We trekked up the stairs to our suite. I pushed the door open slowly, managing to enter without drawing a creak from the hinges. Darkness greeted us. After my eyes adjusted, I noticed shadowed lumps strewn about the floor—flipped tables, upheaved couch cushions, and a broken glass. I curled a fist into my stomach as I pictured the rage that had yielded such wreckage.

A faint glow emanated from the bedroom. I held out a hand and gave Frederick a firm look that hopefully signaled that I wanted him to stay put and allow me to approach first. Thankfully, he seemed to understand the communication.

When I rounded the corner, I caught sight of a single flickering lamp on the bedside table. Its weak light illuminated Baze's cowering form on the floor. With knees drawn up to his chest and arms crossed over them, he sat with his back to the side of the bed and his forehead pressed against his arms.

I crept forward and carefully knelt before him. "Baze?" I whispered.

His body jolted, and his head whipped up. Crazed, bloodshot eyes locked with mine, and his sorrowful expression nearly pulled my heart right out of my chest.

Our eye contact lasted only a second before he buried his face in his hands and spoke, voice muffled. "Al, I'm sorry. I am so, so sorry. I don't know what . . . I should have never . . ."

As his voice cut off, I leaned toward him and placed a hand on his knee. "Baze, you need help. Let someone help you."

"I don't understand." His voice cracked. "I *did* get help. I *want* to stop this. But no matter what I do, it keeps getting worse. I . . . I don't know what to do anymore."

"Maybe you need a second opinion," I said gently.

"I don't know if that will—"

The floor creaked behind me, followed by Frederick's low but harsh voice. "Is this what you've been taking?"

Baze and I looked toward the door. Frederick's tall frame filled it. He held one of the tincture vials aloft. Baze tensed, and I sensed the fury building before it erupted.

"What are you doing here?" Baze vaulted to his feet. He stumbled a bit before finding his balance. I stood with him and held out a hand to steady him, but he batted it away and aimed a finger at me. "*You* called him, didn't you?" The wound in his voice cut deep, but his anger only made my defiance flare.

"Yes, I called him." I balled a hand into a fist. "Because you *need* help. It's help I can't give you, and it's help you're not getting."

"I said I was *trying*." Baze curled his lip. "This was between you and me. We've only been married a few measly weeks, and you're already sneaking around behind my back and betraying my trust— again. Does our marriage mean nothing to you?"

"Of course, it does," I snapped. "I could say the same of you. You haven't been talking to me. You've been lying about your medication. *You* are the one who's been sneaking around."

"That's enough." Frederick raised his voice, shutting us both up. He speared Baze with a glare. "Adelynn was right to call me. This has gotten out of hand. What happened to the regimen I put you on?"

Baze massaged his temples. "It wasn't working."

Frederick passed the vial beneath his nostrils and inhaled, then tilted it to his lips. His face contorted, and he spat to the side, staring at the vial, then at Baze. "*This* is what you've been taking?"

A beat of silence passed before Baze uttered a hesitant, "Yes."

"Basil, this is pure opium."

The air seemed to dissipate from the room. Confusion twisted Baze's face. "No, you're wrong. That . . . that can't be right. The therapist told me it was a weakened dose."

"There's nothing weak about this, I'm afraid. The only thing such a potent substance can accomplish is thrust you deep into the throes of addiction."

Baze's limbs trembled, his gaze darting around in a frenzy. "He lied to me. The bloody fraud lied to me."

"Who lied to you? Who is this therapist that you've been seeing?"

Baze's expression remained fixed, as though he hadn't heard the question.

Frederick clomped to his brother and slapped a hand down on his shoulder. "Basil, snap out of it. Who—"

With a sharp jerk, Baze rammed his elbow into Frederick's ribs, pulled from his touch, and darted out the door.

"Baze!" I shouted and jumped toward the door. I hesitated a moment to consider Frederick—who was curled over and gasping—but chose to pursue Baze. By the time I had made it to the conjoining room, Baze had already escaped out the door.

Coughing, Frederick stumbled out behind me. "Where's he gone?"

"I don't know." Fear steeled my muscles. He could go anywhere, do anything. He wasn't in his right mind. "We have to stop him, Frederick."

We sprinted to the lobby and came across an astonished Mr. Everett. Before he could get a word in, I said in a rush, "Did you see my husband?"

"Yes, he's just gone loping out into the street." Mr. Everett came around the counter, brows crumpled in worry. "What's going on? Can I help?"

Ignoring his inquiry, I ran to the door, burst through it, and peered into the darkness. The scattered lamps did little to illuminate the street, but the area sat empty. Quiet. Foreboding. I couldn't even detect the sound of footsteps.

"How did you get away so quickly?" I growled, kicking a heel into the ground. Helplessness seeped into my core. What had gotten into his head? What could I do? How could I stop him? "Lord God, help me find him," I whispered. "And keep him safe until I can."

A faint chill crawled up my arms, raising the hair and heightening my senses. For the second time since discovering my gift, I prayed for a vision. Yes, there was nothing I'd experienced thus far to make me believe that I could inhabit the body of anyone but Cornelius, Sully, or people they manipulated, but desperation urged me to try anything I could. Maybe—just maybe—I could see *something* that would help me locate Baze.

As I stood waiting, hoping, the darkness grew bleaker, and the chill made its way to my bones. Stiff and defeated, I looked directly into the halo of one of the streetlamps. As its light pierced my vision, I squinted and thrust my subconscious out in one last effort to see something useful.

The scene before me flickered—light, then dark, then light again. Finally, it dissolved into a shadowy scene. I was shuffling, panting, and dragging a heavy object at my feet. In the distance, I spotted a quaint little house, a gravel path, and a tiny wrought iron bench. A signpost reading, "Sebastian Cutler, Physiotherapist," marked the grass a few feet from the house. Then I looked down.

Baze lay limp at my feet, eyes shut, face gray as a corpse.

"Rest well, Inspector," I whispered with a calm masculine voice as I let him drop to the ground in a heap. Then I kicked out, shoving Baze over the side of the path and sending him tumbling into a shallow ditch.

Chapter Thirty-Two

WITH EACH STEP, BAZE'S LEG SHRIEKED with pain, but he couldn't stop. The fog in his mind, the chattering of his teeth, and the weakness in his limbs begged him to take another dose, but Frederick had confiscated his last vial. Besides, according to Frederick, the medicine Baze thought had been healing him had instead been poisoning him all along.

How could Sebastian have misled him? This whole time, he'd been executing a sinister plot to increase Baze's tolerance for the drug, causing him to crave more and more. But why? Why would a man who had devoted his life to helping people have schemed in such a way? Baze had fallen for the ruse like a fool, willingly overlooking any inconsistencies if it meant he would achieve relief from his pain.

Finally, he reached the long gravel path that led to Sebastian's home, which doubled as his office. Hobbling up the path, Baze passed by a man headed the opposite way. A quick glance revealed Charles Caine's surprised face, but Baze didn't have the time to engage him. He couldn't allow the therapist to flee.

A light from within confirmed Sebastian's presence. Baze pounded a fist on the door, but rather than wait for an invitation, he barged in.

The therapist looked up with alarm from where he stood near a far doorway, holding a stack of books. "Basil?" His curly white eyebrows drew together. "What is the meaning of this? Are you all right?"

Chest heaving, Baze left the door ajar and advanced toward Sebastian a few steps, finally brought to a halt by pulsing pain in his leg. "You lied to me," he snarled.

"I did what?" Sebastian set the books on a side table and swiped his hands together. "I think you're confused, Basil. Let's sit down, eh? We can talk—"

"Enough!" Baze pawed at his waistband, drew his gun, and aimed it at Sebastian. "I know everything. You've been poisoning me."

Blood drained from the therapist's face, and his palms lifted. Confusion wrinkled his face. "What do you mean?"

A distant creak sounded behind Baze, but he didn't flinch, didn't stop staking the doctor with his glare. "You know exactly what I mean. You've been poisoning me with opium. You claimed to have been helping me wean off, but you've been doing the opposite. You're trying to keep me addicted." Desperation squeezed Baze's chest. "Why? Why are you doing this?"

Sebastian's voice grew small and uncertain. "The tinctures were potent?"

"As if you didn't know." Sweat dripped between Baze's shoulder blades as he fought to keep his gun-wielding arm aloft. The weapon clacked as his hand shook.

"Basil, if what you say is true, then I am extremely sorry and take fault for what has happened," Sebastian said slowly, deliberately. "I should have been more diligent. Though I am not the one who mixes the tinctures, I prescribe them, and therefore, I take responsibility for their contents."

"You don't mix them . . ." Baze blinked, wading through murky memories. He dug deeper, barreling through recollections until the haze parted and he remembered what Sebastian had said when they'd first met and began the treatment. *"I had a local toxicologist concoct it for you. You might have met him—Charles Caine. He is employed by the Bath Police but often works as a toxicologist for hire in his time off."*

Baze's anger dimmed as he stared at Sebastian. "It wasn't you. You didn't do—"

Something fast and forceful struck the side of Baze's neck. His vision blotted out. The world turned, and he hit the floor.

Sebastian cried out. Grunting and scuffling whirred in Baze's ears, then the stark click of a key in a lock.

When the shock began to fade and Baze regained his vision, he found himself gaping at the ceiling. A heavy object compressed his body. Gasping for breath, he fought to focus his gaze and managed to recognize Caine. With his shins pinning Baze to the floor—one on his chest and one on his neck—the toxicologist sneered.

Baze opened his mouth, but his pinched windpipe trapped his words.

"You should have kept your nose out of matters that didn't concern you," Caine said, voice dripping with calm resentment. "You should have simply allowed the opium to do its job." Caine leaned more weight onto Baze's chest, lifted Baze's right arm, and rolled up the sleeve.

Baze flexed his fingers, realizing he no longer held the gun. He tried to fight back, but his limbs tingled with paralysis, the blow to his neck having rendered him useless.

A needle bit into the skin of Baze's inner arm. As a cool sensation twisted through his veins, he adjusted his head and managed to croak out, "Why?"

"I worried that your meddling would expose me prematurely, but your partnership with Sebastian Cutler offered me a convenient opportunity to keep you out of the way."

Dizziness spun the room. Baze struggled to keep his eyes open. "But you—"

Caine slipped a hand over Baze's mouth. "Shh. Succumb. Let it overtake you. You will be all the better for it. Once you're unconscious, you will no longer feel any pain." Caine squeezed Baze's arm. "It will appear as though you inflicted this upon yourself. Desperate to quell your cravings, you sought a more potent concoction and injected it straight into your bloodstream. An accidental overdose."

Caine's words cut in and out as the poison took hold in Baze's body, filling him with a wave of euphoria followed by a tsunami of fire. He tried to resist it, but the venom was already inside him, attacking every bone, every muscle, every cell.

This was it. He wasn't going to survive this time.

Chapter Thirty-Three

I SAT ON THE VERY EDGE of the passenger seat as we sped across Pulteney Bridge and toward the outskirts of the city, Frederick at the wheel and Mr. Everett leaning forward from the back seat. With the details I'd provided—and the condemning name that had been written so prominently on the sign—we had concluded that Baze had set off toward Sebastian Cutler's residence. As the only person familiar with the city and the therapist, Mr. Everett didn't hesitate to abandon his post in order to guide us in the right direction.

Frustrated, I slapped a palm on the dash. "Hurry, Frederick. Baze could already be lying in a ditch."

"I'm going as quickly as I can," he said through gritted teeth as he veered around a corner.

I closed my eyes, trying not to dwell on the horrific image I'd seen of Baze—unconscious and fading—but it invaded every corner of my mind. Yes, Baze had a head start, but we had left straightaway after realizing he'd gone. Surely we would reach him in time before the worst should happen. I refused to believe otherwise.

Mr. Everett jutted his arm over the front seat and pointed. "There."

Frederick and I braced and stared through the windshield. The dirt road, the house in the distance, the sign out front—this was it.

Halfway up the drive, the tires skidded as Frederick pulled the car to a halt. I forced the door open and hopped out. Slipping on the loose gravel, I made straight for the ditch. My heart thudded in my ribs. I peered through the darkness, praying harder than I ever had before.

That's when I saw him—a mere lump lying in the crook of the ditch. I scrambled down to him, screaming, "He's here!"

Falling to my knees, I reached for Baze. His fully limp body proved nearly impossible to move, but my adrenaline-filled efforts won the battle. I clutched him tight to my chest. With sunken cheeks, pale skin, and blueish lips, he appeared dead. Were it not for ragged, uneven breathing rasping in his throat, I would have assumed the worst.

Frederick dropped to my side and felt Baze's forehead, then pried open one of his eyes. It darted about, the pupil a mere pinprick. "He's overdosed." Frederick swore, but when his gaze landed on Baze's rolled-up sleeve, he stiffened.

"What?" I sucked in a breath. "What is it?"

His face whitening, Frederick thumbed the inside of Baze's elbow above a bruise about the size of a farthing. "He's injected it . . ."

"Injected what? What do you mean?"

Frederick swallowed hard, then spoke, his voice wobbly. "It appears he's injected opium directly into his veins . . . and we don't yet have a substance that can negate it once it has entered the bloodstream."

Crippling fear settled on my chest and labored my breathing. "No. There must be a way. We can't give up."

Frederick's empathetic eyes met mine. "I shall do everything in my power to save him, but our best hope now is that his body built a strong enough tolerance that it can fight this . . . or that he didn't inject enough to kill." Frederick snapped his fingers toward Mr. Everett. "Help me carry him to the car. We have to hurry."

The men lugged Baze up the hill and heaved him into the back seat. I climbed in after him and sat with his head cradled in my lap, caressing his face, smoothing his hair, and praying that he would hold on a little longer.

"Try to rouse him," Frederick said as we careened onto the street. "We can't let him keep sleeping."

I called Baze's name and shook his arm. "Wake up." I patted his cheek, gently but with force. "Please, Baze, wake up." His breath hitched, stopping every so often, but he remained unconscious.

We flew back to the hotel—Frederick said the hospital was too great a distance—and rushed to get him settled in our bed. I sat by his side and watched Frederick hustle about the room, retrieving a basin and swirling a mixture of some kind in a glass. He pushed the basin into my arms and said, "Move." When I obeyed, he took my place and slapped Baze's face with an audible *crack*. Then did it again.

I flinched, but knew it was the only way to snap Baze out of his stupor.

Finally, Baze's eyelids fluttered, and he mumbled incoherently.

"Good. Drink this." Frederick grasped the back of Baze's head and raised the glass to his lips, but Baze smashed his mouth shut and struggled. "Please, Baze. Drink it," Frederick growled. "I'm trying to save your life, you idiot." The words seemed to strike a chord in Baze. He stilled, hesitated, then parted his lips to allow Frederick to pour the liquid down his throat.

"Adelynn, ready the basin," Frederick ordered.

I thrust it out just as Baze curled over the side of the bed and retched. Frederick was using every available advancement in medicine to help Baze, but with the drug already raging through his veins, would induced vomiting truly help? Or was it done in vain? I prayed that the stipulations Frederick had mentioned would prove true—that Baze's body could overcome this poison.

Once Baze had emptied his stomach and his heaves grew hollow, he collapsed back against the pillow.

"Oh, no you don't." Frederick yanked him into a sitting position.

Baze's face scrunched in anguish as he weakly fought against his brother. "Stop, Fred. Please. I need to . . . sleep."

As I watched the man I loved teeter on the precipice between life and death, I found myself numb in both emotion and body. I couldn't imagine losing him. But what could I do to help, to keep him with the living? Nothing, it seemed. I was utterly helpless, unable to do anything useful but pray and watch events unfold.

Mr. Everett touched my arm and whispered, "Is there anyone I can call for you?"

It took me a moment to comprehend his words. "His parents," I managed. "Alistair and Frances Ford. And you could call my mother, Caroline Spencer. Oh, and Emily Bennett. They're all in London. You should also let Chief Inspector Whitaker know."

He nodded. "I shall contact them straightaway."

When I turned back, Frederick and Baze still wrestled with one another. In the midst of their battle, Baze's eyes drifted to me. He froze. Shame drained the color from his face. His purpled lips trembled, mouth opening as though to speak, but he remained mute. When he looked again to Frederick, however, he stopped resisting and allowed his brother to hold him in a sitting position and tip the glass to his lips once more.

I sighed. *Thank you for quelling his stubbornness, Lord. Now, let Frederick's remedies heal him. Don't take him away from me.*

A fierce chill gripped me. My stomach lurched, light flashed, and my consciousness yanked away from the scene.

No, this can't happen now. Not with Baze in such a dire state.

Darkness surrounded me, but I could just make out a small jail cell before me. Within the cell, standing tall in defiance, Katherine glared at me through the bars.

"You should have known you could not escape," I said coolly. "I was tasked to kill you, and I always follow through."

For the first time, I saw fear enter Katherine's eyes. Her chin lifted. "He's using you, you know. You're a mere pawn in his eyes."

"No, I am doing this of my own free will. For if I do this, I can achieve the justice I have so long sought."

The vision faded, and then I was back.

So, the police had arrested Katherine, and now that she had nowhere to run, her pursuer had found her. He had come to finish what he started, exactly as I feared would happen. What should I do? I couldn't leave Baze like this, but if I didn't, Katherine may not escape this final attack on her life. Baze was in the expert hands of his brother. Katherine had no one.

Knowing what I must do, I watched Baze for a time, remembering all of the joyous memories we had created and experienced together. Though I felt confident in my decision, my stomach still clenched in guilt. Unable to stall any longer, I cleared my throat and said, "Frederick, I . . . have to step out for a moment. I shouldn't be long."

The words caused me to wince. In truth, I didn't know how long it would take—or what I would encounter. I could very well be putting my own life in danger.

I passed Mr. Everett in the lobby—he spoke gravely into the telephone and didn't notice me pass by—and stepped out into the night. Unprepared for the stark chill of the evening, I folded my arms and held them close to my chest as I turned right and made for the police station.

Nearing its entrance, I noticed faint black tendrils seeping out from beneath the doors and felt the temperature slowly drop. The cold seized hold of my core and spread out to my limbs. I found myself tensing as though bracing for an impact.

This was the same darkness that had trailed Cornelius wherever he went.

Lord God, go with me into this place.

I forged ahead and entered. My breath turned to haze in the cold air. Eerily quiet, the space seemed to close in as though trying to trap me within. I crept forward, heel to toe, eyes fixed on the open doorway ahead.

As I reached the threshold, a man came careening around the corner. We both let out a cry and drew back. Gathering myself, I recognized Sydney.

The tips of his ears blazed red beneath the golden hair sticking out around them. "Adelynn, I apologize. I didn't hear you enter. Mr. Everett told me what happened. I was about to head that way."

"Good. I think Baze would be blessed by your presence." I glanced behind him, hoping to catch a glimpse of Katherine.

He leaned into my sightline. "Why are you here? Should you not be by your husband's side?"

I tried not to let the guilt unearthed by the accusation in his words show on my face. "I need to speak to Katherine. Baze is in a doctor's hands for the moment, so there's nothing I can do."

"Ah, I see. Well, she's through there in a holding cell." He pointed down the hall. "You don't mind if I make for the hotel, do you?"

"Please. Go. I shouldn't be long."

He nodded. "Our toxicologist is finishing up some work, so if you hear someone milling about, don't be alarmed." He reached forward as though to squeeze my shoulder but must have thought better of it and lowered his arm. "Baze will be all right."

Aggravated, I couldn't help but narrow my eyes. "I know."

"Yes, well, I thought it would do you good to hear it said aloud." With that, he breezed from the precinct and slammed the door behind him. The sound and vibration shuddered through the space and tensed my shoulders.

With Sydney gone, the station fell back into its unsettling quiet, interrupted only by muffled shuffling in the distance—likely the toxicologist.

I plunged into the hallway and found my way to the holding area without incident. An oil lamp upon a desk in the corner illuminated two side-by-side cells. One stood empty, its door hanging ajar, while the other was locked tight to keep its prisoner trapped within. I peered through the bars straight at Katherine.

Dressed in an emerald dress, her hair loose and cascading over her shoulders, Katherine sat in her best posture with one leg crossed over the other and her hands out to the sides for support. Her deep green eyes caught a shine from the lamp, which ignited the fire burning within her.

I folded my arms. "Care to explain yourself?"

She lifted a hand and examined her fingernails. "That depends, angel. Do you trust me or not?"

Not expecting the pointed question, I found myself unsure how to answer. Rather than betray my insecurity, I shrugged. "I haven't decided yet."

In a flash, she bolted to her feet, came to the front of the cell, and grasped one of the bars. "I didn't do this. Despite what you think, I had nothing to do with that magician."

"Then why did the police find one of your treasured cards on his person?"

A look of irritation, shame even, crossed her features. She scratched at the cell bar with a nail. "The day you insisted upon paying me a visit, we were followed, as I feared we would be." Her lips tightened. "Sully found me."

Alarm bells clanged in my head. "He what? But doesn't he . . . how are you . . ."

"How am I still alive?" She snorted. "Sully is a coward at heart. He claimed he couldn't bear to kill me with his own hands."

Afraid to ask but wanting the truth, I whispered, "So what happened?"

Katherine shifted her jaw and hugged her arms tight against her chest. "We did what you might imagine, angel." A bitter laugh rumbled in her throat. "I know what you must be thinking. How could I abandon my morals so swiftly? Well, believe you me, I thought my heart had moved on. I have spent many a night mourning what we once had. But he was—is—my first and only love." Tears sparkled in the lamplight as her eyes met mine. "This was . . . a chance to say my final goodbye." She straightened her back and sighed. "When I awoke in the morning, he was gone. I imagine that while I still slept, he pinched the card from my deck so that he might blame me for the magician's murder."

For the first time in a good while, I found myself at a loss for words. I'd come barging in here so sure that Katherine had pulled the wool over my eyes just as Cornelius had done. Even if the story seemed unlikely, I found myself believing her. The malevolent energy I'd sensed upon entering seemed to end at the jail cell. In fact, all that poured forth from between the bars was warmth—despite Katherine's hardened exterior.

Finding my voice, I asked, "Why does Sully want to frame you?

What does that accomplish?"

"Keeping me trapped in Bath isn't enough. He knows that. Pinning a crime on me puts the police on my trail and flushes me out of hiding."

A creak and a few shuffles emitted from the hallway. I'd forgotten anyone else was here with us, but I kept my focus on Katherine. "So then, what happens next? Where do we go from here?"

"Well"—she planted her hands on her hips—"given that you're the reason I'm trapped here in the city, angel, I'd say you should find a way to break me out of here. I think I spied a ring of keys hanging in the other room."

I grimaced. "I can't break the law like that, even for a cause such as this."

She shrugged. "It's not so hard. I'd pick the lock myself, but they confiscated my . . ." Katherine's gaze latched onto something over my shoulder. Her expression morphed into shock.

I half-turned.

Thwack.

A hard object struck the curve of my neck and shoulder. My vision dissipated. Thoughts fled. The world tipped.

Chapter Thirty-Four

SENSATION BEGAN BLEEDING BACK INTO MY limbs. A pair of hands were hooked painfully under my arms. My body slid along the floor. Then the hands disappeared and let me flop over. A cell door screeched before clanging shut with a click.

Blinking, I struggled to push myself upright. Katherine stood rigid, eyes wide and feral, like a predator caught in the talons of a larger predator. Her gaze locked on a short, hunched man lurking outside the jail cells, one of which now held me prisoner. As the man's face came into focus, I found myself repulsed by the dark features, devoid of emotion. Sydney's parting words echoed in my confusion. The toxicologist had still been in the police station. Charles Caine?

"You're here for me, aren't you?" Katherine said, the accusation a low growl in her throat.

Caine regarded her a moment, then aimed an unnerving stare at me. "I would say that I am sorry for involving you in private matters, Mrs. Ford, but you, unfortunately, couldn't help but involve yourself. You and your husband are two of a kind." His top lip quivered. "If only you had stuck to your holiday and kept to yourselves. If you had, I'd have dealt with Miss Quinn ages ago and brought the murderer at large to justice."

The murderer? Was he referring to the person responsible for the three poisonings? How did he think he could've brought this killer to justice on his own? Wasn't such a notion in direct opposition to the fact that he was the one trying to off Katherine?

Grasping my head, I frowned against the angry pulse in my temples. "How can you reconcile such a thing? Attempting to find the person responsible for these recent deaths while at the same time making attempts on Katherine's life? Do you believe that finding the killer will absolve you of your own guilt and the punishment that would come from killing her?"

Caine breathed a laugh through his nose. "You're thick, Mrs. Ford. I have only ever had one objective, and that is to find the man responsible for taking my son from me fifteen years ago. Killing Miss Quinn is merely the means by which I can accomplish such."

As I retreated within my mind, trying to make sense of the new information bombarding me, time slowed. Mr. Everett's explanation about the nature of the killer from long ago, the meticulous way he went about committing the crimes, came back to me.

"So then, the question we must ask ourselves is this—is the individual copying the last killer out of admiration or out of spite? After all, the case was never solved last time, leaving questions unanswered and justice unfulfilled. Maybe our current killer is purely out for revenge, not against his victims, but against his predecessor."

The lamp flickered. Caine only desired justice for his son, and to achieve that, he had to find a way to draw the original killer out of hiding. He had indeed found a method to do so, but it had cost the lives of three individuals.

Caine was the murderer we had been hunting.

Despite lingering dizziness, I wobbled to a stand and grasped one of the cell bars for support. A cacophony of words fought to escape my lips, but I simply said, "This won't bring your son back."

Caine clenched his jaw, muscles quivering. "You do not have children yet, Mrs. Ford, so you cannot possibly know what will take away this pain that I feel."

"You're right." The brilliant faces of my father and of Bennett filled my mind, drenching me with loneliness. "But I have known loss, and I watched the man responsible for those losses die before my very eyes." I leaned my forehead against the cold bars. "It didn't take the pain away. Only time and the grace of God can dull this hurt we feel."

Caine sneered. "It's too late, and I am too close. I must see this through to the end and draw that monster out of his hellhole so he can face the justice he deserves."

What more could I say? There was no convincing a man so consumed by grief and revenge.

"You're not a killer, Mr. Caine," Katherine said, her tone soft but blunt. "Sully approached you, didn't he? Said he'd help you find a way to uncover the man who killed your boy if you agreed to kill me in return. I am sorry to tell you, but he is using you. Manipulating you."

Caine half-squinted one eye at her. "I'm afraid I can't keep making conversation, Miss Quinn." He speared me with a glare. "I'm close to flushing him out, and I refuse to let you make my work meaningless. I am sorry that I had to incapacitate your husband, but soon you will join him in oblivion."

Fury flared within me. "*You* are the one who attacked Baze?"

The toxicologist paused, and ever so slowly, the blood drained from his face. "The inspector survived?"

I clamped my mouth shut. Caine had thought he'd succeeded at killing Baze. How could I have so foolishly betrayed such precious information?

Jerking as though awakening from a trance, the toxicologist stooped and placed on the floor a small vial with a wick trailing out of its narrow opening.

I jostled the cell bars. "What is that? What are you doing?"

"Do not fear." He rifled through his coat pockets. "Once the fumes consume the room, you will fall asleep quickly. Your death will be painless. It's the best I can do—"

"Put the matches down, Charles."

The stern yet familiar voice tugged my gaze to the doorway. *Mr. Everett?*

With confident steps, Mr. Everett eased into the room and positioned himself between the cells and the deranged killer.

Rigid, Caine straightened slowly, leaving the wick untouched.

"Let there be no more of this." Mr. Everett held out a peace-giving hand. "Because, my friend, I'm afraid it *is* all for naught."

Caine bared his teeth. "What are you on about, Cecil?"

Mr. Everett cast an apologetic glance back at me before focusing on Caine. "The man you seek, the one against whom you want revenge, is dead."

Even more color evaporated from Caine's face. "You're lying."

"The man's name was Joseph Everett. He was my stepfather." Mr. Everett winced as though his own words brought pain. "I was only a young man when he began his murderous spree. Despite having lived with the man for the majority of my life, I knew nothing of his involvement, of his twisted mind. He had spent his life working with chemicals and developing new blends of deadly substances. The murders allowed him the ability to put his concoctions to the test." Mr. Everett swallowed. "Several years ago, Joseph fell ill, and while on his deathbed, he left my mother and I a note confessing to the crimes. She destroyed the letter and made me swear upon her grave that I would never speak of it."

Mr. Everett paused and stroked his mustache, remaining silent for several agonizing moments. When he finally resumed, his voice cracked. "Joseph claimed that your son's death had been an accident. He had been trying to target—"

"Stop." Caine grasped his head.

"No, Charles, you need to stop." Mr. Everett sighed deeply. "I'm sorry that you can't get the justice you seek, and I'm sorry that I kept this secret buried. Had I known you harbored so much hatred that you were willing to stoop to Joseph's level, I'd have confessed long ago. The blood of those individuals is on my hands as much as it is on yours."

"I said stop," Caine growled.

"There is no purpose in this, Charles. All those people. All those lives ruined. You've been chasing a ghost. Do you think your son would have wanted this?"

An animalistic snarl escaped Caine's mouth. He scooped up a stray pen laying upon the table and lunged at Mr. Everett. He snagged a fistful of Mr. Everett's hair, yanked his head to the side, and rammed the pointed tip of the pen into the flesh under Mr. Everett's chin.

A scream burst from my lips as Mr. Everett clutched at his neck. Panicked moans gurgled in his throat. His knees buckled, and Caine kept a hold on him until he collapsed, convulsing. Blood drenched his torso and seeped onto the floor, its thick river racing toward my feet. Mr. Everett's eyes locked on me, and I stared in horror as he grew still.

Caine spun back to the vial he'd placed on the floor. This time, he pulled out a match and lit the wick.

"Stop!" Desperation squeezed my voice. "Don't do this."

But Caine took no heed and escaped from the room without even looking back.

My body froze as I watched dark smoke begin rising from the vial and inching toward Mr. Everett's body—toward us.

Katherine dropped to her knees and reached through the cell bars. She managed to snag Mr. Everett's arm and heaved him closer to her. She pawed at his suit, either not caring or not noticing that blood had transferred to her hands. She came up with a pin. Bending it out straight, she popped up to her feet. Then she inserted it into the keyhole of the cell and began working.

Within seconds, the lock clicked open, and she pushed the cell open, shoving Mr. Everett's body aside. Katherine stepped over him, dodged the vial, and bolted for the door.

"Wait!" I shouted, alert. "You're just going to leave me?"

Her gait hesitated for only a moment. Then, her bright red hair flashed as she fled through the opening.

Plunged into shocked silence, I gaped at the empty doorway. My labored breathing roared in my ears. After everything, after all the time we'd spent learning to understand one another, how could Katherine abandon me so willingly? Though she'd stayed in Bath for my sake, it was clear she'd only been biding her time, waiting for the moment when she could escape me guilt-free. I'd been duped again by another whom

I'd trusted. Would I never learn to hold my trust closer to my chest?

No matter. Everything was about to end.

Thick smoke billowed from the vial. I clapped my hands over my mouth and tried to slow my breaths, but my head had already begun spinning. My skin tingled. I glanced to Mr. Everett, hoping, praying that somehow he yet lived, but the thickening stream of blood and absence of movement confirmed that he was gone.

"God, forgive me," I whispered as my mind grew fuzzier. Nausea roiled.

Footsteps clapped toward the room. "Don't be so dramatic, angel." Katherine emerged, a ring of keys clutched in her hands. She darted to my cell and unlocked it. "Do you really believe me to be so callous that I'd abandon you at the drop of a hat? Come. We have to hurry."

I barely had time to feel relief as her strong grip pulled me from the treacherous cage and helped me escape the room. I clung to her. "You certainly left plenty of opportunity for doubt to creep in."

She huffed. "Really, angel, it's like you barely know me."

When we burst from the police station, I bent over and gasped in fresh air. The clean oxygen cleared my head and chased away the nausea. "Thank you," I said between wheezes.

"Don't thank me yet. That psychopath has a head start, and he knows your husband's alive."

Panic stabbed my stomach as I looked to the hotel. *Baze.*

Chapter Thirty-Five

HOT STEAM SURROUNDED BAZE, COAXING HIS mind to the edge of the shadows but not quite pulling him free. The sensation of water on his skin and strong hands saturating him kept his mind tethered to the earth, when it wanted nothing more than to spiral into the depths.

Everything hurt. Fire raged in his veins. His empty stomach contracted but had nothing left to expel. Was this how he would die?

"Hold on, Baze. Stay with me."

Frederick's distorted voice created an anchor for Baze to home in on. He tried to respond, but he wasn't even sure his mouth moved.

Hands hoisted him up. The world pitched, angering his stomach further. He dry heaved and sagged against Frederick. Water splashed against his shivering form.

Once dried and helped into clothes, Baze felt his brother guiding him back to the bed. When Baze flopped onto his back, the plushness of the bedding seemed to swallow him whole. Through half-shut eyes, he stared up at the ceiling, pulse quickening, as his vision slowly came into focus.

"Look at me, Baze."

Frederick again, but try as he might, Baze couldn't command his eyes to move.

"Hey, look at me."

Thwap.

Light pain stung Baze's cheek. The small strike snapped him out of his stupor, and his eyes jumped to his brother's stern face. Baze grimaced and moaned. "*Ow . . .*"

Shoulders bowing forward, Frederick released a large sigh. "You're all right." He placed a hand on Baze's head and ruffled his hair ever so slightly. "Get some rest, little brother."

Baze tried for a snarky quip but could only twitch one eyebrow.

"Yes, you have my permission to sleep now." His voice sounded heavy, weary. "I'll wake you when it's time." Frederick turned and headed toward the door.

Baze shifted, tilting his head back to allow for as much breath as possible, and managed to croak out, "Al?"

Frederick glanced back. "She stepped out for a moment. I'll send her in as soon as she returns." Then he was gone.

Consuming silence caused Baze to fully focus on the pain constricting his body. Never mind his leg—this pain was worse tenfold. His eyes wandered, rolled back, as sleep tugged at him. His thoughts trekked through unreachable lands. Perhaps he slept. Perhaps not. He wasn't sure.

After an indistinguishable stretch of time, the creak of a door and soft footsteps tickled his ears. Bleary-eyed, he attempted to concentrate on the individual who had entered. "Al?" he whispered.

Rather than answer, the figure moved closer, the shape and features slowly melting into view through the blurriness.

Charles Caine.

Baze's body jolted in shock. He tried to move, to escape—anything—but every little twitch set his muscles on fire.

Caine halted beside the head of the bed and stared with dead eyes. "This is all because of you. You and your wife," he murmured, voice hoarse. "All was going to plan, but that's ruined now." Caine brushed his fingers over Baze's perspiring forehead, and Baze caught a glimpse of red stains on the man's skin. "Apparently, I misjudged the dosage needed to do you in." He grimaced. "I didn't want to do it this way. After all, I promised you a painless death, but it appears I have no choice." Caine curled his hands around Baze's neck.

Baze tensed, opened his mouth to call for help.

Caine squeezed.

Chapter Thirty-Six

A CONTINUOUS STREAM OF PRAYER FILTERED through my mind as Katherine and I sprinted to the hotel. My ribs ached with each frantic inhale as they battled against my constricting corset. *I'm coming, Baze. Hold on a little longer. Hold on.*

I surged through the door ahead of Katherine, took the steps of the grand staircase two at a time, and swerved into the hallway. Up ahead, Frederick and Sydney conversed near the entrance of my room. Still in full sprint, I yelled, "Caine!"

They spun toward me. Frederick's face paled. "Adelynn, what—"

"Caine, the toxicologist." I halted before them, panting. "Was he here?"

"Yes," Sydney replied. "He's gone in to see to your husband."

I bolted. Their shouts of alarm and confusion trailed me as I burst into our room and dashed into the bedchamber. The sickening scene I stumbled upon took a moment to digest. With his back to me, Caine bent over Baze's prone figure on the bed. The toxicologist's hands throttled Baze's throat as his limbs twitched and pumped in a weak struggle.

An inhuman cry tore from my lips. I lunged at Caine, flailing, slashing. My nails found purchase. He reared up, swung his elbow at my face. It cracked my jaw. My ears rang, but I only fought harder. Whirling toward me, he aimed for my face again, but Sydney leapt between us and intercepted the blow.

The room erupted in pandemonium, filling with a cacophony of shouts and a flurry of bodies. Sydney knocked Caine to the floor as Katherine's arms came around me and yanked me from the scuffle.

Coughing, Baze writhed, and Frederick leapt to his side.

With a knee on Caine's chest, Sydney snapped handcuffs onto his wrists. Then he struggled to his feet and wrestled the toxicologist up with him, jostling him for good measure.

Muscles spasming, I tried to pounce at Caine again, but Katherine steeled her arms and held me back. "Easy, angel," she whispered. "Easy."

"He killed Mr. Everett," I blurted, my voice a mixture of fury and sorrow. Sydney and Frederick gaped at me while Caine's lip curled. "And he poisoned all those people. He was trying to draw the killer from fifteen years ago out of the shadows. For his son. For revenge. He's utterly mad."

Strong emotion urged me forward, and this time, Katherine allowed me to pull from her grasp. On wobbly legs, I planted myself in front of Caine and leveled my gaze at him. I reached deep inside myself and tried to sense what lay within this man's heart—the same darkness that had infected Cornelius and allowed him to manipulate others . . . or a darkness of his own?

My probing yielded nothing save for raw malice and violent grief.

I shook my head. "You weren't compelled to do any of this, were you? You did this all on your own accord. You wanted to do it."

Harsh tears glinted in Caine's eyes. "I wanted to achieve justice for Isaac. Someone needed to pay for what was done to him. Is that so wrong? Hmm?"

Pity wound in my stomach. So much resentment, so much heartbreak—but it had manifested in such a twisted way.

"What you did was evil, righteous as your cause may have been," I whispered. "I pray you'll come to see that before the end and turn to the One who can save you."

Teeth bared, Caine twitched toward me, but Sydney jerked him back. "That's enough. It's over, Caine." Sydney caught the man up by the scruff of his neck and steered him out the door.

The tension in my muscles—which had been building gradually

for so long—dissipated all at once. Relief snuffed out my apprehension, and thankfulness replaced my fear. After our holiday had mutated into yet another race to catch a killer, I worried that we would never have the chance to live normal lives or experience a normal marriage.

Of course, considering that my visions appeared here to stay, such a notion no longer seemed possible, even if we never encountered another murderer again. However, I couldn't entirely forget the fact that Katherine's husband, Sully, yet wandered free. Would he continue pursuing her? How long would he give chase before backing down—or would they forever be trapped in a cycle of playing a fatal game of cat and mouse?

For now at least, I tried not to dwell on thoughts of what-if and instead focused on the present. We'd conquered evil, and for that, thankfulness overflowed within me. Thankfulness for provision. For perseverance. For our lives. *Thank you, Lord God. Thank you.*

My eyes drifted to Baze. Frederick sat over him, protective and alert. I wandered toward them. Though Baze's coughs had ceased, his breaths rattled in his chest. Fixed on the bruises marring his throat, I said, "Is he—"

"He'll be okay." Frederick brushed a careful hand over Baze's sweaty forehead. "I don't think the man had enough time to do any lasting damage."

Sudden tears leaked from my eyes. "Thank God."

Baze was safe. I was safe. In addition to that, we had removed a criminal from the streets of Bath. Now that the present danger seemed to have passed, what would Katherine do? Baze and I would soon depart for London, so she would no longer need to stay trapped in the city. Where would she go? And would I ever see her again?

I spun with a renewed smile. "Kath—"

The room sat empty save for Frederick, Baze, and I. She had vanished. I fought the urge to stamp my foot. *Katherine, you cheeky fox. How dare you slip away unnoticed.*

Releasing an exasperated exhale, I looked back at Frederick and said, "I'll be right back," then hurried after the infuriating woman. When I emerged from the lobby doors, the frigid air forced a sharp intake of breath. I caught sight of Katherine's rust-colored hair glinting in a streetlamp's halo a ways down the pavement in the direction of the River Avon.

There you are.

I hastened after her and fell in step with her brisk pace. "I'm rather offended that you planned to disappear without so much as a nod goodbye."

Her single shoulder came up, but she kept her face forward. "No need to cause hullabaloo about nothing. It's better this way."

I threw out a hand and brought her to a stuttering stop. "Your departure is not nothing. I care for you, Katherine. After all that we've endured together, you at least owe me an acknowledgement before simply disappearing."

"Don't get your knickers in a twist, angel. It's not personal." She chewed her lip. "I've . . . never been good at farewells."

My heart warmed at her flicker of vulnerability. So, rather than belabor the matter, I asked, "Where will you go now?"

"I'm not sure." Her gaze became distant. "I hear Ireland's lovely this time of year." A gentle smile tipped her lips, but her tranquility didn't last long, for she shook her head and huffed. "Right then. Goodbye, angel." She tried to move past me, but I snagged a piece of her sleeve, which brought her wheeling around with a sigh. "You have to let me *go*. I cannot stay here."

"But I still have so much to ask you."

"There's nothing more I can tell you that you can't figure out on your own."

"This isn't only about me. We're the same. Would it not bring you comfort to remain near to someone who understands what you're going through?"

The shine in her bright green eyes dimmed slightly. "I'm used to being alone. No need to change my ways now." She grasped my shoulders and squared her body with mine. "Go back to your husband. Go back to your home. And forget about me."

I opened my mouth, but Katherine was quick to continue.

"If there's anything that I hope will result in our paths crossing, it's this—don't let Ciaran have free rein up here." She poked my forehead. "The next time he shows his crooked grin unbidden, chase him out. For good." A kind yet mischievous smile danced on her lips. "You'll do great things, angel. Of that, I am sure. Take care of yourself, and know that I will treasure your friendship for the rest of my days."

After one more reassuring squeeze of my arms, she twirled, her red hair fanning out behind her like a spit of flames, and dissolved into the shadows.

As Baze gradually lifted from unconsciousness, the sound of his own teeth chattering was the first sensation to return. Then a tightness in his neck. Finally, pain coursing through his veins.

Baze peered through his heavy eyelids and noticed Frederick sitting in a chair beside the bed. Even more surprising was the fact that Sebastian Cutler stood next to him. Frowning, Baze swallowed and tried to compose himself long enough to form a question.

"It's over," Frederick said softly, as though sensing Baze's confusion. "Caine's been arrested."

Closing his eyes, Baze said an internal prayer of thanks, then studied the physiotherapist. "How did you . . ."

"Charles locked me in my study after he incapacitated you. I heard your exchange and then listened to him drag you outside. He came back into the house not long after that, likely to dispatch me next, but a car pulled up and caused him to flee. I tried breaking down the door, but it proved futile, so I had to resort to crawling through the window. By the time I escaped, your rescuers had gathered you up and sped away." Sebastian's expression curled in torment. "I am sorry that I did not see through Charles's deception from the start. If I had, I could have prevented you from experiencing such suffering. I shoulder all of the blame."

The pain in Baze's muscles flared as his body quaked. Sweat plastered his shirt to his chest and his hair to his forehead. He strained to lie still, but his body rebelled. Through gritted teeth, he said, "W-what's happening to me?"

Frederick and Sebastian exchanged a glance. Finally, Frederick replied, "You're in withdrawal."

"C-can you stop it?"

"The only way to stop it is to give you another dose—but I'm not going to." Frederick grimaced. "The best thing we can do for you now is allow your body to purge every drop of opium."

"But without it . . . if you do that . . . my leg will . . ." Panic began rising. His breaths became erratic.

Sebastian patted Frederick's shoulder. "Let me have a moment with him, please."

Frederick nodded and permitted the therapist to take his seat, then slipped from the room. Before Sebastian could get a word in, Baze said in a rush, "You h-have to help me, Sebastian. The opium is the only thing staving off the pain in my leg. I c-can't go back to what it was before. I can't."

Sebastian folded his hands in his lap, features compassionate. "Try to breathe deeply, Basil. Breathe."

Baze sucked in air, trying to obey, but his trembling caused his breaths to weaken. Moisture gathered in the corners of his eyes. "I d-don't understand." He clutched the bedding in his fists. "You prayed. You asked God to heal me. But He didn't."

"You are right. I did pray. And God listened."

Baze exhaled a hostile laugh. "I can s-see that."

Sebastian gazed at the floor as though deep in thought. Then, with a calm, even tone, he said, "In the Bible, we are told that the Apostle Paul was stricken with a thorn in his flesh. We are not told specifically what that thorn was, but Paul fervently petitioned God to remove it—three times, in fact. Do you know what God told him?"

Predicting that the next words out of Sebastian's mouth would challenge his inward thinking, would invalidate any complaint he might ever try to conjure about his leg from this moment forward, Baze braced himself and gave a weak shake of his head.

"'My grace is sufficient for thee, for my strength is made perfect in weakness.'" Wrinkles webbed across Sebastian's face as a joyful smile brightened his features. "Is that not incredibly hopeful? Weakness is not a curse. Rather, it is a blessing that allows us to rely fully on God. Now, that does not invalidate our pain or mean that God delights in our suffering. Quite the opposite. He wishes to see us well. How fortunate, then, that He has promised believers heavenly bodies that are free of pain and free of suffering."

Baze covered his face with a hand to hide the tears streaming down his face. He had prayed, had yearned, for so long that his affliction would be taken from him, so much so that he had believed wholeheartedly that it would happen. How could he begin to face the future knowing that pain would plague him every day, every minute, of his life?

Yet, according to Sebastian, he didn't have to experience it alone. There was purpose in his pain, but accepting it would take deep humility that Baze was not accustomed to showing. After enduring such tremendous pain for so long, he wasn't sure he could change his entire mindset at the drop of a hat. In fact, he reckoned it would be impossible, but the therapist's words had soothed an embittered shard of him that had festered ever since the injury and allowed him to finally open his heart to the prospect of true healing—in mind, body, and soul.

Sebastian's stable, comforting hand settled on Baze's shoulder. "As your body fights against this foreign enemy, your symptoms will worsen long before they resolve." His tone grew low yet compassionate. "When that time comes, picture the face of your beautiful new wife. Imagine the blessed future you will enjoy with her once you have conquered this malady. And when it feels as though you cannot continue enduring any longer, turn your eyes heavenward. God will sustain you."

Baze swiped his palms across his face to remove the tears and managed to draw a steadying breath. Then, staring into Sebastian's kind, encouraging eyes, Baze nodded. "I'm ready."

Chapter Thirty-Seven

I CLIPPED DOWN THE TRAIN'S AISLE, tapping each seat and taking note of each passenger—a mother with a young child, a doctor with a medical bag, and a sleeping man with a grating snore. Eventually, I found a suitable place to plop down. Plunking my suitcase next to me, I sat up straight and extracted my worn deck of cards. I'd barely managed to swipe its missing card from the police station before our escape, but I was grateful I had made the attempt. I thwacked the cards together and started shuffling upon the table.

Dear Adelynn. If there had been any reason to linger in the city, it was her friendship and our unique shared gift. However, she would soon be on her way back to London with her husband, and I couldn't stay put. I chafed under the sedentary lifestyle. Besides, the longer I remained in one place, the greater the chance that I would never leave that place alive.

As I reordered the cards, I noticed a glint of red. My practiced fingers snatched out a card and held it up. The queen of hearts—with blood smattered across her face. I paused, breath trapped in my lungs.

An icy chill whispered up my arms and stood my hair on end. Before I could investigate, a waiter appeared and set a steaming cup of tea before me. "For you, ma'am."

I stared up into his hazy, lifeless eyes, and my heart started to palpitate. "I'm afraid you've got the wrong table, sir. I didn't order this."

The man's face remained unmoved, and he pointed. "Enjoy." As he retreated, I spun to call after him, but another voice from the opposite way pulled me to a halt.

"You shouldn't refuse a gift, Kate." Sully sidled up and dropped into the seat across from me in one smooth motion. "It's rude."

With deliberate movements as though I sat upon glass, I faced forward and fixed him with a fierce glare. Seemingly unperturbed, he pushed the cup and saucer toward me before collecting my cards and performing his own shuffling routine.

I flashed him a barbed smile. "Accept a gift from a stranger? How utterly careless that would be."

"Runnin' again." He exhaled softly and looked about the train car. "After the other night, I had hoped that we were beyond this. That we might reconcile."

His voice dripped with false charm, but I shivered nonetheless as melancholy memories of our passionate encounter shot hot currents through me. I grimaced at the fact that my body would betray me so readily. I shook my head. "I am afraid we are past the point of any reconciliation. This is the end for us. We can't keep doing this . . . I can't keep doing this." Unbidden sadness tightened my throat as I caressed the claddagh around my ring finger. I twisted and applied pressure until it popped free and placed it before him with a metallic clink.

Sully paused, cards mid-shuffle. Ever so slowly, he abandoned the deck and gingerly lifted the ring as though it might crumble in his fingers.

"You're going to let me leave this place," I commanded with a soft but firm tone. "And you're either going to turn yourself in or I'm going to expose you. This will all end one way or another."

Sully rolled the ring around in his hand, letting it glitter in the light, then brought it to his mouth and kissed it before slipping it onto his little finger. "I am sorry that it had to come to this, but so be it. I am afraid we don't have much time left, so as your husband, it is my responsibility to ensure that you receive a proper sendoff." He gestured to the teacup with a flick of his eyes and smacked his lips. "Drink up."

Disgust curled my nose. "I shall do no such thing."

"Ahh, Kate. Fiery Kate." He folded his arms over the table. Though his voice held amusement, his expression was anything but. "I have sentinels at every door. There be no escapin' for you this time, sure. Look within yourself, employ those powers of yours. You know it to be true."

Not wanting to give him the satisfaction but knowing that my next move could change the trajectory of my life, I burrowed deep within, extended outward, and felt barriers of darkness blocking every exit. He had utterly consumed this train, taking control of any weakened mind that he could. There was no way out. My thoughts whirled and grappled for a solution.

"Because of what you mean to me, Kate, I shall give you a choice." A glimmer of sincerity bled into his expression. "You could join me. We could stand side by side . . . like we used to. Could even adopt a scruffy brood of orphans like we had once dreamed of doing." The glimmer blossomed into a faint smile. "We have the same goal. We merely disagree about how to accomplish it." He reached out with one hand as though to grasp my own, but he let it rest in the middle of the table, open, inviting. "However, if your heart yet clings to its rejection of me, then you need to flee. Disappear. Remove yourself as an obstacle, vow to never return, and allow me to continue fightin' to bring peace to our home and unite its people in the way I see fit."

I lifted my chin, hot tears threatening to spill. "And if I refuse both of those paths?"

He swallowed hard and withdrew his hand. "Then your only other option is to lay down your life here and now." His eyes grew bitter. "Think long and hard, Kate. Don't choose rashly."

As I stared at the tea, my throat constricted as though anticipating its consumption. Each time I had walked out on Sully, he had begged me to stay, and each time, I had thrown myself back into his arms, hoping and praying that he had changed. The very last time I left, however, I had promised myself I would end the cycle. And I did.

I didn't want to die—not in the slightest—but how could I go back to him again . . . or worse, run from everything I knew? How could I peacefully live out the rest of my days knowing Sully was out there somewhere, tormenting those he deemed his enemies? Knowing I could have stopped him?

Is there a fourth option? There has to be. This can't be the end . . . can it?

Darting my eyes about the space, I noted the exits, the distance between Sully and I, and the loose items that could be fashioned into weapons—the doctor's medical bag, a hooked cane, a child's toy train. Desperation reared its ugly head. Could I really bring myself to attack the man I loved? Considering everything he had done, my actions would surely be justified, but could I allow violence to mar my conscience even if it meant saving myself?

My willpower began to flicker, then weaken—and finally, it snuffed out. Before I could rekindle the flame, I snatched up the cup and gulped down the liquid so quickly I barely had a chance to taste it. My throat and stomach burned. Black tea, perhaps? And poison.

Veiled emotion passed over Sully's face. Was that sadness I saw? Surprise that I'd actually done it? Without a word, he stood and came around to me, but just as he made to pass, he bent, eased a hand around the back of my neck, and kissed me.

I tried to resist but found myself softening into him, wishing once more that our lives could have been different, that we could have been content, merely two ordinary people in love. I'd have lost myself completely to the moment were it not for the poison stinging between our lips.

Sully pulled back ever so slightly. He hesitated, as though not wanting to depart. Then he swiped his tongue over his lips and grimaced. "So passes Katherine Quinn." He straightened. "Thank you for returnin' the claddagh to me. Every time I look upon it, I shall remember what we once had. Farewell, mo ghrá.*" He ambled through the aisle—away from me—before swinging toward a door and hopping off the train.*

Hollow defeat tore a hole in me. God, why? Why would you let it end this way?

But if God had an answer, He didn't speak in time before my stomach seized in pain.

Chapter Thirty-Eight

MORNING. OR AT LEAST I GUESSED it was morning based on the brightness penetrating my closed eyelids. Even so, I couldn't bring myself to rise just yet, for I knew the moment I moved was the moment my body would protest in a chorus of aches. I'd collapsed on the sofa the night before, gown and all, and finally fell asleep in the lonely hours of predawn.

I had remained by Baze's side as long as I could as he began the long, arduous journey of withdrawal, but when he had started mumbling, then convulsing, Frederick steered me into the sitting room and locked me out. Minutes had turned into hours. Morning, afternoon, and evening all came and went. Alistair and Frances Ford had arrived, bringing with them Percy, Aubrey, and several of Baze's nieces. My mother, Emily, and Basil Allan joined soon after.

With each new position of the sun, Baze had grown worse.

When his moans and strained pleas reached my ears, my resolve faltered, and I began pacing. The bedroom door had cracked open, and when Frederick slid through, it allowed me a brief look inside. Baze's appearance had startled me—flushed skin, trembling limbs, rolling eyes.

I had made a dash for him, but Frederick caught my arm and yanked me away. I'd collapsed onto the floor, drawing my knees up and praying with everything I had. Somehow, I had dragged myself to the sofa—or perhaps Frederick had carried me there. Eventually, Baze had grown quiet, and sleep finally claimed me.

"Adelynn?" came a whisper.

"Mmm?" I grumbled, keeping my eyes shut.

"Adelynn, wake up."

I half-opened one eye to see Frederick crouching before me. Yawning, I pushed upright. "What's wrong?"

The corner of his mouth twitched. "He's on his feet."

"He's wha . . ." The words jerked me fully away. I jumped up and ran, leaving Frederick's chuckles in my wake. When I burst into the bedroom, my gaze fell upon Baze standing beside the bed. Though his cheeks had sunken in a bit and his clothes hung a little looser on his frame, the brilliant smile confirmed what I had hoped and prayed.

He was healed.

I lunged for him and wrapped my arms about his waist. I very nearly knocked him over, but he managed to stabilize and hugged me back. A sob bubbled up inside as I burrowed my face into his chest and soaked in his scent, his warmth, his strength.

He rested his head atop mine. "I love you, Al. So much."

"I love you too," I murmured into his shirt.

Hardly any time passed before the sound of Frederick's clearing throat carried from the doorway. "Baze, there are many people here to see you if you'll have them."

The request made me squeeze tighter, not wanting to let go. We had only just been reunited, and they wanted us to separate so suddenly? What cruelty was this? I was his wife, dash it all. They could wait.

Exhaling, Baze loosened his embrace, so I reluctantly slipped back. He studied my face and tucked a stray strand of hair behind my ear before nodding to Frederick. "We can't hold them back forever, I suppose. Send them in."

As I predicted, once the dam broke, there was no holding back the forceful wave of visitors. Frances Ford pushed her way in first—heaven help anyone who stood in the way of a mother trying to reach her son. Next came Percy and Aubrey and several of their daughters. They surrounded Baze, embracing, laughing, shedding tears of joy, and it occurred to me that this was the closest I had ever seen his family. Perhaps some good would come of the misery he endured after all.

"Careful not to crowd him," Frederick warned, but his words went mostly unheeded.

When I noticed Emily lingering near the edge of the reunion, Basil Allan propped on her hip, I approached, both to give Baze and his family time together while also claiming a moment for myself and my dear friend. After subjecting Basil Allan to several quick kisses, I crossed to Emily's other side and drew close. We slid our arms around each other and tilted our heads together. Though we didn't speak, affection and encouragement expanded between us.

Soon after Mr. Everett had completed his calls to London informing everyone of Baze's condition, the Fords had offered Emily transportation to Bath. She'd readily accepted, and they arrived not long after Charles Caine had been taken into custody. Upon seeing Emily come striding through the doors, I had burst into tears and collapsed into her arms.

While we'd waited for Baze's withdrawal symptoms to abate, Emily and I had engaged in several hours of deep conversation, baring our souls and leaving nothing hidden. I had described our grueling ordeal in Bath—the interrupted honeymoon, the horrific murders, and the mysterious Katherine Quinn. In turn, she had detailed her own struggles—surviving the anniversary of Bennett's death, enduring an offer of courtship and near kidnapping by Sergeant Andrews, and receiving unexpected communication from Finn.

I smiled at the thought of the Irish magician. Ever since he left for Ireland, I had worried for him, prayed for him, and based on what he told Emily of his new life, it seemed that he was getting on just fine.

An uncomfortable lull disrupted the hearty gathering around Baze. I searched the group to investigate the reason for the disturbance. Mr. Ford had entered the fray and stood chest to chest with Baze. Neither man moved. Neither man blinked. With his back to me, Mr. Ford's expression remained blocked from view, but I could see Baze's face clear as day, could see myriad emotions waging war.

Finally, in a swift but stiff gesture, Mr. Ford dropped his hand on

Baze's shoulder and squeezed. The older man worked his jaw, swaying as though he might make another move, but he steadied himself. Eventually, he nodded curtly, squeezed his son's shoulder once more, and lowered his hand to his side.

Eyes glistening, Baze relaxed ever so slightly and returned the nod.

With the anxious moment alleviated, Frederick started to shoo people from the room, insisting that it was time for Baze to rest. They complied begrudgingly, but soon, the last of the nieces skipped from the room while Emily and I exchanged our own farewells.

When everyone had gone, Frederick ordered Baze into bed. "Your body's just been through hell. You don't want to push it too far. Trust me." Frederick waited until Baze obeyed before nodding to me. "I'll leave you two with some privacy. Lord knows such a thing is impossible when our family's involved. I'll be in the next room if you need anything." He aimed a finger at his brother. "Rest. I'm serious."

The moment Frederick latched the door behind him, I scrambled to the opposite side of the bed and flopped over next to Baze. I snuggled into his arms and rested my head on his chest. His rhythmic heartbeats tapped against my ear. I listened to his heart for a good, long while, the calming pulse stirring drowsiness and peace within me.

"How do you feel?" I whispered through contented breaths.

"Tired. Sore. Like I just sprinted around the entire perimeter of Bath." His fingers lightly stroked my arm. "But the pain is gone—from the drug, at least."

I blinked against tears, thankful the opium had finally been banished from his body for good but anguished that it meant his leg's original pain had returned . . . and would probably never subside.

He inhaled, his chest lifting my head, and then slowly released it. "I'm sorry, Al."

I wiggled up onto a propped elbow so I could look at his face. "Whatever do you have to be sorry for?"

Moisture collected in his eyes. "For all of this. For allowing my quest for healing to consume me. It became my idol. I was so willing to do anything that I neglected my own body, as well as the people I love. I was selfish. Utterly selfish."

"You were merely trying to find a way to stop the pain. Everything would have been fine if Caine hadn't exploited your weakness."

"Perhaps, but I can't place all the blame on him. I *wanted* to keep taking the opium. It was the only way I could feel normal again." His hand found mine and clutched it tight against his chest. "It will take some time, but I think I'm ready to start accepting what happened, that my injury is a reality that is here to stay. Sebastian helped me see that. He had some . . . difficult words for me."

"I'm sure they were also wise words." I flattened my lips in empathy, then averted my eyes and focused on the buttons of his shirt. "The last time we had a moment alone, I apologized for the hurt my words caused you, but I don't think that, given the circumstances, we were quite of the right mind for such reconciliation. So . . . I want to apologize again. Because I am truly sorry."

Releasing my hand, Baze tilted my chin upward so he could meet my gaze. "I forgive you. Sincerely. Let's put it behind us, eh?"

Relief warmed my heart and bubbled up in a smile. "Let's."

His tender brown eyes searched my face. "What about you?"

I let out a nervous chuckle. "What about me?"

"I'm not the only one who's been battling demons." His gentle stare seemed to pierce right through me and expose everything I'd tried to keep buried deep within.

I looked away, as though that might stop him, and shrugged. "I have it under control."

"What does that mean?"

"It means that I'm taking care of it."

"Adelynn." His voice grew stern. "I know you're still having nightmares. Don't try to argue otherwise."

My mouth grew dry. "Then I won't argue."

"And . . . do you still see Cornelius?"

I winced and looked for disgust in Baze's face, but he only

appeared concerned. Why was I so afraid of sharing this with him? We had agreed from the start that we would trust one another with everything. He had exposed his soul to me, so now it was my turn to reciprocate.

"I see him both in my waking dreams and in my nightmares." I tugged at a loose thread on Baze's shirt. "Our minds had been so closely connected that it's almost as though a little piece of him still has a hold on me. I don't know whether it's actually a piece of him . . . or if I can't quite let him go yet. His death was my doing, after all."

Baze frowned and tilted his head. "I shot him, not you."

"Yes . . . but I had so many opportunities to petition him to turn from his ways. I think, somehow, I feel responsible that he chose to resist in the end." I shook my head. "Katherine told me I was being prideful. That it wasn't up to me—but rather, up to God—to save him. She also said that my gift is strong and that the next time Cornelius enters my mind, I should confront him and banish him for good."

"She's right. You can, and you should."

"I am pleased you have such confidence in me." With a grin, I shifted and leaned across Baze's chest. "Very well. The next time he dares show his face, I shall give him a piece of my mind."

Baze chuckled. "He has no idea the force of nature about to come barreling his way. I almost pity him."

I gaped in mock incredulity, resenting the statement but knowing I couldn't contradict it either. Instead, I edged forward and pressed my lips to his. Laughs punctuated our light kisses. I shivered and sighed contentedly, at that moment realizing just how intensely I had missed his company, had missed his touch.

Our kisses slowed, deepened, making up for the time we had lost. I adjusted, dragging a hand down his chest. Breaths quickening, he shuddered and muscled us upward, then deposited me onto my back. His lips wandered down my jaw to my neck.

As I trembled beneath him, the circumstances of the moment came crashing down upon me. Barely a few hours had passed since his body had purged the last of the opium. How he even managed to keep his head propped up was beyond me.

Halfheartedly, I pushed out with a halting palm. "You're supposed to rest."

"I can rest later," he murmured between kisses.

"I don't want to be held responsible for any harm done to you in your time of recovery."

"You can blame me." He found my mouth again with his.

I snagged a piece of his collar and pushed him back just far enough to make him look me in the eyes. "You do realize Frederick is stationed in the next room?"

This gave him pause. "Ask him to leave."

"I doubt he would agree to vacate the premises simply so you can defy his strict orders. You need to rest. I refuse to be an accomplice in your schemes this time." I patted his cheek, gave him one last quick kiss, and then tried to wiggle free.

Groaning, he rocked away and onto his back. "You're utterly heartless, Al." He draped an arm over his face. "You've no idea what you're doing to me."

"Focus on recovering, and I'll think about revisiting the matter." Smirking, I nudged his shoulder and eased off the bed.

In the next room, Frederick glanced up from a newspaper, took one look at me, and heaved an exasperated sigh. "I told Baze to rest, Adelynn, and I expect you to help with that initiative."

Self-conscious, I smoothed my hair and shook the wrinkles from my dress. "I'll have you know that I was the one who enforced your orders. Baze, however, has some choice words for you."

Frederick rolled his eyes. "I am sure he does."

Giving a curt shrug, I left the room. Getting through the hallways and lobby undetected by Baze's many guests proved difficult, but not impossible. When I passed the front counter, now manned by an unfamiliar host, my chest clenched. That I would never see Mr. Everett's kind smile again filled me with sorrow, but there would be time for mourning later. Right now, I had one final objective to complete.

As I trod outside, fresh air invigorated my lungs and stabilized my racing heart and elevated temperature. Faint music in the distance directed my path toward the abbey. The calm reassurance of the abbey's regal structure kept me moving. My emotions had drifted from Baze to the words he had spoken a moment ago regarding Cornelius, that perhaps it was possible for me to finally be free of him. I paused near the fountain along the abbey's side and stared at the steady stream of water. This time, I intentionally burrowed into my subconscious and sought out the magician—for the last time.

Swelling darkness began tinging the edges of my vision, and the world's colors grew muted. A man stepped around the fountain. Undaunted, I flicked my gaze to the newcomer and focused on those glacial eyes, bright despite the shadows cast by his top hat.

Hands clasped behind his back, he sauntered my way and stopped a few paces from me. As always, the crisp black suit and shaggy raven hair accentuated his handsome face, and somehow, my memory even managed to recreate the tantalizing scents of sandalwood and verbena.

"To what do I owe the pleasure of your summoning, Adelynn?"

His syrupy voice flipped my stomach and nearly made me lose resolve, but I managed to erect a strong barrier between us. *Give me the strength to do this.*

Smiling sweetly, I said, "I only called you here to tell you that this will be our last meeting. I refuse to allow you to remain in my mind. You're unwelcome. Leave. Now."

Cornelius smiled, his sharp incisor flashing. "How could you bring yourself to banish me so callously? Do you not yet harbor immense guilt for the losin' of me soul?"

The barbed words hit their mark, but I tried not to let it show. "You made your own choice. In the end, I am not responsible for your actions."

He tipped his chin and put on an exaggerated frown. "Surely

there's something more you could have done. You torture yourself with that question every day. Have you found an answer?"

Instead of retreating into self-analysis, I straightened my spine and felt a divine confidence rush through me. "I did what I could. It is not ultimately up to me to save souls. I offered you a choice, and you denied it. I will no longer hold on to this or feel responsible for your demise."

Cornelius's eyes darkened as he covered the rest of the distance between us. "But what about me, sweet *cailín?*" That silky voice traced a shiver down my back. His fingertips whispered up my bare arm and came to rest on my chin. "Do you no longer love me?"

The word clouded my thoughts for only a moment. I jerked my head away from his touch. "That wasn't love. That was manipulation. I hold nothing for you now. Except perhaps pity."

The edges around Cornelius's form grew fuzzy, as though something had begun chipping away at him. The darkness that had ushered me into this vision flickered, allowing light to warm my skin.

Cornelius slid his hands into his pockets. "You have grown strong, Adelynn, but you've only scratched the surface of all this." His voice sounded distant, muffled, even though he still stood right in front of me. "Maybe if I had had more time on this earth, you could have led me to the light . . ." His lips distorted into a chilling grin. "Never mind that. I am not the last great force you will encounter, so you'd best reserve some of that power for your next trial."

Resolve welling in my chest, I pushed back against the weakened darkness still trying to prod at me. The push distorted Cornelius's image further, making him transparent. "You have no more power over me or anyone else," I bit out. "So get out of my mind and stay out."

All amusement wiped from his features, and something akin to respect tipped his mouth. He lifted a hand and touched the brim of his hat in a polite gesture. "Good night, Adelynn."

As his image faded and the world regained its original brilliant hue, the soft melody of "The Parting Glass" hummed in my ears. The familiar tune filled me with memories of a time long past, and I found myself caressing my ring's pearl—Father's pearl. Melancholy weighed upon my heart. I didn't grieve the fact that I would never see Cornelius again. Rather, I grieved the idea he represented. Now that our conflict was resolved, there was nothing left for me to do but reflect and move forward. That meant leaving the past where it belonged—Cornelius, Bennett, Father.

Renewed hope lifted the weight inside me.

Yet, the music didn't fade away, nor did a niggling sense that something yet remained unfinished. I focused on the violin melody and realized that it wasn't solely in my head. It was real—and it was nearby.

Skin pricking, I followed the music around to the front of the abbey that faced the Roman Baths. The crowd parted as I walked. Pigeons strutted about. Positioned at the very edge of the fray, near the steps of the abbey, a lone violinist performed.

Dread and curiosity collided in my gut as I crept toward him. I'd seen him here before and around Bath, always playing his instrument in the background yet influencing the thoughts and moods of people around him with his songs. Inconsequential. Unassuming.

Now, I finally looked at him—*really* looked at him.

Brows drawn and eyes closed, he transitioned into the chorus. His wrist rocked in vibrato, and his body swayed. The passion pouring from the violin reminded me of Finn, so joyous and alight in the pleasure of his instrument. But something I couldn't quite name seemed off about this man. Perhaps it was the sternness of his expression and the slight smile that hinted at hidden thoughts.

I stared, rapt, as the violinist played the last phrase of music and let the final note evaporate into the commotion of the square. Sunlight glinted off a simple gold band adorning his left ring finger, but a more delicate silver ring on the little finger of his bow hand triggered recognition—a claddagh.

When he lowered the instrument, several people applauded, and others tossed coins into the open case at his feet. As the crowd around him thinned, I found myself wandering closer like a moth drawn to a flame, breath aching in my lungs.

He loosened the bow strings, knelt, and packed the instrument away. Focused intently on his task, he spoke softly. "You shouldn't stare unless you intend to leave a donation or formally introduce yourself." His calming Irish cadence stirred alarm in me. "I'll go first." He threw the violin case over his shoulder and straightened in one smooth motion. "I'm Shay O'Sullivan."

Time halted. Sounds faded. The air chilled. I stared wide-eyed into his stony blue eyes, darker in hue than Cornelius's. He was taller too, with a muscular build, strong jaw, and a crop of short brown hair sticking out beneath a flat cap.

Shay ambled toward me. I tried to retreat, but my feet rooted me to the spot. The closer he came, the more the darkness I had banished a moment ago regained power. But this felt different. Cornelius had sparked with chaos and arrogance. Shay oozed confidence and control.

"You're Sully." The words slipped past my lips unbidden.

"Shay, actually. Sully is reserved for Kate and Kate alone. Still, it's a pleasure to meet you, Adelynn Ford. I'm chuffed to see my reputation precedes me so." He ducked in a quick half-bow. "Yours does as well. Ciaran had been utterly smitten with you, and Kate wouldn't shut up about you. I feel as though I've known you for a lifetime."

My mind reeled. "You . . . you've been here this whole time . . . and I never noticed. How . . ."

"A magician's whole act lives and dies by his skills of misdirection. It's an art, really—gettin' people to overlook somethin' that's starin' them right in the face." He leaned toward me with a roguish twinkle in his eye. "You did not notice because I did not want you to notice—not until this moment."

My jaw loosened, but no words came. I could only gape. Throughout the entire ordeal in Bath, he had been right in front of us, watching from afar, pulling each carefully orchestrated string.

Cornelius had manipulated innocent minds, but this man had manipulated Cornelius—he had created the monster Cornelius had become. Thus, he bore the blame for every horror my loved ones and I had endured. *He* was the reason Father and Bennett had lost their lives. *He* was the reason Baze now lived as a cripple and I lived in trepidation of murderous visions.

Shay O'Sullivan was the cause of it all.

Deep within the far reaches of my soul, fury began to fester.

"I'm honored to have rendered you speechless." He nipped a finger under my chin to close my mouth. "From what I hear, you are a woman who is rarely without words."

"You did all this," I whispered. "All this death . . . all this pain . . ."

"Ahh"—he angled away—"believe you me, I would love nothin' more than to stay and chat, but I'm afraid—"

"No!" I lashed out and caught a fistful of his shirt. "You don't get to walk away from this."

His mouth tipped in a smirk. "And what be you plannin' to do? Hold me here by sheer willpower until a constable happens by and arrests me?"

"I'll do what I have to until you answer for everything you've done." The malice in my words soured my stomach, but I pressed on. "You set Cornelius upon London. You pushed Caine to wreak havoc here in Bath. You have to pay."

Understanding softened his expression. "Your accusations are unfounded, I'm afraid. Ciaran was his own man. I raised him, yes, but his vendetta was personal. His own power consumed him. He was beyond my or Kate's help. Trust me, we tried to reach him." He grimaced. "As for Caine, I influenced his mind, sure—but only a touch. Like Ciaran, he was driven by his extremely personal need for vengeance. He required no extra proddin' from me."

"I don't believe you." I tried jostling him, but his strong frame resisted my attempt.

"You may believe what you wish, but the truth remains." With a cautious hand, he grasped my wrist and twisted until I released his shirt. "They charted their own courses, allowin' revenge to pollute sound judgment. I, on the other hand, am driven by no such motivation."

"Then what do you want?" My voice cracked in desperation as I yanked from his hold. "Motivation or not, you're still using a power that originates in darkness. You're still using your influence to hurt people."

"I don't hurt the innocent." His angular jaw shifted, and he lowered his voice. "Long ago, I lived every day tryin' to remedy minor injustices, such as carin' for discarded urchins livin' on the street, which is how I came across Finn and Ciaran. But over time, I realized how much my kin have truly suffered. They've been starved, subjugated, cast aside, and now, this foolish fight for independence is pittin' brother against brother. The last thing we need is civil war. Regardless of the outcome of that movement, all I want is peace."

My body quivered with building emotion. "And you think threatening lives and causing people to suffer is the way to achieve that?"

He breathed a mirthless laugh. "You sound so much like Kate. I see why she liked you." He cast a quick glance at the claddagh on his finger, and his throat muscles tightened.

Fear sank like a boulder in my stomach as recognition flared. That wasn't just any ring he wore—it was Katherine's. My breath caught. "What have you done to her?"

Shay adjusted the instrument case over his shoulder and sighed. "I have humored you long enough. Your ignorance in these matters runs deep, and no amount of explanation will change your mind, so it's time I took my leave." He stepped around me and bumped my arm as he passed.

I whirled, biting back a rebuke.

As he retreated, he spun to face me while continuing to saunter backward. "Don't be worryin' your pretty little head about me now. I vow to never bother you again. If you are a wise woman, you will forget all about me in return. You will forget about Ireland, Cornelius Marx, and Katherine Quinn. This is not your fight and never has been. So stay out of it. You have friends and family who deserve your attention more than I." Solemnity darkened his eyes as he touched two fingers to the bill of his cap and saluted. "May the road rise up to meet you."

Author's Note

Ah, history. If I wasn't careful, I would plunge deep into the research rabbit hole and never come out (I'm still considering it, not gonna lie). There are so many little details I have to learn when writing a historical story, and even though I can't use them all in the actual book, they help enrich the characters, setting, and plot behind the scenes. But rather than keep all these details to myself, I thought I'd share some with you!

The Location

Bath was quite a lavish destination of the time, what with its relaxing and healing hot springs. I knew this book would follow Baze and Adelynn right after their wedding, and when wealthy couples of that time got married, they would go away for several months, oftentimes to visit family. It made sense that they might choose Bath for a holiday (and that Baze would want to seek healing for his leg at the hot springs—more on that later).

Quick note about the wedding: from 1662 onward, the Church of England used a revised version of the "Book of Common Prayer" (first used in 1549!) for marriages. What you see in Baze and Adelynn's wedding follows that basically to a T, with some modifications for story purposes. Not to mention, in that proper era, public displays of affection were a no-go—so no "you may kiss your bride" here!

Bath is built around ancient Roman baths and a temple, and the main sites—like the baths, the hotel, and the abbey—are pretty close together, which helped for moving characters from place to place. It was really cool to stumble upon the Empire Hotel with how close the name was to the Empress Theatre. I was able to use that to build a little more tension. The hotel was fairly new at the time, having opened just thirteen years prior in 1901, and as Baze explained, the architecture depicting a castle, a house, and a cottage was meant to represent the three social classes. It's been made into luxury apartments now, with a restaurant on the first floor.

Another cool discovery? The Bath Police headquarters at that time was located literally right next door to the hotel—which made it super convenient for whenever Baze and Adelynn had to pop over to see Chief Inspector Whitaker. That location was used by the police until 1966, and then it was turned into a restaurant in 1998 (and the jail cells are bathrooms!).

The Poison

In my first draft, I originally used arsenic as the poison of choice. You know, arsenic and old lace and all that. Back then, people used to put arsenic in pigments to make them more vibrant. So there would be arsenic in things like wallpaper and clothes—and it was slowly poisoning people! I thought I had a cool plot point there. That is, until further research revealed that arsenic is a *really* slow killer that more often than not just leaves the victim with painful poisoning symptoms (oof, my Google search results must be so dark). Back to the drawing board! That's when I came across cyanide. It was another popular poison of choice at the time, and it could take someone down in minutes. Perfect.

Speaking of poison, Baze and Adelynn were dealing with their own poison—one of the mind and one of the body. In Baze's case, they would have used morphine for his surgery and for the pain, so it was only natural that he might develop an opium dependency. Many people did in those days because doctors didn't yet know the full potential of its addictive effects. It's a terrible thing, and to get in that headspace, I read through journals and personal accounts of opium users, including "Confessions of an English Opium-Eater" by Thomas De Quincy. It was pretty common for people in the early 1900s to ingest opium in the form of laudanum, and some built a strong enough tolerance that they could take larger doses without having severe side effects.

The Healing Waters

I didn't realize it when I first started writing this book, but Baze's journey actually mirrors a journey I have walked myself. When I was a teen, I sustained a back injury while playing softball, and it's an injury that causes me pain to this day. So even though the words in the story crying out to God for healing were Baze's words, they were also my words, words I had repeated over and over and over again. And it made me do some serious soul-searching along the way.

In his desperation for healing, Baze seeks out the mythical healing waters of Bath—and they truly are mythical. The Celts were the first to find the hot springs and dedicate them to the goddess Sulis because they believed she had healing powers. After the Romans arrived on the scene in early 40 AD and founded the city of Aquae Sulis (Latin for "waters of Sulis"), they built a temple to their goddess Minerva and later added an entire bath complex. Several centuries later, the baths fell into ruin.

Fast-forward to the nineteenth century—the baths were rediscovered and excavated, a new bath complex was built, and people started coming from all across the land to find healing for their ailments. It was officially opened to the public in 1897, so it would have been quite the novelty in Baze and Adelynn's time. Fun fact: I got to drink the spring water in the Pump Room when I visited in 2018. It tastes . . . like minerals. And it's really warm. I mean, it contains more than 40 minerals and can get hotter than 100 degrees, so I suppose that shouldn't be surprising.

Writing about hot springs that have mythical healing powers naturally led me to water therapy, which is why I had to include a physical therapist—or a physiotherapist as they're known in England. My dad's been a physical therapist for over 30 years, so I was really excited to explore that profession. Even though I could use my dad for some fact-checking, I had to figure out what they actually knew about medicine at the time—which was surprisingly a lot. I found some old physiotherapy books that detailed specific treatments and exercises that you could do in water (bless you, public domain). The turn of the century is right around when physiotherapy and its American counterpart really took off.

Bonus

Okay, I've been carrying around this crazy revelation from the first book for a long time. It was eating me up, so I finally had to share. The name Cornelius Marx was one of the first things I created when dreaming up the idea for the book (nine years ago!). It just hit me immediately. Through discovery writing, I learned the name was an alias (sorry, spoiler) and found out just how important the Cliffs of Moher were to Cornelius. But why had he chosen *that* name as his pseudonym? Well, there I was, innocently researching the tower that's perched atop of the cliffs, and what might the name of the builder of the tower be? Cornelius O'Brien. *Mind. Blown.* I think I sat there for a solid minute with my mouth open. Sometimes God just moves, you know?

That's just a tiny taste of the research that goes into writing a historical fiction novel. Stay tuned for the third and final book, which will take you to the green shores of Ireland!

If you're interested in learning more fun history tidbits and about the book-writing process, follow me on Instagram or Facebook at @jessicaslyauthor or sign up for my newsletter at jessicasly.com.

Made in the USA
Monee, IL
07 April 2023